HISTORICAL

Your romantic escape to the past.

Scandalously Bound To The Gentleman
Helen Dickson

Alliance With The Notorious Lord
Bronwyn Scott

MILLS & BOON

SCANDALOUSLY BOUND TO THE GENTLEMAN
© 2024 by Helen Dickson
Philippine Copyright 2024
Australian Copyright 2024
New Zealand Copyright 2024

First Published 2024
First Australian Paperback Edition 2024
ISBN 978 1 038 90581 9

ALLIANCE WITH THE NOTORIOUS LORD
© 2024 by Nikki Poppen
Philippine Copyright 2024
Australian Copyright 2024
New Zealand Copyright 2024

First Published 2024
First Australian Paperback Edition 2024
ISBN 978 1 038 90581 9

MIX
Paper | Supporting
responsible forestry
FSC® C001695

Published by
Harlequin Mills & Boon
An imprint of Harlequin Enterprises (Australia) Pty Limited
(ABN 47 001 180 918), a subsidiary of HarperCollins
Publishers Australia Pty Limited
(ABN 36 009 913 517)
Level 19, 201 Elizabeth Street
SYDNEY NSW 2000 AUSTRALIA

Cover art used by arrangement with Harlequin Books S.A.. All rights reserved.

Printed and bound in Australia by McPherson's Printing Group

Scandalously Bound To The Gentleman

Helen Dickson

MILLS & BOON

Helen Dickson was born and still lives in South Yorkshire, UK, with her retired farm-manager husband. Having moved out of the busy farmhouse where she raised their two sons, she now has more time to indulge in her favourite pastimes. She enjoys being outdoors, travelling, reading and music. An incurable romantic, she writes for pleasure. It was a love of history that drove her to writing historical fiction.

Visit the Author Profile page
at millsandboon.com.au for more titles.

Author Note

Scandalously Bound to the Gentleman is the third book in the Cranford Estate Siblings trilogy.

I have thoroughly enjoyed writing this story, which is about Charles, a diplomatic envoy working for the British government, and Lucy Quinn, an independent woman with a troubled past. The beginning of the story is set against the colorful backdrop of India, where Charles's and Lucy's attraction to each other brings them together. It is in the palace of the Rajah of Guntal where they share a magical night of love. Having experienced an unhappy affair in the past, Charles is in no rush to step up to the altar. Lucy has also suffered a trauma in her life and is as reluctant as Charles to wed. It is agreed there will be no commitment and afterward they part, Charles for England, Lucy to remain in India.

Unfortunate circumstances and a child born as a result of their night together force Lucy to leave India for London. Here she meets Charles once more, and after much soul-searching, they eventually resolve their conflicts.

Scandalously Bound to the Gentleman is a story of hope and a passionate search for love and happiness with many pitfalls along the way.

Chapter One

1817—India

Enclosed by hills carrying the bounteous colour of an Indian summer through the glare of the sun, Charles didn't see the danger coming. He rode over rocky ground, his animal guided by his sure hand, its hooves negotiating the loose scree. Suddenly his groom shouted something that sounded like danger, but even though Charles's mind leapt to alertness, it was too late. His horse, spooked by a large snake that slithered from the rocks and across its path, reared, its front legs frantically pawing the air and throwing Charles from the saddle. The next thing he knew he was hitting the ground and rolling down the hillside into a gully below. Pain shot through his thigh, followed by a blow to his head as it made contact with a large boulder, halting his fall. Darkness engulfed him.

How long he had lain there he had no idea as he slipped in and out of consciousness. With a grinding pain inside his head, half opening his eyes, through a haze he saw a bullock cart drawn by two skinny-looking oxen making its way towards him. A woman sat inside the cart, guiding it between boulders strewn on the ground. A plague of flies had descended on him, but there was nothing he could do about it. The cart stopped beside him. The woman spoke to his groom in what he recognised as Urdu. She remained in the cart while someone lifted him inside. The bullock cart began to move off.

It rumbled over the uneven ground in sweltering heat. Each jolt was agony to him. The journey seemed endless. He opened his eyes, his faltering gaze settling on the woman. She was wearing traditional garments—the long skirt with a blouse and a billowing scarf that covered her head and floated in the breeze, the delicate fabric the colour of scarlet threaded with gold.

His gaze became fixed on a long strand of hair that had escaped its confines. There was something not quite right about it, he thought. It was light blonde in colouring, most strange, he thought, for an Indian lady. As he continued to slip in and out of consciousness, in his lucid moments the long strand of light blonde hair—lifting defiantly in the breeze like a ship's sprightly pennant—continued to hold his attention.

He couldn't remember being lifted out of the cart. Some hours later he was aware of a wet cloth being applied to his brow, cooling, welcome. Soft words were murmured, the sound comforting along with the tinkling of bangles.

'Mr Anderson?'

A woman's voice.

'Tilly?' his voice rasped.

Disconnected memories flooded his mind. He was delirious, dreaming of his sister again surrounded by pastures green in the country of his birth. A searing heat tore through his right thigh, combining with the pain inside his head. Where in God's name was he? What had happened to him? He remembered being thrown from his horse and nothing else.

Voices drifted towards him in the darkness. He attempted to move, to raise his head, but his eyelids were weighted and the pain inside his head and leg was unbearable. His bloodshot eyes blinked in puzzlement. He couldn't understand why the face bending over his was shrouded in a swirling haze.

'He has a concussion,' the voice said, a soft voice, a caring voice.

'Perhaps it's as well he's out of it until his wound has been treated. Have him brought to the treatment room. I'll give him something to dull the pain and see what can be done to save his leg.'

'He's in a bad way. Will he make it?' the female voice asked with concern.

'He's strong and healthy. It always helps.'

The agony of being lifted on to a stretcher was too much. A merciful darkness descended once more.

The fever gradually left Charles. There was a babble of voices all around him. His eyes flickered open. As the haze lessened, he brought his gaze into focus. He didn't recognise where he was. Noting the other beds where injured British and Indian men lay, he realised he was in an infirmary, a small, whitewashed affair. Two women and a man bustled about, tending to the other patients. He tried to raise his head, but the room began to spin. He squeezed his eyes tight. The sudden movement made his head feel as though it would explode.

He tried to remember what had happened. When he had set out from Madras, the landscape had stretched out before him, clouds of dust stirred up by his horse's hooves settling on his coat and that of his groom. Mile after mile, hour after hour, they had climbed hills and forded rushing streams. He loved riding over the Indian plains, mysterious, still unknown to him after four years in India, despite his curiosity and desire to know more. They had been riding for four days when his horse threw him.

After a while he carefully blinked his eyes open, relieved to find his sight no longer quite so blurred. A woman approached his bed with a bowl in her hands. She murmured a few words of conventional greeting, placing the bowl on a low table, but when she looked at him a sudden feeling of unease caused him to start, his scalp prickling. It was the woman who had brought him here in the bullock cart, he was sure of it, but she was no longer dressed in Indian clothes. She was studying him with a cool interest, her expression immobile and guarded. His eyes met the steady gaze and for one discomforting moment it seemed that she was staring into the very heart of him, getting the measure of him, of his faults and failings. He had never seen eyes that contained more energy and depth.

'You're awake at last,' she said.

His mouth was as dry as a desert. With patience, she held a cup to his lips. The cool water was a welcome relief to his parched throat. On a sigh he placed his head back on the pillow. 'Thank you. How long have I been out of it?'

'We brought you in two days ago. You are in a small hospital in Nandra in the state of Puna, close to the border with Guntal. Do you remember what happened?'

'My horse threw me. How bad is it?'

'Not good.' She stood aside as a man came to the bed and began removing the dressing from his leg.

'I'm Dr Patrick Jessop—at your service,' he said without raising his head as his piercing eyes scrutinised the wound. 'The muscles in your thigh were badly injured when you fell—thankfully no broken bones, which would have complicated matters. I've managed to suture the wound back together, but it will be a while before you can bear your weight on it. It's a nasty wound and it's possible it will leave you with a limp, but we'll have to see.'

'At least my leg is still attached to the rest of me— thank the Lord—not forgetting yourself, Dr Jessop,' Charles uttered, staring at the middle-aged doctor, for the lilt of the voice was unmistakably Irish. He met twinkling grey eyes in a face tanned dark. He looked at the woman.

She didn't crack a smile or even blink. When she looked at him her stare was forthright. 'You should. You also suffered a head wound and developed a fever.'

'Which I am relieved to see has left you,' Dr Jessop said, prodding the flesh around the wound, causing Charles to grimace with the pain this caused.

Slowly the pain subsided a little and Dr Jessop stood back and looked down at him. 'You're Irish,' Charles remarked, wondering why he should state the obvious.

'Sure I am—from County Wicklow, but it's a long time since I saw the Old Country. I'm a surgeon by profession. I've worked for the East India Company for more years than I care to count, but my work extends beyond the Company. Many residents of Nandra and the villages beyond seek my services when they are in need.'

'I imagine a trained surgeon is a treasure in such a remote place as this.'

'I go where I'm needed. There's no lack of work to be done—soldiers to patch up after some skirmish or other.'

'We're glad to have you at the hospital for a while, Dr Jessop—to make use of your skills,' the young woman said, gathering up the soiled dressings.

'I sure have my work cut out. We can mend broken bones and wounds incurred in fighting, but nothing can keep out the disease, the fevers and the gangrene that creep silently and infect people without notice until it's too late and kills so silently.

'I'm due to leave any time soon—to get back to the regiment in Madras. I can't say I won't be glad to leave the state of Puna. The territory is too unsettled to be easy. I will leave you now. It's been a long day and I'm ready for my supper. I will leave you in Miss Quinn's capable hands. She has been taught how to treat fevers and common ailments and how to clean and dress many types of wounds. You should rest more easily now the fever's left you.' Without more ado he left them.

'Now you're awake I'll fetch you something to eat when I've dressed your leg,' the young woman said. 'You must be hungry.'

When she talked Charles realised the depth of her charm. Her voice was low and beautifully modulated. 'My horse? Do you know what happened to my horse?'

'You will have to ask the man who was with you to tell you that. I believe he is being accommodated in the military encampment on the edge of town. I came upon you by chance and was concerned with getting you to the hospital at the time. Now please be quiet while I dress your wound. It will cause you some discomfort which, I am afraid, is unavoidable. Please remain still.'

Charles watched her as she worked, clenching his teeth when the pain almost overwhelmed him. In an attempt to overcome the agony, he concentrated on the young woman. Her body was lean and sleek as a greyhound's. There was a natural grace about her, almost stately, and a quiet dignity. He'd noted as she walked towards his bed that she moved like a dancer.

An abundance of silky pale blonde hair drawn back from her face was plaited and wrapped in a coil at the nape of her neck. Her cheekbones were high, her features perfect, her eyes huge and the colour being a dark green flecked with gold lights that hinted at hidden depths, reminding him of a tiger he had seen on a hunt when he had first come to India.

The sun had tanned her skin to a golden colour and her mouth was rosy and full. Despite his pain he took pleasure in looking at her. Her face was alluring yet imperious, that told the world that she wasn't to be trifled with. Everything about her fascinated him, drew him to her, and he felt a stirring of interest as he looked into the glowing dark eyes. A large soiled apron covered her grey dress.

Her allure was tangible and he saw the danger of getting to know her too well. She was as exquisite and dangerous as the cobra he had seen emerge from the basket of a man in the bazaar in Madras.

Sitting on the floor cross-legged, the man had removed the lid of his basket and started to play his pipe. Soon the head of a cobra with its spreading hood had appeared, drawn by the mystical sound of the pipe. Its eyes were cold, mesmerising and deadly. Charles had stood and watched, transfixed. His companion had laughed at him when he had stepped back.

'Impressive, is it not, Charles? But be assured that its venom could fell an elephant should its fangs pierce its skin.'

Why Charles should think of that when he looked at Miss Quinn, a woman he suspected was in possession of an intelligent mind as well as beauty, he had no idea. On her part her attention was born of an inclination to minister to his wounds, but in a strange way her attention excited him.

'The doctor referred to you as Miss Quinn. Are you Jeremiah Quinn's daughter by any chance?'

'He is my father. You know him?'

'We have never met but his name is familiar to me. He was a Company factor I believe.'

'He was a Company Resident in Puna and a collector of land revenues. Ill health forced him to retire three years ago.'

'Yet he remains here—in Nandra.'

'He says he is too old to move on. He loves India and Nandra has become his home. It is where his friends are. I am Lucy Quinn. I brought you to this small infirmary. It was fortunate Dr Jessop was here to attend your injury.'

'For which I shall be eternally grateful. Hopefully my recovery will be swift and I will be on my way.'

'You used to work for the Company, did you not, Mr Anderson?'

He nodded. 'Once.'

'But you no longer do so.'

'You—have heard of me?'

'Oh, yes. You are well known. Your reputation has preceded you. Are you as wicked and dangerous as your reputation would lead one to believe?'

He laughed. 'Miss Quinn, I beg you not to destroy my reputation. I have worked very hard at it.' Was that a smile he saw twitching her lips?

'I imagine it wasn't too difficult. However,' she said, on a more serious note, 'I have heard you are a man of attainment, of exceptional courage and resourcefulness, that when you worked for the Company you took your duties beyond what was expected of you. Indeed, such is your prowess with lance and musket that I am surprised you did not make soldiering your career.'

Her remark was a statement of fact, without any form of sarcasm from which he would have taken offence. 'I happen to like what I do now and leave soldiering to the professionals. As for the Honourable Company, it did not take me long to realise the corporate greed of the Company's reign of supremacy, with the most dire consequences for the Indians.'

'Is that why you left?' she asked, curious.

His stare did not waver from her face and he did not immediately answer. All the years of his adult life, working at East India House in London, the only thing he had invested with real importance had been the Company. It had always given a meaning to his life, to everything he did. But all that had changed when he had arrived in India. With no sense of achievement he had left the Company with only the leaden sickness of disillusionment.

When he spoke, his voice was distant, as though all emotion had been carefully erased from it. 'Yes. What I saw about how the Company was run I found unacceptable. I was suspicious of the corruption of British politics by the money and influence that the Company's men have gained in India, which was why I resigned.'

'I see you are a man of principle, Mr Anderson.'

'I know the difference between right and wrong, Miss Quinn, and by continuing to work for the Company it could be seen that I was furthering its corruption. I now work for the British Foreign Office and diplomatic service—which is why I have come to see the Rajah of Guntal at his palace in Kassam. Guntal is an independent state and the Rajah, Naveen Madan, intends it to remain that way. He is not so well disposed to the East India Company and he will not be moved on the issue of Guntal being taken over by it.'

'You have been to Guntal in the past?'

He nodded. 'Once. I was appointed envoy to the court of the Rajah. While no major trading privileges have been conceded by him, I hope the result of my mission will be the beginning of a satisfactory relationship between the state of Guntal and Britain. It is my duty as a diplomat to build up Indo-British relations wherever I am sent.'

'Then I wish you every success.' Her work finished, Miss Quinn collected the soiled linen and the bowl and looked at him, balancing the bowl on her hip. 'You must try to rest now, Mr Anderson. I'll have some food brought to you. You should sleep more easily tonight.'

Charles watched her walk away. Above the smell of antiseptic, the faint scent of rosewater wafted around her, along with an air of hushed calm.

Closing his eyes, he rested more easily in his bed, determined not to be confined for longer than was necessary. He cursed his injury and was impatient to be about his business. India was made up of many territories ruled by different governments. Those not owned by the British and the Dutch separately were ruled by the Princes and Maharajas of the Hindu. As Charles worked for the British Foreign Office, it was his policy to seek better relations with these powers, but before he could further these relations he had to return to England.

Lucy lived with other British residents in the cantonment on the outskirts of the small town of Nandra. It formed a self-contained community, having expanded over the years. Set in smooth lawns dotted with well-tended flowerbeds and shaded with peepul trees, the simple one-storey buildings, wrapped round with deep verandas, were washed in white.

The cool, high-ceilinged house where Lucy lived

with her father was more spacious than most, the rooms still filled with her mother's bric-a-brac. The sweet smell of tobacco from her father's pipe hung in the air in his office, where his work of revenue records and land surveys had once been scattered on the desk. They had a small complement of servants needed to ensure their domestic comfort and Kasim, a man to tend her father now he was confined to bed.

Taking a cool drink on to the veranda, she sat and gazed into the night. Stretching out her legs and supporting her feet on a low foot stool, she sipped the cool lime juice, sitting back in her chair as two mynah birds squabbled raucously. Her thoughts turned to Mr Anderson. Almost everyone had heard of him and his exploits and how he had single-handedly held off a band of raiders when he had worked for the Company. In fact, the ladies of Madras where he had been stationed, married or single, found him quite irresistible apparently. There was no accounting for taste, but Lucy was confident that she would have no difficulty resisting Mr Anderson.

She thought back to the moment she had seen him on the ground, seriously wounded. His eyes were closed. There was blood in his hair from a head wound and blood had pooled on the ground from his injured right leg. His eyes, the colour dark blue, flickered open and then closed. A weak pulse throbbed in his neck. It was clear his life hung by a fragile thread. From the experience she had gained assisting Dr Jessop at the infirmary, she knew if his wound was not properly treated, he could have died of blood poisoning.

She'd assisted Dr Jessop as he'd operated on the leg.

She saw that Mr Anderson, stretched out on the table, had been endowed with a beautiful male body, tautly muscled and toned by years of exercise and partaking in the rigours of training along with the military to keep himself fit for every eventuality.

He was lean of waist and belly, and strong, muscled shoulders rippled beneath his shirt. His hair was thick and a rich dark brown, curling gently into the nape of his neck. His amber skin was clean shaven. It was obvious at a mere glance that he was an arrogant man, bold and self-assured—the kind of man she had learned to avoid.

A shudder ran through her as the memory of what had been done to her seven years ago returned as sickeningly as ever. Tears pricked her eyes. It was no good. She had tried in vain, day after day, to escape from that dreadful day which had destroyed her life, when she had been assaulted by a virtual stranger, a stranger who had brutally stollen her virtue. She had been just eighteen years old at the time, but in worldly experience she was still a child. Then, she'd had such high hopes for the future, her head filled with the kind of dreams every girl dreamed.

Mercilessly, inexorably, the horror of what had been forced on her came back to haunt her again and again. The man had taken his pleasure where he found it, for instant gratification, to be discarded and forgotten soon afterwards. Not so for Lucy, who had felt dirtied and corrupted and beyond redemption.

The warm sunlight bathed the small infirmary in soft light. Miss Quinn had just arrived and Charles leaned back on his pillows, watching her with interest, amazed by the gracious ease with which she tended the patients. He studied her profile, tracing with his gaze the classical lines of her face. She was quite extraordinarily lovely. He had never seen the like of her. She had an untamed quality running in dangerous undercurrents, a wild freedom of spirit just below the surface. For Charles Anderson, she represented everything most desirable in a woman. There was also something quite regal about her and she possessed a single-minded determination and a quiet will which he admired.

There was no doubting the sincerity of her tone whenever she spoke to him and he had begun to feel drawn to her, watching for the moment when she would appear and he could feast his eyes on her—and he didn't like the feeling. His present mode of life as a diplomatic envoy suited him. No ties. No regrets as he moved from town to town. And, most importantly, no emotional involvements.

Unbidden, a familiar ache returned to his heart, one he had long since buried. Sucking in his breath, he sternly dismissed the memories that threatened to overwhelm him, memories of Amelia, the woman he had thought was the love of his life, a woman to share his home and bear his children, a woman who was beautiful, gifted, only to discover she was also a callous and ambitious schemer with a highly refined sense of survival, who had betrayed his trust when she had left him for a man of wealth and superior rank.

That experience had left him wary of women. There was nothing to be gained from dredging up the past, or to waste time on what might have been. He knew the folly of placing his trust in womankind. But this did not stop his eyes searching for Miss Quinn when she did her daily rounds of those afflicted with illness and injury.

When she came to dress his wound, he stared at her bent head as her hands diligently removed the dressing. The sunlight shining in through the open window brought out all the glorious shades of her hair, from pale gold to silver. His experiences of life had conditioned him to react to any situation with lightning reflexes, yet now he didn't move, didn't think—and damn if his traitorous heart didn't beat faster and a spear of lust pass through him. The sensations spreading through him were like nothing he'd ever experienced before. They came in waves, each faster and stronger than the last.

There was something deep within Miss Quinn that made her sparkle and glow like a precious gem, a gem that needed only the proper place and setting to complement her exquisite features and alluring body. Suddenly the old, abandoned dream of having a wife to light up his life with warmth and laughter, to banish the emptiness inside him, returned.

He quickly caught himself up short, disgusted with his youthful dreams and unfulfilled yearnings, dreams and yearnings he had carried with him into adulthood, stupidly believing Amelia was the woman to make them come true, only to have them dashed like a storm-tossed sea breaking against the rocks. Suddenly pain shot through him when Miss Quinn began to redress the wound and he scowled as he realised she was bringing all those old yearnings back to torment him.

Aware of his sudden tension, Miss Quinn raised her head and looked at him, her eyes large and intense in her flushed face. 'I apologise if I hurt you. The wound is still raw, but knitting together nicely. You will be up and about in no time.'

'That's good to know,' he replied tightly, dreading the moment when he would have to test his leg's ability to carry his weight. 'How is your father?' he asked when she paused and handed him some water.

'No better, I'm afraid.'

'And your mother?'

'She is no longer with us. She has been dead two years now.'

'You miss her?'

'Yes, daily. We were close. Father is a quiet man, a clever man, who took his work with the Company seriously, even though, like yourself, he did not always agree with how things were run.'

'What has life been like for you in the cantonment?'

'Pleasant enough. People entertain at each other's houses. Father would entertain his friends and drink too much, but then most of the men in the cantonment drink too much and many suffer from damaged livers.'

Charles smiled at the seriousness of her expression. 'I can see you love your father, Miss Quinn.'

'I do—passionately. He is the only person in the world I do love. His love of India he has passed on to me,' she told him as she began to wrap a clean bandage around his leg, 'educating me with the enthusiasm which comes of real affection for one's subject so that I quickly accumulated a fair knowledge of India's complex history. I learned to appreciate and respect the traditions and customs of what to many will always remain a land of mystery, with its unique culture, beliefs and superstitions and its ancient gods.'

'If he is up to it, I would like to meet him when I am back on my feet. I am surprised that you work in the hospital,' he said as she put the finished touches to his dressing. He was curious to know more about her. 'Is it not frowned upon by the ladies here in Nandra?'

'Absolutely, but I don't let it concern me. I help in the hospital when I am needed. There are always wounds needing attention and Dr Jessop values my assistance.'

'And I imagine all the patients fall in love with you, Miss Quinn,' he remarked with a desire to know how she interacted with other patients in her care.

Her face hardened. 'I sincerely hope not, Mr Anderson. If that were to occur, then they would be disappointed and learn to stifle their amours. I have neither the time nor the inclination for such dalliance.'

Charles lifted a brow to regard her with some amusement. 'You have an uncommon honesty about such matters—unlike most women.'

There was a gleam of battle in her eyes as she held his gaze. 'Many men see my independence as a threat. I protect my honour,' Miss Quinn countered.

'And to add to your accomplishments you speak fluent Urdu.'

'How do you know that?'

'I heard you speak to my servant before I lost consciousness. There are few people of my acquaintance who make any concession to learning local languages or customs. You are an exception.'

'I have been in India long enough to know these things. When I came here with my parents, knowing that I was to be here for a long time because of my father's work encouraged me to speak the languages. Some people who know this think it peculiar and are amused by it. I find it amusing for different reasons. If I were in France or Spain for any length of time and failed to learn to converse in French or Spanish, it would be regarded as neglectful. Urdu is a serviceable language to begin with.'

'You think that, do you, Miss Quinn?'

She looked at him, ready to argue, but found him regarding her seriously and with some interest. 'You don't find it peculiar?'

'Why on earth would I do that? I am impressed.'

'Do you speak it—or any of the other languages of India?'

'A little—I am determined to be more conversant. So you see, you, Miss Quinn, have me at a disadvantage—which is a first for me. You are also a forthright young lady—and your eyes are quite remarkable—unusual—as dark a green as I have seen before.'

Miss Quinn stiffened and averted her eyes. 'I have never thought there to be anything remarkable about my eyes—apart from the necessary fact that I can see through them very well. I don't like empty flattery, Mr Anderson, so please do not insult my intelligence by using it on me. I *do* have a truly direct nature.' He raised an eyebrow at her reproach. She imagined he was not used to a woman questioning a compliment.

'And you, Miss Quinn, insult my honour. I never say what I don't mean.' His tone was serious.

'You are very sure of yourself.'

'Not so sure as you might think. Accept the compliment for what it is. You are a lovely young woman and, for the time I am indisposed, I look forward to getting to know you better. My instinct tells me that you are a woman with spirit, with the face of an angel. I truly believed when I opened my eyes that I had indeed died and gone to heaven.'

When Miss Quinn spoke her voice was cold. 'You are too forward by far, Mr Anderson. As for becoming better acquainted with me, you are Dr Jessop's patient and will be treated as such and no differently from any of the other patients. Have you a wife waiting for you at home?'

Apart from a darkening to his eyes, his features remained impassive. 'I do not have a wife, Miss Quinn. I doubt a woman would be happy to share the life of a nomad and I'm never in one place long enough to put down roots and settle down. That is just one of the reasons I have yet to take a wife.'

He spoke quietly with a placid indifference to his bachelor state. He possessed a natural desire for a beautiful woman, but never for more than a passing affair. Yet Miss Quinn appeared to capture the very essence of the perfect woman who could tempt a man to bind his very soul to own her. He quickly recollected himself as he was beset with self-reproach. The bang on the head must have been more serious than he had thought to allow his thoughts such meanderings.

* * *

'I apologise if I have offended you, Miss Quinn,' Mr Anderson said as she finished her task. 'It was not my intention to scare you away, but for us to become better acquainted.'

He was watching her intently and Lucy tried to ignore the shiver that ran down her spine, which put her on her guard. She had felt something she had rarely experienced before when she had listened to his compliments—embarrassment. She was dishevelled and her hair was all mussed up, yet this man found her attractive.

Nobody had been so wholeheartedly complimentary before and she felt a small tingle of excitement. She was disturbed by Mr Anderson. He evoked feelings and conflicting emotions she did not welcome. He emanated vitality and masculinity that was so potent it sent an involuntary tingle down her spine. And yet with just one infuriating lift of his brows, one mocking word from him, she lost all decorum and dignity and turned into a virago, prepared to say the most appalling things so as not to give him the upper hand.

Then she was angry at herself for allowing the weakness. Like all the men she knew he was predictable and she was disappointed. She despised his type, men who thought all women were theirs for the taking. Their handsome looks and soft words masked something else, something sinister. The light-hearted banter was meant to hoodwink and posed a persuasive threat.

Normally she found it easy to fall in with anyone's desire for conversation, but Mr Anderson kept his eyes on her face with a sort of frank, unsmiling curiosity that embarrassed her. But she would not weaken. She would not allow him to see her wounds.

His reputation having preceded him, she knew him to be a man of action, fearless and ruthless, a ladies' man and an adventurer. His eyes were as turbulent and as enticing as the winds that blew down on Puna from the vast snow-capped mountain peaks in the north, the beautiful and mysterious Himalayas, their colours ever changing in the light of day. Her instinct also told her he was a man of passion. The insight made her shudder. She realised the implications of his presence at the hospital. He was a man to avoid getting too close to, so, after much deliberation, she came to the simple conclusion to act towards him with private and stringent reservations.

Raising her chin, she gave him a haughty stare. 'It will take more than you to scare me, Mr Anderson. As for becoming better acquainted with me, I will not be coming here again—not for a while. I have other commitments that take up my time.' Recognising the obvious admiration she read in his eyes, she was acutely aware of the boldness of his body stretched out on the bed, his maleness. There was a vibrancy about him that was like no one she'd ever met before. Too bold, she thought. Turning on her heel, she walked away.

Chapter Two

When a man tried to get too familiar, without warning blurred shadows of the assault on her person several years ago forced bitter memories to return, intensifying pictures of her weeping mother holding her. Lucy had wept with her and, once she had started to cry, she couldn't stop. She'd cried for herself. She'd cried for the loss of her virtue.

She'd cried for the death of the man she would have married, his humour, his caring of her, his gentleness and his hopes for them. She'd blamed herself for his death, for, by her actions and his need to avenge what had been done to her, he had lost his life. She'd cried for the pain he must have suffered and she cried for the dreams she had lost and the future she'd so blindly believed in. Her mother had told her everything would be all right. But it wasn't. It never would be again—not for her.

Silence had followed in her household. It seemed there was an unspoken decision that it would be unwise to speak of it, to put what had happened out of her mind—out of all their minds—and in doing so all memories would die.

For a long time, she had been frozen with shame and outrage, retreating into herself, going through the motions of living day to day. When her father had asked the Company to move him to another district, they had come to Nandra. Here she had learned to live again— not happily, but her life went on. There had been no more wild crying of rage, only an icy calm, a new strength to face what was ahead of her.

In Nandra, it was easy to hide away from the society of her former life. Only Dr Jessop knew what had happened to her. He had been there as she had battled with her demons. She had been bruised and traumatised, dirty and sullied, and he had tried to put her back together again. In fact, along with her parents, he had been her salvation…when the worst of things that could happen to a woman had happened to her.

Physically he had succeeded, but the mental scars were for her to deal with. Logically she knew it had not been her fault and yet the feeling of blame that Johnathan, the man she would have married, had lost his life avenging her lingered, lurking in the darkest corners of her mind. She yearned to go back to how it had been between them. How he had made her heart sing with joy and she had felt such passion the like of which she had never known.

She recalled the moment she had dressed Mr Anderson's wound and touched his flesh and the way he had watched her through half-closed eyes. She had been under some kind of narcotic when that awful thing had been done to her, but she could imagine it. Would she ever know what it would be like to experience passionate, mutual bliss—or even to know if it existed at all? Lucy could not imagine there might be any pleasure in such a procedure. Although, she mused, had she not enjoyed Johnathan's kisses and caresses? They had been sweet and tender and left her wanting more.

She knew there would come a time when she must reconcile with her past or she would be lost for ever, a crucial part of her missing. Was it time to be brave and push herself to become strong, someone worthy of her parents and Johnathan, to do something she had thought she couldn't?

Charles watched Miss Quinn go, feeling a rush of anger including disappointment that her departure had been so abrupt. Then he laughed at himself, bemused as to why he should feel that way, why he should feel anything at all. The woman was nothing to him, yet he was certainly not indifferent to her, which could apply to many women he had known—women who had enjoyed his attentions and shared his bed for a while.

He couldn't think of anyone, male or female, who would have stood up to him the way she had done, verbally reproach him and walk away as regal as any queen. She had spirit, a fiery spirit that challenged him. Her arrogance was tantamount to disrespect, yet in spite of himself he admired her style. Nor was she afraid of him. That was the intriguing part about her. The primal rush of attraction he felt for her surprised him. She was a beautiful woman whose grace would have won her many beaus on the London social scene.

But what he felt for Miss Quinn wasn't lust. This

was different. The feel of her hands on his flesh had stirred in him a powerful sensation that was unwelcome. When her cheeks were flushed from her exertions she reminded him of a rose and she smelled just as sweet. The perfect comparison.

Then he smiled wryly, for the rose might have a delicate flower, but its barbs were sharp and could draw blood. Why did she have to appear and complicate his life? She disturbed him in a way that could be diverting and dangerous and he needed to crush those feelings. He had a job to do, but first he had to recover from this damned injury and get back on his feet. As if to remind him the pain intensified.

'With the amount of work to be done here at the hospital, you must find Miss Quinn an enormous help,' he uttered when Dr Jessop came to look at his wound.

'She surely is—she's also a distraction, I'll say that, but she takes no notice of the besotted young gentlemen who pass through the hospital. Some of her time she spends teaching the British children in the cantonment, but she comes to the infirmary to help when needed, like now, when I haven't enough assistants to take care of all those who come through the doors. Medicine and staff are a problem, with not enough assistants to tend the numerous wounded from battles fought both here and in other field hospitals. It's a problem.'

'Miss Quinn works tirelessly—I've noticed.'

Doctor Jessop nodded. 'I wish I had a dozen like her. She's an absolute treasure. She is also a law unto herself. Miss Quinn is a brisk, no-nonsense soul who, since the death of her mother, has devoted her time to her father.

She's strong willed and has butted a few heads among the community with the work she does here. She's efficient and useful and cares not a fig for convention. Not even her father can control her.'

'I admire her for what she's doing. It takes great courage to go against convention. She appears to be a serious young woman. She has never married?'

'No, she hasn't,' Dr Jessop replied, directing his gaze elsewhere. 'As much as the bachelors who pass through Nandra admire her looks and open manner and her excellent seat on a horse, they are shy of her—which suits her. Unlike other young ladies who come out to India, she has opinions on everything—from the education of the children the families place in her charge to the way the Company is run. In short, she makes gentlemen uneasy and is fast heading towards that sorriest of all fates—spinsterhood—which would be a tragedy in my opinion. I admire a woman with a clever mind.'

Alone once more, Charles tried to close his ears to the moans of a man who had been badly wounded in a street brawl. He lay back wearily, contemplating his future and hoping it wouldn't be too long before he could continue with his journey to see the Rajah of Guntal.

Miss Quinn had nursed him through the initial dangers and the long bouts of agony that followed his injury, so Charles was disappointed when he didn't see her at the hospital again. She had told him that she wouldn't be returning to the hospital, but he did wonder if her reason for not doing so was because she wanted to avoid him, and if so, why? Had he offended her in some way? He sincerely hoped not.

Once his wound began to heal and the pain was less severe, until he placed his weight on it, he decided he had wallowed in bed long enough. Gritting his teeth, he sat on the edge of the bed, prepared to endure the agony of forcing the injured muscles in his thigh to function. He drove himself on, walking with the aid of a stick, but Dr Jessop warned him his leg might never function as well as it had.

After one week he had recovered enough to move into more comfortable accommodation in the cantonment, procured for him by Dr Jessop, in a bungalow to himself and a seemingly endless supply of servants— a luxury he seldom enjoyed in any of the stations he visited. Considering the seriousness of his injury, he made a remarkable recovery, for which his constitution, as much as Dr Jessop's ministrations, could take the credit. The time he had taken exercising and trekking in the mountains had paid dividends, for they had toughened him as nothing else could have done. His leg pained him still and he returned daily to the hospital to have his dressing changed.

Unable to get Miss Quinn out of his mind, setting his jaw, he set out to find her. He was directed to the military encampment close to the cantonment, where Miss Quinn, who was a frequent rider, kept her horse. It was also where Captain Hugh Travis, already known to him and who had been appointed to accompany him on his journey to Guntal, was staying. Hugh had been to the hospital on several occasions to enquire after his health and was content to pass his time with other military men until Charles was sufficiently recovered to resume his journey into Guntal.

Charles arrived at the military encampment where rows of military tents stood in regimental lines. Servants cooked the midday meal over open fires and the soldiers not on duty lounged about, talking and laughing among themselves. A company of soldiers were about to be put through their drill, the company commander watching them. Captain Hugh Travis, standing at the side of the drill sergeant, told him to continue. The drill sergeant immediately began barking out a series of commands. The soldiers all marched as one in perfect synchronisation.

Seeing Charles, Hugh beckoned him over. Hugh was a fair-skinned robust man with a pleasant face that suggested a kind and genial disposition. Having spent a good deal of time together in India, the two men were good friends and he greeted Charles with a friendly slap on the back.

'Good to see you back on your feet, Charles. How's the leg?'

Charles grinned, leaning on the cane he used to aid his walking and swinging his injured leg as a point of defiance. 'Getting better by the day, Hugh—better by the day.'

Hugh laughed. 'I'll take your word for it. Come to check on your horse?'

Charles nodded. 'I'm keen to be back in the saddle, Hugh, and be on my way.'

Standing by the Captain's side and observing the sweating soldiers being put through the drill, Charles shook his head. 'I thank the Lord I'm attached to the Foreign Office and not a soldier having this kind of practice day in and day out. This heat at this time of day is enough to fell a man.'

Hugh laughed. 'The best way to help them is to make sure they're fighting fit and ready for action. They'll thank the drill sergeant for it in battle.'

'And when not in battle the curse of peace time is boredom when a soldier can indulge in his pleasures—drinking to excess.'

'When they've done here it's time for musket practice. How is the leg really, Charles?' Hugh asked as they sauntered away from the drill, slowing his walk to accommodate the invalid. 'It is healing all right?'

'If you want the truth, it's damned painful. The muscles of my thigh tighten like wet leather when I remain immobile too long. Doctor Jessop explained the healing process would be slow—that I'll have to be patient. As you know, Hugh, patience is not one of my virtues. Thought I might take a short ride—get used to being back in the saddle.'

'Your horse is in the pen but don't you think it's a bit soon?'

'I don't think so. Have you seen Miss Quinn by any chance—the young woman who helped nurse me back to health? I was told she keeps a horse in the encampment.'

'She does. In fact, I saw her riding out about half an hour since—in the direction of the river.'

In no time at all Charles had his horse saddled up and was riding at a careful pace away from the encampment.

She left her horse grazing close to the shallow river, which meandered its way through the valley, flowing sluggishly over a stretch of shallow stones. Strolling past a row of tamarind trees with bright green feathery foliage and down a steep bank, Lucy stopped at a place where she often came to sit and put her mind in order. Removing her hat and jacket, then unfastening the top buttons of her blouse, she dipped her handkerchief into the water and, turning her face up to the sun, she bathed her face and neck, some of the water trickling down between her breasts.

The water was cold and refreshing. How she would like to strip off her clothes, to lie in the river's shallow depths and let the water wash over her naked body. She dared not, but she did remove her riding boots and stockings and dangled her feet into the cool depths. Content to sit and dream and survey the mystery of the plains stretching out in all directions, she smiled broadly when she looked down and saw tiny silver fish swimming between her feet. Turning her head, she watched as a lizard scuttled across the ground.

When stones rolled down to where she sat, she looked up the bank to see Mr Anderson standing there, looking down at her. His powerful masculinity was an assault on her senses. As if he had reached out and touched her flesh, a tiny erotic trickle coiled through her, startling her, as if a switch had been thrown deep inside her. Impatiently she tried to shake off the effect he was having on her. She had tried not to think of him, wishing she could treat him with detachment, with indifference— but she was powerless to prevent him slipping through her guard, to force her into an awareness of him. Why had she allowed herself to be attracted by him?

Charles stood looking down to where Miss Quinn sat at the water's edge. On finding her he was content to simply look at her and was sorry he had disturbed her. She was the most baffling, beguiling woman he had ever come across and, for his sins, she fascinated him. Observing her day after day as he had lain in his hospital bed, he had become ensnared by her allure. Her profile was soft against the setting sun. She was beautiful, exquisite. Yet there was something else about her that intrigued him. It was not easily apparent.

Having one failed and painful love affair behind him, he had decided not to become caught up in another serious relationship, that his work would come above all else. He was now master of himself—he was sure of that—or perhaps not so sure when Miss Quinn suddenly turned her head and looked at him, a half-smile on her lips.

The effect on Charles was as potent as the full smile she had given him on coming out of his delirium. He felt the tingling in his neck and then down his spine, as intense as any he had ever known. He was bewitched, utterly enchanted by this new picture of Miss Quinn as she smiled, her lovely face suffused with pleasure and her soft lips parted and lifted with laugher. He was relieved to discover she had not lost her ability to smile after all.

Spellbound as he was, the tingling turned to heat, a curious, inflaming heat. The heat grew as she continued to look at him—he was aroused by that smile. For a moment he felt his resistance waver. It pulled him up short. It was a small warning, but a warning all the same. Too often for his peace of mind, Miss Quinn could get beneath his guard. He would have to keep a tighter rein on his attraction to her, but she was not an easy woman to ignore. Her manner and personality along with her beauty, of which she seemed unaware, remained unblemished by self-interest. Until that moment he had not fully realised the extent of the emotions she aroused in him, but, seeing her like this, immersed in her own thoughts, at ease and uninhibited, he knew it was going to be no simple matter leaving her behind when he left for Guntal.

When Lucy saw who it was who had come to disturb her peace, her smile was fleeting, vanishing from her lips. Immediately she withdrew her feet from the river, pulling down her skirt, no doubt feeling extremely vulnerable that he should find her with her bare legs dangling into the water.

'Mr Anderson!' she said, glancing to where he had left his horse, close to her own. 'You take me by surprise. I did not expect to see you back in the saddle quite so soon.'

'I'm impatient to regain the strength in my leg. The sooner I can continue with my journey into Guntal, the better. Do you often come down to the river?'

'When I can.' Grasping her boots and stockings, she scrambled back up the bank.

'I came to find you. I hope you don't mind.'

She seemed surprised. 'Did you? What on earth for?'

'To apologise for any offence I may have caused—which I hope was not the reason you haven't been to the hospital of late. I've come to make amends,' he told her, sitting on a convenient boulder and lounging back in an indolent manner.

She eyed him warily. The amazing eyes still focused on her as he waited for her to reply. She drew a deep breath. 'You have? You seem unsure.'

He raised one well-defined eyebrow, watching her, a half-smile playing on his lips. 'I'm quite sure. You are well, I trust.'

'As you see,' she replied evenly, 'I have survived our previous encounters without scars—and my absence from the hospital has nothing to do with you. I have other duties, teaching children here in the cantonment, which keeps me busy most days.'

Charles noted the softening of her expression that was currently replacing her normal hauteur. No man could not be moved by the lovely features of this woman, who possessed a spirit equal to his own. It really added to his admiration of her. He'd known it from the start by just looking into her eyes and realised the spirit of her there, the intelligence. 'Hasn't anyone told you it isn't advisable to go wandering off alone?' He looked down at her feet. 'I see you have removed your boots and stockings as well.'

'Clearly,' she replied, her sarcasm not lost on Charles. 'I couldn't resist the pull of the cool water.' Her look challenged him to argue.

'Now that I can understand. I have noted that since

our meeting at the hospital, things have been somewhat strained between us. If I have been at fault and offended you in any way, then I beg your pardon. I would dearly like us to promote a deeper understanding and friendship between ourselves—if you are in agreement, that is?'

Sitting on the ground and proceeding to pull on her boots, Lucy stiffened. 'No, of course not. But I think we understand each other well enough—and I was not aware that our friendship needs promoting. You will be leaving for Guntal as soon as your wound is healed enough to withstand the journey and we will never see each other again.'

'I did not intend to cause you any…puzzlement. When I came across you and took you to the hospital, to me you were no different to any other wounded man or sick child who needed care. If you find me quiet, that is because I am a private person. I have much on my mind.'

Perched on his boulder, he continued to watch her, his eyes dark and brooding. 'I have no wish to break into your privacy, but you have erected a barrier between us which puzzles me. You appear to have formed an adverse opinion of me and keep me at arm's length for some reason, which I find hard to understand. I believe I have expressed my gratitude with all sincerity for what you did for me when you found me wounded.'

'For which I thank you. I have never wished to be hurtful or unfriendly towards you, Mr Anderson,' she said, having pulled on her boots and standing up, 'and I do not believe I have been either. You misjudge me and my motives. I apologise if you find my manner and my character at all unfriendly. I do not mean to be. It is as I am and I cannot guess how else you would have me be. My father is very much on my mind at present. With that and the work I do, I can think of little else.'

'I can understand that. It cannot be an easy time for you.'

'It isn't. I appreciate your concern.'

'How long have you been in India, Miss Quinn?'

'Since I was ten years old. Father was born here. He didn't like England when he finally got to go there—he said it was too cold and always raining and he couldn't wait to get back to India. Sadly, my mother, who was an only child and was brought up in London, couldn't settle in India. She couldn't stand the dust, the humidity and the poverty she found here.'

'You still have relatives in England?'

'My maternal grandmother—whose health has deteriorated of late. My grandfather, who was in banking, died of a seizure several years ago. I correspond with my grandmother on a regular basis—although as you will know from your own experiences regarding any correspondence from England, by the time letters arrive here, it is old news.'

'That is true.'

'Grandmother hated it when Mother left for India. She missed her terribly and lived in hope that she would return home. Sadly, they never saw each other again.'

'And what is your opinion of India, Miss Quinn?'

'I like it very well. When I first came here, I found it a magical place to be and very exciting. I loved the vibrancy of it all. It all seemed very exotic to me. It quickly became my home.'

'And you are still unmarried.'

She nodded, turning her head away, but not before Charles had seen a dark shadow enter her eyes. 'Yes, and that suits me very well.'

There was some history there, Charles thought, and he was tempted to probe further. But it wasn't his business and he knew there was no point pressing her to reveal more than she wanted to reveal. If she felt like talking about it, she would.

'How unconventional you are, Miss Quinn.'

'I'm afraid I am,' she agreed with an unregretful sigh. 'The ladies in the cantonment, with nothing better to do, discuss me over their afternoon tea all the time, having already decided I am beyond redemption, that I have utter disregard for the rules that govern the conduct and outlook of other young ladies. And you, Mr Anderson?' she said, swinging the conversation around to the safer ground of asking him about himself. 'Are you as popular with the ladies in Madras as you are portrayed as being?'

'No one is ever quite what they seem, Miss Quinn,' he replied, sidestepping the question. 'Not even you. Besides, since leaving the Company I have not been to Madras. You know,' he said, his gaze never leaving hers, 'you have a unique distinction.'

'I have? What is that?'

'You have the distinction, apart from my sister, of being the only woman to have reminded me of my less than honourable reputation to my face.' His lips twitched with ill-suppressed amusement. 'I recall you accused me of being wicked and dangerous. Lying there in the hospital, I felt wounded to the quick and deflated, as though I'd been pricked all over with thorns.'

'You have a hide thicker than an oxen's, Mr Anderson,' Miss Quinn retorted drily. 'I'm sure you'll heal. Why did you come to India?'

'Because I wanted to. I was working for the Company in London and when the opportunity for me to come to India arose, I leapt at the chance—which was as well. It is only by being here—working for the Company—that my eyes were opened to the corruption that went on.'

'Which is why you left and became a diplomat—a much more honourable profession.'

'I think so.'

'And you get to go to wonderful places. The Rajah of Guntal's palace is renowned for its beauty.'

'You have been there?'

She shook her head. 'No, but I would love to. You can see it from here—see?—far in the distance.'

Shading her eyes, she looked across the shimmering expanse that separated Nandra from Guntal, to the blue mountains topped with snow. The pink walls of the Rajah's palace could just be made out over the miles, sleeping under the open blue sky, basking comfortably in the heat haze.

'There,' she said, pointing in the direction of the palace. 'That is where the Rajah of Guntal lives in fantastic splendour in the city of Kassam. You should get there in less than a day's ride.'

'Which is fortunate considering my injury.'

'Yes—you are so lucky to be going there.' Tearing her eyes away from the object of her dreams, she looked at Mr Anderson, who was watching her closely. 'You mentioned that you would like to meet my father.'

He nodded. 'I would—if it is convenient.'

'I told you he is unwell, but I know he would be pleased to meet you. Perhaps tomorrow evening.'

'Of course. I will look forward to it.'

'Then that's settled. You have family here?'

He shook his head. 'What family I have is back in England.'

'Who is Tilly?'

'Tilly? She is my sister. Why do you ask?'

'Because in your delirium when you were at the hospital, you kept repeating her name. You must be close, I think.'

'You think correctly. Tilly is younger than me—she married an earl and went to live in Devon before I left to come to India.' He looked at her sideways, squinting his eyes in the sun. 'You remind me of her,' he said suddenly.

'Do I? How?'

'It is a compliment, Miss Quinn. Believe me. Tilly is like a free spirit, but she is also a fierce individual.'

Miss Quinn smiled. 'So you are saying I am fierce— but I'll accept the compliment. You miss her, don't you?'

He was silent for a moment, his gaze shifting to a place beyond her. 'Yes, very much. I haven't talked about her in a long time.'

With the sun settling on them both, Miss Quinn waited for him to go on.

'I remember the joy of her, the way she had of teasing me mercilessly, the sound of her laughter—and the way her eyes would sparkle when she was happy.'

'I see the way you love her.' She felt his gaze steady and searching on her face, as if he wanted her to know his sister.

'I also have a half-brother—he's a marquess.'

Miss Quinn raised her eyebrows in mock surprise. 'A marquess? How very grand.'

He grinned. 'He is. He came out to India with the Company before leaving and going off on his own, before returning to England to take up his inheritance.'

'And where do you live, Mr Anderson, when you are in England?'

'In London—although I do have a house in Devon.'

'Devon is a long way from London.'

'It is—and I have yet to see the house, which is close to the coast. I inherited it on the death of an uncle. I did consider selling it, but Tilly lives close by—she lived in the house for a while and loves the place. She persuaded me not to sell it—not until I've seen it.'

'And will you go and see it?'

He shrugged. 'I have no idea. Probably—when I return to England.'

'Who lives there now?'

'At present my aunt is in residence—along with a couple of servants. She has fallen in love with the place, so I expect I shall have to please them both and hold on to it for the present.' He struggled to his feet when Miss Quinn began to walk towards the horses, bringing a scowl to his face. 'Do you have to walk so quickly? My wound forbids me to move at a faster pace,' he said when she glanced back at him with suspicion.

'You do not look to be in great pain, Mr Anderson, so

I am inclined to think your wound is healing.' Then she frowned at the guilty smile that flitted across his face. 'Although, it would seem you are not above playing on your infirmity to garner sympathy and to get your own way,' she said sweetly but pointedly.

His grin was disarming. 'You read me too well, Miss Quinn. I will not lose any opportunity to gain your attention in the hope that on better acquaintance you might get to like me a little better.

As they rode side by side back to the encampment, looking straight ahead Lucy thought of the strange conversation they had engaged in. Had she been too ready to judge, to believe the gossip she'd heard about him? Was he so different from what she had assumed? For the short time she had known him, she decided that none of it described him or did him justice. There was a powerful charisma about him that had nothing to do with his honed physique or mocking smile.

There was something else, too, something behind that lazy smile and unbreachable wall of aloof strength behind his dark blue eyes, that told her that Charles Anderson had done, seen and experienced all there was to do and see, that to know him properly would be exciting and dangerous, and therein lay his appeal—an appeal that frightened and unnerved her.

She told herself that he was nothing to her, just a spectacularly handsome man who happened to have entered her life when he had taken an unfortunate tumble from his horse. As soon as he was recovered, he would leave for Guntal and any association between her and the infamous Charles Anderson would cease.

Yet all the time Lucy rode beside him or followed him along narrow, winding paths, she was burningly aware of him in ways that she had never been with Johnathan. She was shaken to the core by the bewildering sensations racing through her body. She tried to turn her head away, but his extraordinary presence would draw her back. These feelings and emotions disconcerted her and made her feel strangely lightheaded. It was as if he invaded her very being.

Vaguely she realised that, despite what had happened to her and her youthful romance with Johnathan, she was an innocent when it came to physical desire. She had never experienced anything even vaguely resembling what she was experiencing now. All about them was the sweep of the landscape and a sky full of birds rising and wheeling in glittering formations against the puffs of cloud. Her increasing preoccupation with Mr Anderson troubled her. Better to keep him at arm's length, prudence whispered—but since when had she listened to prudence?

Chapter Three

~~~~~~~~~~

Seated in her usual chair on the veranda awaiting the arrival of Mr Anderson, Lucy saw him coming towards her, his firmly marked eyebrows drawn together as he concentrated on placing one foot in front of the other, steadying himself with his cane. As her thoughts raced, he paused and looked at her, then carried on walking towards her.

In that moment she noticed the startling, intense blue of his eyes and again thought how extraordinarily attractive he was. Her heart seemed suddenly to leap into her throat in a ridiculous way and she chided herself for being so foolish.

She was lightly clad in a shimmering green and gold sari. A curling lock of gleaming blonde hair had come loose from its arrangement in the nape of her neck and curled over her shoulder, resting on her breast. Lucy knew instinctively that he was just as aware of her as she was of him and bent her head so that he should not see her confusion. After a moment, quite composed now, she lifted her eyes and rose and stood at the top of the steps to wait for him, flicking the lock of hair back over her shoulder. His direct masculine assurance disconcerted her, but she was determined not to show weakness.

'I trust it's still convenient to meet with your father?'

'Yes, of course. He's awake now and looking forward to meeting you. Excuse me while I go in and tell him you are here.'

Lucy paused in the doorway of her father's bedroom. The punkah, suspended over the large bed with its richly embroidered silk cover that stood in the centre of the room, swayed gently in the draught from the door. Seated in a curved-back armchair close to the window overlooking the garden at the back of the house, was her father. He was wearing a long, loose robe of saffron silk, with a pair of soft slippers on his feet. His eyes were closed as if asleep or in deep thought.

Lucy paused for a moment to take in the sight of him. His face was drawn and there were dark rings round his eyes. He looked so frail and elderly. He had lost weight and his skin was an unhealthy yellow.

As if sensing a presence, he opened his eyes. On seeing her a smile spread across his face.

'Mr Anderson has arrived, Father, and is eager to meet you.'

'And I him. Doctor Jessop speaks highly of him.' He squinted at his daughter. 'Tell me, what is this Mr Anderson like? Is he to your liking?'

Taken by surprise by his question, Lucy averted her eyes, but was unable to quell the flush that mantled her cheeks, which did not go unnoticed by her father and brought a frown to his brow.

'Yes—I mean—he is well liked and highly thought

of by those who know him—but I do not know him very well.'

'But well enough to have formed an opinion, surely.'

Lucy shrugged complacently. 'You will soon see for yourself what kind of man he is.'

He nodded, studying her closely. 'I dare say I will. It pleases me when visitors come to call. It provides me with the opportunity to talk about the old days in India.' Tilting his head to one side, he said, 'You look well, Lucy—more relaxed somehow—different. Happily, I believe I am beginning to see the old Lucy slowly emerge from her shell.'

'I'm trying, Father. Every day I try.'

'Of course you do. It's time to move on. It's been long enough—too long. Don't let what happened to you steal your future. I would not want that for you. You are too young to shut yourself away.'

'I know. I know. It's all I've thought about of late. But—it's hard, Father.'

'Of course it is.' He patted her hand affectionately. 'But knowing you, you'll get there. Now—we have a guest I am looking forward to meeting. You'd better show him in.'

Going out, Lucy thought of what her father had said about what had happened to her in the past and realised with shock that he was right. She was beginning to feel like her old self, an insight into how her life could be if she would let it and move on. It was up to her to take the initiative.

Mr Anderson turned to face her when she reappeared.

'We'll go in now...' She smiled. 'He has a habit of dropping off to sleep, I'm afraid. He is extremely poorly.

Doctor Jessop sees him on a regular basis, but there is little to be done.'

'I'll try not to tire him.'

Charles levelled a steady gaze at the silver-haired man, noting the unhealthy yellowing of his skin. Silently they took stock of each of each other before shaking hands.

'Mr Anderson.' Jeremiah Quinn spoke to him amiably because his daughter would not have lied about his character. 'I'm sorry I was not there to receive you, but as you see I am incapacitated just now. My health is not good. Jessop has ordered me not to overtax myself. It's more than my life is worth to defy him.' He looked at Lucy standing at the side of his chair. 'You've met my daughter.'

Charles's gaze passed warmly over her, bringing a slight flush to her face, which did not go unnoticed by her father. 'It has been my pleasure.'

'I'm proud of her. She's grown into a fine young woman.'

'Alas, I fear I'm not that, Father,' Lucy retorted. 'Mrs Marsh still thinks I'm a hopeless hoyden and her friend, Mrs Senior, says my manners are deplorable and I am a disgrace. I fear they are both right.'

Her father chuckled softly. 'They are just two old ladies with nothing to do with their time other than gossip.'

He fixed his attention on his visitor. 'I never did keep a tight rein on my daughter, which I have oft had reason to regret, but she has a single-minded determination and a will to match—in addition, she is a courageous young woman with a particular brand of quiet fortitude. You were injured, Mr Anderson—fell off your horse, Lucy tells me.'

'I did and I am grateful to your daughter and Dr Jessop for putting me back together. My wound still bothers me, but it's nothing I can't deal with. I hope to be on my way to Guntal shortly.'

'You must take care. Skirmishes both in Puna and Guntal occur on a regular basis.'

'Father is right,' Lucy said, looking at Charles. 'These raids happen all too often—by such wicked people, who seem to be a law unto themselves.'

'There are good and bad people everywhere.' Jeremiah looked at his visitor. 'You're no longer a Company man, Mr Anderson—not that I blame you. Your new position as a British envoy you must find rewarding. You have met the Rajah of Guntal, I believe. What is the nature of him?'

'I think you'd like him. He's a benevolent sort—but one shouldn't be fooled. He's as shrewd and cunning as an old fox and misses nothing. As you know, Guntal is an independent state and the Rajah intends it to remain that way. Thankfully the two of us get on reasonably well.'

After speaking of diplomatic issues a while longer, Jeremiah's eye lids began to droop. Tactfully Charles left.

Back on the veranda, Lucy indicated the cushioned wicker seat opposite. 'Please take a seat.'

Mr Anderson did as invited and sat opposite her, biting back a curse at the discomfort this caused him. He had turned white around the mouth, Lucy noted in dismay, while his hand rubbed his right thigh. After a moment his pain must have eased because he relaxed and stretched his legs out in front of him.

Recognising the obvious admiration she read in his eyes when he looked at her, she suddenly became aware of the boldness of his body, his maleness and the impropriety of entertaining a gentleman alone at this time of night. Mrs Marsh would consider such behaviour scandalous. Lucy smiled inwardly, uncaring what Mrs Marsh would say.

'You appear relaxed,' Mr Anderson said softly, his gaze appraising.

'I love this time of day, when smoke and dust hang over the town. I love the cool of the evening and often sit and look at the lazy meandering of the river below the sloping lawn and watch the colourful sunsets and the stars come out, which I used to do with my father before he became confined to his bed. We would sit and listen to the crickets and the night birds and the sound of unoiled wheels on the dusty road—all contributing to the murmur of the Indian night. It's a time for dreaming.' She fell silent for a moment as her gaze swept appreciatively over her surroundings.

Cool drinks appeared before them, offered by a young Indian serving girl dressed in a bright pink sari, her shining black hair plaited down her back. A broad smile stretched her lips and she dipped her gaze when she saw the imposing visitor.

'Thank you, Nisha,' Lucy said.

Nisha left as quietly as she had appeared. Accepting the drink Lucy handed to him, her visitor drank gratefully. After a moment's silence he managed to stand.

As he did so his expression was pained, betraying the effect of his exertions. He stood looking down at the river, his tall, lean body clearly delineated by the moon-lit night. 'You are in a good position here, with no over-looking neighbours.'

'Don't you believe it,' Lucy said with irony. 'There are few secrets here. Everyone knows everyone else and what is happening. Your appearance in Nandra will have been seen and noted, and, come breakfast, everyone will be gossiping about it and speculating on the reason for your visit to the house.'

'And will be met with censure, I suppose.'

'You suppose correctly. The British and their an-tiquated ways of doing things—ways that dominate women's lives especially—needs reforming.'

'Forgive me, Miss Quinn, but you seem to have done that all by yourself.'

'Only because it suits me and because I don't give a fig for anyone's opinion. Boredom can set in if one is not careful, which is why I began teaching the children of the British community their lessons and helping Dr Jessop in the infirmary. Before my father's retirement, sometimes I would accompany him on official trips that were not too far away. At other times I ride out in the cool of the day, keeping to the confines of the town for my own safety.'

'You ride alone?'

'Maya, one of the house servants, loves to ride and often accompanies me.'

'And on occasion you even take to wearing Indian dress'

Lucy smiled. 'As you see. I find the light fabrics cooler

and more suitable to the Indian climate. They are also far more comfortable to wear than being trussed up in yards of cumbersome skirts and undergarments and whale bones that restrict the freedom of movement of a healthy female form.'

'Indian dress also shows the natural shape of a woman's body and brings out in her an innate femininity,' Charles said softly. 'I think you are the most unconventional young lady I have ever met, Miss Quinn. You are your own person. It is a relief to find a woman who has dispersed with ridiculous conventions.'

'Not all of them,' she denied indignantly. 'There are still some that I abide by—otherwise my life would not be worth living.'

Charles chuckled softly. 'I do believe you,' he said, his expression telling her he was not convinced.

Lucy smiled. 'I must confess that I find it hard to submit to the taboos and restrictions that govern the conduct of an unmarried English lady in a small station. My lack of convention at first shocked the English ladies of the community, especially one, who scrutinised me thoroughly through her lorgnette when she called on my father one day, and declared it was an outrage that I should flaunt myself so shamelessly. As if that weren't bad enough, another lady, Mrs Marsh, almost suffered an apoplectic fit when I began assisting Dr Jessop in the infirmary. As far as she and the other stiff, elderly ladies who make up the British community were concerned, I broke nearly every rule that dictates the lives of young ladies.'

'Is it not the opinion that a woman should not find herself independent?'

'What? And be governed by the fears and restrictions that blight so many women's lives? I do not share that opinion. I have a mind and will of my own and make my own decisions—for which I am condemned by the likes of Mrs Marsh.'

'How did you react to such condemnation?'

'I simply shrugged off the recriminations and ignore their censure, uncaring what others think of me.'

'And who exactly is Mrs Marsh?'

'She is the doyenne of the British community here. She believes she has the right to dispense orders and judgement like a queen. There are so many rules an English woman in India must abide by—most of which I have broken. A young lady must never voice her opinions in public or discuss politics, which should be left to the men, and she must never appear in public without a servant. In other words, all young ladies must show decorum, prudence and the virtues of sobriety at all times, both in public and in private. She has the young ladies quaking in their shoes.'

'But not you, Miss Quinn.'

'Absolutely not. I am no eighteen-year-old miss, but a woman with a mind and a will of my own. I will not be dictated to by women of Mrs Marsh's ilk.'

Mr Anderson laughed. 'Or anyone else who does not gain your good opinion. You are certainly no delicate, pampered young woman, that's for sure.'

'Precisely. Despite the likes of Mrs Marsh, if you are to remain in Nandra for some time, on the whole you will find a spirit of kindliness and hospitality among the British community. We've had to learn the value of society and don't be surprised when you begin receiving invitations to attend social functions and entertainments. As handsome as you are, Mr Anderson, you will have every lady buzzing round you and wanting to partner you in the dance.'

'Dancing is not one of my favourite pastimes.'

'No? Well, you have the perfect excuse not to—your wounded leg has put paid to that. I do have many friends here—we are all in the same boat, after all, and Mrs Wilson, who came to Nandra with her husband at the same time as my parents and has a married daughter living in Madras, takes me under her wing from time to time, for which I am grateful.

'But I often wonder if the English will ever realise that their customs and values cannot work here in India, where the old gods rule. Few make concession to local custom—beyond the gentlemen smoking hookahs. The fact that I go my own way and don't always listen to the dictates of my father has crystalised all my sins in Mrs Marsh's mind. My father says I am too wilful and unconventional—and I suppose I am. Which is why all the old ladies in Nandra are always complaining to him about me and giving him advice on the best way to deal with a wayward daughter. But he likes me the way I am and wouldn't like it if I were to change.'

'Your father is quite right. You are what you are. You can't please everybody. One's true character springs from the heart and dwells in the eyes. Unconventionality is an invitation to disaster in the world we inhabit.'

Lucy stared at him. 'How very profound.' Gazing into his unfathomable eyes, she saw cynicism lurking in their depths. She had the uneasy feeling that his indolent manner was nothing but a disguise to lull the unwary into believing he was civilised, when he wasn't civilised at all.

Hearing a lilting voice singing in the nether regions of the house, Mr Anderson rested his hips on the rail and folded his arms across his broad chest and cocked a curious brow. 'Someone sounds happy.'

'That's Nisha. She's a great help—although she is to be married shortly and will not be coming here when she is wed. All she's talked about for weeks is the wedding, what she is going to wear and the preparations.'

'It was arranged, I suppose.'

'Of course. It was arranged between the bridegroom's family and her own some time ago. It is the custom—and she is fortunate to have fallen in love with her future husband at first sight.'

'You think that, do you, Miss Quinn—that she is fortunate?'

'Of course I do. A marriage based on love is more likely to withstand the trials and tribulations of the future. Don't you agree? Although I imagine your opinions on that particular subject differs from mine.'

'I have told you previously that I have no time at present for marriage and affairs of the heart. A man who loves too well is vulnerable.'

'When has love anything to do with marriage?' Lucy returned, deriding his cynicism and going to stand beside him at the rail. 'Marriage is a contract based upon oneself for security and property, whereas true love must be free—uninhibited—and have the foundations of trust and fidelity.'

'Ah, but love is inconsistent,' Mr Anderson proclaimed. 'Desire is a more honest and recognisable emotion.'

Lucy lifted her chin as her eyes caught his flickering appreciatively over her from the top of her head to the slippers peeping from the hem of her sari. She shook her head. 'Desire is fleeting, while love is all-consuming.'

'And when love and passion burn themselves out, nothing is left but a shedload of bitterness.'

There was a deep blush on Lucy's cheekbones, as much to her gathering annoyance she found she did not mind his calm, unhurried appraisal of her. 'It doesn't always end like that.'

'Love is not the only side to a relationship.'

'I know. But it is the most important one. I realise that for some, money and gain in some way is the only consideration, but there is more to marriage than that. Two people should marry because they love each other, because there is a longing to be close to each other.'

'You really are a romantic, Miss Quinn.'

'I suppose I am. When I marry, I will settle for nothing less.' When he gave her a sceptical glance, she raised her brows in question. 'I see you find something wrong with that.'

Shaking his head slowly, he smiled thinly. 'In my opinion love is a common passion, in which chance and sensation take the place of choice and reason and draw the mind out of its accustomed state.'

'That is your opinion, but I will not under any circumstances reduce myself to living in wifely obedience in a loveless marriage.'

His gaze returned to her face. He gave her a long slow look, a twist of humour around his beautifully moulded lips. The smile building about his mouth creased the clear hardness of his jaw and made him appear in that moment as the most handsome man in the world. 'And there speaks a hopeless romantic,' he declared softly. 'Love is for the young and idealistic. It is magnificent while it lasts, but once it is appeased it is soon reduced to the boredom of familiarity.'

Lucy laughed despite herself. 'And those are the words of a rake and confirmed bachelor. You should have a care, Mr Anderson, for the day will come when you venture too close to love's flames and get burned. It will bring you more heartache than you can ever imagine.'

'I see that you are determined to think me some kind of reprobate,' he said coolly, 'which is quite untrue I hasten to add. But if so, does it not concern you that to be seen in such bad company might rebound on you?'

There was more than a hint of mockery in his eyes though he continued to smile.

'Not at all. I may be unconventional, but I am far too independent to be concerned whether the company I keep is good or bad. I run my own life.'

'Run it or ruin it, Miss Quinn?' He grinned, his eyes twinkling with mischief. 'Unconventional ladies are always the most exciting.'

A smile twitched the corners of Lucy's lips. 'You may be right. How can I argue with an experienced man of the world? The ladies appear to be enamoured of you. Enjoy your popularity while it lasts.'

'But you will never be one of them, will you, Miss Quinn?'

'Never.' She laughed to dispel the seriousness of the moment. His words were flippant, but Lucy heard an edge to his voice. Some woman in his past had caused that cynical note, she was sure. 'Your words and the seriousness of your expression tells me that whatever has befallen you in the past—perhaps an unrequited love affair—has left scars, as yet unhealed.' What had happened to harden his heart so? she wondered.

He turned away from her. His body was tense, the tendons of his neck corded. Lucy stifled an impulse to reach out to him. The content of their conversation had revived memories for him and she regretted that. She had bitter memories of her own she had no wish to discuss, so she knew exactly how he felt. She continued to stare at his profile, uneasy at the tension which lay between them.

His voice was mocking when he eventually spoke. 'You are right, Miss Quinn. Aren't you curious about her? Aren't you going to ask me who she was—what terrible deed she committed? You are a woman—is that not what all women want to know?'

'It has nothing to do with me. If you want to tell me, you will. You are well travelled, Mr Anderson, and must have been to some interesting places and seen much. You must also have made friends and enemies along the way. Your comments prompted me to draw a conclusion. I didn't mean to pry.'

Drawn by the sincerity of her words, he turned and looked at her. The intensity of his gaze was so profound that Lucy thought he was about to tell her more of the woman who must have got under his skin at some point.

'There are some things one prefers to forget.'

Lucy respected his privacy. She had her own demons to deal with. His gaze was drawn to the scoop of the low neckline of her bodice, which displayed the gentle, upper swell of her breasts. Seeing where his gaze had settled, she put a hand to cover her decolletage.

Suddenly, his direct masculine appearance disconcerted her. She was vividly conscious of his proximity to her. She felt the mad, unfamiliar rush of blood singing through her veins which she had never experienced before, not even with Johnathan. Immediately she felt resentful towards him. He had made too much of an impact on her and she was afraid that, if he looked at her much longer, he would read her thoughts with those brilliant eyes of his.

Clearly amused by her haste to defend her modesty, he chuckled softly. 'Devil take it, Miss Quinn. How am I ever going to regard the woman who nursed me back to health in the same light again?'

She laughed. 'Don't they say restraint is good for the soul?' she challenged.

'I believe they do, but I have yet to find it so. Why do you remain unmarried?'

Lucy turned her head away, having no wish to tell him how she had wrapped the pain and the grief of Johnathan's loss about her like a blanket. 'I—I lost someone—we were betrothed. It—was difficult. He was killed,' she said quietly, a faraway look in her eyes. 'There was an—an incident that led to his death.'

A shadow crossed her face and, for a moment, her companion knew she was recalling the pain that was inflicted on her of her betrothed's death. An incident, she said. She wasn't telling him everything. There was some history there, he thought, and he was tempted to probe further. But it wasn't his business and he knew there was no point pressing her to reveal more than she wanted. He set it aside, for now. There was a desperation about her that he had not witnessed before. She was usually so composed.

'My father always said I hid my feelings and he was right. It has become a habit with me and perhaps a form of defence, too.'

'A defence against what?' The bravado fell away from her, like a cloak, and she transformed before his eyes into someone much more vulnerable.

'Becoming hurt again. At the time it seemed so unfathomable to me that someone whom one had strong feelings for could die so suddenly.' Mr Anderson reached out and touched her arm. Their eyes met and something passed between them. She half smiled. 'To lose someone you love in such a brutal manner is the worst thing that can happen. It's made me more determined never to experience the pain—such distress—like that again. So you see, I have relegated myself to the proverbial shelf for ever.'

He nodded, looking at her from beneath hooded lids. 'Until someone comes along to pluck you off that shelf.'

Again, there was that flirtatious touch in his words

Miss Quinn so distrusted. 'It's a very broad shelf, Mr Anderson. I very much doubt anyone will do that.'

'You are very sure of yourself, Miss Quinn.'

'Not as sure as you might think. I have my weaknesses just like everyone else.'

'You accused me of being a libertine—are you not afraid to be seen in the company of a man with an unsavoury reputation?'

Although Lucy could feel her pulses racing, she somehow managed to maintain her calm expression. 'I haven't thought about it. Should I?'

He arched an eyebrow. 'No. You are quite safe.'

'As you said yourself, Mr Anderson, no one is what they seem. Perhaps you are a scoundrel with a sudden urge to reform.'

A low chuckle preceded his reply. 'Heaven forbid! I confess that I find this unfortunate development a nuisance, but one good thing has come out of it.'

'It has? And what is that, pray?'

'I get to spend time getting to know you better.'

'Why? Do you find my company pleasant?'

'When you're not being stubborn and temperamental.'

'I am never temperamental.'

'I disagree. There's no question about it.'

'Only if I'm driven to it.'

'You know, Miss Quinn, despite what you say about living on a very broad shelf, a lovely young woman like you should be surrounded by doting swains.'

She looked away. 'Why on earth would I want that? I wouldn't know what to do with them. I have my work at the school, which I enjoy, and helping Dr Jessop, which is important to me—and now, perhaps, my father to take care of. I will allow nothing to interfere with that.'

'Not even love,' he murmured softly, his gaze capturing hers.

'No.'

'Are you afraid of love, Miss Quinn?'

'No, of course I'm not.'

'I don't believe you.'

'Believe what you like. It's true,' she retorted.

'Then if you are not afraid of love, why do you hide behind your work at the school and the hospital?'

'I am not hiding—and it is not my school. I just happen to teach there.'

'Now you are prevaricating, Miss Quinn. I think if you didn't have to mix with others on the cantonment, you would be quite happy to make yourself invisible—to fade into obscurity.' He smiled at her sudden look of indignation that his words had provoked.

'I apologise if my opinion is unkind, but you must admit that it does have the ring of truth about it.' She appeared to think about what he had said for a moment. He hoped there was something in his face that would invite her confidence, but it was not forthcoming.

'Whether it is true or not, I would not admit such a thing to you. The man I loved and would have married was killed. I am no longer interested in forming any kind of relationship.'

His eyes narrowed on her face and he spoke softly. 'Then as a woman you are truly unique.'

She looked at him warily, swallowing nervously. 'You

are not trying to seduce me by any chance, are you, Mr Anderson?'

'Would you allow me to seduce you, Miss Quinn?'

Something stirred deep within her—the need for this man that increased with every moment she spent with him. And she had to stop this, needed to remember that he was soon to leave for Guntal. In spite of the fact that his eyes were touching her in a way she hadn't been touched in a long time, she gave him a defiant look. 'Now you're mocking me.'

'I wouldn't dream of doing that. You are far too adorable to mock.'

Her lips curved in a reluctant smile. 'And you really are a complete rogue, Mr Anderson, arrogant and overbearing.'

He grinned. 'I am. I admit it. What I need,' he said, moving closer to her, 'is a lovely, patient and extremely tolerant young woman to take me in hand, to make me see the error of my ways and reform me.'

'Then I wish you luck.' Turning her back on him, she clutched the rail with her hands. 'Intolerance and impatience have always been two of my failings, but there must be a female somewhere who will fall for a silken tongue and an accomplished womaniser, who will be willing to expend so much energy, time and effort on such an unenviable task.'

He laughed softly. 'Maybe there is, but she will never be bored, I promise you that.'

'So, you admit it—what they say about you is true after all.'

When she fell silent, his hands clenched and his eyes

hardened. 'Let me assure you that what you have just accused me of being—a philanderer of the worst possible
kind, I believe—is exceedingly exaggerated and I would
like to set the record straight. I am a man of pride and
honour and with a strong sense of responsibility. You
really shouldn't listen to gossip. I am sorry to disappoint
you and shatter the illusion you appear to have of me,
but I must tell you that it is with some regret that I find
I have little time for the kind of pleasures you speak of.
Much of my time is taken up with the more important
matter of furthering British relations with India.'

Her expression became serious and she nodded slightly.
'I apologise if I have wrongly maligned you. Despite what
I have said to the contrary in our short acquaintance, I
have never been one to listen to gossip, only facts.'

He moved to stand closer to her. 'You are a lovely
young woman, Lucy Quinn—a temptress—a dangerous
temptress I am finding increasingly impossible to resist.'

Suddenly Lucy sensed danger. Her spine prickled.
The air between them was alive with tension. She felt
every moment with such heightened sensuality that she
knew if he were to continue speaking to her in this
manner, she was in danger of releasing all the tensions
and worries she'd been carrying for so long. The need
to be away from him was strong and frightening in its
intensity.

She hesitated. Reaching out, he took her arm and
drew her closer to his side. Should she let him prevail
in his hunger, his desire? No, she didn't want it—or did
she? Her confusion, her passion and her pain rose to a
pinnacle as she stood trembling against him. To be this

close to Mr Anderson felt as though she was suffocating. She didn't think she could survive it. But she would survive it. Her instinct told her that this man wouldn't hurt her. She trusted him. Could he be the one to lead her back to normality, to a normal life, to take away her fear of what to expect from any man who encroached too close?

Tentatively turning to face him, her slender jaw hardening with resolution, she met his gaze directly. 'Mr Anderson,' she said very clearly, 'I would like you to kiss me.'

Chapter Four

⟨ decorative flourish ⟩

Mr Anderson stared at her, clearly wondering if he had heard her correctly. 'What did you say?'

'I want you to kiss me,' Lucy repeated quite clearly. From the way he was looking at her, Lucy realised that he could see she was in the grip of some powerful emotion, for he must be able to feel her trembling.

Involuntarily, he dropped his gaze to her mouth. It was a tantalising mouth, made to be kissed, generous, that begged for a man's caress. 'You don't know what you're asking.'

'I know very well what I'm asking. And it isn't particularly flattering for me to have to plead with you—and if you refuse my request then such will be my embarrassment that I shall have to ask you to leave and will never be able to look at you ever again.'

The roguish glint that must surely be what had charmed half the females he had ever met made his blue eyes dance with an inner light. 'Then I should hate to disappoint and cause you any embarrassment.'

Lucy stood there, gazing at him, shocked to the core by her own audacity. But she had done it now. There was no going back. Suddenly everything seemed to happen in slow motion. Taking her arms, he drew her close, his hands gentle and controlled, yet unyielding. She did not have time to change her mind before he lowered his head and found her generous mouth with his own.

The kiss was brief, little more than a meeting of lips, yet before it ended, she felt him stiffen slightly, as if he had found something surprising. And when he raised his head, she could see that he was frowning down at her, his heavy brows drawn together as if in puzzlement. Momentarily stunned, Lucy returned his gaze, shock holding her motionless. He didn't release her, but continued to stand there, appraising her.

'I'm surprised,' he said huskily. 'It's the first time a lady has invited me to kiss her. It's usually me who does the asking.'

'I expect it is—but—well, I suppose there's a first time for everything—even for you.'

'Having tasted your offering, it has left me dissatisfied and craving more.'

She smiled softly, her eyes warm and glowing as they settled on his lips. 'Oh, dear me—then to avoid any kind of discomfort you are experiencing, I think you should kiss me again, don't you?'

Their lips met again. His mouth was pure and sweet, gentle and tender. Her breasts were flattened against his broad chest, her legs pressed intimately against his muscled thighs. Her senses were dazed—perhaps it was the scent rising from the damp earth and greenery in the garden—or perhaps it was the distinctively clean scent of his skin.

She could not remember Johnathan affecting her in

such a manner—leaving her breathless and trembling. Nor had he ever kissed her the way Charles Anderson was doing now. His strong hands moved up her arms to her slender shoulders as he kissed her in an almost leisurely way—deeply, thoroughly, gliding his long fingers along her delicate jawline to tangle them in the silken tresses of her hair.

Lucy felt the wildest urge to respond to his overpowering maleness, to the warm animal magnetism that radiated from him. His mouth was warm and exciting. How very different this kiss was from what she had expected, she reflected with one part of her brain. The other had been full of trepidation and more than a little pain, but this kiss was the kind of kiss she had dreamed of and helplessly she responded to it. Sensations coursed through her.

When the kiss ended and he raised his head, she stared up at him, her composure shattered, wondering at the amazement she saw on his handsome face. Then, like an animal shedding water, he shook his head, as if to clear his muddled senses.

The movement brought Lucy to her own senses. She felt a slow, painful blush rising to her face as she realised she had allowed—asked—him to kiss her. With quiet deliberation she drew back. Terrified of making an overestimation of her ability to carry out the course she had chosen for herself, somehow she managed to take a step away from him.

'This is a mistake,' she whispered, knowing that if she allowed some tenderness between them, she would be lost. 'I think I must have taken leave of my senses. I cannot believe I did that—and that I—I actually asked you to kiss me. Why didn't you refuse?'

'Because you asked me—and because I didn't want to.'

'It's been a long time since I was kissed—not since...' She sighed, unwilling to discuss her relationship with Johnathan or what had occurred that had led up to his death lest he thought her flawed in some way.

'Not since the man you would have married,' he said with quiet understanding.

She nodded, stepping round him and moving away. Folding her arms, she stood on the veranda and looked into the distance, towards Guntal, where Charles Anderson would soon be, Charles Anderson who radiated sensual hunger in every glance, every move and every touch, but she could not deny that something had passed between them that would change their relationship for ever.

And yet, she thought, why shouldn't she want to feel such things? Johnathan wouldn't have wanted her to wallow in grief for ever. The bitterness that had consumed her for so long helped no one, least of all herself. Despite what had happened to her at the hands of the monster who had molested her, Johnathan would have wanted her to wade through the sea of sorrow and pull herself out of the quagmire of shame and loss and grief she had been floundering in for far too long.

What she and Johnathan had shared had been a wonderful, very special thing, but he was gone now—and she would not allow the man who had violated her to undermine her. He was not worth remembering. Yet the blame for depriving Johnathan of his life and the happiness that should have been his was still with her, denying her happiness for herself.

Charles moved to stand by her side, taking her shoulders and turning her to face him, then looking down at her upturned face. The colour on her cheeks was gloriously high. Her eyes were sparkling. They were the most brilliant eyes Charles had ever seen, their golden flecks so bright they seemed to be lit from within.

He was not a man of such iron control that he could resist looking down at her feminine form, which she held before him like a talisman. Noticing things like how her sari clung to her round curves so provocatively, concealing the beautiful treasures beneath, gave him a clear sense of pleasurable torture. Being so close to her, he could feel her warmth, smell the sweet scent of her body, all in such close proximity, and the memory of her responsiveness to his kiss sent heat searing into his loins.

Why did this explosion of passion happen every time he was near her? Why could this one young woman make him forget the treacherous woman who had gone before? It dawned on him as he looked down into her face that he wanted her more now than he had ever wanted any woman, if that were possible. He couldn't bear the thought that when he rode away from Nandra and into the state of Guntal, he would never see her again.

He was unprepared for the moment when she raised her head and looked at him, her eyes filled with curious longing. He was also unprepared for the question that sprang to her lips.

'Who was she, Mr Anderson? Who was it that hurt you, that made you speak so scathingly of love? Did you fall in love with her?'

Charles stared at her hard, his body tense, unwilling to answer her question, but knowing he must if he didn't want to lose her just yet. He would face that when they had to part, but for now he wanted to keep her with him for as long as possible. He thought of Amelia and the type of woman she was—self-confident, sexually alluring to every man she came into contact with, never for a moment doubting her power over the opposite sex and her ability to control and manipulate them to her advantage.

After a moment he said, 'Her name was Amelia. She was the daughter of a colonel in a Company regiment. In the beginning she appeared innocent and shy—she was also beautiful and I fell in love with her. To my deep regret I later found out that I didn't really know her at all, so blinded had I been by her beauty. Then I began to realise how ambitious she was, how she thrived on duplicity and deception. I didn't know how treacherous she could be until I told her I was to leave the Company.

'We were to have been married—but to Amelia the Company and all the pleasures it provided—the society, the balls, the admiration she needed to thrive—were too important, too much a part of her life to give up. She had no wish to become the wife of an envoy, constantly travelling the length and breadth of India. In no time at all she became attached to a titled, high-ranking officer.' His voice hardened. 'All we had shared, every word she had uttered, were meaningless.'

'I see. I'm so sorry.' Miss Quinn's eyes were large and misty with regret. They mirrored his own sense of loss. 'That must have hurt your feelings terribly. I can understand your cynicism—that it is why, because of what she did to you, you despise what romantics call love?'

He nodded. 'Something like that. Until I met Amelia there always had to be the ideal. Not only must I love the woman who captured my heart, I must be loved by her with equal measure. Anything else was unacceptable.' He paused and stared down at her.

Raising her head, she looked at him. It was a special look just for him. It seemed to beckon with strange energies. It seduced him absolutely and left him bewildered in the most sensual way. He was intrigued by the enigma of this young woman, whose naive personality concealed a mysterious core of which Miss Quinn herself was perhaps not aware.

On the spur of the moment, he said, 'Come with me. Come with me when I go to Guntal. I'm not ready to be separated from you just yet. Come and see the palace in Kassam, the palace you have dreamed of seeing for so long.'

He was close once more, his head lowered, his warm breath caressing her cheek. She didn't move. After a moment's thought, she said, 'I can't. I can't leave my father.'

'Four days, Miss Quinn. Four days is all it will take—two days for the journey and two for you to spend in the palace before you make the journey back to Nandra. I will stay on to conduct my affairs with the Rajah before I have to leave for Madras where I will have to take ship for England. We can ride to Kassam together. I'll arrange for a small military escort so you will be quite safe.'

He moved away. 'I'll leave you to think about it, to speak to your father. I'll come and see you in the morning.' Going down the steps, he followed the path to the gate where he turned and looked back at her. 'My name is Charles, by the way. After what we have just shared, for you to continue addressing me as Mr Anderson is too formal. Will you allow me to address you as Lucy?'

'Yes,' she murmured. 'Yes, I would like that.'

Lucy stood on the veranda and watched him walk away, trying to come to terms with her emotions. She thought of what he had told her, and what had been between him and the woman called Amelia, and wondered if a man ever recovered from such a love. Her eyes were narrowed as her thoughts swirled about inside her head and she wanted to reach out her arms and draw him back, knowing she was as foolish as all the other women who had fallen prey to his allure.

Her attraction to Charles was scaring her, yet boosting her. It felt so good being with him and she wasn't ready to be separated from him either. His charm was his ability to make every woman fall for his attraction, to make her feel that she was the only woman important to him.

Going to her room, she crossed to her dressing table and sat before the mirror, contemplating her features as she had done so often in the past. She was deeply disturbed by what Charles had said as she tried to see what he saw in her. He had said she was a temptress. Was she? Somehow the wide, lustrous eyes staring back at her looked alien to her, but determinedly she plunged her gaze into their depths.

And suddenly, like a will-o'-the-wisp, it seemed that someone else gazed out at her, someone almost child-like in her innocence, but at the same time seductive—a temptress, who seemed to grow from a tiny seed in a recess of her personality, a seed that had lain dormant in fertile soil until this moment. But she vanished as quickly as she'd appeared, too shy, too coy, to be caught, but far too real to deny.

She sighed wistfully, continuing to study her face. Charles Anderson had cast some magical enchantment over her. His dominance was accomplished by tender-ness rather than by force and she instinctively sensed that if she were to succumb to the mesmeric force of his personality, she would then be at his mercy.

The opportunity to see inside the Rajah's palace was a great temptation. She wanted to go. She wanted to be with Charles until they had to go their separate ways—he to return to England, she to return to Nandra and her ailing father. She would never see him again and, while he was still here, she wanted to see as much of him as was possible, to absorb every part of him. Her mind made up, she went to inform her father.

It was decided that Lucy would go with Charles when he left for Guntal, leaving her father in the care of his loyal servant, Kasim. Indeed, he encouraged her to go, trusting that she would be well taken care of by Mr Anderson and with Maya as chaperon.

Two days later, the night before they were to leave, Lucy had been too excited to sleep. The morning found her up early and dressed. A chattering Maya was more than happy to accompany her, her excitement to see the Rajah of Guntal's palace as great as Lucy's. She saw to it that their tough little ponies were saddled, with bags containing their needs for the short time they would be in Kassam, the city where the Rajah had his magnificent palace. In the early light, with a thin mist trailing over the land, the mountains on the horizon were jagged crests of moving shadows, sharp edged against the northern sky.

Captain Travis and a small escort, all mounted and armed, gathered in the military encampment to begin their short journey to the town of Kassam. Lucy slanted a look at Charles as he approached on his mount. He wore a tan riding coat, a pair of buckskin breeches and highly polished brown boots. A broad-brimmed hat covered his dark hair. He dismounted, his eyes darting to Lucy. The final preparations made, after making sure Maya was settled on her mount, Lucy led her horse to where Charles and Captain Travis waited.

'You are ready, Miss Quinn?' Captain Travis asked.

'Yes, I am impatient for us to be on our way,' she replied. Lifting her head, she met Charles's gaze squarely, her face now bright with anticipation of the journey.

Hoisting herself into the saddle with an agility that both astonished and impressed both men, Lucy prepared herself for the ride ahead. The journey would take up most of the day. She loved travelling anywhere and the idea of travelling across India's vast landscape always excited her. The sun had already risen behind the hills in the distance, staining the sky red and pink with streaks of gold.

Lucy rode a small grey mare—it was unusual to see a woman riding astride. Charles's gaze took in her buff-coloured breeches and riding boots beneath the skirts of her dark brown riding habit spread out over the horse's rump. He wore a look of scarcely concealed appreciation on his handsome face as he surveyed her. Her stout-hearted mount matched the other horses stride for stride as they headed in the direction of the border with Guntal.

They spoke little as they left Nandra behind. The horses were frisky and eager to exercise their legs. Their route had been carefully worked out. They rode across the hot, parched land, the heat somewhat lessened by a light wind that blew down from the hills. Lucy was gripped by the excitement of the journey. Nothing could detract from this exotic land of mystery and beauty.

They passed abandoned homes and temples, the vegetation intense with rampant vines clinging to the crumbling walls. Entering Guntal, they rode over plains and pastures and thickly wooded countryside. Towards midday the heat was relentless. It rose in waves from the rocky ground. Lucy dabbed at her face with a handkerchief. They finally stopped beneath the shade of some trees on the edge of a small village to take refreshment and to rest the horses.

* * *

As the day drew on the ride began to take its toll on Lucy. She tried not to let her companions see it, but she was exhausted with fatigue and her inner thighs were so sore that she felt as if she would never be able to ride again. She could hardly remember the girl who would ride almost daily, cantering on her horse. That girl was a lifetime ago. She glanced at Charles who was riding alongside Captain Travis, allowing her gaze to linger, wondering what went on behind those dark blue eyes.

She noted that he absently kneaded his aching leg. He had removed his hat and the sunlight glinted on his hair, giving it a lighter touch and accentuating the nobility of his features. If not for the shadow of pain in his eyes that gave him an air of vulnerability, she might have been intimidated by him. When he looked at her, the keen blue eyes seemed to see much more than she wanted him to see.

All the while Lucy had kept her eyes on the distant horizon as they got closer to Kassam and the Rajah's palace. It was early evening when they reached the outskirts of the town. Coming to a river, they crossed over an arched stone bridge. Along the banks mahouts were bathing their elephants and children splashed about while mothers busied themselves with piles of washing. They entered the town through one of the gates. Charles halted and looked about him, careful to keep Lucy close by while he took in the layout, memorising what he saw.

A wide street acted as the main bazaar, where food

vendors cooked on open fires and every sort of produce seemed to spill in profusion from the colourful stalls on either side. Lucy inhaled the heavy air, bursting with spices and other beguiling scents. Eventually they came to the main arched gateway to the palace—sprawling and vast. It was wide enough to allow four elephants to pass through at once. They paused and looked ahead. Guards stood on either side.

Lucy was infected by a heady mixture of anxiety and excitement and the tension mounted the closer they got to the guards. 'I do so hope we won't be sent away,' she whispered.

'My arrival is expected,' Charles replied, without taking his eyes off the guards.

They were met by a minor official who had been informed of Charles's imminent arrival. He was to take him to the Rajah directly. Dismounting, Hugh Travis and the escort left them to set up camp outside the walls, while Charles, Lucy and Maya went deeper into the palace.

As they moved along wide, cool marble corridors bristling with armed men, the grandiose interior did nothing to settle Lucy's nerves. Turbaned servants and people walked by in both directions, deep in conversation, lending what they saw an air of intrigue and conspiracy. They emerged now and then into internal courtyards. Cascades of brilliant coloured plants hung from galleries and latticed balconies.

At one point there was a huge marble tiger spouting water from its mouth into a crystal-clear pool. Orange and lemon trees rose out of huge terracotta pots and the scent of flowers was heavy on the air. Lucy and Maya kept stopping to look around in wonder. Charles took Lucy's arm, pulling her along, as the official marched quickly ahead of them. Lucy had to run to keep up with his long strides.

'What a glorious place this is,' she whispered as her feet passed over glittering mosaic floors. The palace was exactly as she had imagined it to be. 'I can hardly believe I am here and what I am seeing.' To be allowed inside the Rajah's palace was a great honour, even she knew that, and to be taken to his presence was doubly so.

Coming to the inner sanctum of the palace, they were ushered into the Hall of Public Audience. Here the air was heavy with the aroma of almonds and spices, of jasmine and musk, along with an air of tradition and history. Magnificently attired councillors and courtiers were milling about. Everyone turned briefly as they walked in, eyes darting towards these English strangers. Lucy could not tear her eyes away from the Rajah, Naveen Madan, as she bobbed a respectful curtsy. Never had she seen the like.

Charles bowed with respect. The warmth of the Rajah's welcome was sincere. Maya hung back when Charles drew Lucy forward. The Rajah's eyes passed over her and he smiled broadly.

'I am delighted that you spare the time to visit Guntal again, Mr Anderson, and I am happy to receive you, Miss Quinn,' he said in a light sing-song voice. 'You are most welcome. I trust you had a safe journey?'

Lucy was impressed by his fluency in English. He was decked out in splendid clothes studded with precious gems that reflected the light. His robe, which fell straight from his shoulders, was made of silk dyed deep blue and edged with gold and was extremely beautiful. A blue sash encircled his large waist, exposing the jewel-studded hilt of his imperial dagger. On his feet he wore turquoise slippers and his fingers were heavily weighted with spectacular jewelled rings. She placed his age somewhere between forty and fifty years and his dark hair shone lustrously. His features were fine cut and his eyes dark and glowing.

Surrounded by a small army of servants and officials on a raised dais, he sat cross-legged on a low divan spread with bright rugs and surrounded by a heap of brightly coloured silk cushions.

'We did, Your Highness,' Charles replied in answer to his question. 'I compliment you on your English. It is much improved since last we met.'

The Rajah laughed good humouredly. 'I have been working hard to improve it every day. With the rise of the East India Company, my father made sure I was taught to converse in English and understand the language from an early age, telling me it is a skill I need when entertaining the English. I also have a good memory. I value your coming here to see me. We had some interesting discussions on your previous visit—I hope we can do the same this time—about your King George and England—and I will show you some more of Guntal. You will remember how I enjoy hunting with hawks for game and wild boar when I have the time. Tomorrow is to be such a day. You might like to join me—and

Miss Quinn, too. You are a competent horsewoman, Miss Quinn?'

'Yes—and thank you. I would love to join you.'

'We have an early start. You may not care to be woken at that hour.'

'I will be there,' she assured him, smiling. 'I will look forward to it.'

While Charles continued to converse with the Rajah, Lucy's face burned as she felt those in the Rajah's privy circle scrutinising her. The Rajah's easy manner put Lucy at ease, giving her an insight into the man behind his position and all his finery. He was a man who had the weight of ruling his province upon his shoulders, but was still someone with a heart and, she sensed, a capacity to show pleasure.

A woman entered, drawing Lucy's attention. She seemed to appear from nowhere, gliding across the floor, her bare feet making no sound on the black marble floor and, save for the silvery tinkle that accompanied her movement, Lucy might have imagined her an apparition. Her skin glowed between the yards of pink and orange silk in which she was draped and dozens of gold bracelets jangled on her arms and legs. Her skirts were so fine they floated around her as she walked. She was blessed with womanly curves and she walked with grace and was light of foot.

Her features were sultry and unlined and showed humour and kindness. Her dark eyes crinkled as she smiled and her black hair hung in a thick glossy plait to her waist. Above her soft almond-shaped eyes, strands of fine beads and precious stones hung over her forehead and around her neck. Lucy suspected she was the Rani, the Rajah's wife, her suspicions confirmed when Charles bowed to her with respect.

She was accompanied by a group of ladies who hovered around her. A dazzling smile broke out on the Rani's red lips. 'You honour us with your presence,' she said in broken English, her voice rich and deep. Her eyes slipped to Lucy. 'And I see you have brought with you a companion, Mr Anderson? How delightful. You will by hungry after your journey. We will eat and then you will relax.'

In an atmosphere that was pleasantly friendly and informal, the food was served by an army of servants in white robes and blue silk turbans. It was carried on large silver trays—fish and meats and sweetmeats dripping in honey. It was spicy and delicious and washed down with spiced wines. The Rajah was the perfect host while his eyes constantly watched those about him like a hunting hawk noticing everything. Lucy was quick to compliment him on the food that set her tastebuds tingling.

The talk was of political matters, small skirmishes and rebellions and the need to crush them, and how the Rajah continued to keep the East India Company out of Guntal. As the meal progressed, the conversation went on more slowly for, comfortably settled with good food and the wine's sweetness, Charles was in no haste to move. In fact, it might have gone on all night long had Lucy not voiced her desire for sleep. But the Rani, who insisted on being addressed as Ananya, had other ideas.

'You must come with me. I have just the thing for

you after the journey you have made today. Afterwards you will sleep the sleep of the gods.'

Intrigued and with a nod and a smile from Charles, Lucy went with Ananya and her giggling ladies who floated in her wake, all moving at the same time. She was taken to a gold and blue mosaic chamber that she soon discovered was a luxurious bath house. The ceiling was domed and in the centre of the floor, surrounded by slender pillars, was a tiled, large sunken bath in which water was steaming.

Lucy gasped, her eyes alight with excitement. She had heard about these bath houses in the princely palaces but had never imagined them as being so luxurious. Thick, fluffy towels were to hand, while all around were vials of oils and soaps.

'Why, I have never seen the like,' she exclaimed, delighted. 'I never imagined anything that looks so tempting and pleasurable.'

Ananya laughed, pleased with Lucy's reaction. 'There is enough luxury for a person to wallow in for as long as they wish. Now come—don't be shy. There is no need for that. We are all ladies together.' She led Lucy to the edge of the tub.

Her ladies were chattering excitedly and, before Lucy could protest, they were undressing her as if it were the most natural thing to do. There was a great deal of giggling as her clothes were partially removed, but before they could remove them entirely, alarmed, Lucy put up her hands to stop them, trying to hold on to her modesty, but the more she protested the louder they laughed. Standing back, they began to undress themselves to show it was quite natural in the world they inhabited to bathe together in the nude.

They slipped into the scented water, beckoning for her to join them. Unable to resist the temptation of joining them, deciding to throw caution and all her inhibitions to the wind and to give herself up to the slow tempo of this life, Lucy began to relax and finished undressing swiftly. Squeals and gasps of admiration were drawn from the beautiful ladies when her pale slender body was revealed and her glorious mane of pale blonde hair, freed from its pins, snaked down her spine.

'You really are the loveliest woman,' Ananya enthused. 'Such a pretty face—and such milky skin—with hair like the purest silk and the colour of desert sand. You are quite perfect, Miss Quinn. Mr Anderson must find it difficult being close to you and not touching you.'

Lucy gasped, shocked that she should think that. 'Mr Anderson and I are not…not together,' she said, in an attempt to explain their relationship, but it was clear from the expression of disbelief on Ananya's face and her intelligent, all-seeing eyes that she did not believe her. Deciding not to dig herself in any deeper, Lucy slipped gracefully into the pool where she readily abandoned herself quite passively to the ministering of two of the young ladies' gentle hands.

A smile on her lips, Ananya sat on a low stool at the side of the pool, content to watch as Lucy's hair was washed and she was soaped all over.

Wallowing pleasurably, feeling the water about her like a caress, Lucy was astonished at the strange sense of well-being that spread through every part of her body.

Some of the ladies were chattering away in their own language, their laughter and cries echoing off the tiled walls. The abandon of these women and their brazen and unashamed nakedness shocked her, but after a while as she began to relax and she ceased to think about it.

When she stepped out, one of the ladies was waiting with a thick cotton towel to dry her, before taking her to a divan where she began to massage her body with hands that were amazingly gentle, rubbing in a strangely pungent oil that relaxed her muscles and gave her skin a soft patina.

While most of the ladies lounged about indulging in idle gossip, she relaxed and, spreading her arms, opened her eyes and gazed at the ceiling, at the colourful designs with a picture in the centre, of stars and a moon representing the heavens, and a golden sun in the middle. Pressing her eyes shut, she held her breath to hold on to the pleasurable sensation. Her body seemed to have broken all its earthly moorings. She was like a marionette, moving to the strings that pulled her, only her brain functioning slowly as her body was ministered to as never before and in ways she could never have imagined.

Beneath the massaging boldness of the woman's hands, a woman who had the air of a priestess carrying out some ancient ritual, she was honest enough to admit her treacherous woman's body was coming breathlessly alive, not even against her will. She sighed with contentment.

'You use such wonderful scents,' she murmured, as the woman proceeded to apply more oil to her skin. The air in the bathing chamber was warm and thick and redolent of perfume, not flower-like, but compounded of ambergris and musk—intoxicating and languid, artful weapons to entrap a man. That she should think such things just then did not surprise her, for Charles occupied her mind.

'Where did you learn to speak English?' Lucy liked Ananya. She was sure she'd met someone who, in different circumstances, could be a good friend.

Ananya's full lips stretched in a broad smile. 'My husband. He taught me. He said it was important that I learn to speak the language of the English should we find ourselves entertaining them in the future. And here you are,' she said with tinkling laughter, 'so you see, it is fortunate for me and you that I learned the language of the English.'

Bathed and scented, Lucy's body was soft and supple, her skin bloomed. They draped her in a flowing gorgeous white robe, the fabric so fine as to be almost shockingly transparent. Feeling more feminine than she had ever felt in her life before, Lucy stood back for the ladies to inspect their handiwork.

Ananya beamed broadly, well satisfied. 'You are very beautiful, Miss Quinn. Mr Anderson will not be able to resist you when he sees you out of those unflattering English clothes, which are too restricting and not at all suitable for the Indian climate. I suspect he is like my own husband in many ways—honourable and noble, as well as very handsome—all the things I cherish in a man. I have observed how he looks at you—how protective of you he is. You are a long way from England

and have plenty of time to be together, so it will be interesting to see what happens between the two of you while you are here in Kassam.'

Having no intention of remaining in Kassam for more than two days at the most, Lucy merely smiled and let the matter rest for the present. She suspected Ananya could ferret out secrets the owner had no notion of.

She spent the rest of the evening lounging on a divan in conversation with Ananya and nibbling on delicious sweetmeats. Eventually she was shown to a room of sumptuous luxury where she was to sleep. She still wore the robe and went barefoot, luxuriating in the feel of the soles of her feet against the cool marble floors. After making sure Lucy was comfortable and she was unlikely to need her, Maya left her to explore the environs of the palace and chat with the other servants.

With Lucy being taken care of by the Rani and her ladies, Charles went to join Hugh encamped outside the palace walls. Hidden by the darkness, Charles lounged on the ground, staring across the starlit plains. The night wind smelt of woodsmoke from the campfire and a hundred other scents that drifted from the town on the night air.

Hugh and the rest of the escort sat around the fire, talking quietly among themselves. He could envisage the Rani introducing Lucy to the bathing chamber and he knew how she would look, her naked body glistening with fragrant oils and with her white-blonde hair combed out—in fact, he was aware of every single thing about her. Too aware, he thought disgustedly, his eyes narrowing.

He'd hoped that upon closer association his interest and preoccupation with her would fade. The opposite had happened. If anything, he was more fascinated by her than he had been when they had left Nandra and he was thoroughly annoyed by the fact and beginning to think that perhaps he should not have invited her to accompany him into Guntal.

During the journey he had expected to see her at her worst, but even covered in dust and with her hair in disarray beneath her hat, her long legs beneath her skirts astride her horse and urging it on with an energy that confounded him, she still managed to look appealing. She had made no unnecessary demands, had not complained or made a nuisance of herself—except to disrupt his peace of mind, he admitted grimly.

Chapter Five

In the cool freshness of dawn, the Rajah of Guntal's hunting party patiently waited for the signal to depart. Excitement prevailed, beaters assembled, restless horses whinnied and champed at their bits, eager to be off.

Lucy stood in the shadow of an overhanging tree, enjoying the rich confusion going on all around her. She slanted a look at Charles as he approached on his mount. He wore a riding coat, a pair of buckskin breeches and highly polished brown boots. A broad-brimmed hat covered his dark hair.

'After our ride yesterday, I thought you might have had a change of mind and stayed beneath the covers.'

'Not a bit of it,' she said. 'I woke this morning and it was so fresh and beautiful that the thought of riding out with the hunt was too tempting to resist.'

'Then stay close at all times.'

Lucy galloped along with the rest, jungle fowl rising, fluttering from the long grass and screeching as they thundered by. They came to a place where there was little sign of habitation. Lucy was aware of the remoteness of it all. When the party began hunting game birds, she found the sport not to her liking and had no wish to be in on the kill.

Seeing a river in the distance, its gleaming waters beckoning as it meandered its way leisurely across the landscape, Lucy rode off, enjoying her own leisurely pace. Becoming lost in the beauty of the distant hills and the vast expanse of the plains, she felt at peace, without any sense of how far she had ridden. That was when the rain came and a fierce wind rose so suddenly, she was taken completely by surprise. It blew about her with a viciousness that almost unseated her from her horse.

Within just a few minutes it was coming down in sheets. After such a long spell of dry weather, the ground quickly soaked it up. Lucy could smell the rich scent of earth as the rain quenched its thirst. Normally when the monsoons came, her inner self would feel at one with nature, but she didn't any more. This deluge couldn't have come at a worse time and in no time at all she was soaked to the skin. In danger of losing her hat she removed it and attached it to the saddle. Her hair was soaked, hanging down her back in sodden strands.

With the rain pouring down and the hunting party looking for shelter, Charles rode around looking for Lucy, hoping she'd had the sense to find shelter herself. Searching frantically, he soon realised she was missing, but forced himself to stay calm. Reason flooded back and his sense of anger and frustration was subdued beneath a firm grip of will as his concern for her safety increased. His gaze was drawn to the river in the distance. Dear Lord, don't let her have ridden as far as that. He knew how easy it was for a person to get swept away when monsoon rains poured down.

The landscape became almost invisible. Straining his eyes, he could just make out the shape of an animal in the distance—a horse, he was sure of it—it had to be.

'My God! The little fool—' he gasped, urging his mount into a gallop, his mindless terror giving way to blind panic as he went after her, sliding and skidding over the now sodden ground.

Lucy scolded herself for riding on ahead of the rest. Charles had specifically told her not to become separated from the party. Oh, Lord, why hadn't she listened to him? She glanced back, hoping to see the others following closely, but if they were the rain obscured them. Seeing a dark shape ahead of her that looked like the rocks she had seen earlier, with a renewed spurt of energy she urged her horse on.

On reaching the rocks, she threw herself out of the saddle and, taking the reins of her terrified horse, dragged the animal into the shelter. Wiping the water from her eyes, seeing a gap that looked like a cave in the rocks some yards ahead, where peepul trees had conspired to form a canopy over the entrance, almost hiding it from the world, she struggled to reach it, holding on to the reins.

Suddenly two strong arms were around her, helping her to remain on her feet and hauling her into the dank interior of the cave. Once there she fell to her knees coughing the water out of her mouth. When she finally managed to speak, she staggered to her feet and faced her rescuer—Charles.

'You little fool,' he chided, furiously, glaring at her, elbows akimbo. 'What the devil do you think you were doing riding off like that? I told you not to leave the hunting party—but would you listen? If you had gone anywhere near the river, you could have drowned. Didn't you see the clouds gathering overhead? No. You always think you know best.'

Undismayed Lucy glared at him with stubborn, unyielding pride. 'When it happens to concern me then, yes, I do. I wasn't in any danger,' she retorted, trying to ignore the enraged glitter in his eyes. 'Were—were you worried about me?'

'Of course I was worried. Anything could have happened to you. Thank God I saw you come in here, otherwise I wouldn't have known where to look.'

'As you see, I am still in one piece,' she said, trying to remain calm. Her chest rose and fell in agitation, but she tried desperately to appeal to his reason. 'You need not have worried. I do ride extremely well, you know, and I will not be dictated to by you or anyone else,' she retorted, seeing the fury her defiance ignited in his features.

'Now why doesn't that surprise me? You're too stubborn to listen to sound advice. You should have known better,' he chided crossly. Moving towards her, he leaned forward deliberately until blue eyes stared into dark green from little more than a foot apart. His eyes grew hard and flintlike, yet when it came his voice was soft and slow. Almost gently he warned, 'Before you consider going off again on your own, pause to consider there are tigers in these parts—man-eating tigers. Unless you want to provide a banquet for them, you'd do well to heed my words.'

Lucy felt the colour drain from her face. Charles's presence filled the small cave. He looked like a dark, invincible god, formidable, intimidating and yet strangely compelling. With his hair a cluster of dark wet curls, all she could do was stare with a bemused intensity. But then, his arrogance to assume he knew what was best for her raised her indignation and, highly incensed by his words, a feral light gleamed in the depths of her eyes. She was like a kitten showing its claws to a full-grown panther.

'Oh, I will. I didn't realise I had ridden so far. I didn't think the rain would come just yet—or so fast and hard.'

'You were wrong—and just look at you. You're soaking wet.'

'I am not the only one. You're as wet as I am.'

She was about to move away, only to find herself halted when he came up behind her with the sure-footed skill of an animal on the scent of its prey. She stood there, frozen, his strong hands on her shoulders. Unable to turn, she could feel his closeness, the muscular hardness of him, the vibrant heat of his body pressed close against her back and his warm breath on her neck.

'For God's sake, Lucy. I was scared out of my wits when I couldn't find you. I was afraid something might have happened to you. I'd no idea in which direction you'd ridden—not until I saw your horse.'

Lucy swallowed and wet her lips, her anger subsiding. 'I didn't mean to frighten you,' she whispered, her voice shaking with emotion as she tried to maintain the friendly relationship that had existed between them since they had left Nandra. 'I'm sorry, but I didn't think I was in any danger at the time. Truly. Don't be angry.'

'I'm not—at least not any longer. But I was concerned. When the rains came and I couldn't find you, thinking you might have gone to the river, I was beginning to fear the worst.'

Lucy thought he was going to chastise her some more, but suddenly all his anger seemed to disappear. She was touched by his obvious concern for her safety and deeply sorry and mortified for not having listened to his advice about becoming separated from the hunting party. Charles was right. She should not have ridden off on her own.

His hands on her arms were soothing, caressing her. She jerked her head slightly when she felt his hand on her head, but his fingers only threaded through her wet hair, freeing the strands, careful not to tug and hurt her, patient as he took several long strands at a time, all the while holding her with the other hand against his chest, easing her closer. The unconscious gentleness of the gesture touched and warmed something deep inside her.

Captivated by the heat of his breath on her neck, she trembled when he drew the heavy, wet mass of her hair to one side, feeling defeated, afraid when she felt his mouth gently touch the soft warm flesh on the back of her neck. But instead of stepping away, she leaned into him, the action encouraging him to continue to hold her. On a gasp she sucked in her breath when he parted his lips and touched her skin with the fiery tip of his tongue. Her heart was pounding when his voice spoke very quietly into her ear.

'Shall I tell you what I think when I look at you, Lucy?'

'I—if you like,' she said, trying to answer lightly, but her voice was low and husky.

'I see an extremely beautiful young woman with lovely hair like a shimmering cloth of gold.'

Lucy wanted to step away from him, but an answering quiver that was a combination of fright and excitement was tingling up her spine.

'Would you like me to stop now, Lucy, or would you like me to continue to hold you close?' he murmured.

Charles's closeness and his physical presence scorched through her and she could not move away if she tried. 'H-hold me a while—I would like that.'

She lowered her head, the floor of the cave becoming the focal point of her concentration, a misshapen image tugging at the heart of her memory, conjuring indistinct, cloudy visions in her mind. They blended in a confused jumble of events that took her back to another time, another place, when other hands had touched her, when she had wanted to flee before darkness had mercifully engulfed her, rendering her helpless and unable to escape the brutality of what was being done to her.

She fought a welter of unwelcome emotions that threatened to drag her down to a new depth of despair. But she was not immune to Charles standing behind her, of the hard rack of his chest pressed against her back, making her feel things that added to her confusion. He remained close, so close she could feel the heat of his body scorching through the clothes on her back to her flesh, along with an alarming, treacherous warmth creeping through her body, a melting sensation unlike anything she had felt in a long time.

For one mad moment she wanted to relax back against him, to feel his arm close around her, but because she could still feel those powerful emotions that seemed to have been drawn into her heart and soul from that day when she thought her life had ended, she could not bring herself to make that move.

The moment was oddly intimate. Maybe it was the way Charles was holding her, or maybe it was the way his closeness made her feel. She was nervous, but what did it matter? Yes, she was afraid—but it wasn't like before. While she didn't doubt for a moment that she was safe with Charles, that she was in control of this situation, she was afraid of the things she felt when he looked at her, afraid of the feelings he had awakened in her when he'd kissed her on the veranda of her home in Nandra.

She had concealed everything for so long, tried to stamp it out. She thought she might succeed with time, but this man made her think of the past and the uncertainty she was still living in. Since he had appeared in her life, she found she was returning more frequently to her memories of that dark day she wished she could forget—yet their shared kiss had been so sublime she was curious to experience the same again. A warm trickle of a familiar sensation ran through her, overwhelming her anxiety. It was that same stirring she had felt when he had kissed her.

With desire crashing over him in tidal waves, Charles

looked down at Lucy's bent head, his lips brushing her shining wet hair. Having no concept of her thoughts, he slipped an arm about her waist and drew her tightly against him, feeling a shimmering tremor in her slender body.

'You are as irresistible to me now as you were when we kissed, Lucy—which I am sorely tempted to repeat.'

Slowly she turned to face him, meeting his gaze, seeing the desire he felt for her in his eyes. Without warning his hand lifted and curved tenderly round her cheek. Gazing into those fathomless eyes, she felt a curious sharp thrill run through her as the force between them seemed to ignite. She was entranced, hardly breathing, wet strands of hair drifting over her face, and she thought his face bent over her was more beautiful than she had ever known. She saw the deepening light in his eyes and the thick defined brows and wanted to touch him as one touches the soft flesh of a newborn babe.

'Then kiss me again, Charles—it might be better this time.'

When she fell silent, his hands tightened on her arms and once again he drew her close, his lips settling on hers. They were cool and surprisingly smooth as they brushed lightly against her closed mouth. A jolt slammed through her as they began to move on hers, thoroughly and possessively exploring every tender contour. She found herself imprisoned in a grip of steel, pressed against his hard, muscular length, her breasts coming to rest against his chest and there was little she could do to escape. Alternate waves seemed to run through her body, but there was also another far more disturbing sensation.

His lips increased their pressure, becoming coaxing as he slipped the tip of his tongue into the warm sweetness of her mouth. She gasped, totally innocent of the sort of warmth, the passion he was skilfully arousing in her, that poured through her veins with a shattering explosion of delight. It was a kiss of exquisite restraint and, unable to think of anything but the exciting urgency of his mouth and the warmth of his breath, she felt herself falling slowly into a dizzying abyss of sensuality. His hands glided restlessly, possessively up and down her spine and the nape of her neck, pressing her tightly to his hardened body.

Trailing her hands up the muscles of his chest and shoulders and sliding her fingers into the crisp curly hair at his nape, with a quiet moan of helpless surrender she clung to him, devastated by what he was doing to her, by the raw hunger of his passion. Inside her an emotion she had never experienced before began to sweetly unfold, before vibrantly bursting with a fierceness that made her tremble. His kiss became more demanding, ardent, persuasive, a slow erotic seduction, and Lucy, lost in a wild and beautiful madness and with blood beating in her throat and temples that wiped out all reason and will, responded with equal passion.

When at last he lifted his mouth from hers, his breathing was harsh and rapid, and gazing up at him Lucy felt as if she would melt beneath his scorching eyes. Slowly she brought one of her hands from behind his neck and her fingers gently traced the outline of his cheek, following its angular line down to his jaw and neck.

'Well?' Charles asked, his voice low and husky, recovering more quickly than Lucy. Her face was bemused, her eyes unfocused, her soft pink mouth partly open. 'Do you like being kissed?' When she did not reply immediately, he grinned and murmured, 'Surely I cannot have rendered you speechless.'

'It certainly took my breath, and, yes, I like it very well,' she confessed, still drifting between total peace and a strong, delirious joy, while at the same time a feeling of disquiet was creeping over her as her mind came together from the nether regions of the universe where it had fled. Slowly she disentangled herself from his arms, stepping round him and moving away.

'I—I can't believe I kissed you like that,' she murmured. 'I—I don't usually…'

In a daze of suspended yearning and confusion, she hesitated as his eyes held hers in one long, compelling look, hiding all her frustrated longing and unfulfilled desires. That one kiss had been too much and too little, arousing deep feelings she did not fully understand. What had happened between them had been a sudden overwhelming passion, heightened by the intensity of the knowledge that it shouldn't be happening.

Turning abruptly, she started to walk away from him, her feet driven by panic. She stepped outside and took hold of her horse, vaguely aware that Charles was following her. She didn't look at him, but she sensed he was bewildered by her behaviour. It didn't matter. Nothing did just then. Let him rant and rail and chastise her to his heart's content if he wanted to—anything. Just let him never look at her as he had just then, or touch her with such tender intimacy. She would not let herself be at the mercy of a man like Charles Anderson, who radiated sensual hunger in every glance, every move and every touch.

As she was about to mount her horse, Charles steadied her by placing his hand over hers. 'Do not hurry away. Give me a moment, Lucy.'

'Why? Have you not said all you have to say?'

'Not quite.'

'Is it that you want to kiss me again?'

'Yes, I do, very much, as it happens, but I'm not going to. I enjoyed kissing you, but there will be no repeat of it. When—if, I kiss you again, I will do the asking.' He turned her round to face him, frowning when he saw the look on her face. 'And don't look like that. You're like a disgruntled hedgehog and just as prickly.'

Lucy continued to glower at him, her fingers slipping away from his face. It was taut, his eyes fixed squarely on hers. Now the rain had ceased, the light behind him made an aureole around his dark head. He regarded her in silence. She was profoundly aware of him and the wet state she was in. There were too many feelings struggling to come to the fore to resurrect feelings and emotions, which was disconcerting.

Trying not to let any of those emotions show on her face, she folded her arms. 'Just what does a disgruntled hedgehog look like? I really have no idea.'

'Had I a mirror to hand, I would show you.'

'I think I get the picture. I see there's no danger of my head swelling from any compliments from you.'

'I apologise,' he said simply.

'There is nothing to apologise for,' she answered quietly.

For a long moment Charles's gaze held hers with penetrating intensity. It was as enigmatic as it was challenging and unexpectedly Lucy felt an answering frisson of excitement. The darkening in his eyes warned her that he was aware of that brief response. Something in his expression made the breath catch in her throat and the warmly intimate look in his eyes was vibrantly, alarmingly alive. Not for the first time since he had come into her life, she found herself at a loss to understand him.

'You really should not go riding off like that, Lucy. You gave me one hell of a fright.'

'I'm sorry. I didn't think.'

'There are so many dangers when it rains like that,' he said quietly. 'I just want to keep you safe.'

'No one can promise that.'

'I can be very determined,' he answered with a half-smile. 'I am not perfect. Far from it in fact. But I will do all in my power to see that you come to no harm.'

'Thank you for your concern, Charles, but I can do that perfectly well myself. I am not helpless.'

'I'm not saying you are. You are accomplished in many things. You are also wise enough to know a fool when you see one. You have confidence, too, as well as a sense of humour—although I have seen very little of that of late. And your compassion for others compels my admiration and respect.'

Lucy trembled, staring at him.

'You are also brave,' he continued as she turned her

head away. 'The fact that you have worked your way through adversity in life and your profession as a teacher and the care you take of your father is commendable and bespeaks your courage and good sense. It makes me feel that I can trust you in your integrity, which is a rarity for me. It is not often I come across a person I can trust.'

She looked at him, listening like a doe in the woods, but poised to flee from him. She was rendered helpless by his words. It was difficult to argue with a man who praised her not for superficial things, but for the very qualities that she valued in herself. Mounting her horse, she looked down at his upturned face and half smiled.

'I'm an ungrateful wretch. I don't think it even occurred to me to thank you for your concern.'

He smiled back at her, happy to see a softening and friendliness in her eyes. 'You're welcome. Now I think we should get back to the others before they send out a search party.'

Lucy cantered on, Charles loping easily in her wake. A disturbed fowl rose with a flutter and a squark. Bent low over her mount's neck, Lucy's response was to urge it into a faster pace, its hooves kicking up the wet earth.

Looking straight ahead and uncomfortable in her saturated clothes, she knew something was happening within her, something overwhelming over which she seemed to have no control. How could it have come to this—finding herself fascinated, angered and beguiled by Charles Anderson? A man whose mere touch and the sound of his voice woke turbulent emotions she hadn't known she possessed.

Yet an inexplicable heaviness weighed on her heart—probably, she thought, because she hadn't yet determined how the kiss had affected Charles. It didn't help, either, that her own thoughts kept returning to it. Perhaps he hadn't been as affected by it as she had been. Perhaps Charles Anderson was the kind of man to whom kisses meant little, the kind of adventurer with a woman in every town. Maybe by now he would have forgotten about it entirely. Yet she couldn't forget. Sensations she had not felt in a long time, and never as strong as this, coursed through her. It was a new kind of madness she was unable to resist.

She suddenly wanted to feel Charles's arms around her again for reasons she could not understand, but had everything to do with his hard frame pressed against hers, to feel his breath on her neck. It startled her, this reaction to his nearness. It would not go away and she was left with the insane desire to taste that kiss again. But these new feelings Charles had aroused in her frightened her—she was aware that he was far more dangerous to her now, now that her own body was betraying her.

Her heart beat rapidly when she thought about him. He had stirred an excitement that had been lacking for a long time. She fought the battle within her, but something stronger pulled at her senses and with a groan of defeat she left whatever it was to have its way.

For too long, she now realised, she had avoided anything other than the daily routine at the school and assisting Dr Jessop, too afraid to feel happy or excited. Her father, with his wise old head, had told her time and again not to worry, that it would all work out, that time healed all wounds. But could she move on? Her life didn't have to stop because of what had happened to her, she told herself.

Growing up, she'd had so many dreams, like most girls dream, of marrying the man you fall in love with, having children, watching them grow up happy and carefree, just as she had. Except it didn't happen that way. When Johnathan had died all her dreams lay in tatters. But there was no reason why she couldn't have children, although they would never be Johnathan's.

As an innocent, naive girl, before the assault on her person, she had seen no wrong in the man who had violated her. But because of her actions she had deprived Johnathan of any chance of happiness as well as his life and, for as long as she lived, she would never forgive herself. She did want a child of her own, she couldn't deny that. But it couldn't happen unless it was with someone else.

Riding a horse length behind Lucy, Charles looked ahead in deep reflection. With frustration he attacked his sentimental thoughts until they cowered in meek submission, but they refused to lie down. When he had found Lucy missing, in the space of a heartbeat, a fury had replaced his calm composure. He was furious that she'd worried him with her recklessness, furious that she was able to evoke any kind of emotion in him at all, but he had been more concerned by her disappearance than he'd cared to reveal. He'd known instinctively that she must have ridden off alone.

Panic had beset him. With the torrent of rain unleashed on them he knew she was in danger, immediate and terrible, and with every instinct in him, he had ridden after her, ready to berate her—or hold her close in relief, to comfort her.

His growing attraction to Lucy was disquieting—in fact, it was damned annoying. If he wanted an affair or diversion of any kind, he had a string of some of the most beautiful women back in Madras to choose from—so why should he feel this insanely wild attraction for a woman he hardly knew? Only Lucy Quinn would have done something so outrageous as to ask a man to kiss her and then dared to confront him so magnificently.

A reluctant smile touched his lips when he remembered her standing valiantly against him when he had come upon her in the cave. She had been soaked to the skin, her hair hanging about her face and down her back in wet profusion, but he thought she had never looked so heartbreakingly lovely or so young, with those mutinous dark eyes flashing fire, seeing nothing wrong in what she had done.

Something in his heart moved and softened, then something stabbed him in the centre of his chest. What the hell was wrong with him? Her behaviour had made him angry, and at the same time he had been overwhelmed by the realisation that if he didn't take care, she would come to mean something to him.

Lucy Quinn was an unusual female, intelligent, opinionated and full of surprises. She was also the epitome of stubborn, prideful woman. Yet for all her fire and spirit, there was no underlying viciousness. She was so very different from the sophisticated, worldly women

he took to bed—experienced, sensual women, knowledgeable in the ways of love, women who knew how
to please him.

No, Lucy was different, a phenomenon. She had a
touching self-belief. He sensed a goodness in her, something special, sensitive—something worth pursuing.
There was also something untapped inside her that not
even she was aware of—passion buried deep.

Reaching the hunting party, the unseasonable storm
had created a stir among the men, which had been so
severe that there had been no time to spare a thought
for the missing Miss Quinn or that Charles had ridden
off to find her, for everyone had been frantically seeking shelter and securing the animals before the worst
of the storm was upon them.

Returning to the palace, Lucy paid another visit to
the bathing chamber, hoping the pampering and ministrations of Ananya's ladies would relax her. But sleep
evaded her that night. It was impossible to sleep after
such a day. She stood on the latticed balcony, where
anyone could look down on life below without being
seen. The night was glorious—an Indian night, the sky
indigo blue and rich with stars that glittered softly. The
walled garden was filled with mango trees and pine-
apple bushes, the air heavy with the sweet fragrance
of frangipani. From somewhere, a peacock sounded its
melancholy cry above the buzz of cicadas. There were
thousands of them all around, but they kept out of sight.

Looking down, she saw a figure standing alone. She
could see at once it was Charles. He was leaning against

a bench, relaxed, as if he belonged there. She took a moment to observe him, admiring the fine figure he made. A white shirt, opened at the throat and ruffled at the cuffs, contrasted sharply with his bronze skin, and his lean, muscular build was accentuated by the close-fitting breeches and white stockings. As if sensing her watching him, he looked up. An amused smile twitched at the corners of his mouth.

His presence lightened her heart. Encouraged by the sudden startling wish for something different, something new, she saw a star shoot across the sky. Something *new*. Was it really possible? Charles Anderson disturbed her in ways that surprised her. The more time she spent in his presence, the more she wanted to be. How could she equate this truth with the awful thing that had happened to her when she had resolved never to be drawn to a man as she had been to Johnathan ever again, that she would never speak of it, to keep it inside her head.

She continued to look down at him, resolute, all the more determined to make changes to her life. She would not let what had happened to her determine her life, the person that she was. For too long she had kept a part of her mind closed even to herself. If, after years of pushing it away, she embraced it, perhaps the pain and the shame that had plagued her since that time would ease and she would be able to live her life without feeling tormented. She refused to spend her life feeling frustrated and angry, her only outlet the children that she taught and her work at the hospital. It was time she put an end to this tedious monotony that had dominated her everyday existence for far too long and had become her fate.

She watched Charles shrug himself away from the bench and cross the courtyard, moving with a sensuous grace and a sureness in his stride, as if he carefully planned where each foot would fall. He appeared relaxed and at ease.

After several moments there was a soft tapping on her door. Knowing with a certainty who it was and that she should not answer, ignoring her own advice and knowing she shouldn't be alone with him at this time of night, she opened it. Unbeknown to her, she was between Charles and the light, so that her slender form was outlined through her thin robe. His admiring gaze took in her fashionable *toilette*, lingering on the gentle swell of her breasts beneath the thin fabric. Lucy felt herself grow hot with embarrassment.

'Charles—can't you sleep either?' The dark liquid of his eyes deepened as he became caught in the warmth of her presence and she read in his face such evident desire that heat flamed for a moment in her belly.

'Can I come in?'

Lucy hesitated. His stance was casual, but his eyes were intense, penetrating. Again she experienced the depth to which her mind and body stirred whenever she was in his presence. Then a feeling of carelessness took over and she opened the door wider. He stepped inside. Closing the door, she stood perfectly still as he came closer. There was an aura of calm authority about him. His expression was now blank and impervious and he looked unbearably handsome. The sight of his chiselled features and bold blue eyes never failed to stir her heart.

Taking her hand, he raised her fingers to his lips, enjoying the scent and taste of her. When he looked at her there was a twinkle in his eyes. 'Are you happy being here, Lucy? No regrets?'

'I am glad I came—I have no regrets.' And she meant it. With every moment she spent in this gorgeous palace with Charles Anderson she grew more comfortable with him and more intrigued by him. And felt more free.

'I can't believe the change in you. You look like some eastern princess and very lovely.'

'And you, Mr Anderson, are extremely handsome,' she said with a teasing glint in her eyes.

He grinned wickedly, sauntering over to the balcony. Perching his hips on the balustrade, he folded his arms across his chest. 'As a lady you're not supposed to say that to a gentleman—but, I have to admit to having known a lady or two who have admired my charms.'

She laughed, joining him on the balcony, sitting in a cushioned chair and looking at him candidly. 'As to that I don't doubt, but I'm sure you always behave like a perfect gentleman.'

'Always.'

Perhaps it was the magic of the night, the warmth and subtle floral scents, or her need to be close to him, but whatever the cause, Lucy's heart doubled its pace.

In a voice like rough velvet, he said, 'I meant it when I said you are a lovely young woman, Lucy. Where has the woman I met in Nandra gone?'

Mesmerised, she stared into his fathomless dark eyes, while his deep, husky voice caressed her, pulling her further under his spell. 'Nowhere. She is still here.'

'The robe suits you. Ananya told me of your visit to the bathing chamber after we had eaten.'

'I was quite ravenous when we got back to the palace.'

'I noticed.'

'You did?' She recalled how he had watched her with some amusement as she ate her way through dish after dish of the delicious food set before them, as if she had eaten nothing for days.

'For a young woman of such sender build, you have a remarkably robust appetite.' His eyes narrowed and one dark eyebrow rose in amusement.

'After a long day with the Rajah's hunt and having eaten nothing all day, I was starving.'

'So it would seem. And to put the finishing touch to the day, you were once again bathed and pampered by the Rani's ladies.'

'And what is wrong with that?'

'Nothing at all, for I must admit to finding the end result very pleasant. There is a glow about you and you smell quite divine.'

Acknowledging the compliment, Lucy smiled sweetly. 'Why, thank you, Charles. You do say the most charming things, although you say it with a curl to your lips which makes me not quite sure how to take your compliments. It's as if it gives you immense enjoyment to tease me.'

But it was not malicious or hurtful, for there was a wicked gleam in his eyes which she could not interpret. He was a complex man who allowed no one to see the hidden depths of himself.

'No doubt you enjoyed the pampering?'

'It was delightful. It is one of the things I shall miss

when I leave here. It's so far removed from anything I have ever known or could have imagined. I have been bathed, scented and oiled so much that should anyone try to get hold of me, I will slip out of their fingers.'

Relinquishing his perch and stepping forward, he winced suddenly. Thinking of his wounded leg and the rigours he had endured on the journey, Lucy said, 'Your leg still pains you, I see.'

Charles ran a distracted hand through his hair. 'It does somewhat, but I am also weary after the hunt. It has been a long day.'

'And yet, like me, you can't sleep.'

'It would appear so.'

'So—what should we do about it? What do you suggest?'

His eyes were partly hooded as they fastened on her face, his voice soft and seductive when he spoke. 'My night is free. You have me all to yourself—if you want me.'

Chapter Six

Unable to ignore his suggestive remark—Charles knew how to use his potent charm to lethal effect—Lucy couldn't help but catch her breath.

He was gazing at her hard, looking like a man in the throes of some internal struggle. 'Is it possible that you are even more lovely now than when I first saw you?' he said in a lazy, sensual drawl that made Lucy's heart melt.

She laughed uneasily, getting to her feet. 'Fancy waiting until I'm in the Rajah's palace with nowhere to run, to tell me that—dressed in nothing but a robe and my hair unbound. It puts a woman at a disadvantage.'

'I like you in your robe and your hair unbound,' he breathed.

Lucy realised just how perceptive this man was. She was disturbingly aware of those warm blue eyes delving into hers as if he were intent on searching out her innermost thoughts. Placing his hands on her shoulders, he held her at arm's length, his eyes, full of intensity, refusing to relinquish their hold on hers. For an instant she thought he was angry, but then she saw a troubled, almost tortured look enter his eyes.

'I've known many women, Lucy, and ventured far

and wide, but no woman—not even Amelia—has provoked my imagination to such a degree as you do. You are a temptress, dangerous in your innocence. It's hard for me seeing you on the occasions we've been together, knowing you are almost within my arm's reach and not touching you as I want to do.'

His voice had softened to the timbre of rough velvet and made Lucy's senses jolt almost as much as the strange way he was looking at her. Suddenly her sense of security began to disintegrate. 'Did you really bring me all the way to Kassam to say that?' she asked quietly, feeling a treacherous warmth slowly beginning to seep beneath her flesh.

'I wanted to be alone with you. Because we are soon to part, I wanted to prolong our relationship. Can you understand that? Does it alarm you?'

'And—and why should you think I want to be alone with you?' she whispered shakily.

His relentless gaze locked with hers. 'Neither of us has anything to gain by pretending the other doesn't exist—that the kisses we have shared never happened. I remember them and I know damn well you remember them, too.'

'I haven't forgotten them. How could I?' she added defensively.

'So far, I have managed to convince myself that my memory of how sweet it was is exaggerated. Now I'm curious to know if it really was that good and ardently wish it might be repeated—and to finish what we began.'

'Are you telling me you want to make love to me?'

The sweetness of her question was almost Charles's undoing. 'It is my fervent desire. It is not just a question of wanting you, but of wanting you too much. The mere fact of being alone with you now is torture for me. But worry not, Lucy. I am not in the habit of seducing gently reared, virginal young ladies. I have developed a high regard for you—no, more than that—an attraction and a strong and passionate desire for you. I will not dishonour you. I came to your room to spend a pleasant hour in your company. Nothing more than that.'

He spoke in that soft, cajoling tone that charmed Lucy. She shivered when she recalled the touch of his lips, which she was consciously yearning for. Breathing deeply, she savoured it once more, feeling the hour of her defeat approaching. She became thoughtful, observing him with earnest attention. Remembering the ugliness of what had happened to her in the past, she shuddered.

Charles noticed. 'Is something wrong?'

'No. Just a memory.'

'An unpleasant memory?'

She looked at him and he stared into the depths of the dark green eyes, open so wide, so filled with fear and at the same time with trust. 'Yes, but it doesn't matter now.' By some hidden force she became gripped by some powerful emotion. Having removed his hands from her shoulders, she moved a little closer to him and lifted her eyes to his, holding his gaze with her own. This was the moment. Unbeknown to him, he had just presented her with the opportunity she had been waiting for.

'There is something I want to tell you,' she said, trying to keep the nervousness out of her voice and failing completely. 'I didn't intend to—but now I think I must.'

'What is it?' he asked, watching her closely.

She took a deep breath. 'It—it's about the time when Johnathan died—about what happened to me—that made me who I am today—why the way people see me is not always…pleasant. I cannot believe that I have spent all the years since he died living in the shadows.'

'Why? What are you trying to tell me, Lucy?'

'When I met Johnathan I was an ordinary girl. I wanted all the things girls want—parties and balls and excitement—to share it all with the man who was to be my husband. I wanted romance—to be held and kissed…' She sighed. 'I had all that, but then…'

His dark brows almost joined in a frown. 'Then? What happened, Lucy?'

His voice was softer, more tender than she'd ever heard it. Her heartbeat quickened to a frantic rhythm and time stood still. Once again, she was back there, all that time ago. She wet her lips and tried to speak, but the words stuck in her throat. She swallowed and gathered her courage.

'Something unpleasant happened to me. I was having supper with my parents at the residency in Bhopal— that was where we were living at the time. Having finished my meal and leaving my parents to chat over their coffee and brandy, feeling stifled and in need of air, I wandered out on to the veranda. I remember how quiet it was with just one young man lounging at a table. He invited me to join him.

'Already acquainted with him, but knowing nothing

of his character and unable to see anything wrong with sitting with him until my parents were ready to leave, I accepted. He ordered me some coffee. We exchanged pleasantries. I remember feeling sleepy and then, apart from being manhandled and seeing a shadowy face looming over me, I knew nothing else until I woke in the hospital.

'That was when I met Dr Jessop. With my mother present, he told me what had been done to me—but I already knew. One cannot be raped and not know. I wanted to die, but I had to go on living. I blotted it from my mind, only to suffer further trauma when Johnathan, intent on revenge, sought out the perpetrator, only to lose his own life by the hand of the man who had violated me.'

'Dear God!'

Charles stared at her, his shock so plain for her to see. She wanted nothing more than for the earth to swallow her up. All her courage fled and painful embarrassment took its place. 'I can see how shocked you are—and I cannot blame you. What happened to me cannot be erased or changed. I have to accept it, live with it and get on with my life.'

She spoke with a tired resignation, without anger or resentment. Charles understood all too well what she was saying. With their disparate lives, their completely different experiences, they had something in common. He reached out and placed his hand on her cheek in a comforting gesture that surprised him. It surprised her, too. Reaching up, she placed her hand over his.

'Thank you,' she said.

'For what?'

'Listening to me. I've never told anyone about what happened to me. I couldn't. I have never spoken of it. It was too difficult.'

Lowering her eyes, she turned her face half away from his penetrating gaze, still unable to tell him of her guilt—the deep and terrible abiding guilt that still consumed her—that by her actions of allowing her abuser into her life, she had unwittingly signed Johnathan's death warrant. Had she not sat with a virtual stranger and invited conversation and drank the coffee he'd placed before her, Johnathan would not have died. A terrible despair had engulfed her and with it the shame. She still felt trapped by her guilt, knowing her impulsive action had endangered not only her future, but had led to Johnathan's death.

'I was too ashamed,' she whispered. 'I couldn't speak of it—not to anyone.'

'And yet you have told me.'

'Yes. You see—since meeting you I began to realise all that I have missed, to experience all the things once more that I so enjoyed before...before Johnathan lost his life avenging what had been done to me.'

'Tell me how it was—to help me understand—and about the man who committed the crime.'

'He was a Company employee. What he did to me was in retaliation for Johnathan reporting him to the Company for embezzlement. As a consequence, he was dismissed.'

'Was it proved that he killed Johnathan?'

'No, but a close friend of Johnathan's at the time,

who knew others who were there when the attack on Johnathan took place and intimated the fact, was in no doubt. Before that, when I went missing, I was found in quite a state, wandering in a disreputable district. I was disorientated and, mercifully, with no idea where I was or what had happened to me at that point. I—I had been drugged and raped. Demented with anger and anguish, in an act of vengeance Johnathan went looking for the perpetrator. Unfortunately, he lost his life in the fracas that ensued.'

'And the man responsible?'

'Was found in an opium den. As I recovered from my ordeal there was pain and misery and the dark and unmistakable bruises—a legacy of the violence inflicted on me. It was ugly.'

Charles stared at her as he tried to take in what she had told him. He was entirely unprepared for what she had disclosed. He was incapable of any kind of rational thought. What he felt at that moment was raw, red-hot anger. He was horrified—horrified at what that monster had put Lucy through. Where there was rage at what had been done to her, there was tenderness and sorrow, and he felt a surge of deep compassion as he realised how distraught and anguished she must have been at the time.

He could not bear to think of the pain Lucy must have experienced because of that horrendous act. The pictures thrust through his brain like knives. Lucy had been bound up in the secrets of the past for far too long. Clearly it was too private, too painful, something she was locked into, for her to speak about. Not that he could blame her. No doubt she felt that to confess she would be punished without mercy and she had learned to keep her secret so well that she hardly knew her motives for doing so. He could well imagine how her betrothed must have felt and understood his need to avenge Lucy.

His heart ached with the enormity of it all. The thought of Lucy knowing a moment's terror was too agonising for him to deal with just then. Had the rape left such an indelible scar on her that it went deeper than the surface? That was the moment he realised he didn't know her mind, what went off inside her head. She wouldn't admit him into it. She was an enigma.

'After what he was guilty of? Was he not apprehended for that?'

Lucy shook her head. 'You must understand that it was a highly charged, sensitive situation at the time. Apart from my parents, and a couple of Johnathan's close friends, no one knew of it. Had it become known my violation would have fuelled vicious tongues and tarnished me for ever. My parents and Dr Jessop, who put me back together, thought I had suffered enough. My father wanted the whole affair hushed up. For my sake they wanted to escape a scandal. Afterwards I retreated into myself, refusing to speak of it, but I was deeply traumatised by what had been done to me. When my father was moved to Nandra, I threw myself into working with the children and helping at the hospital in an attempt to forget.'

'Why have you decided to tell me this now, Lucy?'

'I want to experience what I missed because of what

happened to me.' Her jaw hardened with resolution and she said very clearly, 'You kissed me—showed me how it could be. I want you to show me again—I want you to make love to me.'

Charles stared at her, clearly wondering if he had heard her correctly. He could not believe what she had asked him to do, the enormity of the responsibility she was placing on him. Touching her cheek tenderly with the tip of his finger, he shook his head. 'I don't know if you are being serious or just teasing me, Lucy.' Seeing the courage she had mustered to expose her inner self disintegrate, like a flower wilting in the hot sun and how she moved away, he watched her turn her back on him, her shoulders drooping.

'I—I'm sorry if this is not what you want.' She kept her face averted, not wanting him to see how it hurt. 'After what I have told you, knowing what you do now, if you find the whole idea of making love to a woman who has been raped abhorrent, then we will stop now and never speak of it again. I will understand absolutely and apologise for any embarrassment I have caused.'

Charles moved to stand behind her. Though he wasn't touching her, she felt the heat of his body behind her as if it were a touch. His warm breath fanned her cheek as he bent his head.

'Nothing about you is abhorrent, Lucy—or the fact that another man took from you that most precious thing a woman has to give to the man she loves.' Placing his hands on her shoulders, he turned her to face him, tenderly wiping away the strands of hair fanning her cheeks and tucking them behind her ears. 'Since that time, what you have done, the way you have dealt with it, has been no more than an act of personal survival—something anyone with the same kind of courage would have done, faced with the same situation.'

Having emptied her heart, Lucy almost broke into a sea of tears and emotion. The pull of Charles's gaze was too strong for her to resist. It was as though he were looking into the very depths of her heart and soul. She felt the touch of his empathy like healing fingers touching and soothing her pain like a balm. She had seen in his eyes the reflection of her torment and now, as though he were God's own advocate, he was offering her redemption.

'Thank you, Charles. Your words mean a lot to me.'

'I hope you realise what you're really asking for,' he murmured.

'I was not joking, Charles,' she said quietly. 'I was being serious. My feelings are comparable with yours, but that is all. I will not expect any kind of commitment from you. I do not want it. That would only complicate things.' She met his intense blue gaze squarely, searching his eyes to guess his mood. They were dark with desire and a hunger.

'No one need know of this but us. I have no inhibitions and no pretences. I am doing this for myself. I am twenty-five years old and I don't have my virtue to worry about. I *want* you to make love to me. I ask nothing from you other than that—no commitments. I know your views on what you consider to be a debilitating emotion called love—you told me in no uncertain terms. I know the rules and I expect nothing from you that you are not prepared to give. Afterwards we will go our separate ways—no recriminations and no regrets.'

In the warm intimacy of the room, Charles was beginning to see another side to Lucy emerge, pushing the old one away, a Lucy without conscience, without shame, as if she were feeling something that was completely physical, hinting at joys that could be hers, telling herself this was a moment not to be missed—a night of the kind of pleasure she had never experienced before.

Involuntarily, he dropped his gaze to her mouth, a mouth lush and generous, a mouth that tantalised, a mouth made to be kissed. He remembered how soft and warm and inviting those lips had felt when he had kissed them before. It had surprised him. He never would have expected the fierce desire that had shot through him. Lucy Quinn was a lovely young woman, with her light fair hair spilling down her spine like a waterfall, and the exotic scent of her recently pampered body intoxicating. She had a mysterious allure he found hard to ignore.

'I think the palace and the attention showered on you by the Rani and her ladies has affected you more than you realise, Lucy. You don't know what you are asking of me—the responsibility you place on me. You tell me you were raped—that no man has touched you since that time. How do I know you won't run screaming from my arms?'

'I promise you I won't do that. I know very well what I am asking—and it is not particularly flattering for me to have to ask you. After the kisses we have shared, I wouldn't have thought you reluctant to carry on where we left off.'

'And I recall telling you that if there was to be a next time we kissed, then I would do the asking.'

'Then ask me.'

Seeing the determination on Lucy's lovely face, Charles frowned. He couldn't believe she was offering herself. It had been quite some time since a woman had warmed his bed and he was more than tempted by the slender body beneath the almost transparent robe before him.

When he didn't reply Lucy moved even closer. 'Why do you hesitate? Don't you want me, Charles? What must I do to persuade you?'

He studied her bathed in the glow of the moon and the lamps. Her large dark eyes were wide and wary. She looked completely vulnerable. Which was exactly what she was. Vulnerable and still innocent, despite what had been done to her, and without any idea of what she was asking for. He could show her. He wanted to show her, more than he had ever wanted anything before. His desire for her was driving him mad.

But now, when she had asked him to make love to her, when all he had to do was take her to bed, he was unable to move. It was no easy matter. He didn't want to hurt her. He respected her too much. He had never made love to a woman who wasn't willing. She only had to say no and he would stop.

'Lucy—what you are asking me to do is a huge undertaking on my part. The last thing I want is for you to hate me afterwards should you have any regrets.'

'I could never hate you, Charles—and I think I'm perfectly capable of deciding what I want.'

'At this moment, perhaps. But not when I leave Kassam—when I leave you and move on.'

'I'm not asking for tomorrow,' she murmured. 'I told you—no commitments. All I'm asking for is tonight. Help me move on from the past.'

Seeing the way she was looking at him—the softness in her eyes—he knew he should leave now, tell her no, but instead, taking her face between the palms of his hands he lowered his head and kissed her lips. 'Then that is what you will have,' he murmured against her mouth. 'Tonight.'

His arms went round her with infinite care, bringing her in close contact with his lean, hard frame, savouring the warmth of her body against his. His mouth came down on hers. Her lips parted freely and, with that instant response from her, the taste of her, Charles knew there was no turning back.

Sliding his fingers through her hair, revelling in the silken feel of it, he kissed her long and deeply. Her voluptuous bloom of womanhood evoked in him a strong stirring of desire. He could not believe how much he wanted her, that the body his own had so fiercely craved from the moment he had first laid eyes on her was in his arms.

Sensitive to her vulnerability, he knew that if he was to dispel the memory of the terrible thing that had been done to her, then he had to take it slowly, to be patient, to wait until she was ready. He tore his lips from hers and buried his head in the curve of her neck, his hands sliding down to her slender waist and drawing her close.

His fingers caressed the small of her back, pressing her body closer still.

Scooping her up into his arms, he carried her to the bed, settling her on the cool covers. With her hair spread about her in lustrous waves, he had never seen her look lovelier. He looked down at her face. 'Is this what you want, Lucy? Are you sure?'

She nodded, taking his hand and placing her lips on his open palm. 'I do—more than anything. Just the two of us, here, in this room.'

He smiled. 'Two lonely people finding solace in each other arms.'

'I would like to think it is more than that,' she murmured, losing herself in those blue eyes gazing down at her, now hazy with desire.

Slowly Charles's hand slipped about her waist as he drew her body against his and kissed her gently, amazed and intrigued by the mixture of innocence, boldness and fear which fired this woman. He would like to make her body sing before they were done, to shatter her demureness and reserve and lay bare the woman of passion.

He kissed her again and again, lost in the heady beauty of her. By God, she was lovely, and he wanted her with a fierceness that took his breath away. An uncontrollable compulsion to make love to her overwhelmed him and he kissed her until she was moaning and writhing in his arms and desire was pouring through him like hot tidal waves, but he had to contain himself, to be patient, to wait until she was ready.

Slowly he shoved aside her robe, exposing the softness, the curves of her naked body. He bent his head, again covering her mouth with his, his hand gently caressing her neck. Her eyes darkened and she tried to cover her breasts with her arms, Charles gently caught her hands and pulled them away. He knew he must be gentle lest her fear destroyed the moment.

'No, Lucy. Open your eyes and look at me.' Slowly, she met his gaze and his heart sank on seeing the apprehension and fear in their dark depths. Leaning up on his elbow, reaching out he tenderly smoothed the wayward strands of hair from her face. Pride surged through him at her courage. The beautiful, brave young woman was prepared to give herself to him, and him alone. He wanted to make up to her all that she had suffered in the past, when her virginity had been taken with brutal swiftness.

'I don't know what you're thinking,' he said softly, 'but you look terrified. Don't be afraid. I'm not going to hurt you, I promise,' he said reassuringly. 'I want to please you.'

Lucy swallowed, lowering her hands, but she continued to clasp the edges of the robe to her body. He wondered if she was going to change her mind. He wanted her, wanted to continue kissing those soft lips, to span that invitingly narrow waist with his hands and draw her hips beneath him. The fierceness of his wanting startled him, but he would not force her. Hearing her faint inhalation, he held back, looking down at her.

'What's wrong, Lucy? Keep your robe on if you like. But if this is not what you want, then it is not too late. We can stop now.'

'No—don't stop, it's just—I—I don't know what I'm supposed to do.'

'Then I'll show you—slowly—every step of the way. Any time you want me to stop, just say the words and we will go no further. You have my word.'

His hands stroked downwards, over the curve of her hip, and then upwards along the velvet softness of her inner thighs. She gasped, reflexively tensing her muscles and clamping her legs together. Once more, Charles stopped what he was doing.

'Lucy,' he said huskily. 'You don't have to do this.'

Above her, Lucy could see his face was tense, his eyes dark with passion, yet there was so much tenderness in their depths that her heart ached. 'Yes,' she murmured, 'I do.' The pull of his gaze was too strong for her to resist. It was as though he were looking into the very depths of her heart and soul. It was as if he knew her fear that twisted within her chest, as if she were so transparent, he could see all she had kept hidden laid bare. She felt the touch of his empathy like healing fingers soothing her apprehension like a balm.

Like a celestial being she raised her arms and wrapped them about his neck. Charles gathered her to him in reverence. Her fear was like a cutting edge and yet sublime, and when it left her and she felt the warmth of his lips, she was wide open in a flood of wondrous new emotions.

He took her soft lips she was offering in a long, sweet kiss that was almost beyond bearing, then, releasing her, he divested himself of his clothes and slipped his naked body on to the bed beside her.

Tentatively she moved her fingers over the furring of dark hair on his chest and felt the slight increase in the steady thudding of his heart. Very slowly he began to kiss her, long and lingeringly, with all the aching tenderness in his heart and she, after a few moments of tense passivity, began to kiss him back. Her slender arms slid up his chest and went around his neck and she pressed herself to the full length of his hard, unyielding contours.

Charles groaned, his mouth opening passionately over hers. Gently moving her robe aside, his hand slid to her midriff, then moved upwards, cupping the ripeness of her breast. She trembled beneath his touch, but instead of pulling away, as Charles expected her to do, the stiffness flowed out of her body and she relaxed, surrendering to his gentle, insistent persuasion.

She moved closer to him, fitting her body against his, her heartbeat increasing with a mixture of pulsing pleasure and fear when she felt the demanding heat of his maleness pressing against her thigh. Instead of pulling away, she gave herself up to his caresses until there was no more fear, only an exquisite, aching need to have him inside her. His hand continued to caress her, glorying in the softness of her flesh, and when he shifted her on to her back and leaned over her, what Lucy was feeling was drugging, delirious and quite wonderful.

She looked up at him, her eyes enormous and unblinking in her small, flushed face, and her mouth was rosy, as though waiting for further instructions on how to proceed, as if she wanted to take a more active part in what was slowly becoming a pleasant pastime, but was not sure how to go about it. It was as though what Charles was doing to her unlocked her heart.

She could sense the need in him, the need he had of

her and her body, and she gloried in it, but when his fingers reached that part of her that was totally private, she stiffened and bit her lip, briefly recalling he was not the first to touch her like this. Even though she could not remember what had happened to her at that time, she doubted that other man had treated her as lovingly and gently as Charles was doing. Immediately she thrust the unpleasant thoughts away and concentrated on what he was doing. She had to. She owed this to herself and would not let what that monster had done to her take away her capacity for loving.

The sensations Charles was arousing in her were utterly erotic, burning her flesh to a compelling, melting, quivering need, to go on until the very core of her ignited and inflamed every part of her body. Nothing else in the world mattered. They were completely absorbed with each other.

Leaning on his forearms, Charles gazed down at her lovely face. 'I want you, Lucy,' he whispered against her parted lips, his voice hoarse with tenderness. 'I want you very badly. Are you ready for this?'

Lucy nodded. 'Yes,' she whispered. 'Please—don't stop now.'

A fierce exhilaration swept through her as he slowly, tenderly entered her, filling every vein with liquid fire. She wrapped her arms around him, lost in incoherent yearnings. With his lips devouring hers, more eloquent, more demanding than before, he moved inside her, his eyes never leaving her face.

Some essential part of her that Lucy had not been aware of until now awoke and she ceased to think at all.

She felt something unfold inside her, spreading and filling her with warmth, with colour and light and reaching every nerve in her body, when suddenly a shudder rocked him and he let out a gasp as he thrust against her one last time.

A shimmering ecstasy pierced Lucy's entire body, sending sparks of pleasure curling through her that increased until they became a flame inside her and they lay together in sweet oblivion.

They lay for a long time, not speaking, reluctant to shatter the tranquillity and completeness of what they had found with one another during this magical night. After a moment when their bodies ceased to tremble, with an overpowering wave of tenderness, Charles rolled on to his side, taking her with him, cradling her in his arms, reluctant to let go of her. With her face resting in the curve of his jaw, Lucy experienced a joyous contentment, a languorous peace—and exultation, that the terrible thing that had been done to her had not taken away her capacity for loving.

'Are you all right, Lucy?'

Hearing the concern in his voice, Lucy felt an overpowering wave of tenderness wash over her. 'Yes—at least—I think so.'

'What are you thinking?'

'That now I am indeed a fallen woman—and I feel no shame, no regrets, just an incredible joy that has opened like a flower inside me—and I have you to thank for the way I feel now and I shall be forever grateful. For the first time since...' She faltered. 'I won't speak of that. I have no wish to tarnish the exquisite joy I feel now with the past. I feel vibrant, alive, and I want nothing more than for this moment to go on for ever—even though I know it must soon end.' Closing her eyes, she pressed her cheek against his chest and sighed, listening to his heartbeat.

'It must—when the time comes for you to return to Nandra.'

'Don't,' she whispered. 'Don't say it, Charles—not now. We'll deal with that when the time comes.' She nestled closer to him. She would allow nothing to steal the joy, the quiet glow of absolute bliss, which was with her now.

The room had become a magical place, their own private heaven. Sighing now, she placed tantalising little kisses on his chest, their naked bodies fitting together in sweet perfection. Lucy could smell him now she had her senses back, smell his skin, the scent of his cologne and a musky odour she could not identify, not an unpleasant odour—an odour of sensuality, one she knew she would always associate with this moment. She heard him sigh with contentment.

'You were a delight, Lucy. Something truly special.'

'And I am delighted to hear it,' she murmured.

'Do you realise how desirable you are?'

'Am I?' she whispered curiously. 'I'm amazed you can say that, for I never thought you felt anything for me but irritation—at least that's the impression you gave me when we first met.'

He chuckled softly. 'Was I that bad? I suppose you were irritating at times—and I was in a great deal of pain, don't forget,' he teased, tightening his hold on her.

'There you are. I was right.'

'Call it self-defence.'

Laughing delightedly, she wriggled away from him and stretched her body for him to inspect. 'I don't think I care for that remark. I think I'm going to have to punish you.'

'And how do you intend to do that?' he asked, devouring her with his eyes, his fingers tweaking a lock of her hair.

'By insisting that you make love to me again.'

'You call that punishment? I call it pleasure.'

And to prove his point, leaning over her he took her hands and held them above her while he carefully inspected her breasts, her waist, the curve of her hips. He knew her now, every part of her, knowing the true nature of her.

His senses were alive to every inch of her form languorously stretched out before him and, desire pouring like boiling lava through his veins, he kissed and nuzzled and caressed her until she felt the heat return to the pit of her belly. She sighed with absolute delight as he took her again with a lovely languor, consumed in a passion infinitely more powerful than before.

Afterwards, Lucy felt sleepy with contentment and her eyes fluttered closed. For a long time, she had been like a captive bird and now Charles had opened the cage and let her fly free.

The golden glow of the night washed over them as they lay clasped together, their moist skin cooling in the night air. They were breathing heavily as they waited for the slow and powerful beating of their hearts that follows climax to return to normal and to preserve the moment of their union a moment longer, as though afraid to disturb their fragile link by moving.

Gazing at the incredibly lovely young woman resting in the crook of his arm, her satiated body aglow from the force of her passion, Charles felt strangely humble and possessive. The enchanting temptress who had yielded to him without reservation, who had writhed beneath him as he had made love to her, was gentleness and goodness personified. He revelled in the sweetness of her as he stroked her spine, trying not to think and to hold on to the fading euphoria. He had been surprisingly enchanted with her and her body's responses to his own, and recognised the needs of the flesh without the complications of the heart.

Lucy asked for no more of him than he did of her. So why did it bother him that they were to go their separate ways? The answer was a mystery. He admired her tenacity and resolve. She had the ability to amuse him and he liked being with her. She was also honest and kept her word, which was somewhat rare in the women he had known previously. She was exciting to be with and he enjoyed her company, but it was time to put a stop to it before she began to expect more of him than he was prepared to give.

Besides, she was not free. She was still caught up in a web from which she could not escape—a web which the man she had been betrothed to and the man who had ruined her had woven round her. She could lead a happy and dignified life—but always her thoughts would turn to Johnathan. For the first time in his life Charles experienced a real, bitter jealousy. It was a cruel emotion; one he was not accustomed to.

With the dawn came the reminder that he had promised to accompany the Rajah on another hunt. Lucy wasn't aware when he reluctantly slipped away from her, kissing her bare shoulder before pulling on his clothes and leaving her to slumber.

When Lucy awoke, little remained of the girl who had been a victim of a rapist. She was a creature of the past. The mysterious alchemy of her inner self, mixed with elements inside Charles, had worked the miracle of transformation. The change in her was clear, and for the first time in years she felt at peace with herself.

A great burden had been lifted from her and she felt so happy it was like walking on air. It was as if she was waking up after a long dark sleep and what her soul had craved for the past seven years. She realised that she had turned a corner in coming to terms with the events of what had been done to her and it was Charles that had helped her to do that.

Her mind was filled with images of Charles and she held the memory of their loving as it wrapped itself about her like a warm blanket. Her mind and her very soul had been possessed by that perfect body, a body without flaw. It was no use hiding from the fact that they had been attracted to each other from the beginning, despite her initial show of indifference, but she must not mistake the kindness and tenderness he had shown her for something deeper.

Charles had the infuriating ability to pluck at the worst of her nature, to see what no man had ever seen before. But, she thought, on a warm tide of feelings, he also had the ability to tease, to cajole, to delight her senses in a way no other man had succeeded in doing before. He had created yearnings inside her she was a stranger to, yearnings she wanted to satisfy, and only Charles could do that.

Yet no matter how intense her feelings were for Charles, how constant, dominating her every thought, the burden of guilt she still carried in her heart over Johnathan's death, that he would still be alive if not for her, continued to plague her and she felt undeserving of any kind of happiness.

Throwing back the shutters, she noticed the flush of rose and apricot in the sky, along with a tinge of lilac and orange. A flock of small birds came and settled in the trees. She glanced at the sun rising behind the low hills, now the colour of ochre and gold. It enchanted her. It seemed as if they were living things, changing colour depending on the sun and the time of day. This was the colour of India in all its magical glory, she thought.

Chapter Seven

Lucy was in the garden along with Ananya and several of her ladies. This was where Charles found her. She was seated alone on a bench, watching the colourful scene of the ladies happily lounging on the grass, laughing and talking among themselves. Drinking in the fragrant tranquillity, he took a moment to observe her, admiring the fine figure she made. For a moment he felt as if she had reached into his chest and squeezed his heart. And then he blinked and shook off his strange abstractions.

Looking up from where she was seated on a wooden bench, she smiled on seeing him. 'Charles? Are you looking for me by any chance? I was wondering when you would show yourself.'

Her familiar voice rose above the sounds of the chattering ladies. Charles did not realise how much he had missed her until he heard it, or how the sight of her warmed his heart—and it had not been twelve hours since he had left her. He ached for her—to touch her, to gaze on her lovely face, to hear the sweet, soft sound of her voice. When they had made love, she had touched a tenderness and protectiveness within him he hadn't known existed.

He stood before her and his eyes glowed, complimenting her appearance, and a smile hovered on his mouth. The dark liquid of his eyes deepened as he became caught up in the warmth of her presence. Outwardly she appeared composed and very calm, making it impossible to determine her feelings and emotions generated in her following their night together.

'Here you are. I've been impatient to see you again, Lucy.'

'Oh? I missed you when I woke and found you gone,' she said, getting to her feet. 'Although perhaps it was as well. Maya is an early riser and would have scolded me severely had she found us together at that hour.'

'I'd arranged to go hunting again with the Rajah this morning and he wanted to make an early start. I've just returned. Later on today he is eager to show me his domain—and to spend the night with some of his friends at a hunting lodge. We will be back before you have to return to Nandra.'

'I see. Well,' she said, beginning to saunter away from the chattering ladies in the direction of a fountain spouting water high into the air, 'that is the reason why you are here, to spend time with the Rajah to promote better relations between Britain and India.'

'Our talks have been favourable so far.' He looked sideways at her as he fell into step beside her. 'Did you sleep well?' he asked quietly.

'Like a babe after you left me.'

Her tone, her very posture, were cool and aloof. Charles

peered at her, trying to read her expression. He wasn't sure what he had expected. An acknowledgement of what had passed between them, he supposed. His appraising gaze swept slowly over her once more, as if he couldn't get enough of looking at her. 'You look adorable. The sari suits you. I imagine you will be reluctant to get back to wearing English garb.'

'Indeed, I will,' she said as they continued to stroll along the quiet paths. 'I took advantage of another session in the bathing chamber earlier. In fact, I find myself remarkably transformed. The comfortable, indolent life at the palace, the rich food, the leisurely strolls in the flower-filled courtyards and gardens, and all the dexterous attention of Ananya's ladies have worked wonders. I have spent a good deal of time resting. I'm just not used to having so much time on my hands with nothing to do. I shall find it hard readjusting to the many duties that occupy my time in Nandra.'

'I have enjoyed our time together. I shall miss you, Lucy.' He looked down at her. 'Will you miss me?'

'I dare say I shall—although I expect you will soon find another diversion.'

'Diversion? Is that how you think of yourself?'

'No, of course not. It is what I intend not to be.'

Charles stopped walking and looked down at her, his expression serious, searching. 'You were never that. Do you regret it, Lucy—what we did?'

Her wide-eyed look was one of complete innocence. 'No, of course not. It is right that you should know how I feel. When I gave myself to you I did so gladly—without shame or remorse. In fact, it was quite wonderful—the most wonderful thing that has ever happened to me,' she confessed.

'I am relieved to hear it. You know how I feel about you.'

'Do I, Charles? Do I really?' Tilting her head to one side, she gave him a teasing look. 'I do hope you are not saying that you love me, Charles?'

'Love?' He slowly shook his head. 'I despise the idea of what the romantics call love. How does one define love? I've told you before that I no longer know what the word means. I care for you—a great deal, as it happens—but don't confuse physical desire with love. I have lived through one disastrous relationship, which taught me that it is an unpleasant experience I have no desire to repeat. The woman in question wrung almost every emotion out of me.'

'And so you judge every woman to be the same,' Lucy said quietly.

'No, not all of them, but I realised a long time ago that poets may write about love and balladeers may sing about it. It exists for others—but not for me. Despite the feelings and emotions we aroused in each other, do not fool yourself into believing it had anything to do with love.'

'Don't worry, Charles, I don't and I thank you for being honest with me. But I would have imagined you would have too much common sense to attribute to all women what you have experienced in one.'

'You would say that. You, who showed me so much vulnerability, so much generous passion.' He looked at her, wondering what the change in her attitude was all about. Was she ashamed of what they'd done? He didn't

think so. On recalling the passionate, irresistible temptress he had aroused in her bed, of the pure bliss they
had each felt in their union, he believed her when she
said she had no regrets.

'But what of you, Charles? Do you have regrets?'

He shook his head slowly. 'I refuse to regret or apologise for what happened. We wanted each other—we
were attracted to each other. It was as simple as that. I
well remember what your body looks like, Lucy.' His
eyelids were lowered over his eyes as he looked down at
her upturned face, gently flushed a delicate pink by his
remark. 'I remember everything about it—every curve,
every hollow and every inviting, secret place.' He smiled
at the shock that registered in her eyes.

Lucy's attempt to chastise him for his forward remark, when Ananya and her ladies had fallen silent and
were watching them with curiosity, failed. 'Please be
quiet, Charles, lest we are overheard.'

'Worry not, Lucy. Apart from the Rani and perhaps
an odd one of her ladies, our exchange will not be understood.'

His voice was deceptively soft and Lucy cast her eyes
away, registering her unease. 'Nevertheless, I think you
should leave. I will see you in the morning before I depart for Nandra—if you get back in time, that is.'

'I will make a point of it. But there is something I
would like to say before we part.'

'Oh?'

'I hope you find someone who will show you a way to
a new life. Someone who will bring you out of the past.
Someone who will give you a chance to put all that hap-

pened behind you. Do you intend to mourn Johnathan for ever?'

His words seemed to take her off guard. Clearly she had not expected this. He saw the hurt and despair in her eyes. He felt something inside him, some strange emotion that was unrecognisable to him just then, and unconsciously his hand went out to her. His expression became one of mixed emotions, strangely gentle, and his eyes softened and were filled with sorrow and compassion, telling her of his regret that his words should give her pain.

'You are right. I have lived too long in the past. I might have been Johnathan's wife now. I would have been happy with him.'

'You were in love with him.'

'Yes, I was. How could I not be? He was handsome, kind—a gentleman and highly thought of by everyone.' She looked at him gravely. 'There are some things in my life I cannot set aside, Charles. Johnathan is one of them.'

Charles paused to collect his thoughts and marshal the facts, for that was the moment he realised her betrothed's loss remained a gaping wound. There was nothing in Lucy's attitude to give him any encouragement and he had no intention of trying to compete with a dead man.

In some way, he was reminded of his own situation. With his instinct for self-preservation, he was suddenly furious with himself for having succumbed so easily and foolishly to a woman's charms once more. Tentatively he made a move towards her, but he could almost feel the alert tension of all her muscles. Her very stillness was like a positive force.

'I would have said more, Lucy, as I could now, but I do not have the right.'

'The right? No, Charles, you don't. It's best not to say anything else.'

'Just one thing. Johnathan has been dead these past seven years. It is time you accepted the fact.'

Lucy met his gaze. His blunt words were cruel and hit their mark. 'I do accept it, Charles, but that doesn't mean I can forget him—or the fact that it was my own actions that brought about his brutal death.' Drawing a deep breath, she stepped away from him, unwilling to discuss the matter further. 'Tomorrow I shall return to Nandra. I shall not forget our time together.'

'I sincerely hope not. I shall not forget it either and, whatever the future holds for you, Lucy, I sincerely wish only for your happiness.'

The attraction of his handsome face and deep blue eyes, which could be as stormy as India during a monsoon or warm with depths of tenderness, had been irresistible. Whenever they were together Lucy's feelings had intensified until they brought an ache of emptiness to her heart. He did not love her—not that she expected him to, but his consideration as a lover had brought her to a pleasure that Johnathan had never achieved.

That night had held a thousand unexceptionable and unexpected pleasures for them both, but she would not allow herself to become caught up in a romantic dream. Her emotions were torn asunder and she could find no solace in the depths of her thoughts. Knowing they must part had strengthened the barrier about her heart, but

that barrier was not made of stones. Their first kiss had
brought some of them tumbling down. Now, as he walked
away, with an awful lump of desolation in her throat,
her heart ached.

The following morning, having reverted to western
dress, as though adopting armour for the journey back to
Nandra, Lucy said her farewells to the Rajah and Ananya.
She was sorry to be leaving her new friend.

'I will miss my English friend,' Ananya said. 'I will
remember you always. But you are not far away and will
be welcome any time at the palace. I have a gift for you
to remember me by.' She clapped her hands and a servant rushed forward with a package.

'But I can't possibly accept it. I shall be for ever
grateful to you and the Rajah for the kindness you have
shown me.'

'It was our pleasure. Now open it. You will like it,
I know.'

Lucy did as she asked and gasped when she saw the
carefully folded sky-blue silk finely threaded with gold,
so fine yet so delicate that if filtered through her fingers like liquid. She gasped. 'But—this is so beautiful.
I—I cannot—'

'Yes, you can. It is my gift to you. You cannot refuse.'

'Thank you, Ananya. I will treasure it always.'

Accompanied by Maya, who had found so much wonder within the palace that she would speak of it for ev-
ermore to her children and grandchildren, Lucy found

Captain Travis and the small military escort waiting for them with the horses.

She had not seen Charles since they had parted in the garden the previous day. Now, as she was about to leave Kassam, he suddenly appeared, looking harassed in his haste to see her before she left. He came towards her, his expression grim. There was an unusually brooding expression in his eyes.

Taking her arm, he drew her away from the others, 'You are ready to leave?'

'Yes. It is time—although I am sorry to be saying goodbye to Ananya and all those who have shown me kindness.'

'Kassam is just a day's ride away. I am certain the Rani would welcome you again.'

'Yes, she had invited me to return. When do you leave for Madras?'

'A couple of days here and then I shall be on my way. I hope to obtain a passage quickly. I don't relish the thought of having to kick my heels in Madras for any length of time.'

'Then I wish you a safe voyage.'

He nodded, his brows drawn together in a frown. 'There is a matter you should give some thought to, Lucy, which must be considered seriously.'

'And what is that, pray?'

'It is possible that a child may be the result of the night we spent together. Has it crossed your mind?'

'A child? Yes, it has.' Unconsciously her hand went to her abdomen and for a moment she could think of nothing more wonderful than to give birth to his child. 'I will give the matter some thought if that should happen.'

'And if you are carrying my child? What then?'

'I will deal with it.'

His frown deepened. '*You* will deal with it?'

Lucy flinched at the bite of his tone. 'Yes, I will have to—although it is not a situation I wish to find myself in. But I suppose like everything that has gone before, I shall weather the storm and hope for the best.'

The flippancy of her remark provoked Charles's eyes to flare with anger. 'No, Lucy, you will not. *We* will deal with it. Should it happen, the child you will be carrying will be mine, too, don't forget. I *will* have a say in how it is raised. You will write and tell me?'

Lucy felt anger and frustration rising within her. 'Of course I will tell you—I would not deprive you of seeing your child. I know you to be an honourable man who would give support and provide for it. But I will not have what I do in the future and the destiny of my child—should there be one—dictated by circumstance,' she said, suddenly boldly audacious in her maturity. 'Really, Charles, I cannot see why we are having this conversation now when in all probability I have not conceived. You must understand that I have some control over this—which I shall have no choice since you will be hundreds of miles away in England.'

'I shall not be in England for ever. I intend to return to India at the earliest possible time.'

'Well, there you are then. But a baby is not on the agenda at this crucial part of my life,' and, she thought, certainly not with a man who would stand by her out of nothing but a sense of duty. 'What we did was a mutual decision—my feelings comparable with yours. We had a strong desire for each other, nothing more than that.'

'It was more than that and you damn well know it. If you find yourself with child, then I have a duty to both you and the child and I insist that you inform me.'

'If that is what you want, then so be it. If there is a child, then I promise you I will write and tell you of the fact.'

'I think you misunderstand me. If I do not hear from you, then I shall call on you when I return to India—however long it takes—to make quite sure there is no child.'

'I understand you very well, Charles, and you insult my integrity if you think I would keep such an important matter from you. But do not think you have a right or a responsibility to arrange my life because of what happened between us. Do not put yourself out on my account. It is over, Charles. I am a grown woman. I can take care of myself. I will not be any man's duty. I thank you for your consideration and, should I find myself with child, I will inform you. That is my final word on the matter.'

He was standing very close. She had to look up to him. Impatiently she tried to shake off the effect he was having on her, regretting the harshness of her words and reminding herself that if it had not been for Charles she would still be battling her nightmares.

Without relinquishing the hold he had on her eyes, he looked down into her face. 'Of all the women I have known, Lucy, none has possessed the fire of heart and mind as you do and I am going to miss you like hell. You are beautiful. A temptress. We are to part and may never see each other again, so there is nothing left for us to say other than to bid each other farewell.' His gaze settled on her lips. 'A parting kiss, Lucy, as a farewell gift?'

As he bent his head, his firmly chiselled lips began a slow, deliberate descent towards her. She did not draw away—in fact, she raised her face to his, too tempted to forbid him a kiss. At first, he kissed her lightly. She tried not to show surprise or emotion, but that first touch was exquisite. His lips were warm, his kiss soft, and he kissed her long and lingeringly, a compelling kiss that made her head swim.

That was the moment when Lucy's mind went blank as his sensual mouth seized hers in an endless, drugging kiss that quickly built to one of demanding insistence and shook her to the core of her being. The world began to tilt as he crushed her tighter to the hard length of his body, parting her lips and exploring the honeyed softness of her mouth. Whether from fear or desire, Lucy moaned softly. She clung tighter to him, raising her arms and sliding her fingers into the crisp hair above his collar.

By the time Charles finally raised his head, Lucy's weakened defences crumbled completely. She felt dazed and her body quivered with all the raw emotions and the mindless pleasure he had aroused in her in her bed.

He tipped her chin. 'Look at me, Lucy.'

That deep voice saying her name was capable of making her do anything. She dragged her wide, wary gaze up to his smouldering blue eyes. 'Please let me go, Charles. You go too far.'

He smiled lazily, his white teeth flashing from between parted lips. 'Come now, Lucy, you are being unreasonable.'

'Unreasonable? Because I don't want you to kiss me?'

'But you do. You wanted it just as you wanted me in your bed. Be honest with yourself and admit it.'

The amusement in his tone angered Lucy further. She faced him squarely, her eyes flashing. The memory of that burning kiss, and the dark, hidden pleasure it had stirred in her, roused her to fresh paroxysms of anger.

'You think I am so easy to manipulate, don't you?' she said, choosing her words with great care in the hope of preserving what little was left of her pride. 'You have got it all wrong. You have misunderstood me completely. I will not be bullied.'

One eyebrow lifted in sardonic, arrogant enquiry. Seeing fire flame hot and sure in her eyes, a smile curled his lips. 'Ah, I appear to have stirred your temper.'

Lucy could feel the anger begin somewhere in her breast, a hard knot just where her heart lay. She found his hostile manner and egotistical attitude outrageous. She also felt a dreadful resentment that he should feel he had the right to speak to her as though she were nothing at all. Stiffening her spine, she raised her head defiantly, proudly, her pride being her strength. 'I do lose my temper and I am hurt just as easily as anyone else.'

His expression softened. 'I know. We cannot leave things as they are between us.'

'We have to, Charles. You should concentrate on leaving for England.' She was glad that he could not see what an effort it was for her to be close to him. Why else would she be experiencing this painful yearning that was equal parts rejection and want? 'I think everything that needed to be said has been said. Talking about it will not change anything. I'm sorry if you feel you have wasted your time, but it is hardly a tragedy.'

His eyes darkened in his anger. 'Be careful what you say,' he said harshly. 'And don't be misled by the fact that I once showed myself indulgent in my dealings with you—'

'You might say more than indulgent,' Lucy snapped back. 'It infuriates me that I allowed such liberties to be taken by a man who thinks of me as no more than a moment's pleasure when you get me alone.'

'I don't recall you complaining at the time. You were the one who invited me in, don't forget.'

Something welled up in Lucy, a powerful surge of emotion to which she had no alternative but to give full rein. It was as if she had suddenly become someone else, someone bigger and much stronger than her own self. Her eyes flashed as cold fury drained her face of colour and added a steely edge to her voice.

'Which, if you are not careful, I will begin to regret. As a matter of fact it did mean something to me. To you, what happened may have seemed commonplace,' she upbraided him, her words reverberating around them, 'just another one of the many flirtations, romances and infidelities that give others something to gossip about. But I am not in the habit of sleeping with gentlemen who are relative strangers to me, or any other kind for that matter.'

'I was not accusing you of such.'

'You, Charles Anderson, may hold a lofty position with the British government and not for one minute would I aspire to wanting to get to know you better than I do now. But after saying that, there is nothing about you that intimidates me. You may be an envoy and mix in the highest circles when you are in London, but you are not the sun around which the world revolves. I know who I am and what I am and I do not need anyone to remind me. You will soon forget me when you return to your duties at the Foreign Office—forget that you ever came to Puna and met a woman called Lucy Quinn.'

'Your judgement of me is harsh to say the least. It is completely false and you know it. I think this journey— with you—will remain with me for a long time.'

'I am honoured that I have given you such food for thought.'

'Of course you have. It is quite natural when I consider that you are different from anyone I have ever known.'

'That is usually the case. No two people are alike.'

'Nevertheless, most of the people I meet arouse little interest in me.'

'Maybe that is because you are too self-absorbed.'

Her words angered him. He stood before her, tall and powerful, his face austere. His eyes focused on her with a clarity that seemed to gain strength from his anger, his eyes searching hers for the truth of her words. 'That is the last thing I want. I would not hurt you in any way.'

'I do not doubt it,' she uttered caustically, feeling more hurt than she cared to admit. In his expression there was no affection, only a resolute determination to have his way.

They looked at each other in a struggle that racked them both and Lucy clung to the sudden coldness between them as a shield. Drawing herself up proudly, she raised her chin. He would never know how much she was hurting.

'Very well,' he said, stepping back. 'What can I say except goodbye and please take care. But remember your promise and contact me at the Foreign Office if need be.'

'Yes, I will. Goodbye, Charles.'

He walked away without turning to see her. Her heart leaden, Lucy's eyes followed his tall figure helplessly. He looked so handsome with the sunlight casting a warm halo about his dark head. She wanted to go after him and tell him how sorry she was for all her harsh words, but her pride came forward, forbidding her that comfort.

Not for one moment did she regret having known him. Until then her heart and body had been dormant, waiting for the spark that would make it explode into life. And if Charles had not ignited it, she would have spent her whole existence not knowing what it felt like to have a fire inside her soul, would never have known that such a wild, sweet passion could exist. Better by far to experience that passion for such a short time than never to have known it at all, even if it brought such pain and heartache, or to die not knowing such joy was possible.

The thought that she would not be with Charles again tormented her and she could not bear to think of a day, a month, let alone an eternity beyond that, without him. The weight of it was almost more than she could bear. Her heart ached with the desolation of it and with the loss that must come next. Her mind was filled with thoughts of him, just as her eyes were filled with tears. The great black void of her parched existence threatened to swallow her up once more.

On her return to Nandra, Lucy was surprised to find Dr Jessop waiting for her. He looked tense. Clearly, he had something on his mind, something unpleasant to impart. Alerted by a quivering tension in the air, she became still.

'Doctor Jessop? What is it? Is something wrong?'

'I have some sad news, Lucy. You must prepare yourself.'

'For what? Is it Father? Is something wrong?' She looked around her, not understanding. Before he even uttered the words, she knew her father was dead.

He nodded. 'I deeply regret to inform you that your father passed away during the night. I am so sorry.'

Bright tears filled her eyes. She swallowed and held herself very erect. Without uttering a word, she went past him and hurried to her father's room. She stood close to the bed in which her father lay, still in his night attire, his eyes closed in his waxen face. Kasim, his loyal servant of many years who had been keeping vigil, appeared from the shadows, his elderly face etched with grief.

'Leave me for a moment, will you, Kasim?' Her voice

was broken with sorrow. 'Please,' she entreated. 'Leave us alone.' Mercifully he went.

Alone now, the silence settled around her like a shroud in the room with its elegant and colourful hangings. As she looked at the bed where her father lay so still, grief welled up within her. She was absolutely mortified that she had left him, that this had happened when she was away. So extreme were her thoughts that her brain retreated into some kind of limbo.

She waited until her breathing was normal before she let herself out of the room, but she had no clear recollection of leaving it, for the insensibility nature provides to protect the mind fell over her. She thought she would wake any moment and find that it had all been a hideous nightmare, not more than that, and that her father wasn't dead after all.

In the unforgiving heat it was necessary to inter Jeremiah Quinn without delay. It was a small, sorry company that gathered to witness his final interment. After a brief ceremony in the small church, he was laid to rest in the small cemetery outside the cantonment.

Lucy held herself in check as the coffin was lowered into the deep pit. It was laid next to that of her mother. A cleric who lived in the town intoned the final words of interment, reminding them all of where they had come from and where they would return to, then it was over.

Devoid of her father, the house no longer felt like home. Lucy was feeling lost and unusually tired and depressed. Even with all there was to do and think about, she could not help wondering what awaited her in the future.

Her days were consumed with packing up her life in Nandra—her life and her father's. She had almost finished when she received a letter from her father's lawyer, Mr Fleming, in Madras. He had written to inform her that he had heard from her grandmother's lawyers in London of the old lady's demise and that she had left Lucy a substantial legacy.

Lucy was deeply saddened to learn that her grandmother had died. She had been her only remaining relative. However, Lucy hadn't known her very well, being just a child when she had stayed with her. She had been ill for some time and at eighty-five years of age her demise was to be expected.

Her husband, Lucy's grandfather, had left her a wealthy woman. All that wealth, along with her grandmother's house, had now passed on to Lucy. Lucy had given little thought to such matters. Her parents had never spoken of such things to her. But with that and the substantial wealth her father had accrued over the years with the East India Company, to suddenly find that she was a wealthy young woman in her own right and that she need not fear for her future, was such a wonderful feeling and such a tremendous relief that she could not believe it at first.

Fixing her gaze on the distant horizon beyond the cantonment, she made her first decision about her future. Where could she go? What could she do? She had done nothing but help her father with his work. For the first time she began to wonder if there were other possibilities for her future besides teaching and looking after the sick. She decided it was time to stop believing she had no choices in her life. It was time to begin deciding her own destiny.

When Mrs Wilson went to stay with her daughter in Madras she would go with her—and maybe consider accompanying her when she left for England, even though it would break her heart to leave India. Mrs Wilson had two daughters: Celia, who lived in Madras, and Alice, who lived in London. Alice had recently been delivered of Mr and Mrs Wilson's first grandchild and Mrs Wilson was to go to England to see her. She was to spend twelve months with her before returning to India to be with her husband.

When the day came for Lucy to leave Nandra, tears flooded her eyes as she closed the door, realising that she was finally leaving the only place she had called home. She left Nandra with Mrs Wilson and others embarking on the week-long journey to Madras, with a regiment of soldiers making for Fort St George. One of the hardest things she had to do was to say farewell to Maya, who had been with her since she had come to Nandra.

Lucy would miss the life she'd led there and Dr Jessop, who had become a good friend to her and seen her through the darkest days of her life. She forced herself not to think about it. She couldn't afford to or she knew she would fall apart because of all she had lost. She couldn't allow herself to get sentimental now. She just had to keep going until she reached Madras and had found safe haven somewhere. A chapter of her life had closed, but the memories would linger.

Chapter Eight

M adras was all a bustle after the small parochial atmosphere of Nandra. White, colonnaded buildings of grace and proportion bespoke a dignified wealth. Lucy had stayed there with her parents when they had arrived in India. She had found it an agreeable town, where the English conducted themselves exactly as they would in London. The way they promenaded themselves in their fine equipages along Mount Road of an evening rivalled anything to be seen in London's Hyde Park.

Lucy was staying with Mrs Wilson's daughter and her husband in a house extensive and elegant along the shoreline and within sight of the massive walls of Fort St George, with its bastions, its Government House and gardens.

The days passed in a blur of activity as she assisted Celia in civic and church activities. Charles was never far from her thoughts. Despite the acrimony of their parting, she found it extraordinarily difficult, even after this considerable time, to think about much else. She saw his face, heard his voice, remembered him—oh, dear Lord, she remembered him, everywhere, all the time.

Mrs Wilson was a kindly soul and had been glad to

take Lucy under her wing. 'You have been to see your father's lawyer, Lucy,' she said over tea and cakes in the afternoon. 'Have you decided what you will do? Will you remain in India?'

'No. There is nothing here for me any more. Now I have been to see Mr Fleming I have decided to book a passage on the first available ship bound for England.'

'Then we will travel together. I would value your company on the journey. At least you have a house to go to, which must be a relief,' Mrs Wilson remarked, sipping her tea. 'And I must say, the way you have described it to me, it would be foolish of you not to take up residence.'

'Yes, it would. Although I know no one in London.'

'You will soon make some friends. Whenever I've been in England, I always found London such a delight. I loved seeing the sights and galleries and attending the many social events and the theatre my husband insisted upon.' She laughed, placing her cup and saucer on the table in front of her. 'I am so glad you will not be far away. And you must call on me and Alice. I look forward to introducing you to her.'

Lucy smiled across at her. 'And you and Alice must visit me, Mrs Wilson. I remember the house as being quite large, large enough to accommodate guests and central to the city's pleasure gardens and theatres.'

'We will visit, my dear, and how convenient to be close to all the city's pleasurable amenities.'

'You have always been very kind to me, Mrs Wilson—especially when my mother died. I am going to miss you when you return to India.'

'And I you, my dear. The cantonment won't be the same without you and your dear father. But I know you are going to love London.'

Lucy felt all was not as it should be with herself and there was a nagging fear in her that could not be discounted. She felt unwell and was often plagued by bouts of nausea. As the days progressed, disbelieving and shocked, the thought that another life grew within her crept in unbidden. It was a thought that could not be shaken. It filtered through her brain like some unwelcome shockwave.

She was unprepared for this sudden explosion in the quiet landscape of her life. It was a tenacious, terrifying reality. Charles loomed even larger in her thoughts. It was almost two months since they had made love. The pleasure and intensity she had experienced then was now too painful to contemplate. Her face became pale and drawn and there were dark circles beneath her eyes. She could not sleep, her predicament and her future causing her to lie awake night after night worrying, pondering over what she should do.

Mrs Wilson was not as shocked by Lucy's predicament as she had thought she would be, nor was she surprised on being told of the identity of the father. In fact, she was goodness and consideration personified and insisted on taking care of her. It was decided that they were to remain in Madras until the baby was born before leaving for England. And Lucy was eternally grateful, if a little guilt-laden that Mrs Wilson was to delay her own journey to England for so long.

Now, more than ever, Lucy needed the strength of her forceful personality to keep her sane in the days, weeks and the months to come. Charles had told her that this might happen and that if she found herself with child he wanted to know—Lucy would not dream of keeping something of such importance from him. Now that she was to have a child and feeling a love so powerful for that tiny being inside her and that she would do anything to keep it safe, to do what was right by it, it was her duty to inform Charles that he had fathered a child.

With the hope that he had not yet left Madras, enquiries were made. Unfortunately, he had sailed for England a month earlier. She did as he had told her and wrote to him at the Foreign Office, informing him that she was to bear his child and providing him the address in London where she could eventually be reached. If he did not receive it, she would have to wait until she arrived in London and make enquiries as to where he could be contacted.

Lucy was thankful that she now had enough money to care for herself and her child. The stigma of bearing a child out of wedlock would no doubt hit her eventually. Yet it gave her a strange, rather agonising joy to know that Charles's blood was at work somewhere deep inside her. Whatever he did now, he was bound to her by the ties of flesh and blood, so, now that the shock of the revelation of her condition had worn off, nothing could destroy her happiness in the knowledge that she bore his child.

Edward Charles Quinn smiled his wide, beaming, toothless smile and his dark blue eyes narrowed in his sweet face, before fastening his hungry mouth on his mother's breast. With a mop of dark curly hair, he was adorable, Lucy's pride and joy, and when she gazed down at him with a passion of love, she couldn't believe he belonged to her—to her and Charles. Her emotions for her son were so powerful that she shuddered at their strength. She loved him from the moment he was put in her arms.

The vessel on which Lucy and Mrs Wilson embarked from Madras took five long months to reach the Pool of London. It was a grey, miserable day in March when they finally put ashore and very cold. The contrast between it and the country they had left was astounding. And made her miss it all the more.

It had almost broken Lucy's heart to leave India. She would miss the colours of the sunset, the star-spangled night skies, the lilac and blue and soft pink of the dawn. She would miss the storm clouds that heralded the months of the monsoon, of mists and the curtains of rain. When they had set sail, the breeze carried the scent of Madras far out to sea, of flowers and spices and the ever-prevailing dust.

But she must forget about that now and focus on the future.

Lucy's grandmother's house in Kensington was an attractive manor house set in its own well-tended grounds. It was where her mother had been born and had lived until she had met and married her father. Inside it was just as Lucy remembered when she had been here as a child. It was warm and inviting. Fortunately, Mrs Yates, her grandmother's housekeeper of many years, was still in residence, along with two servants and a groom who lived above the stables to the rear of the house and looked after the two carriage horses.

Edward was soon ensconced in the nursery, where he was cooed over by an adoring nursemaid and Mrs Yates, who was delighted to have fresh life injected into the house regardless of Lucy's unmarried state.

Accompanied by her daughter Alice, Mrs Wilson was a frequent visitor. Alice was married to a Company employee who worked at East India House on Leadenhall Street. Their lives had been enriched by the birth of their daughter. Alice was a slender young woman and a brunette like her mother, with winged brows over friendly grey eyes. Learning of Lucy's troubled last days in India and the birth of her adorable son, not being one to judge, she had befriended Lucy from the start and was determined to introduce her to her circle of friends.

During the short time Lucy had lived in the house she had come to love it and soon began to look on it as her home. Whatever came about, she must be independent and do the best she could for Edward. She must become accustomed to the fact that she would never marry, for no man would take on a woman who had fallen so far from grace and given birth to an illegitimate child.

Lucy scarcely had time to catch her breath before Alice happily and enthusiastically transported her into a world of high fashion. They went to the most fashionable milliners, hosiers and glove makers to be found near the Exchange, then to the smartest drapers, where they purchased the finest linen petticoats and nightdresses, going on to the silk mercers on Ludgate Hill before finishing in New Bond Street, Alice advising and superintending the choice of colours and materials for her new gowns.

Having finished their shopping for the day, and feeling pleasantly exhausted, Alice suggested that, before going home, they drive through Hyde Park, which was an integral part of London's social life, one of the ways to see and be seen, to show off fine carriages and clothes. Leaving the carriage, they walked at a leisurely pace along the paths.

When Alice paused to speak to an acquaintance, two riders, a man and a woman entering the park, caught her attention. The woman was riding a chestnut mare and the man a grey stallion, a huge beast, a thoroughbred and no mistake. The pair made a handsome picture. She continued to watch in fascination. To her the perfectly groomed man was every inch an elegant, relaxed and poised gentleman. His dark blue jacket set off his broad shoulders and his snowy white neckcloth emphasised his dark hair and dark looks.

Suddenly Lucy felt the pull of those looks, her eyes drawn to them like a magnet, feeling her body freeze when she recognised those chiselled features printed indelibly on her heart. Like a stone statue, unflinching, her eyes unblinking, she watched him turn to the incredibly beautiful woman in an emerald-green habit. Leaning towards her, he bent his head to hear what she had to say and what Lucy took to be an affectionate gesture broke a hold in her emotional barricade. The woman's face was alight with laughter as they rode off at a cracking pace.

Lucy stared at the scene in ringing silence, filled with admiration for the woman's ability and daring. It was clear that she was utterly fearless. As she watched Charles, her face lost what little colour it had.

Alice, noticing her friend's strained profile beside her and sensing that she was not enjoying the park, leaned towards her. 'Lucy, are you all right? You're not ill, are you?' she enquired softly.

Pulling herself together, Lucy forced a laugh, turning to her friend. 'No. No—I'm quite well, Alice. I have a slight headache, that's all. I saw someone I thought I recognised. I was mistaken,' she said, watching as Charles disappeared among the trees.

In one fell swoop, all the hope and confidence, which had upheld her throughout her pregnancy and the voyage to England to the moment when she would behold Charles once more, crumbled to nothing. That glimpse of him with another woman had been like a dagger thrust to her heart. Never before in all her life had Lucy felt so agonisingly, unbearably jealous of another woman as she did of the one she had seen with Charles.

She gulped, swallowing down the tears that accumulated in her throat and threatened to choke her. She felt overpowered by an immense weariness and disappointment, born of the accumulated fatigue of the past months together with this shock she had just received. Disappointed, dazed and unable to form any coherent thought, wanting nothing more than to seek refuge, playing on her headache, she asked Alice to take her home. All she could see in her mind's eye was the touching scene she had witnessed between Charles and the beautiful woman.

One thing that Lucy was determined to do now she was in London was to visit Anna, Johnathan's sister. Before Johnathan had died, he had told her his sister would have to return to England to live with their Uncle Robert and Aunt Constance at Melcot Lodge in Kensington. It wasn't difficult to locate the house, but she was disappointed when told their niece had married and was now the Marchioness of Elvington. She and her husband, the Marquess, resided in Berkshire, but had a house in Mayfair.

Impressed by Johnathan's sister's high status, Lucy was apprehensive about meeting her, but, keen to do so all the same, she instructed the driver to take her to the address of the Marquess of Elvington.

The footman who admitted Lucy to the fashionable residence informed her that the Marchioness was at home and if she would care to wait in the drawing room he would see if she was available to see her.

With a lump in her throat, Lucy watched Johnathan's sister enter, not knowing what to expect. One thing she had not expected to find was that this was the woman she had seen in the park the previous day with Charles. Bewildered and curious at the same time, she decided not to mention this for the time being. They were strangers to each other and she didn't want to cause her any embarrassment should she feel the need to explain.

Lucy saw that the Marchioness moved with a regal grace not often met with. What she saw was a slender woman, slightly older than herself, assured and quite lovely in an understated way, her skin as white as milk, her eyes a warm shade of amber. She held her head high on its graceful neck, her golden hair exquisitely coiffed. There was an air of kindliness and generosity about her—she wouldn't have expected anything else from Johnathan's sister. Her resemblance to Johnathan was so striking that it brought back all Lucy's memories of the man she would have married.

Lucy stared at her. She could hardly breathe. Her chin trembled against her will and her eyes were awash with tears. She dashed them away as they began to fall and crossed her arms across her chest. So overcome was she with shock and heartbreak on meeting this woman whose connection to Johnathan reminded her of what might have been had he not died, that she couldn't trust herself to speak.

In her mind, Anna Harris was still the young sister of the man she had loved with all the innocence of her youth—which seemed so long ago now. How silly to think this was still that young girl who had written long letters to Johnathan. This was a woman—a beautiful woman, with eyes that were so incredibly like Johnathan's, so incredibly kind.

'Lucy?' Anna whispered, as overcome with emotion as she was. A deep sadness for the loss of her brother filled her eyes, but then a smile touched her lips and her eyes brightened a little when she said, 'I cannot believe it's really you.' Settling on the sofa, she indicated that Lucy should sit beside her. 'If only you knew how often I've thought of you over the years. I wanted to write to you, but I didn't know where to send the letter to. I never thought we would meet. I often wondered what had become of you. Did you remain in India after— after Johnathan...?'

'Yes—yes, I did,' Lucy replied, sinking down beside Anna, facing her. She wondered how much Anna knew about what had really happened to Johnathan—and the assault on herself. She prayed she didn't know, that Anna had left India unaware of the sordid details of the circumstances leading up to her brother's death. 'After what happened to Johnathan, my parents left Bhopal. My father was given a position in Puna. When my mother died, I remained with my father. When he passed away, with nothing to keep me in India and receiving a legacy from my grandmother, I came to England.'

'And were you sad to leave India?'

'Very much so. It had been my home for so long.'

'I didn't want to leave either, but I had no choice.' Anna lowered her eyes, her expression becoming grave. 'Lucy—I—know what happened to you in India,' she said softly, raising what Lucy had feared most.

Lucy swallowed, shaking her head slowly. 'You do?' she whispered.

Anna nodded. 'Yes, my husband told me.'

'Your husband? How—how would he know that— unless he was there.'

'My husband is William Lancaster. He was Johnathan's closest friend. Johnathan placed me in his care for the voyage when I returned to England.'

Lucy stared at her in shocked amazement. 'William? You married William?'

'Yes. As the heir of the Marquess of Elvington, he came back to England to take up residence at Cranford Park in Berkshire.'

'I remember William. He—he was very kind to me when it happened. I—I knew him as William Lancaster—although not all that well. I had no idea he was the Marquess of Elvington.'

Anna smiled. 'He wasn't then—not until his grandfather died when he returned to England.' She placed her hand on Lucy's arm. 'There is no shame, Lucy. None of it was your fault. I knew James Ryder, the man who—who...'

'Raped me,' Lucy managed to say bitterly. 'I was just eighteen years old, Anna, and he—he drugged me and raped me. How could he have done that—how could anyone?'

'I know. I met James Ryder on board ship. I didn't know what he was, who he was, what he was guilty of, until later. He—he tried to molest me also, Lucy. Fortunately, William found me in time—along with James Ryder's father, who banished him to America, and as far as I know he remains there to this day.'

'Good riddance, I say.'

'Precisely.'

'Poor Johnathan. He had good reason to despise him before that, but after what happened to me his hatred knew no bounds. But he shouldn't have gone looking for him—to avenge what he had done to me. He would not have died had he not done that. I blame myself to this day for what happened. I was stupid and naive— James Ryder was no stranger to me although I did not know him well. He asked me to sit with him—brought me some coffee. I stayed with him while I waited for my parents—and I drank the coffee—which he must— have…'

'Oh, Lucy, my dear,' Anna murmured, moved by her distress. 'There is no blame attached to you. You cannot continue letting this rule your life. Johnathan would not want you to suffer and neither do I. Johnathan lived life to the fullest and he would want you to do the same.'

'But I can't—even after all this time. Because of my actions, I deprived him of his life—of happiness. I will never forgive myself for that.'

'You are too hard on yourself, Lucy. Ours is a shared loss—given that you lost the man you were to marry and I lost a beloved brother. This is a tragedy that binds us for ever. Like me you will carry on.'

Lucy gulped down her tears and nodded. She was completely taken with the easy friendliness of this attractive woman and accepted the feeling as mutual as Anna's fingers squeezed her own before releasing them. 'I know—and I have tried, Anna—but it has been hard—it is still hard.'

'Then we will help each other. I look forward to furthering our friendship—and to you meeting William. He will be so delighted to meet you again—to know you are here in London. He's still at Cranford at present, but I expect him in London any day.'

Hearing a child's happy laughter from somewhere in the upper echelons of the house, Anna smiled. 'That is one of my offspring.'

'You have children?'

'Two, and they are adorable. At four years old, Thomas is quite the young man, while Sophie is just beginning to walk.' She tipped her head to one side. 'And you, Lucy? Do you have any children?'

Lucy nodded, looking down at her hands. 'Yes—a son. He—he is seven months old now.'

'And—your husband? Is he here in London with you?'

Lucy shook her head, raising her head and looking directly at Anna. 'No. I am not married. My son's father and I—didn't see eye to eye, I'm afraid.'

Anna's expression was pained on hearing this. 'I'm sorry to hear that. It—must be difficult...'

'Being an unmarried mother?' Lucy sighed. 'Yes, I'm sure there will be many hurdles to overcome in the future, but that's the way it is. Since what happened to Johnathan I—I feel a great reluctance to place my well-being in another's hands—to have to rely on someone else.'

'Oh, Lucy, you shouldn't feel that way. I've told you, you were not to blame for any of it. You deserve happiness. Should you need any help and support, I will always be here for you.'

'Thank you. You are very kind, Anna.'

Anna smiled. 'I feel that you and I are kindred spirits, Lucy. Perhaps when you feel up to it you could share your stories of India—of your time with Johnathan, as memories are all that remain of him.'

'I should like that very much,' Lucy whispered. 'Johnathan was a good person—the best of men.'

'Praise indeed.' Anna smiled. 'Now I will have some refreshment brought in and you must tell me a little about India before you leave.'

This they did. When Lucy got up to leave, Anna walked with her to the door. Lucy turned to her as she stood on the steps. 'I—think I saw you yesterday, Anna—in the park. I didn't mention it at first because I wasn't sure it was you. You were riding a chestnut horse?'

Anna smiled with delight. 'Yes, it would have been me. I was with Charles—my brother-in-law. We often ride in the park. It's the only place one can have a good gallop here in London. He's due to leave for India shortly— works for the Foreign Office. You must meet him. I'll arrange for us all to get together when William gets here.'

Lucy's heart skipped a beat. How she managed not to reveal how shocking this pronouncement was to her she would never know. At times like this, her self-imposed training in outward control set in. She put an expression of interest on her face, kept her spine straight, but it was the thinnest of veneers. Beneath it her emotions were in turmoil.

'Yes—of course. I would like that.'

Relaxing against the upholstery in the carriage taking her back to Kensington, Lucy felt as though a huge weight had been lifted from her. She had been completely mistaken in thinking that Charles was in a relationship with the woman she had seen him with in the park, whom she now knew to be his sister-in-law. Nothing could be further from the truth, but his close ties to Anna and William Lancaster had come as a surprise to her and she wasn't sure how to deal with it right now, but at least she now knew how to contact Charles when she was ready.

Lucy sometimes went riding in the park with Alice and her husband, Henry, which she loved. Visits to the theatre and walks in the park with her new friends were also added to her agenda. When she was invited to accompany them to an exhibition of a prominent artist at the art gallery in Pall Mall, she accepted, even though she knew very little about the subject and did not have an educated eye for art.

The occasion was attended by the wealthy, artists, writers and journalists. Ladies and gentlemen were dressed in full splendour. It was an animated crowd, with laughing, gossiping and whispering faces. Never having seen anything quite like it, Lucy was all agog. There were no outsiders, everyone present having been issued with a gold-embossed invitation. Liveried footmen moved among them, bearing salvers of glasses brimming with champagne. The paintings on display drew a great deal of interest, although they did not appeal to Lucy.

Feeling out of her depth as she looked around at the animated throng, she glanced at Alice and Henry for reassurance. 'Goodness! I never imagined there would be so many people present.'

Henry's attractive face relaxed into a faint smile as

his eyes swept and absorbed the full length of the gallery. He was a great admirer of art and his eyes lit up, as always when he found himself surrounded by such illustrious company and fine works of art.

'These occasions are always well attended. If you will excuse me, there is someone I haven't seen in a while. I will go and have a quick word.'

Watching him thread his way through the throng to the other side of the room, Alice smiled, shaking her head. 'You must forgive my husband, Lucy. I always find myself neglected when he is surround by works of art and illustrious company. Come, let us circulate and I will introduce you to one or two people I know.'

This Alice did, but after a while of engaging in social chit-chat with friends and acquaintances of Alice, Lucy found it difficult to take it all in and the faces became a blur. Looking about her, hoping to catch the eye of one of the servants for a glass of champagne, Lucy focused on a couple of gentlemen who had just arrived.

Suddenly and inexplicably Lucy's heart gave a joyful leap at the sight of one of them and the familiar fine-boned, taut, bronzed face. Her whole being reached out to him across the distance that separated them. Being quite the tallest man there, Charles Anderson was a man who dominated his environment and his mere presence forced people to notice him. He and his companion were in deep conversation at the opposite end of the gallery, seemingly oblivious to the noise around them.

Lucy's feet became fastened to the floor as if they had roots as she looked at him across the room. The very air around him seemed to move forcefully, snapping with exhilaration and the restless intensity he seemed to discharge. He was splendid in a bottle-green frock coat that clung to his shoulders, which were broader and more muscular than she remembered. There was lace at his throat and his dove-grey waistcoat was embroidered with silver thread.

Suddenly Charles was looking down the length of the room, his gaze drawn to her. Their eyes met and she felt the strange shock of recognition shake her as it always had when he'd looked at her. Then he was striding towards her and she couldn't take her eyes off him. Her mind ranged through the evocative memories left over from the days they had spent together in Guntal at the Rajah's gorgeous palace. Though sorely lacking experience in the realm of desire, instinct assured her the wanton yearnings gnawing at the pit of her being were nothing less than the cravings that Charles had elicited during that lustful night they had spent together.

The vision that appeared in the room made Charles pause in his stride. The sure knowledge of Lucy's presence interrupted the conversation he was having with his friend, Sir David Henderson, a man of his own age and an extremely wealthy industrialist from the Midlands. David was saying something important, but Charles heard not a word. With her hair elegantly coiffed and her figure attired in a simple but fashionable gown of sky-blue satin, with her back to the open doorway, Lucy looked like a heavenly apparition, a radiant silhouette with the light shining from the adjoining room behind her.

The exultation he felt at the sight of her almost overwhelmed him. There was a new maturity about her, her figure more rounded. It suited her. She was beautiful, even more beautiful than she had looked when they had last met—a radiant sunburst in a city choked with darkness. My God, he had missed her.

In India they'd had no time to get to know each other. Yes, they had made wonderful and passionate love, but their deeper feelings had remained very much hidden. Seeing her now, he felt a world of feelings flash across his face—disbelief, surprise, happiness, but only fleeting. Unsure of how she would receive him, as he came closer his expression cooled.

Chapter Nine

Trying to ignore the treacherous leap her heart gave, Lucy stepped forward with a quaking reluctance, clutching her reticule in her gloved hands, her lips curved in an uncertain smile. Drop by precious drop she felt her confidence draining away, especially when the thoroughly piercing eyes locked on her and slowly appraised her.

She lifted her head and looked into his eyes, then wished she hadn't. She had forgotten what looking directly into those deep blue eyes was like. Rather weakened, she took a deep breath. In some strange way they seemed capable of seeing right inside her. It was all she could do to face Charles's unspoken challenge and not turn and flee.

'Lucy? It's been a long time. I did not expect to see you here.' His voice was soft, though his smile was knowingly chiding.

For an instant Lucy could not move. She felt herself relax, every limb slowly settling into its usual posture, her eyes still fastened on his, drifting on the enchantment of being in the same space as him. 'I did not expect to see you here either, Charles. I—I wondered if you might have returned to India.'

'I'm due to go back at any time soon. Why have you left India?'

'I had no reason to remain any longer. My father died—the night before I returned from Guntal—which came as a dreadful shock to me.'

'I'm very sorry to hear that,' he said sympathetically. 'I know how close you were. You will miss him.'

'There was nothing that could be done—but I wish I had been with him at the end.' She swallowed hard, but her voice was husky. 'It was a while before I accepted that he was gone. When my mother died, he became the centre of my world, so, yes, it was hard at the time but, as you will remember, his health had been deteriorating for a while.'

'Yes, I do. And now here you are, in London.'

Lucy managed a smile. 'Yes. When one door closes another opens—isn't that what they say? When I received a letter from my grandmother's lawyer informing me of her demise, as the only member of the family remaining, she left everything to me. Her legacy was substantial and gave me no choice but to come here.'

'Like you, there has been a death in my own family— my aunt—Aunt Charlotte. She went to live in Devon in the house left to me by my uncle, which was where she died.'

Lucy saw the pain slash its way across Charles's features and at that moment she knew he had loved his aunt with the same everlasting devotion she had felt for her father. 'This can't be easy for you either, Charles.'

'I loved her dearly. She will be sadly missed, particularly by my sister Tilly, who, as I told you, also lives in Devon. Aunt Charlotte left me her house in Chelsea, which is where I'm living.'

'So, you have acquired two houses.'

He nodded. His eyes softened. 'I've missed you, Lucy.'

Her heart was touched by his admission. 'You have?'

He nodded. 'More than you will ever know. How long have you been in London?'

'Just three weeks. I live in Kensington.'

'Then, if you will permit, I will call on you.'

For a moment she stared at him. There was so much she had to tell him, so much she wanted to explain.

'Yes—I would like that.'

'Are you glad to see me, Lucy?'

'Yes, of course I am,' she murmured with nervous apprehension. 'We knew each other for such a short time and I will always remember how it was between us.'

The sound of his warm, masculine voice never failed to bring her senses alive. Close to him at last, she was powerfully aware of everything that was masculine, primitive and demanding about him, which was always so strong it seemed to be an almost physical force. She was more aware of him now than she had ever been and here, with the whole world looking on, stood the man whose child she had given birth to, a child he didn't even know existed.

With so many people looking on, she wouldn't tell him now. She wanted to be alone with him to do that. Nor would she tell him about seeing him in the park or her visit to Anna. Clearly, he hadn't seen his sister-in-law since their ride in the park, because Lucy was certain Anna would have mentioned her visit to see her and, if she had mentioned Lucy's name, he would have known she was in London. Time enough for that later. Introducing Charles to his son was paramount at this time.

'When I think how easily you dismissed me from your life when we parted, I am encouraged by your reply.' A wicked twinkle sprung up in his eyes. 'Had you said otherwise, then I would probably have hotfooted it back to India without a by your leave.'

'Is what I feel so important to you, Charles?'

'Yes,' he replied on a serious note, his eyes holding hers. 'I'm afraid it is.'

'I didn't dismiss you from my life or my mind when you left India—quite the opposite, in fact. When I received my grandmother's legacy, I did write to you, telling you of my change in circumstances and where I could be reached here in London.'

'You did? I never received it. Where did you address it to?'

'The Foreign Office. I thought it would be passed on to you.'

A frown furrowed his brow in puzzlement. 'It should have been. I will make enquires—although the post between India and London is pretty poor at the best of times and mail does get mislaid.' He uttered a few words of quiet annoyance when a group of boisterous young men pushed their way through the throng, causing him to step aside to let them pass. Taking Lucy's elbow, he drew her out of the way. 'We have matters to discuss— things to say to each other that cannot be said here.'

'Then you can call on me tomorrow, Charles.' She looked past him to see Alice coming towards her. 'Here is my friend Alice. She is Mrs Wilson's daughter and has become a good friend to me since coming to London. Mrs Wilson and I travelled together on the voyage. She is to return to India very soon to be with her husband. Come. I will introduce you.'

When Lucy left the exhibition and returned to Kensington, there was a new lightness to her heart. Seeing Charles had everything to do with this and she was looking forward to introducing him to their son. She refused to think any further than that.

She would never forget Johnathan and their betrothal, which had ended so tragically, and since her feelings for Charles had not lessened since their parting, she had thought of him more and more. But that did not mean the guilt she still felt for the part she had played in Johnathan's death had lessened or that the pain had gone away. There were still chains around her heart. True happiness would continue to elude her until she could find forgiveness for herself.

The following morning Lucy awaited Charles's arrival with trepidation, although why she should feel this way she couldn't say because she had done no wrong. It was unfortunate that Charles had not received her letter informing him that she was to bear his child.

He appeared at eleven o'clock. Mrs Yates showed him into the sitting room where she waited. She stood up to receive him, watching the way he moved. For a man of such imposing stature, he had an elegant way of moving in his casual clothes. He wore a dark blue coat, his long legs encased in biscuit-coloured trousers and highly polished black riding boots. He had removed his tall hat and his hair was slightly dishevelled, brushing the edge of his collar.

She watched him raise his hand and, as he absently rubbed the muscles at the back of his neck, her treacherous mind suddenly recalled how skilfully those long fingers had caressed her own body and the exquisite pleasure he had made her feel. She could still taste that hungry mouth on hers, still feel his hands on her body, which had aroused such an intensity of desire within her. In her heart she yearned for him, as if he had put his own dark brand upon her soul.

And how he was here, coming towards her, smiling almost suavely, as if it were the most natural thing in the world that he should be there.

'Charles,' she said. 'Welcome to my home.'

'It's a charming house—so different from where you were living in India.'

'I think so. It's a different world to the one I knew there. Please sit down,' she said, indicating a chair opposite the one she sank into drawn up to the hearth—her manner was polite and proper when all the time she wanted to fling herself into his arms. 'I came here often when I was a child to visit my grandmother. I suppose, there being no one else for her to leave it to, I always knew I would inherit it one day, but I never gave it much thought.'

He sat across from her, his eyes settling on her face. 'And you intend to live here permanently?'

'Of course. I like the house and it serves all my needs. Why do you ask?'

He shrugged, crossing his long legs in front of him and steepling his fingers. 'No reason, although I could never imagine you living in a metropolis.'

'After India, you mean? I cannot go back. There is nothing for me there any more. Did you enjoy the art exhibition?'

'It was interesting—if one likes that sort of thing.' He paused, before continuing, 'I may be mistaken, Lucy, but when I saw you, I got the impression that there was something you wanted to speak to me about. Are there any secrets lurking in that pretty head of yours that I should know?'

She stared at him, a soft pink flush mantling her cheeks. With a raised brow he waited silently, expectantly, for her answer. She swallowed audibly, knowing the moment had come when she must tell him he had a son. 'Why—I—yes,' she said softly. 'Since you ask, there is just one very small secret you should know about. If you had received my letter, you would already know.'

'And? What is it, Lucy? What is it you have to tell me?'

'It—it concerns a baby. Our baby,' she said quietly. 'You—we—have a son, Charles.'

Whatever Charles had been expecting her to say, it wasn't this. Not a muscle of the handsome, authoritative face moved. He recovered himself quickly. 'And am I to believe this?' he finally said into the reverberant silence, which to Lucy seemed almost a lifetime later. 'The child is mine?' He stopped abruptly, aware that what he had said would be deeply hurtful and offensive and that now the words had been said they could not be retrieved.

Lucy bristled with indignation, suddenly angry that he might doubt his part in Edward's parentage. 'Yes, Charles. What I have just told you is the truth. I am not trying to deceive you. I did not get myself pregnant. I did not do it alone. You had some part in it—it was not all my doing. It takes two to make a child. We—you and I—made Edward.'

'Of course—and I'm sorry if you think I doubted you. I don't—not for one second. But—good Lord!' he said, getting to his feet and shoving back the heavy lock of hair that had fallen forward on to his brow with his long fingers. 'You are telling me that I have a son?'

'Yes, Charles. You have a son. Edward. Although, when I sent the letter informing you I was to bear your child, I truly thought you might have forgotten all about me.'

'I confess that when I returned to England it was with mingled fears of regret and concern that you might be pregnant. If you remember, I did mention that it was possible that it would be the result of our night together,' he said.

Then he smiled in disbelief of the very idea that he had a son, shaking his head as he tried to absorb the fact. 'Of course I couldn't forget you, Lucy. In fact, every day I have been here I hoped a letter would arrive from you telling me exactly this—that you were to bear my child. When no such letter arrived, I was resolved to return to India. Can I see him?'

'Yes, of course you can. Come with me. He has a nap at this time so he will be asleep, but he should soon be awake.'

As if in a trance, Charles followed Lucy into the nursery. She spoke quietly to the nurse, asking her to give them a moment. Charles's gaze went straight to the crib, where his son was deep in slumber. Slowly he moved towards it and stood looking down. Edward was lying on his back, his arms flung out on either side, breathing softly, his lips slightly parted. The child was so perfect it was as if a sudden pain twisted Charles's heart—as if it had been pierced by a sharp blade. Unable to tear his eyes away from him, he stood quite still in those first moments, his eyes seeking the truth, which in his heart he already knew. This was indeed his son.

There was a silence, a stillness. The moment seemed to go on for ever, though it lasted only seconds. The child was the most beautiful child Charles had ever seen. Charles could not yet speak, for his throat was clogged with words he wanted to say but couldn't.

He touched a tentative finger to the child's rosy cheek, then to his hair and finally, with a gesture that was lovely to see, to one of the tiny hands shaped like a starfish on the pillow. To his delight Edward's hand gripped his finger.

'Is he not beautiful, Charles?' Lucy whispered, returning his smile. 'The most beautiful little boy you have ever seen?'

'Most certainly,' he said, his voice hoarse with every kind of emotion as he stared down, feeling an immense closeness and love for the child. As if sensing he was the focus of someone's besotted admiration, Edward stirred, opening his eyes and blinking at his father for the first time. Without more ado Charles gathered him up and held him in the crook of his arm, his face soft, the softness melting away the harshness, the determination that ruled his everyday life. His expression was loving and proud.

'This is my son—such a handsome little chap. He is perfect—and he looks like you, Lucy—although he bears my likeness.'

'He is your image, Charles. One only has to look at him to know whose son he is.'

Edward's eyes opened and he blinked and blinked again, then blue eyes stared into blue eyes, the child's steady and curious, and then he smiled, a wonderful, toothless smile. With a great wave of tenderness washing over him, Charles placed a kiss on his forehead before carefully placing him back down in his cot. He reached down and touched the tiny hand.

For the first time in his life, he was experiencing new and confusing emotions. He saw the world in a different light, a world that no longer centred around himself, but around his tiny son. He looked at Lucy and smiled, this little boy holding them together with a thread, however fragile.

'Thank you, Lucy. I wish I had been present at his birth.'

'Now you are here you will have to make up for the time lost.'

'I can imagine you have not had an easy time of it.

But our son is a beautiful child, a credit to you, and I thank you for what you have done for him in my absence. I have missed seven months of his life. Believe me when I tell you that had I known of his existence I would have moved heaven and earth to come to you before now. From now on Edward's interests will be paramount. So you see, Lucy, already he is very precious to me. I am an utterly devoted and besotted father.'

When the nursemaid came back into the room, they left the nursery. Mrs Yates brought refreshments to them and when she had left a silence stretched between them, filled with the intensity of the emotion that suddenly linked them.

Placing his cup on the occasional table that separated them, Charles looked across at Lucy. 'It cannot have been an easy time for you when you realised you were pregnant,' he said calmly after a short pause in which neither of them seemed to want to break the silence.

'No, I confess it wasn't. I was living in Madras with Mrs Wilson's daughter at the time. They were very good to me. Indeed, I don't know how I would have coped without them. When I got over the initial shock of my condition, my duty was to the child. I remained in Madras until Edward was born. When he was two months old, I came to London. I decided to look to the future, to my new life—with or without a father for Edward—life is too short to squander on ifs and wherefores. My day-to-day life would change, I knew that, and that in all probability I would be shunned. But after much soul-searching I discarded any resentment and self-pity I felt about my situation. Now I spend as much time with my beautiful son as I possibly can.'

Charles gave her a look of admiration. 'It appears to me that you are a capable young woman. I can only apologise for not being there to support you. However, things have changed. I have much to think about before I have to leave for India.' There was a tension about his mouth. He hesitated, as if searching for the right words, then, getting to his feet, he said, 'I will leave you now and consider how best to proceed.'

Lucy watching him go, wondering in what way he wished to proceed. Perhaps he would offer some kind of financial settlement for Edward's future. The only other way she could think of that would put things right would be if he were to offer her marriage, but somehow, she doubted he would do that—or that she would accept.

The following day it was a worried Charles who arrived at his brother's town house in Mayfair. The instant he saw the tall man with dark hair coming towards him, his handsome countenance lightened. The two strode across the hall towards each other, where they clasped arms and hugged warmly, laughing.

'Good to see you before you have to leave for India. When? Do you know yet?'

'Not the precise date, but it won't be long—although I have some loose ends to tie up before I go.'

'Bet you can't wait to get back.'

'How are things with you, William? You look tired. Working too hard?'

'You might say that. It's backbreaking work running an estate the size of Cranford Park.'

Dismissing the subject with a casual wave of his hand, William drew him towards the sitting room. 'Anna will be sorry to see you go. I think she's got used to having you around.'

They entered the sumptuously furnished sitting room, where Anna was sat at a desk writing letters. Since the birth of her last child, she had bloomed like a beautiful English rose. On seeing Charles, with an exclamation of delight she went to embrace him.

'Charles! This is a wonderful surprise. I hope you're staying for dinner. Come and sit down. William will pour you a drink. I envy you going back to India. I would love to go back.'

They sat in a companionable threesome, conversing on familiar matters, the sun slanting through the tall windows. The brothers each held a glass of brandy from which they sipped appreciatively, while Anna preferred a cup of tea.

'And how are the little ones?' Charles asked, crossing his long legs in front of him.

'They are very well—though a handful. They're up in the nursery. You must go up and see them before you leave, otherwise Thomas will never forgive us if he knows Uncle Charles has called and not seen him. They're a delight, are they not, William?' Anna said, looking lovingly at her husband.

They talked of things that were of interest to them all, until Anna placed her cup down, a serious expression on her face. 'I almost forgot to tell you. I had a visitor the other day—Lucy Quinn, would you believe—Johnathan's betrothed. I was most surprised.'

Charles stared at her in shocked amazement, staying his glass halfway to his lips. It was as though all the air had been sucked out of the room.

'Lucy Quinn?' William said. 'Good Lord! I didn't expect to hear of her again—although I always did wonder what had become of her.'

'Yes—well, you'll be able to meet her again. She's a delightful young woman—such a tragedy what happened to her.' Her eyes filled with sadness on being reminded that they might have been sisters-in-law. 'I'm going to invite her round for dinner—you must come, too, Charles. I'm sure you'll find her interesting and have much to talk about.'

'Yes,' Charles said tightly, having recovered himself from the shock of realising who she was. 'I imagine I will—since Miss Lucy Quinn and I are already acquainted.'

Anna stared at him. 'You know Lucy?'

'Yes. We met in India.'

'You never said anything.'

'I had no reason to. I had no idea she was girl who had been betrothed to your brother, Anna. At the time, when you and William arrived in London, I had other matters to take care of. I was unaware of all the details concerning your brother's death.'

'But—you know what happened to her—which resulted in Johnathan's death?'

'I do now. She told me. I'm sorry, Anna. I really did not connect the Lucy I know with your brother. And she had no idea who I was. I didn't even know the name of the girl your brother was betrothed to.'

'Lucy came to see me, Charles. She was severely traumatised by events back then. But—I am curious. How well do you know her?'

Charles shifted uncomfortably in his chair. 'We—we met when I was wounded and ended up in the hospital she worked in. She was a nurse.'

'That wasn't what Anna asked you, Charles,' William said. His expression was one of calm speculation as he regarded his half-brother. He quirked a brow in amused enquiry, waiting for him to speak. 'I recall Lucy as being a very attractive young woman. You cannot have failed to notice what a dear, sweet girl she is.'

Charles got up sharply, agitated suddenly, as he put some distance between them. 'I would not describe Lucy Quinn as sweet,' he replied, turning to face them, his tone impervious, irritated because William seemed to be enjoying his predicament enormously. 'It has taken me a year and a half to appreciate that high-minded young woman is the most exasperating female I have known in my entire life.' He paused, becoming thoughtful. After a moment, he said, 'She is also the woman I want for my wife.'

Anna gasped. 'Your wife?'

William laughed. 'Pardon me, Charles, but I have to say that you do not look in the least like a man in the full flush of love.'

'I am not.'

'Then why do you want to marry her?' Anna asked. 'Have you come to care for her?'

'Of course I care for her—more than I have cared for any other woman, which is why I want her to be my wife,' he replied, annoyed when he saw William's victorious smile widen on hearing his confession. 'Lucy and I have a son—Edward. He was born in India and is seven months old. I did not find out about his existence until yesterday—but,' he said on a softer note when an image of his precious son entered his mind, 'he really is the most beautiful boy.'

Anna and William both stared at him in amazement, speechless. After a moment William let out a low whistle and said, 'Good Lord, Charles, I'm stunned—surprised— even shocked. You say you didn't find out about him until yesterday. Did Lucy intend keeping it from you?'

'Apparently not. She wrote to me from India via the Foreign Office. I never received the letter. I have looked into it. She did write, but they failed to pass it on.'

'I knew that Lucy has a child, but I'd no idea that he is also your son, Charles. She hinted that there was some bad feeling between her and the father. However, whatever has passed between you two, I look forward to meeting our new nephew,' Anna said, as shocked and surprised by Charles's news as her husband. 'Have you proposed to her, Charles?'

'No—not yet.'

'Is there a problem?' William asked. 'Are you afraid she will turn you down? Although with a child between you, it is the obvious solution.'

A wide smile lit Anna's face. 'But—that would be wonderful. I would love Lucy to be my sister-in-law— which she would have been had she married Johnathan.'

'Not so very wonderful,' Charles replied drily. 'She might very well turn me down.'

'I can't imagine why. Most women would be happy for the chance to marry a British diplomat.'

'Lucy is not most women.'

Suddenly Anna frowned as a thought occurred to her. 'Charles, when you ask her—do that, will you? Don't *tell* her. Knowing you and your autocratic manner, she might very well tell you to go to the devil.'

Charles found it irritating that Anna might be right. 'She can be very stubborn. She is a very independent young woman with strong opinions regarding marriage—and even after all this time, she is also still very much in love with Johnathan.'

'I don't believe that is so. She is still consumed with guilt about what happened, believing it was all her fault and that, having deprived Johnathan of his life, she does not deserve to be happy. But things have changed. She now has her son to think about. It is in the child's best interests that he grows up with both his parents. She hasn't been in London two minutes, Charles. Perhaps it would be a good idea to court her before you propose to her. You do want her, don't you?'

Of course he wanted her, his mind raged. Seeing her again was like a sunburst in his life. Suddenly he was catapulted backward through time while the image of Lucy abruptly blended into another image—that of an enchanting golden-haired young woman who had once looked up at him with unconcealed desire glowing in her eyes. All that passion was within her still. It simmered just under the surface. He had been driven to unleash it and that was coming back to taunt him now, for he wanted to unleash it again.

Within him, he felt a pang of nostalgia mingled with a sharp sense of loss because the woman he had known was gone now. His worry and confusion of the previous day when he had called on her had been replaced by a deeper, darker feeling of uncertainty. It was still a new emotion to him and one of which he was not particularly fond.

'Yes, I do,' he replied quietly, in answer to Anna's question.

'Then you must use all your powers of persuasion. Charm her—which shouldn't be too difficult, having seen how the ladies fawn over you. Show her that you care. Do not forget that you are to leave for India very soon so unless you want to say goodbye to her and your son, missing out on his childhood, then you must woo her in earnest.'

'Anna is right, Charles. And whatever happens, you will have our support,' William said on a more sombre note.

'Yes, we must,' Anna agreed softly. 'You are right when you say she still feels the guilt for what happened to Johnathan after all this time. She is reluctant to place her well-being in another's hands after what happened before—to rely on another person is difficult for her. But Johnathan would have wanted her to be happy.

'I realise that after what happened to her, she found it difficult forming any kind of relationship—and who can blame her—until she met you, Charles. She must care for you a great deal even if she does not show it.'

Going to him, she stood behind his chair and put her arms about his neck, fondly resting her cheek against his. 'I do believe it will come right in the end.'

'Thank you, Anna. I hope you are right.'

'It's very important that we make her feel welcome and unafraid of the kind of reception she will receive.' She looked at her husband, noting his pensive look. 'You knew her, didn't you, William?'

He nodded. 'I did—but not all that well. I wasn't always with Johnathan when they were together. What I do know is that Johnathan thought the world of her and they would have married had he lived. Of course we will do our best to make her feel welcome. She deserves our absolute support.

'There is the Rutherford ball coming up. They're close friends of ours so I doubt they'd object if she accompanied us. It would be an opportunity for you to begin courting her properly, Charles. Out in India she never had the opportunity to enjoy the luxuries in life and I imagine she could do with a few.' He grinned across at his brother, raising his glass. 'A few flowers wouldn't go amiss.'

Charles looked at his brother as if he'd taken leave of his senses. 'Flowers? You are joking? What the—' He broke off and his eyes narrowed as the suggestion took hold. 'Oh, I hadn't thought of that.'

Anna laughed. 'Clearly. Although Lucy deserves all the niceties life has to offer.'

'You're right, Anna,' Charles agreed, a positive light entering his eyes. 'You always are and, by God, I will shower her with all the luxuries I can afford.'

'There's no time like the present,' Anna said, pleased to see his enthusiasm. 'Flowers are as good a place as any to start.'

'Very well, Anna. I will take the task of courting Lucy seriously. I shall be politely considerate, attentive and indefatigable in my attempts to please her. I know exactly how to treat a woman and to adjust my attitude to what I believe will please her best. In fact, I shall be patience and consideration personified.'

'Goodness me, Charles! With so much consideration, I am almost tempted to divorce William and marry you myself,' Anna said, laughing and winking at her adoring husband.

Later that same day when a beautiful bouquet of red roses had arrived, Lucy couldn't believe her eyes. The note that came with them told her they were from Charles. Her surprise deepened the following day when two more bouquets arrived, each banded with a red ribbon. Reading the attached note, she saw they were also from Charles, telling her how he was looking forward to calling on her shortly. Touched by the extravagance of the gifts and wondering what he was up to, but unable to think of an answer, she gave them to Mrs Yates, telling her to accommodate them where there was room.

Going into the quiet, scented garden while Edward was taking his mid-morning nap, deep in thought she wandered along the paths, absently touching flowers, then sitting on a bench in a small arbour. The garden was well established and her grandmother, who'd had a love for all things that grew, had stocked it well with flowers and fragrant shrubs.

When Charles appeared on the terrace, instantly all her anxieties returned. She had not seen him since he had left two days ago—enough time for him to consider the best way for them to proceed into the future. Standing up, she waited quietly and calmly for him to reach her, her eyes enormous in her pale face. With his dark hair and tan coat and buff trousers, he looked incredibly attractive as he strode towards her. How handsome he was, how striking. Her heart wrenched as she allowed her eyes to dwell on his face.

It was never easy to remain composed when she was with him, for his face was so intense that she was affected by the force of passion that emanated from him, that seared her flesh and melted her bones. She wanted to tell him how deeply she had come to care for him, how much he had come to mean to her, but until she knew he would reciprocate her feelings she would keep them locked in her heart.

His eyes looked directly into Lucy's, his expression unreadable, neither warm nor cold. The torment in Lucy's mind showed on her face and, seeing it, he didn't have to guess at the reason.

'Anna told me of your meeting, Lucy. I was never more surprised to learn that Johnathan was her brother, that there was a connection between the two of you.'

'Why should you be surprised? I didn't know you were William Lancaster's half-brother either. I thought it only courteous that I should make Anna's acquaintance since I was betrothed to her brother. I always wondered what she was like. She's nice and very gracious—just as I imagined Johnathan's sister to be.'

'She is. Did you like the roses?' he asked, seating himself on a bench and pulling her down beside him.

'Yes, thank you, Charles. They were exquisite. They were the first flowers ever given to me. Somehow, I didn't associate you with presenting ladies with flowers.'

'I don't. You are the first.'

'What message did you hope to convey to me by sending them?'

'I wasn't conveying anything. I merely thought it would be nice to send you something. Red roses, I am told, have a significant meaning. Although I believe the flower reigns as the ultimate symbol of passionate love.'

Lucy stared at him, not having expected him to say that. 'I believe it also began its symbolic history in Greece, where it was associated with Aphrodite or Venus—the goddess of love.'

He grinned. 'There you are then. At least I've got that right. In some countries I believe it is the custom for a married woman to wear a flower on her dress to tell her husband of her desire.'

Lucy laughed. 'Since I don't have a husband that doesn't apply. Perhaps I should put one behind my ear.'

A wicked gleam appeared in his eyes. 'I believe that means an unmarried lady is available.'

'In which case I shall leave the roses where they are. In a vase.'

'I'm happy you like them.'

'Hmm,' she breathed, giving him a suspicious glance.

'Now why do I think Anna might have had a hand in your sudden decision to send me flowers?'

'She might have said something,' he answered nonchalantly. 'I am to return to India very soon, Lucy, so I would like to spend as much time with Edward as I can—and you, of course.'

'I see. So, what do you suggest?'

'I've come to take you for a drive. It's a fine day, so we might as well make the most of it.'

She raised her eyebrows in surprise. 'What? Now?'

'No time like the present.'

'Then I will go and get my bonnet.' Standing up, she looked down at him, her brow puckered in a frown. He was watching her with a strange and tender smile on his lips. 'Why, Charles, if I didn't know you better, I would think you are intending to court me,' she said in soft amusement. Her mouth curved into a tantalising smile. 'Of course, we both know such a thing is quite ridiculous.'

Getting to his feet, Charles caught her eyes. 'I thought you would think that—but would you mind if I did?'

'Goodness me, I have no idea. Apart from being betrothed to Johnathan—being very young at the time— I've never really been courted before—not properly.'

'Would you welcome my attention?'

'It would be...challenging, I think,' she said, giving him a thoughtful look. 'And the outcome might be... interesting.'

'Then we will see what happens—and Anna told me that if I am to court you, then I have to do it properly.'

'Hence the flowers,' she said drily. Was he set on a course in which he was to play the part of a considerate betrothed, because if so then he seemed completely assured of his success. 'It's all right, Charles, I understand perfectly. It's reassuring that you've decided to do things properly—but please don't imagine for one minute that there is anything to be gained by it. While you're waiting you might like to take a peek at Edward. He's having his nap. He likes his sleep and I swear a string of stampeding horses wouldn't wake him.'

It didn't take Lucy long to tidy herself and put on her bonnet, and in no time at all Charles handed her up into a shiny black carriage. When she was settled and her skirts arranged properly, he instructed the driver to head for St James's Park.

'You were right, Edward was asleep,' Charles said, seating himself across from her. 'I would like to spend more time with him—when he's not sleeping.'

'Perhaps when we get back to the house he'll be awake. You can go up and see him then if you like.'

Lucy sighed, relaxing into the upholstery and tingling with exuberance. A warm breeze floated across the park. People and rosy-cheeked children were milling about, some strolling while others gathered and sat in clusters to gossip. Flowers in beds and borders added a splash of colour to the park and the grass was like soft green velvet.

Charles suggested they leave the carriage to stroll along the paths, which they did, her arm in the crook of his elbow.

'While I remain in London, I would like to show you more of the city.'

'I have lived here before, Charles. I am no stranger to it.'

'I mean the real London. I want you to look on this time as a holiday.'

'And how much longer is it before you have to return to India?'

'Roughly about four weeks. I want to remain here until Tilly and her family come up from Devon. They're due any time soon.'

'Then I hope she arrives before you have to leave.' Lucy was aware that they were attracting some attention. 'I can't help feeling conspicuous,' she said. 'I'm sure everyone is staring at us.'

Completely impervious to the curious eyes flashing their way, Charles cast a glance around them, then shifted his gaze to Lucy's flushed face. 'Don't let it worry you. No one will know who you are.'

'Maybe not, but you are recognised in society and everyone will be curious who it is you have on your arm. It's a good thing I'm a nobody, otherwise my reputation would be destroyed.'

'When we have decided on the best way forward for us both—what is best for Edward—then you may do as you please. Which, as I remember from India,' he said with a conspiratorial smile, 'you did anyway, always prepared to cock a snook at anyone who dared to criticise.'

'I did, didn't I? Most unashamedly. The best way forward, you say. You have given it some thought, Charles? If so, then perhaps you would enlighten me.'

'I will—very soon,' he said with absolutely finality.

Lucy opened her mouth to argue, but he turned his

head to acknowledge an acquaintance in a passing carriage. Sternly, Lucy reminded herself of the arrogant and high-handed way he had negotiated this carriage drive, then she shrugged the thought aside. Charles was determined they were going to be together in whatever form. He had decided that and his indomitable will was going to prevail as surely as night followed day.

On returning to the house, Lucy removed her bonnet and asked Mrs Yates to have refreshment sent into the drawing room while Charles went to the nursery to see his son. It was a while before he came back down, looking quite pleased with himself after, he told her, frolicking on the rug with a wide-awake Edward.

To Lucy's chagrin, instead of seating himself in one of the many chairs in the room, he chose to sit beside her on the sofa and watched as she poured the tea. Beneath his watchful gaze he was making her nervous, so much so that she almost dropped the teapot.

He sat with his long legs stretched out, studying her imperturbably. His body, a perfect harmony of form and strength, was like a work of Grecian art and most unsettling to Lucy's heart. Unable to endure his scrutiny a moment longer, with the teapot poised in mid-air, she turned and looked at him, her eyes locking on his.

'Why do you look at me so closely when I am trying to pour the tea? You're making me nervous.'

Quite unexpectedly he smiled and his eyes danced with devilish humour. 'You don't have to look so uneasy to find yourself the object of my attention. As a matter of fact I was admiring you.'

Unaccustomed as she was to any kind of compliment from the opposite sex, the unfamiliar warmth in his tone brought heat creeping into her cheeks. To divert the conversation away from herself, she said, 'What do you do when you are in London—besides driving unattached ladies around in your carriage?'

'I have business meetings to attend as well as taking instructions from ministers at the Foreign Office and in Parliament as to what is expected of me when I travel to foreign parts.' A faint smile touched his lips when he observed Lucy's expression of bewilderment. 'I realise that spending most of your life in India, you will know very little about English politics.'

'You are a politician?'

'No—at least not in the professional sense.'

Lucy was impressed. 'It all sounds extremely grand to me.'

'I imagine it does and I take my duties very seriously, but I like what I do.'

Lucy leaned back on the sofa and they sipped their tea in companionable silence. When Lucy placed her cup and saucer back on the tray, Charles did the same.

Turning sideways to face her, seeing she had her eyes closed, he said, 'You look tired, Lucy. Have a nap if you wish. I promise not to disturb you. I can return and play with Edward and wake you when I leave.'

Lucy's eyes shot open. She was tired and would like a nap, but she wouldn't do so in front of Charles. 'I don't feel in the least like sleeping. Anyway, I could not sleep with you sitting next to me.'

'Why on earth not?'

'It's not often I'm alone with a gentleman—in fact, I'm never alone with a gentleman.'

'We have been alone together in the past.'

'That was different,' she said, her cheeks turning red when she recalled the passionate moments they had spent alone together in India. 'That was then—this is now. Things change.'

'They needn't. Why are they different, Lucy?'

Lucy also asked herself the question and to her consternation found the answer. It was because he encroached so closely upon her, because he seemed too near, because she was afraid of him coming closer still. Her body reached out to his, wanting to feel his lips on hers, but if that were to happen it would be her undoing. However difficult it would be, she must learn to resist these feelings and step back.

Quietly, in answer to his question, she said, 'Because now we have Edward.'

'I agree. Edward changes everything,' he agreed. The smile vanished from his lips, his expression became grave. 'But what there is between us, Lucy, is too special to deny.'

'Special? How special?'

'I think about you constantly. I don't want to lose you.' Meeting her steady gaze, he uttered a sound of exasperation. Her calmness provoked him. 'Damn it all, Lucy. What I feel for you is…different to anything I have felt before. Perhaps I am halfway to being in love with you—I don't know the answer,' he said, having great difficulty in putting his feelings into words. 'What I do know is that you make me forget that accursed affair with Amelia. I admire and respect you and I am never more content that I am when I am with you.'

His words took Lucy off guard. She had not expected this. Desire was there in his vivid blue gaze and something more, something so profound that it held her spellbound.

'I want to marry you, Lucy. I want you to be my wife.'

Lucy stared at him. He had it all worked out. She remembered his views on marriage and love when they had discussed it in India. She could not imagine they had changed. She knew she should be gratified that he had offered to marry her, but she did not feel particularly flattered or complimented by the manner of his proposal. What he offered was not enough.

He was watching her reaction from beneath lowered lids. 'Marry you? But—I can't marry you, Charles,' she said, getting to her feet and looking down at him. 'We agreed that night—no commitments. Nothing has changed.'

'Yes, it has,' he said, his voice adamant. 'We have a child. His birth changes what we said. It is right that we wed.'

'Why?' she said with a proud lift to her chin. 'Because you say so? Marriage is important and serious and not something to be undertaken lightly—especially not for me. I comprehend perfectly how you feel. But what makes you imagine I want to be your wife? You have certainly said nothing that can tempt me into accepting your proposal.

'I reciprocate your feelings. I am strongly attracted to you and desire you, but to marry without love is not for me. I have always made no secret of the fact when we've been together. You said you might already be half in love with me. That is not enough. When—*if*—I marry, the man I will choose for my husband will have to love me completely—or be more than *half* in love with me. I will settle for nothing less than that.'

Getting to his feet and shoving a heavy lock of hair back from his forehead, Charles sighed heavily. 'You are a stubborn woman, Lucy Quinn.'

'You have no idea how stubborn I can be. So far you have only scratched the surface.'

'Have you any idea how unreasonable you are being?'

'Why? Because I won't be coerced and cajoled by you? You are the one being unreasonable. To give myself in marriage now, without love, would not seem right for me.'

As if he was aware of the struggle she was battling with, as if to add oil to the flames, he said, 'You do not mention Edward in all of this, Lucy. For his sake, if nothing else, you will have to marry me. You do realise that, don't you?'

'I don't *have* to do anything I don't want to do. Are you asking me, Charles, or ordering me to marry you?'

'I am asking. Who else could possibly suit but the woman who inspires me with feelings and emotions I have never felt before—a woman who has given me the most precious gift of all. A child.'

Had he declared his love for her and told her he couldn't possibly live without her, Lucy would have been suffused with happiness. But he didn't. Raising her chin, she looked at him squarely, resolute in her determination not to weaken. 'Edward's birth doesn't change anything for me. I am not without wealth. I will see that he is properly raised. He will want for nothing.'

Charles's expression tensed. 'You insult my honour and your own. Damn it, Lucy! I am not asking you to become my mistress. I am asking you to be my wife.'

'Because you feel obligated. Well, you needn't,' she retorted coldly. She didn't want him to ask her to be his wife because he felt obligated, as if it were some kind of duty now they had a child between them. She wanted him to ask her because he loved her. But he didn't. Perhaps he felt affection for her, but no more than that. That realisation was what hurt the most. 'Please do not feel you have a duty towards me. Whatever I want, it is not that—to hold you through some obligation that would make a mockery of what we shared in India, however brief it was.'

Charles stared at her, his eyes like chips of ice. 'This is no longer about you and me, Lucy. It is about our son and doing the decent thing by him.'

'Do you think I don't want that, too?'

'Then what are you saying? That I set aside my own child?'

'No, that is not what I am saying, but you don't have to sacrifice yourself on the altar of matrimony for my sake or Edward's. Accepting your support for him is one thing. Marrying you is something else. When we were in India, I told you that I expected nothing—I wanted nothing from you. You are not required to marry me, Charles. It was never part of our agreement to go beyond that one night. What happened was entirely my fault when I invited you into my bed. I accept that and you are under no obligation to marry me.'

Charles's jaw tightened, his eyes burning furiously down into hers. 'In all conscience it would appear I have no alternative,' he said, his voice harsh in the quietness of the room. 'But it is certainly not to save your reputation that I do so. Marriage between us is in the best interests for Edward—who is paramount to all else.

'You imply that you have made your decision. I am asking you to reconsider and I will not ask you again. I strongly suspect that you are still living in the past, Lucy, that you still carry a candle for Johnathan—that you continue to blame yourself for his death and that you do not deserve happiness because he was denied the same. Don't you think it is time you laid him to rest and to look to the future?'

Lucy paled visibly. 'That was uncalled for,' she flared, even though there was a great deal of truth in what he said. 'You know nothing about it. Whatever I carried in my heart for Johnathan is my affair and nothing to do with anyone else.'

'I apologise if my words cause you pain, but they had to be said. I will not compete with a dead man, Lucy. What I am offering you is also a way of maintaining your honour and dignity.'

'Do not assume that marriage to you is a solution to all my troubles,' she flared, deeply hurt and angry at his comments about Johnathan, even if there was a ring of truth in what he said.

Charles's eyes blazed suddenly, with the incredible blueness of a sapphire, as her words goaded him to further anger. 'I don't, but it is the truth. You are right on one count. You brought this on yourself. You chose your own fate when you asked me to take you to bed. You wanted it so badly that you were prepared to run any risk. If you play with fire, you must be able to take the consequences. As I must do.

'I do not blame you. I never have. I was equally to blame. The time we were together was too precious to me to want to hurl recriminations at each other now. Can't you see that I am trying to make the best of a situation which involves our son and to me that means the obvious solution is for us to marry?'

'Do not press me further on this, Charles. You know my feelings. I am not ashamed of what we did, nor do I regret it—not for one moment. I will not marry you, because, despite this attraction, this desire you have for me now, you do not love me, nor care enough for me in any way that would make for a happy marriage. I hope you understand my reasons for refusing your—generous offer. Try to see it from my point of view. Should I accept your offer, I should lose all respect for myself—and for you, too, for putting me in a position of feeling obligated to you and for that I would not forgive you.'

'Yes, I can see that now. Believe me, the last thing I want is for you to feel obligated to me in any way.'

'Good. At last we understand each other. I will not live the rest of my life with any man in a loveless marriage made as a result of a temporary passion, to expunge his guilt.'

Charles's anger began to melt and he looked at her thoughtfully for a moment, moved, despite himself, by

her argument. 'Lucy, you must be sensible,' he said on
a gentler note, his expression grave. 'You cannot bring
up a child on your own. You will never endure the disgrace and humiliation when it becomes public knowledge. People can be extremely cruel in such situations.
The scandal will be intolerable. You will never withstand it alone.'

Anger rose up like flames licking inside Lucy. 'Why
not? I have withstood much worse,' she flared. 'I could
do so again.'

Her stubbornness provoked Charles's eyes to blaze
with renewed fury. 'Edward belongs to me as well as
you, don't forget. I *will* have a say in how he is reared
and I refuse to have him brought up a bastard, being
forced to endure the scourge of public scorn just because his mother—in her abominable stubbornness and
pride—refuses my offer of marriage. It is not an offer I
make lightly, Lucy, and believe me when I tell you that
you are the only woman I have ever asked to be my
wife—the only woman I have *wanted* to be my wife.'

Without another word he turned and strode to the
door, where he turned and looked back at her. 'I won't
accept your refusal. I know from your responses to me
that you're far from immune to me. I will not ask you to
be my wife again, but I swear this is not the end of it.'

'As to that we will have to see,' she retorted angrily.
'I think that now we understand each other.'

When he had gone Lucy stared at the closed door,
her chest heaving as she tried to conquer her emotions.
There was a silence occupied by her examining the
words they had exchanged in anger. When he had asked

her to be his wife the words had been forced from his unwilling mouth. As though he had not wanted to ask them, but had felt obligated. Tears clogged her throat. He should have fallen in love with her. He should want to marry her for herself—for love. He didn't want her because he worshipped her. That was all she had hoped for, all she had wanted.

Deep inside her she knew that Charles was right, that they had Edward to consider in all of this. The stigma of his illegitimacy would strike a bitter note. People would avoid them. Innocence was a technicality when loose morals were involved. Did she want her son to grow up without a father to guide him?

Was it time to sacrifice her pride and marry Charles? If so, what kind of future could she expect, living in a loveless marriage with a man who was a diplomatic envoy for the British government, riding hither and thither across the Indian plains, while she withered away for months at a time in some distant town awaiting his return? The thought was intolerable to her.

Chapter Ten

The following days were a kaleidoscope of shifting emotions for Lucy. Determined to take her under her wing, pointing out that it was what Johnathan would have wanted, Anna insisted that she accompanied her and William to social events. More often than not Charles was present.

On their first theatre attendance, Anna and her husband arrived on time to collect her. Coming out of the drawing room, Lucy saw William Lancaster for the first time in seven years and all the old unforgettable memories of Johnathan and that awful time came flooding back. Swallowing down a lump of nostalgia in her throat, she stepped forward to welcome them. William strode across the hall to greet her. Unexpectedly, tears gathered in her eyes. She dropped a small, polite curtsy.

'Lucy, my dear.' His voice was deep and he extended both hands and drew her close in the warmest of welcomes. 'How charming you look and how wonderful that you were able to join us this evening. I can't tell you how much I've looked forward to meeting you again. You haven't changed. You're just as lovely as I remember.'

Raising her eyes to his, Lucy saw he was sincere.

'Hello, William.' She held his gaze, sensing his pleasure at seeing her again. 'I haven't changed, although I feel as if a lifetime has passed since last we met.'

'I'm sure it must feel that way and I do understand, Lucy. I was sorry to hear of your father's death. You must miss him.'

Her smile did not falter, though the unexpected reminder of her loss stabbed at her heart. 'Yes, I do. When he died there was nothing to keep me in India any longer.'

'And you had your grandmother's legacy, which brought you back to England. Charles, who is to join us later, tells me he has asked you to be his wife. I sincerely hope you accept his proposal. How ever it came about, I cannot express my exultation that, by meeting you, it has prompted him to take a more serious interest in marriage.'

Try as she might, Lucy couldn't suppress her smile. 'I haven't accepted his proposal.'

William gave her a knowing smile. 'That is between you and Charles, Lucy, but I cannot deny that Anna and I are hoping for a happy outcome. Charles has told us about young Edward—proudly so. My brother is a lucky man.'

Dressed in a fashionable gown of saffron silk, Anna embraced Lucy warmly. 'What a pleasure it is to have you with us tonight, Lucy. I'm so pleased you agreed to come.'

'Thank you for inviting me. It was thoughtful of you.'

'Not at all—and how charming you look. Now come along. We mustn't be late.'

* * *

Lucy hadn't seen Charles since he had proposed marriage. He drew her aside when they were in the foyer. Theatregoers mingled around them and William and Anna had paused to speak to some friends.

'You look lovely tonight, Lucy,' Charles said, drawing her to a quiet place. 'I'm glad you don't intend what passed between us on our last meeting to stop you enjoying yourself.'

She looked at him squarely. 'I don't. It was very kind of William and Anna to extend the invitation for me to accompany them to the theatre. I knew you would be coming along and I have no intention of avoiding you. Despite what you think and regardless of our differences, I like being with you, Charles.'

He smiled wryly. 'That's something, I suppose. It doesn't change what I said, Lucy. I want you to consider my proposal of marriage seriously.'

'I've already given you my reply.'

'I'm hoping you're open to persuasion.'

'You said you weren't going to ask me again.'

'I'm not. All I ask is that you reconsider. I will always keep you safe.'

'No one can promise that,' she said, snapping her fan open and beginning to fan her face vigorously, already feeling the heat of so many bodies milling about. This really was a ridiculous situation. She had thought Charles had more pride than to come after her, especially when she had refused him so finally. Maybe that was the reason he was persisting—his pride. She had dented it badly by turning him down and now he meant to repair the damage by trying to get her to change her mind.

'I can be very determined,' he answered, his expression grave. 'I am not perfect, far from it, in fact. But if you become my wife, I will do all in my power to see that you come to no harm. You have many attributes, Lucy—confidence, as well as a sense of humour, although I have seen very little of it of late. And your compassion for others compels my admiration and respect.'

Lucy trembled, staring at him. 'Anything else?' she asked, hoping he would say something of a romantic nature.

'You are also brave. The fact that you have worked your way through adversity in your life inspires my admiration and bespeaks your courage and good sense. It makes me feel that I can trust you, trust in your integrity, which is a rarity for me. It is not often I come across a person I can trust.'

Lucy looked at him. It would seem he did understand her a little better than she had given him credit for, but he still did not speak of the romantic love she wanted to hear.

The tantalising channels in his cheeks deepened as he offered her a smile that seemed every bit as persuasive as it once had been. 'Will you relent, Lucy?'

'You have given me much to think about, Charles—but not now. This is neither the time nor the place.' The way he looked at her told her he was not done yet and that he would try another method of persuasion. His eyes delved into hers, seeking she knew not what.

'We have much to reminisce over.'

His voice was low, incredibly warm, melting her, Lucy feared, from the inside out. She couldn't believe what he was able to do with her emotions and with such little effort.

Sighing softly, he touched her cheek with the tip of his finger, uncaring that they were being observed. 'I remember our time together and our conversations and the first time I ever heard you laugh—the first time we kissed and the first time we made love,' he said, his voice low and fierce and wrenching to hear.

'I have an image imprinted on my mind of an enchanting golden-haired woman who once looked up at me with unconcealed desire glowing in her eyes. I remember the feel of her arms around my neck, the delicate aroma of her perfume, the heat of her body pressed close to mine. Most of all I remember her face after we made love, the genuine pleasure of her smile, pleasure that my kisses had given her, pleasure she gave me willingly.'

Flushing hotly, Lucy looked away, wafting her fan more vigorously. 'Please stop it, Charles. I refuse to listen to this.'

'But you will,' he murmured, leaning closer to her ear. 'All that passion is within you still, Lucy. It simmers just under the surface. I feel driven to unleash it again. You cannot blame me for feeling a pang of nostalgia mingled with a sharp sense of loss if I find that woman has gone now. You see, I remember how it felt to hold you, how your skin felt to my touch. I remember how you looked in the moonlight with your face upturned to mine—wanting to kiss you.'

'Stop it,' she repeated. Lucy felt her body burn beneath his eyes and she turned from him, trying to still the trembling in her limbs. The sheer wickedness of the slow lazy smile he gave her made her catch her breath against the tightness of her buttoned bodice.

All of a sudden, she longed to be rid of it, rid of all her clothing, when he looked at her that way. Her strong determination to hold herself from him, which she thought had worked when she had turned his proposal down, was completely overwhelmed by his palpable expertise and she thought again of what it was like to have him make love to her, to caress and kiss her boy into insensibility—she was tempted.

Charles moved closer to her, bending his head so that his mouth was close to her ear, his breath warming her neck. 'I remember how you liked me to touch you, how you would say my name over and over again, of how you filled my senses until I could not think straight.'

'Be quiet, Charles. You are cruel,' she told him in a fierce whisper. 'You should not say these things to me when we both know it is only to get me to do what you want that impels you to say them.'

'*You* accuse *me* of being cruel when you are trying to keep my son from me.'

'But I'm not. That is the last thing I want. But—please stop. I will not listen to this.'

'Then close your ears all you like, but I remember everything and I cannot believe you have forgotten. If you have, I will make you remember. I swear on my life I will.'

Staring into those vivid blue depths that ensnared her

own, Lucy felt as if she were being swept back in time. Drop by precious drop she felt her confidence along with her resistance draining away. How could she have deluded herself into believing she could sway him from his purpose? 'I dislike this situation, Charles, and I have decided that it would be for the best if we did not speak of it just now.'

Elevating a dark brow and folding his arms to restrain his hands from touching her, he continued to gaze down at her. His eyes narrowed because he could not link the figure standing before him with the woman who had given herself to him with such passion.

'Do you think that making love to you meant nothing to me, you foolish woman?' he said abruptly, his lips curling in slight mockery. 'Do I look like a man playing games? The hell I am. How dare you dismiss me without any sort of explanation? Exactly who, Miss Quinn, do you think you're dealing with?'

Lucy fought the urge to shrink from his show of bluster and forced herself to sound as calm as possible. 'I know precisely who I am dealing with. That's the trouble. We do not suit.'

'Why?'

'Because we are too different. We have been through this when you first proposed. I don't want to go through it again.'

'And neither do I. But it has to be discussed at some point.'

'Do we have to do this now, Charles?'

'No, we don't,' he said, brightening suddenly and

stepping back. 'You will be relieved when I tell you that I have decided not to speak of marriage again.'

She stared at him with surprise at this sudden change in him. 'You have?'

'You are right. We have come to enjoy the play, so smile. Here come William and Anna. I think it is time we went to our box and settled down.'

'And you really are not going to pressure me about marrying you.'

He held up his hands in a pose of surrender. 'You have my word. I will not speak of it.'

Lucy sighed and pinned a smile on her lips, glad that the uncomfortable moment had passed.

When Charles's time was not taken up at the Foreign Office, as a foursome they visited the theatre once more and went to the gardens at Marylebone where they drank tea. Anna accompanied him to the house on a couple of occasions when he came to see Edward. True to his word, he did not mention his proposal of marriage, but he was always watchful.

Lucy was as happy and carefree as she had ever been and revelling in Anna's company in particular. She was aware of Charles's moods, but always at the height of her pleasure she was aware of a warning voice telling her to have a care. She knew she was falling completely under Charles's spell, but she need have no fear, she told herself firmly. She was not an innocent girl. She would always remember the man she was dealing with—worldly and determined—and she would always pride herself on her common sense.

There were days when she learned a great deal about him. He was extremely knowledgeable. He was something of a connoisseur of music and the arts. But, she reminded herself every time they were together, it was ephemeral. It would end when he returned to India, so she clung to each moment, savouring it to the full, although she had an uneasy feeling that she was becoming his victim as he had all the time intended that she should.

Lucy was nervous about going to the ball, her nervousness superseded by a blissful sense of unreality. Taking particular care to choose what to wear, she selected an off-the-shoulder emerald and eau de Nil silk gown. It suited her, its colour catching the glow of light in its folds, shading the richness of the silk from light green to a dark shade. It fit her perfectly, with a fitted bodice and a tight waist that dipped into a vee.

Martha, one of the maids she had set on to take care of her clothes and assist her to dress when she attended social events, had been right about this particular colour. It set off her hair and the dark green of her eyes. Her hair was demurely swept back into a coil at the nape. A touch of rosewater perfume and she was ready to face whatever the evening had in store for her.

William and Anna had come to collect her. The scene that confronted them at the Rutherfords' fashionable house in Mayfair was a kaleidoscope of colour. The house was ablaze with light, with large urns of sweet-scented flowers overflowing. They climbed the curving staircase to the ballroom, where she was met by a wave of light and heat and music. The buzz of conversation was punctuated by the fluttering of fans and the swishing of silk gowns. Footmen dressed in formal dark green velvet livery stood at attention. The ballroom with its tall windows and marble pillars was very grand.

Set against this background of unashamed opulence, the rooms of the house were swarming with titled, wealthy and influential guests, their beautiful gowns and jackets competing with each other. The whole house resounded with careless gaiety and glowed with the brilliance of the immense chandeliers dripping with sparkling crystals reflecting the dazzling kaleidoscope of gowns and jewels. Lucy felt strangely inadequate, knowing she could never compete with the worldly experience of these people. She felt vulnerable and gauche. Dancing was in progress, ladies and gentlemen dipping and swaying in time to the music.

Expecting Charles to appear at any moment, a warm, aching sensation of anticipation spread through her.

Taking two glasses of sparkling wine from a footman, William handed them to Anna and Lucy.

'If Charles does not show himself soon, you will have no shortage of partners, Lucy.'

'I fully expect to spend my time observing the dancing rather than taking part.' Taking a sip of her wine, she glanced around, her gaze arrested by a gentleman across the room. 'I think Charles has already arrived.' She felt his gaze light upon her.

Charles stood with his back to the open doorway through which bright lights from beyond were shining, his face partly in shadow, the light gleaming on his dark hair. He had been there for several minutes, observing William and Anna as they introduced Lucy to people they were acquainted with, but he only had eyes for Lucy.

The loveliness of her smiling face was flushed and, when she moved her slender, though softly rounded form, she moved with a fluidity and grace in the simple elegance of her dress over the highly polished floor. Charles's breath caught in his throat as he watched the irresistible curve of her generous lips as she laughed with Anna. He had never thought to see her looking so at ease, so provocatively lovely, glamorous and bewitching. He yearned to hold her in his arms, to feel her warmth, smell her hair, her skin.

He recollected himself, his dark eyebrows dipping alarmingly and his lips thinning. Every time he thought of her, of kissing her, he felt a sharp needle of exasperation drive through him, directed at her, as though, like a witch, she had cast a spell on him, which was totally absurd.

It was not her fault that he couldn't seem to put her out of his mind. No woman had clouded his judgement and stolen his peace of mind so completely. Never in his life had he felt a bond so great and a feeling so all consuming. He had told her he was half in love with her. After much soul searching and deliberation, he now realised it was more than that. He loved her with his whole heart and soul, more than he had loved anyone in his life, but until she could banish her past love from her heart, then it would remain his secret.

Jolted from his reverie when the centre of his attention looked his way, he forced a smile to his lips.

Charles would be surprised if he knew how Lucy was feeling as she looked at him, how her heart skipped a beat when her eyes met his. His mouth was a firm, grim line and there were shadows under his tumultuous eyes. He was splendidly dressed in a well-cut coat of dark blue superfine cloth edged with silver trim, his dove-grey waistcoat was embroidered with silver thread and he wore a pristine white neckcloth. He was more magnificent, more intimidating, more brooding, more remote than Lucy had seen him. Never had any man looked so attractive or so distant and never had her heart called out so strongly to anyone.

She wanted to do something to make him look at her, to see she had the ability, the mind, perhaps, to capture his masculine attention. She so wanted to see that look in his eyes that would tell her she was the most important person in the world to him at that moment. Somehow, she forced herself forward, her head held high, wishing she could cool the waves of heat that mounted her cheeks.

'I can't tell you how delighted I was when Anna told me you had agreed to come tonight, Lucy. Where are they, by the way?'

'Dancing, which is the whole point of being here.'

His expression softened as his gaze swept over her. 'You look lovely. Are you enjoying the ball?'

'We've only just arrived—but I would like to.'

'And yet I notice how you seem to prefer to stand on the fringe.'

'The truth is, that as a woman of limited importance, I am apprehensive of being among so many important people. I'm the proverbial wallflower, I'm afraid. I confess to feeling a little overwhelmed by it all. I'm unused to such a grand gathering. When I entered the house, it reminded me of a tableau set up to tell a story. I find it rather awe-inspiring to stand on the edge of a gathering such as this and simply watch everyone.'

'You really are the most unconventional woman,' he said, his lips twisting.

'I have to agree with you. A conventional woman would not have done the things I did in India. I have never been to a ball before and I am finding it all rather overwhelming.'

'Then we must do something about it right away. Come, we will have our first dance together—the first of many, I hope.'

Lucy gave him a wry look. He was watching her, his teeth showing in a lazy smile. 'I don't think that would be wise—at least, not if you value your feet.'

'I'll risk it if you will.'

Unable to refuse, not that she wanted to, Lucy placed her hand on his arm and allowed him to lead her on to the dance floor. 'I hope your leg doesn't still cause you any discomfort, Charles.'

'It is quite recovered—thanks to the ministrations of a wonderful nurse,' he said, taking her in his arms and spinning her round, as if to prove the point.

Gazing openly at him, Lucy decided she liked the

crinkles at the corners of his eyes caused by smiling. He had lovely eyes and she wondered if he knew it. Then, pulling herself together, as he drew her into his embrace, she wickedly chose that moment to lift her head and turn the full impact of her brilliant smile upon him. It was a waltz, a swirling, exciting dance that brought couples into close contact as no other. Charles swung her into the rhythm with a sureness of step and she followed with a natural grace.

'Everyone loves to dance the waltz. Do you remember how it was between us—that magical night we spent together at the palace in Guntal?'

'Yes, I remember it all too well. How could I forget?' Her body was heating up because she could not forget what they had done that night. She wanted to think about it, linger on it, close her eyes and squirm with pleasure at the thought of those hot, blissful moments.

'You were not telling me the truth when you implied you were a poor dancer, Lucy,' Charles said at length. 'You dance as beautifully as you make love.'

Lucy felt a sudden warmth infuse her body and she knew her cheeks had pinked. 'I must say, Charles, that you do pick your moments.'

'I meant what I said. I will not accept your refusal to marry me, Lucy.'

Leaning back in his arms the better to see his face, she met his gaze. 'I know.'

'And I never say anything I don't mean. At some point very soon, I will have persuaded you to overlook your refusal.' The heat of his desire lent the weight of truth to his words.

'You are so sure of yourself, Charles. Have I given you reason to believe my feelings have changed since you made your proposal?'

'The days I've spent calling on you to see Edward combined with the evenings I've been squiring you around to this and that with William and Anna, we have come to know each other better, so it is something that I sense.'

'So you persist.'

'Because I cannot get you out of my thoughts—and I now have a son to think of and must do what is best for him—which is two parents, not one.' He halted by the French doors leading out to the terrace and the garden beyond.

'Perhaps you will honour me by taking a turn about the gardens. You will find it cooler outside.'

Lucy did not have a chance to refuse. She found herself drawn through one of the long open doors and out on to the terrace.

'Charles—I don't think…'

He grinned wolfishly. 'I want to talk to you, Lucy. I cannot do that when we are surrounded by so many people and constantly on the move.'

In the diffused moonlight he took her hand and led her down a flight of shallow stone steps. He pulled her along a path into an ornamental shrubbery, hiding them from view. It was a place for lovers hiding from the lights and music.

Lucy came to a halt. 'I think we have come far enough, Charles. Why have you brought me out here?'

'It is my hope that I can persuade you to be my wife

without being watched by the whole of London's elite while I am doing so.'

Lucy sighed with exasperation. 'Please do not speak of it tonight, Charles. We are here to enjoy the ball after all.'

'We can do both. Have you any idea what you are doing to me—holding yourself from me? I can't stop thinking about you. I remember the times we were together—the time we made love,' he said, his voice low and fierce and wrenching to hear. 'I remember everything about you—the softness of your flesh, the way you responded to my touch, to my kiss, the way you filled my senses until I was unable to think. Yes, Lucy, I remember everything.'

'Stop it, Charles.' Her face was flushed under his watchful gaze. Memories of him and their night together were etched into her brain like carvings on a stone. 'You are trying to provoke me.'

'We made love, Lucy. Afterwards, when I discovered the consequence of that night, my whole concern was for you—that I do the honourable thing. I see now that I should have chosen my words more carefully.'

'You were being honest. I would ask for nothing less. You have meant well for speaking so plain, but somehow it seemed to me like the worst insult of all. I do not want to marry any man if it is all for duty and consideration—without love.'

'If my words have hurt you, then I'm sorry. It was certainly never my intention. I care for you deeply and I will not give up on you, Lucy, or our son. I am determined. And what of you? You hide your feelings well.'

His words, carelessly thrown on her already roiling emotions, ignited like oil thrown on to a fire. 'How ever I may seem to you, I am neither cold nor indifferent,' she said in a shaky, indignant voice. 'And with the birth of our son things have changed since—since we parted in India. What do you think I am? I am not made of stone. I am not without feeling. I have desires and needs just like any other woman. How could you think I do not?'

'Perhaps that's because you turned me down. When I first met you, you were so lovely I was attracted to you like a moth to a flame. For a time, I held it against you, which was stupid of me. But I was on my guard. Suddenly you posed a threat, a danger to my peace of mind—which somehow made you different, gave you added appeal. I had no wish to become shackled in that way to another woman ever again.'

'Regardless of that you still asked me to marry you.'

Lifting his hand, he traced the outline of her jaw. 'When Amelia left me, I persuaded myself that I would never fall in love again, that I would have the strength of character to withstand such a debilitating emotion.'

'And now?'

'Everything has changed.'

'It has? How?' she asked, awaiting his answer with bated breath.

'When I sent you the roses it was the truest way of expressing my feelings that I could give you. I know you, Lucy. I believe that marriage between us is the most sensible course to take. Get used to the idea, to the knowledge that you are very special to me, that I will make a decent life for us as a family, that I will take care of you and Edward and that you have nothing to fear. What we feel for each other is quite unique, that is evident, and all it needs is time—and we have plenty of that. I'm hoping you come to understand, too, before it's too late.'

'You're speaking in riddles, Charles.'

'No, I'm not,' he replied. 'It merely seems that way because you refuse to see what is before you—what is in your heart.'

'I know what is in my heart. I know who I am.'

'If only that were true.' He spoke softly, tenderly. His eyes were sad and reflective. He claimed to know her, but he didn't, not really, and she realised she didn't know him either. He was complex, a man of many moods. Beneath that handsome façade were depths she had never fully appreciated. Looking towards the house, she saw others coming out into the garden. She shivered when a cold breeze touched her bare shoulders.

'It's coming in cold, Charles. I'll go back inside if you don't mind.' She smiled up at him. 'Just think, you'll soon be back in India so you won't have to suffer the cold English winter.'

Charles looked into the distance. His face, sculpted in moonlight, was without expression now. He seemed remote, untouchable. 'You're right. I will,' he said. His voice was hard. 'And you will be here in London, still dreaming and grieving about your past love.'

'Charles, I...' She hesitated, feeling suddenly deflated. 'It isn't like that...'

He looked at her, his eyes hard. 'No? Then what is it like, Lucy? I had hoped there might be a chance for us. I hoped that you might come to your senses. I was wrong. I was a fool to hope.'

'I'm sorry. I hadn't meant to cause you pain...'

'It's not your fault. You cannot help how you feel,' he said tersely. 'Each of us creates our own kind of hell. We've no one to blame but ourselves. We just have to get on with it.' He scowled and looked towards the house. 'You're right. It's blowing cold. Come, we'll go back inside.'

After that the night passed in a haze for Lucy. She danced with people she did not know, people whose names she could remember, and she danced with William, but Charles did not ask her again and left before the end of the ball. Soon the night was over and she was thankful.

Charles, travelling with William and Anna in their carriage on their way home from the ball, was to spend the night at William's house. Staring fixedly out of the window, he was despondent and more disturbed than he realised over his angry dispute with Lucy, to such an extent that he could think of little else.

Concentrating on what Anna was saying proved difficult, because he couldn't stop thinking about how he was going to get that stubborn, headstrong, beloved woman to agree to be his wife. Whenever she was in a room with him, he had trouble keeping his eyes off her. When she was absent, he couldn't seem to keep his mind off her. He'd wanted her from the moment he'd first laid eyes on her.

The revelation of just how much she had come to

mean to him, how much he loved her, pounded in his brain, but in the face of her defiance to keep on rejecting him, he felt helpless. Meeting her again in London, he had tried desperately to reach out to her, but his own stupidity over Amelia, and his pride—along with Lucy's determination to cling on to Johnathan—had been between then.

But there was Edward to consider, so something must be put in place between them before he left for India. Lucy was not immune to him, he knew that, but time was running out. With the revelations of how deep his love was for her, it was as though his mind had become free of its burden of pain, the kind of freedom he hoped and prayed Lucy would feel when she finally let Johnathan go.

'I couldn't help noticing that you and Lucy seemed to be avoiding each other, Charles,' Anna remarked, dragging Charles out of his despondency. 'You hardly spoke to her all evening. You—do have feelings for her, don't you?'

'Of course I do. I have the kind of feelings for her that a man can only feel for one special woman, though what the hell I'm to do about it I don't know. She continues to turn me down, Anna. What more can I do?'

Chapter Eleven

When an opportunity arose, in the true spirit of a match-maker, two days after the ball Anna went to see Lucy. As always Lucy was delighted to see her and after Mrs Yates had placed light refreshment before them and left the room, Anna came straight to the point. 'Charles has told us that he has proposed marriage to you, Lucy.'

'Yes, he has,' she replied, her expression guarded, wondering just how much Charles had divulged to William and his sister-in-law. She was uneasy about people gossiping about her behind her back and would like to hear Anna's account of what Charles had told her. 'Has he told you that I refused his offer?'

'Yes, he did.'

'What else did he tell you, Anna?'

Anna gave a wry smile. 'Charles is always so guarded about his private life, but having found out that he had a son, he felt marriage was the only solution to a difficult situation. Are you quite certain that you don't want to marry him?'

'No, Anna, I am not—in fact, I am quite confused about the whole idea of marrying Charles. So please do not counsel me on the wisdom of my refusal and tell me how foolish I am being.'

'I wouldn't dream of doing any such thing. You are a grown woman with a mind of your own. You do have a great deal to consider, I accept that,' she said, watching Lucy closely. 'You have only recently arrived in London and wish to make your life here. But then, you do have Edward to consider—both of you,' she said pointedly. 'This is no longer just about the two of you, but how your estrangement will affect him in the future.'

'Exactly. Edward's well-being is paramount.'

'Of course it is. So you must consider this carefully. A woman alone with an illegitimate child is prey to all the pitilessness of society that believes the sin is all the woman's fault, that she is to blame for conditions she has brought on herself.'

'I know that, Anna. I have thought about nothing else.'

'You know, Lucy, I find it strange how the two of you met. It was as if it was meant to be. When he was wounded, it was fortunate that you were there to nurse him back to health.'

'There were others, Anna, not just me.'

Anna sighed, placing her hand over Lucy's folded in her lap. 'Johnathan wouldn't want this, Lucy. He would want you to be happy. Most women would be delighted to accept a proposal from Charles.'

'Then the world is full of silly women,' Lucy replied flippantly.

'And yet you abandon him, the father of your child,

so you can continue mourning a man who has been dead for seven years.'

'I am not abandoning him—and—and I no longer grieve for Johnathan. He is in the past, I accept that now.'

Anna studied the dark eyes regarding her solemnly from beneath a heavy fringe of dark lashes and asked the question that had been plaguing her ever since she had known of Lucy's connection to Charles, for she was not convinced by anything Lucy had told her. 'You have feelings for him, don't you, Lucy?' she said softly.

Lucy looked down at her hands resting in her lap, her throat aching with the tears she had refused to shed. She nodded, unable to deny it any longer. 'Is it so very obvious, Anna?'

She smiled. 'It's written all over your face.'

Lucy gave a wobbly smile. 'Oh, dear. I thought it might be. I cannot ignore what I feel.'

'Why would you want to, if you love him?'

'Sadly, I cannot choose who to love, but love Charles I surely do with all my heart and soul.'

'Then what is the problem?'

'Charles does not feel the same way. It's his inability to return my love that makes me hold back, because I will settle for nothing less. I love him and I want him to love me. Is it so very wrong of me to want what my mother and father had—that perfect love?'

Anna heard the anguish in her voice, saw it in her eyes. 'Of course not. It's quite natural to feel that way. I am not convinced that Charles doesn't love you. I believe he does—although perhaps he doesn't realise just how much just now. I believe his pride might have something to do with that. He believes the reason you turned him down is because you are still grieving for Johnathan—that you continue to blame yourself for what happened to him—which is what you told me when first we met.'

'Yes—that did have something to do with my decision. But not any longer.'

'That's good.' Anna got up, picking up her gloves and pulling them on. 'I must go. I promised William I would accompany him to visit friends just out of town.' Lucy followed her to the door. 'I hope you enjoyed the ball, by the way?'

'Yes, I did—very much.'

'Then I will make a point of seeing you are invited to the next. Pity Charles won't be there,' she said as she was about to depart the house.

Lucy looked at her retreating back sharply. 'Oh? Why…?'

'At present he is on a ship in the London docks.'

Anna had Lucy's full attention. 'Ship? What ship?'

'A ship that is about to sail for India.'

'When?'

'Today.'

'Today?' Lucy gasped, unable to comprehend her words. 'But—he said he wasn't leaving for another month—until after his sister arrives from Devon.'

Anna turned and looked at her. 'There must have been a change of plan. The vessel sails later today.'

A stone seemed to hit Lucy a heavy blow over the heart. 'But—he—he can't possibly… How can he do that—without telling me? Without saying goodbye.'

'I believe he called on you yesterday, but you weren't at home.'

'No—I had taken Edward to the park with Alice. Oh, Anna,' she cried, gripped by panic when Anna was about to climb into her carriage, 'what shall I do? He can't leave like this.'

Anna smiled at her. 'He can and he will, Lucy. I believe the ship won't depart until later this evening—depending on the tide, of course. So, it is up to you. Now I must be off,' she said, kissing her cheek lightly. 'But remember what I said, Lucy. Charles cares about you a great deal. I am sure of that.'

Alone, Lucy paced the room in anguish as she tried to fight off the burden of doom which was descending on her. She was unable to comprehend why Charles was doing this to her at a time when she could no longer deny her love for him and at the very moment when happiness seemed finally within her grasp. Memories of Charles stirred as she stalked the house, unable to settle her thoughts.

The past came back to haunt her now that he was about to leave for India. She saw again Johnathan's beloved face, blurred now and fading. On a cry, she banished his image from her mind. What a fool she had been not to grasp what was before her eyes.

Impatience and anguish had plagued her since Anna had told her Charles was leaving. Lucy suspected that this was the reason for her earlier visit, so she had time to do something about it if she wanted. *'I believe Charles does love you,'* she had said. Anna's words had brought her closer to this moment and a flood of joy swept over her.

It was time she faced the fact that she did want Charles, that she did love him quite desperately. What she wanted now was to hear Charles say that to her. Had she been seduced, not by Charles, but by her desire for him? She knew in the depths of her heart that it was a most pertinent distinction. This desire was of the kind that had trapped women since time began into loveless unions. She had every reason to distrust the emotion, to avoid it, to reject it.

But she could not—perhaps before today, but now this rogue emotion was too strong, too compulsively within her, for her ever to be free of it. But this in itself brought no sadness, no pain, and indeed if the act itself could elicit such power and joy, such boundless excitement, such pleasure that she was addicted to it, then given the choice she would have the experiences rather than live the rest of her life without it.

Having made her decision, she was aware of a kind of peace stealing over her. But like a dark cloud coming over the sun, she knew this small sense of peace and happiness she had felt so briefly in Charles's arms would be short lived if she did not speak to him before he sailed for India.

The noise and bustle of the East India dock was jarring and chaotic. It was a scene of great variety. The smell of tar and coffee beans, timber and hemp, permeated the air, along with other aromas which titillated the nostrils. Stevedores carrying crates and trunks swarmed up and down the gangplank. Charles stood on the deck of the giant vessel that was soon to depart for India. He surveyed the crowded dockyard below him, his eyes sliding over the people milling about, then his glance instantly came to a halt and froze when it reached a breathtaking vision. It was Lucy.

She was attired in a dark green dress, the colour complementing the pale blonde of her hair which was swept back off her forehead and held in place by a clip, then left to fall artlessly about her shoulders in a wealth of luxurious glossy curls. Charles saw only perfection. She was too exquisite to be flesh and blood, too regal and aloof to ever have let him touch her. But, he thought, drawing a strangled breath, what in God's name was she doing here?

'Good Lord!' exclaimed Sir Humphrey Lloyd beside him. 'See that young woman, Charles? Who is that gorgeous creature? Is she real?'

'My thoughts exactly,' said Sir Humphrey's companion, helping himself to a pinch of snuff. 'She shines like a light in the midst of all that chaos below. I hope she's sailing with us. Her company will certainly make the voyage more enjoyable.'

At that moment the lady in question looked up at the ship, her eyes searching, finding and fastening on Charles.

Charles smiled, turning to the two gentlemen who were about to embark on this, their first passage to India. One of them, Sir Humphrey, was a diplomatic envoy like himself, the other gentleman a businessman going out to India where he hoped to make his fortune.

'I can confirm that the lady is perfectly real, gentlemen, and I'm sorry to disappoint you, but she is looking for me. She is my future wife,' he said with a confidence he was far from feeling, but he continued to live in hope. 'If we meet up in India, it will be my pleasure to introduce you, but for the time being I wish you *bon voyage*.'

With that he left the ship, unable to believe that Lucy had done something so foolhardy as to come to the docks alone. On reaching her, he took hold of her elbow and led her to her carriage and only when everyone's attention was taken up with what was happening on the dock did he lean towards her.

'What the hell are you doing here?' he demanded, his voice low. 'It's not the place for an unaccompanied young woman to be.'

Beneath his icy calm Lucy flinched, but in the face of his anger her own fury rose. 'I'm sorry if you're not pleased to see me, Charles, but what do you think you are playing at, leaving London without a by your leave to me? How could you do that?'

Taken off guard by both her anger and her words, he cocked an eyebrow in puzzlement. 'What are you talking about?'

'You—deciding to go back to India at a moment's notice, leaving me here with Edward and failing to put anything in place for his future.'

Suddenly Charles understood what had happened, that she must have been speaking to Anna and had got hold of the wrong end of the stick—which was what Anna would have intended to snap Lucy out of her stubborn refusal to marry him. 'I told you I am here for another four weeks, Lucy. I have no intention of leaving before we have settled our issues.'

She stared at him in surprise. 'You're not leaving?'

'No. I am here merely to bid a friend of mine farewell. Hopefully we will meet up in India some time.'

'But—but Anna said...'

'I think you will find that Anna's intention is to bring us together by whatever means at her disposal, Lucy.'

'Oh—yes,' she said, bemused by the whole thing. 'I think I see it now.'

'Don't be downhearted,' he said, opening the carriage door. 'You can give me a lift to my house in Chelsea. Not knowing how long I was going to be with my companions, I sent my driver away.'

After giving Lucy's driver directions, they left the docks behind. They were silent as the carriage rattled its way along the rough roads to Chelsea village. They both had things to say, but not in the carriage with the driver listening in on their conversation. Arriving at the house, Charles sent the driver back to Kensington, telling Lucy his own driver would take her home later.

Charles's home was a charming house that stood in its own grounds back from the road. It was quiet when Charles let them in. He explained that it was the housekeeper's day off.

'We don't have to stand on ceremony with each other,' Charles said harshly. 'We are, after all, almost family.'

There was a tense silence in the room for several seconds before Lucy looked at him. 'Why?' she asked bluntly. 'Do you really think that I am going to marry you?'

'I do not,' he said easily, 'see how you can get out of it. Not if you want to live in society, which cannot happen if you are seen as a fallen woman.'

'I can always return to India—or go somewhere else. It's unlikely the story will follow me. I can afford it now.'

'But you will never be sure. What will you tell Edward when he asks about his father? That he is dead? You won't be able to lie, Lucy. You are too honest and honourable to do that.'

As he removed his coat and flung it over a chair, Lucy looked at his handsome face and thought of him waiting at the altar for his bride, a man brought to his knees by shattered pride because she had rejected his proposal of marriage. He was waiting for her to go to him. That he was hurting deep inside she could see in his eyes. A lump of poignant tenderness swelled in her throat and she unthinkingly walked towards him. She felt the heat of his eyes upon her and they warmed her more than any verbal reassurance. The message in those compelling eyes was as clear as if he were whispering it.

You will marry me.

'I'm so sorry,' she whispered achingly when she stood before him, wanting so much to reach out and touch him, but it was as if her arms had lead weights attached to them that kept them planted firmly by her sides. She gazed at the sensual mouth only inches from hers. It was an inviting mouth.

The eyebrows snapped together over cool blue eyes. 'Sorry? Sorry for what? Sorry for refusing to marry me and leaving me to kick my heels?'

Her lips curved in a wobbly smile and she had to

clear the tears from the back of her throat before she could go on. 'Which tells me you are as determined to marry me as you were when you first proposed. I deserve to be thrashed to within an inch of my life for daring to provoke you, but all that would achieve would be a delay in the wedding, for it would be unthinkable for a bride to walk down the aisle covered in bruises.'

'I would never harm a hair on your head and you know it.' His heated gaze seared her. 'Does that mean you will marry me, Lucy?'

'I shall be proud to be your wife, Charles.' Stepping closer, she slipped a hand behind his head and pulled his face close to hers and kissed his lips until his sanity began to slip away.

The desire Lucy had ignited in him and which been eating away at him for so long… He lifted his head and looked at her. 'I think an arrangement to our problem can best be solved upstairs?' he said, a half-smile curving his lips.

Lucy's excitement was almost unendurable as she let him lead her up the stairs to his bedroom. Once there he closed the door and leaned against it. The air inside the room was sultry and warm and the gentlest of breezes stirred the curtains. Lucy was the first to break the silence, looking at Charles wide-eyed and uncertain, relieved to see his mood had lightened.

'Well, Charles, here we are,' she said softly.

He sauntered towards her, scrutinising her intently, his eyes drawn to her mouth. 'This is what you want, isn't it? This is what all this is about—the reason why you hastened to the ship in case you were too late and I had sailed for India?' His eyes were beginning to glint with wicked amusement. 'I should hate to disappoint you,' he murmured, his voice low and husky.

'You won't—but if you have changed your mind and prefer it if I left...'

'And if I don't wish you to leave?' he breathed, reaching out and very slowly tucking a thick strand of her hair behind her ear, the warmth smouldering in his eyes as he looked at her, emphasising his desire to remain. 'If I want to find out if what we experienced together once before can be as good between us again? If it is, then I think that should settle the argument about whether or not you will be my wife. Do you wish to leave?'

'No, I want to stay,' she whispered, her heart beginning to pound with helpless anticipation.

Charles placed a finger under her chin, turning her face up towards his. He searched the depths of her glowing eyes for a moment, seeing the pupils large and as black as jet in their centres, then he sighed, shaking his head. 'You wanted this all along, didn't you, Lucy—along with a little collusion from Anna, I don't doubt.'

'Not really. I didn't know what she was playing at until you told me you weren't about to sail for India. She's a very shrewd lady is Anna. But after we parted at the ball, I realise it was foolish of me to try to distance myself from you. I couldn't. I'm glad Anna came and gave me the impression you were about to leave. It was what I needed. I couldn't bear the thought of you not being here and it does not suit me to live the life of an unmarried mother.'

He arched a sleek black brow. 'I see. Well, what are you going to do about it? Show me.'

Lucy stared at him, unsure how to proceed now the moment had arrived when it was within her power to win him over. He was so incredibly masculine and stood so close that she was overwhelmed by him. A faint mocking smile curved his mouth as he waited patiently for her to make a move, his heightened senses darkening his eyes and tensing his features, but she would not be afraid of him.

Following her instinct, she rose to the challenge in an impulsive attempt to communicate with him the only way she knew how. With an enticing smile, she raised herself on tiptoe and left her hands slide slowly over his silk shirt, feeling his muscles tauten as she placed them lightly on his shoulders and began to spark the passion that had lain dormant between them for too long.

'I would do this,' she whispered, reaching up and placing a kiss on his mouth with gentle shyness, her lips as light as a butterfly's wings, her heart hammering like a wild, captured bird's. 'And this—and even this.'

And she continued to place tantalising little kisses on different features of his face, her warm breath caressing his skin, before stepping back.

Charles responded with another questioning lift to his brows, giving no indication of the feelings her soft lips had aroused in him. 'No woman I have ever known has been capable of igniting such an uncontrollable rush of lust with just a few featherlight kisses. But I'm sure you can do more?'

Lucy's delicate brows drew together in confusion. 'Are you criticising me? What else would you have me do?'

'Oh, I'm sure you can think of something. I'm in no hurry. You can take your time—as long as you want.'

Tentatively she put a hand over his and smiled, drawing a deep breath. With no notion of whether what she was doing was right or wrong, she moved closer, love her only instinct to guide her. All along his arm his muscles were tense as he watched her, a savage, wolf-like look in his eyes. Slowly she uncurled his fingers that were clenched in a fist, raising his hand and stroking the palm with the tip of her finger, lifting it a little more and placing her lips to its warm centre, feeling the sinews tense and then relax. She slid her fingers through his, lacing them together, feeling his eyes watching her, burning into her bowed head.

Still holding his hand, she drew him towards the bed, sitting and pulling him down beside her. They lay back and, smiling softly, she leaned over him, her breath warm as she kissed his mouth, and then held back a little, looking to see if she had reached him. His breathing had quickened and his eyes held hers like a magnet, but when she lowered her head and would have kissed him again, he took hold of her and pushed her back on to the bed, suspending himself above her, the sudden ferocious depth of his desire for her roaring in his ears.

'No, Lucy. No more,' he said huskily, unable to resist temptation, to withstand the glorious beauty of her. 'This is where I take over.'

Lucy gazed up into his smouldering eyes, while his

hands plunged into her hair on either side of her face, holding her captive as he looked down at her. 'I may have given you reason to think otherwise, but I am still a novice at all this,' she breathed after his mouth had claimed hers in a kiss of violent tenderness.

'You seem to be doing very well to me, but I am sure you can do better. I remember I taught you well and it is not too long ago for you to remember.'

'And if I don't?'

'Then I shall have to teach you all over again.'

'And you will continue to do so when I am your wife,' she whispered.

'When you are my wife,' he repeated softly, trying to control his hungry passion, looking down into her velvety eyes, now huge with desire. 'Enough conversation for now. That is not what I want from you.'

'Then what do you want from me, Charles?' she asked, a provocative smile curving her lips.

'Only that you let me love you, my adorable lady of pleasure,' he murmured, proceeding to make love to her, pausing only long enough to discard his clothes and remove hers, flinging them to the far corners of the room in his impatience to be with her.

Lucy became lost in the beauty of his body, his touch, with a sensual joy she had not felt since that night when Edward had been conceived. His lips were warm, first on her mouth and then sliding down the long, graceful column of her neck, gentle, harmless, with the merest whisper of a caress. Then slowly, easily, where his lips had led, his hand followed and stroked, cradling her breast, soft to his touch, and then to the smooth flesh of her stomach.

Completely absorbed, she was aflame, her body responding to Charles's caresses like an explosion of raging thirst. He held her in a state of bemused suspension, the sensations she had experienced once before melting her inside and out. He raised his head and looked down at her, his eyes travelling in wonder and rediscovery over her body, ripe and more mature after the birth of their child.

He pressed her back against the pillows, his breath warm on her throat as his arms dragged her fully against his hardening body, which moved over hers. Their skin touched with a burning warmth and Lucy moaned under the power of his body as her own unfolded and opened to him, like a flower opening in the warmth of the sun, and they made love as passionately as they had done before.

Afterwards Charles rolled on to his back, pulling Lucy close so that her cheek rested on his chest. She sighed, sleepy and languid, her expression one of perfect tranquillity, her slender, silky limbs entwined with his. Lifting a hand, she brushed her fingers lightly over his chest, smiling serenely as she raced the outline of his muscular shoulders, wanting this moment to go on for ever. With the sheet draped carelessly over them and his arms around her, Charles gently kissed the top of her head, glorying in the sheer heaven of holding her.

'Well,' he murmured, 'was it as good between us as the last time?'

'Yes. Better, I think.'

'And it will get even better—when we are married.'

'Yes,' she agreed, 'for marry we must, otherwise we might find another little Edward on the way and I doubt I could withstand the stigma of being an unmarried mother of two illegitimate children.'

'There is that, I suppose,' he said, chuckling softly. 'I cannot believe you actually thought I would leave you here alone and go to India without you. I couldn't do that. I would have resigned my position with the Foreign Office and sought another occupation to remain close to you.'

'You would have done that—for me?'

'Yes. You see, my darling, when I saw you refused to marry me, I was the most wretched of men. The plain and simple truth is that I wanted you so much I was miserable when I was away from you and I realised how much you had come to mean to me—how much I care for you. I love you, Lucy. Deeply. And I know you love me. I can feel it when I hold you in my arms.'

'Yes, I admit it. I do love you, Charles. I love you as much as it is possible for a woman to love a man— although I was so wrapped up in the past and reluctant to let go of it that I didn't realise how much. The past has not been easy and the years have been filled with tragedy, but when I met you, I knew a happiness as well as joy that sang in my blood without my being aware of it. I know with a certainty that I have survived the past and, in doing so, I have experienced a shattering love that reaches my very soul.'

Charles sighed with contentment. When he clasped Lucy in his arms the bewildering melancholy that had had him in its grip for so long vanished for ever. 'You belong to me, Lucy. Your place is by my side along with our son. You will come with me when I go to India?'

'Gladly. I have been a part of India for so long. England could never stir the feelings I have for that country inside me.' A swift vision of that lovely, mysterious country with all its smells, its vibrancy and blistering heat sprang into her mind with a mixture of pleasure and pain. England was a plain comparison.

'In India, you will forget everything that has gone before and share with me a future that will be filled with joy few women are fortunate to know. All the anguish and conflict of the past will be behind us at last. You are a beautiful and truly wonderful woman,' he said, with a raw ache in his voice, bending his head and kissing her lips tenderly, all the love that had been accumulating over the years since Amelia's betrayal delivered in that that kiss.

'And am I to believe you love me for my beauty alone?' she teased gently, her lips against his.

His features became solemn. 'No. I am not so stupid that I would have let your beauty alone make me love you. You have a multitude of other assets that I admire and love. You are a rare being, Lucy Quinn. You are everything I dreamed a woman, a wife and a mother could be—and more.'

Lucy tilted her head up to his and could see he was perfectly serious. 'That is a compliment indeed, Charles. Thank you.'

The following afternoon Charles arrived to collect Lucy. They were to dine with William and Anna. Having been let into the house by Mrs Yates, he stood in the hall and watched as Lucy descended the stairs, aware of the sudden pounding of his heart and the way his breath caught in his throat. Silver threads gleamed in her hair and her eyes sparkled bewitchingly.

The low cut, scooped neckline of her gown framed her shoulders and gave a provocative hint of her breasts. She looked quite exquisite and the exultation he felt at the sight of her nearly overwhelmed him. He realised with a start that all that really mattered was that she was to be his wife.

He nearly groaned aloud at the surge of désire that swept through him. Stepping forward, he took her hand as she reached the bottom of the stairs and drew her close. After kissing her lips, he held her from him.

'Is Edward awake? I would like to see him before we leave.'

'Yes, you're in luck. He's woken from his afternoon nap.'

They entered the nursery to find Edward sitting on the floor with his favourite bricks around him. Charles knelt down on the carpet by him. He saw the dark curly hair clinging in tendrils around a rosy face which was squared at the jaw, a little like his own. Standing up, he took hold of the child and held him in his arms. Grasping a brick to his chest, Edward smiled. Charles gazed at him. He had the same startling blue eyes framed with long black lashes. Feeling all the instinctive poignancy, the yearning love he had felt when he had first laid eyes on him in his crib just days before, he could not tear his eyes away from him.

'He's a fine boy, Lucy.'

'He resembles his father,' she remarked with a smile. 'Even at so young an age he has the same arrogant way of holding his head, the same jut of his chin as his father.' With mock severity she sighed. 'I suppose I'll just have to get used to having two such men in my life.'

Charles gave him a kiss on the forehead, then put him back on the carpet, placing his arm about Lucy's waist without taking his eyes from Edward. 'Count yourself fortunate. With two such men around you'll never be bored.'

She laughed, punching him playfully on the shoulder. 'That's just the kind of reply I can expect from you. Now come along else we'll be late for dinner with William and Anna.'

Reluctantly Charles dragged himself away from his son, determined not to miss a day of seeing him. He had been deprived of him for far too long as it was.

The four of them went into the sitting room where a sherry was put in Lucy's hand and the conversation was about the ball and then became general mostly. William and Anna were highly delighted that the two of them were to marry—and Anna blushingly apologised for deceiving Lucy when she had implied that Charles had been about to leave for India. Lucy laughingly told her that it was forgotten. Without her interference they would not be where they were now.

It was mentioned that Tilly and Lucas with their little family were travelling up from Devon within the next week, give or take a day or two. Charles was impatient to see her again. Tilly, the Countess of Clifton, was his sister and he loved her dearly, although he had yet to meet her children, two boys, Gideon and Andrew. Tobias at six years old was Lucas's nephew, who lived with them. His parents had died in Spain while Edmund Price, his father, had been a soldier in Wellington's army.

When dinner was announced they went into the dining room to take their places at the large formally laid table. The food was sublime, the wine superb, the conversation relaxed and about anything and all things that came to mind. Anna was the first to mention the wedding when the last course had been served and eaten and they had retired to the sitting room.

'Now,' she asked, as they settled on two sofas facing each other, a low table between them, 'when would you like the event to take place?' She glanced from Lucy to Charles, who looked a little bemused by her question. 'I take it you have discussed it with Lucy, Charles?'

'Not yet, but we will. As far as I am concerned the sooner the better.'

'How soon?' Lucy asked, turning to look at her betrothed who sat beside her.

'Three or four weeks at the most—if Lucy is in agreement.'

'Three or four weeks! But that's far too soon,' Anna exclaimed. 'You can't possibly mean that. It's virtually impossible. Clearly you have never had to arrange a wedding before, Charles.'

Charles laughed. 'No, Anna, I haven't, and I sincerely hope I never have to arrange another. You must take into account that we have to leave for India shortly so the sooner the wedding takes place the better.'

'Have you any idea what has to be done? A guest list has to be drawn up, the flowers and bridesmaids—Lucy's dress to be made—the church.'

'The church. Do you have a preference, Charles?' William asked.

'Not at the moment. I haven't given it a thought.'

'St George's Church in Hanover Square, where Anna and I tied the knot, is Mayfair's most fashionable church. How does that strike you?'

Charles looked at Lucy, who was quietly listening. 'Do you have a preference, Lucy?'

'No, not at all—only—I don't want a fuss. The mere thought of anything ostentatious terrifies me. I would prefer a small affair with few guests. My father has not long been laid to rest—albeit over a year now, but I feel I must respect that.'

'Of course you must, Lucy,' Anna said, 'and I apologise for not taking that into account. I can understand you not wanting a fuss. That was exactly how I felt when I married William. Might I make a suggestion that I hope you will consider? It might be the solution.'

'Please do,' Lucy answered.

'Cranford Park has its own chapel. It's not often used these days—the local village has a fine church that we attend most Sundays when we are in residence. If you want a quiet wedding, then I'm certain it would be suitable.'

Charles looked at Lucy. 'I can't say that I've seen this chapel, but I'm sure it would suit. What do you say, Lucy?'

'It sounds perfect. I would like that. Thank you.'

'Then that's settled,' William said, draining his glass and nodding to the hovering footman, who went to an alcove where a huge trough of Sicilian jasper was filled with iced water and bottles of champagne. Taking out a bottle, he filled glasses and handed them out before leaving the room.

Lucy and Charles made scant conversation on the journey back to Kensington. They were both preoccupied with their own thoughts. For Lucy, the evening had been eventful. It had been an evening of stirred memories, each one bittersweet—some welcome and nostalgic, others not so welcome and better to be set aside.

Over the following days Lucy saw little of Charles. His work at the Foreign Office kept him occupied. They were to travel to Berkshire shortly. In the meantime, Anna was a constant visitor. And then it was time for them to leave for Cranford Park.

The Lancaster crested coach carrying Charles, William and their ladies passed through huge, wrought-iron gates bearing the distinctive Lancaster insignia. From there the road wound its way through meadow and pasture to the great house itself.

Cranford Park was set in the county of Berkshire, with a commanding view of the surrounding countryside where honey-toned cottages were tucked away into folds of the land. It was a brilliant late summer's day, with fields gilded with ripening corn. Surrounded by breathtaking parkland and glorious gardens, there was power and pride in every line of this gracious house that stood like a silent, brooding sentinel, the home of the Marquess of Elvington. Lucy was enchanted by it all.

'Oh, my,' she whispered, her eyes wide as they took in every detail. 'I've never seen anything quite so beautiful— and there's a lake. See how it glints between the trees like a rush of quicksilver?'

Anna, seated beside her, laughed at her enthusiasm. 'I felt exactly the same when I saw it for the very first time. It really is a beautiful house, Lucy. I will enjoy showing it to you.'

At the main entrance the four bay mounts pulling the coach at last danced to a halt and William got out, gallantly extending his hand to help Anna and Lucy. The coach carrying nursemaids and children pulled up behind them. Uniform-clad footmen appeared out of the house and descended on the coaches to strip them of the mountain of baggage.

'Welcome to Cranford Park, Lucy,' William said, taking her arm and escorting her inside.

'I'm sure you must want to freshen up and see Edward settled, Lucy,' Anna said, looking back at the door as the children were ushered inside, fractious after being confined for so long, Martha carrying a sleeping Edward. 'I'll ask the housekeeper to show you to your rooms.'

Charles disappeared into William's study to partake of liquid refreshment while Lucy was shown to their rooms. At a glance, she became aware of the rich trappings of the interior. The opulence and elegance of what she saw took her breath away. It was like nothing she had experienced before.

* * *

During the first few days she familiarised herself with the house, but what she liked most of all was exploring the extensive grounds. She became a familiar sight at the stables where Charles joined her and, together, they rode further afield to enjoy the delights of the countryside. There was great excitement when Tilly and Lucas and their boys arrived, expressing their surprise and absolute delight on seeing Charles.

After Tilly had thrown herself into her brother's arms and declared passionately how much she had missed him, as the nursemaids ushered the children up the stairs she was introduced to Lucy. When Charles gave her the news of their impending marriage, she expressed her delight and was more than happy to welcome Lucy into the family. Tilly was gay and spirited and it was clear she loved her brother deeply and had worried about him being so far away in India.

Later, when the family were gathered together on the terrace, the eldest of Lucas and Tilly's three boys came to Lucy and smiled up at her. At six years old he had a mop of dark brown curls and deep blue eyes.

'Hello,' Lucy said, smiling down at him. 'And what is your name?'

'I'm Tobias and I'm going to build boats when I grow up.'

Lucas laughed, playfully ruffling his curls. 'Like his father before him. His parents would have been proud of him.'

'Tobias has been with us since his birth,' Tilly explained, placing her arm protectively round the child's shoulders. He fell into her embrace before running off to join Thomas scampering about after a small dog beneath the trees. 'He's the son of Lucas's sister—who died in Spain along with her husband—he was with Wellington's army. Tobias is a delightful child and we love him dearly. He already has a sense of what his life will be.'

'You have lovely children,' Lucy remarked. 'Although I imagine they're a handful.'

'They are—but I wouldn't have them any other way. Lucas disciplines them as best he can, but he's a softy where they are concerned. I'm just going to check on Andrew—he was rather tearful when I left him and I want to make sure Florence has settled him down and he's not about to go down with something awful, then I'll be back.

'I want you to tell me all about India and how you and that brother of mine got to know each other. We have a lot of catching up to do. Perhaps now he's home you'll come and see us in Devon. Honestly, Lucy, it's so lovely down there that you'll never want to leave.'

Lucy watched her disappear into the house, wondering what she had done to deserve to be welcomed into this warm and loving family. Charles had told her so much about Tilly, the sister he adored. With her shining black hair and warm violet eyes, she was just as she imagined.

Three days before the wedding, the few guests accompanied by their personal servants arrived and were easily accommodated in the great house. It was Charles and

Lucy's decision to limit the wedding guests to immediate family and close friends only, which avoided offending the sensibilities of friends and made it a quiet, intimate affair. Lucy had insisted on inviting Mrs Wilson and Alice and her husband Henry, along with their daughter, who was more than welcomed in the nursery. Anna was ready to greet them and insisted Charles and Lucy were by her side.

'Let them get a look at the bride and groom right away,' she said.

The following day, with the house ringing with the children's voices and laughter, everything had taken on a sense of urgency as wedding preparations got under way. Some members of the house party who wished to ride jaunted off to the nearby village, then settled down to cards and the like in the evenings.

Lucy had found herself spending a great deal of her time with Anna and Tilly. She had become very fond of them both and would be sorry when they had to part. Anna spoke of Johnathan when they were alone, but she accepted that Lucy had Charles now and was sensitive of his feelings and careful not to dwell on Lucy's past.

Sitting under the trees where tea tables had been laid, Lucy sat drinking tea out of china cups and eating dainty cakes with Mrs Wilson and Alice before they left her to stroll along the garden paths. When Mrs Wilson left for London after the wedding, secure in the knowledge that Alice was well and having seen her grandchild, she was to make arrangements to return to India to join her husband. She was to travel with Charles and Lucy, much to Lucy's delight. Lucy sighed, watching mother and daughter, arm in arm, saunter across the lawn. She tilted her face to the sun, her thoughts melancholy as memories of her time in that wonderful land crowded in to her mind. She was so happy to be going back.

Seeing her sitting alone, Tilly's husband Lucas came to sit with her, stretching his long athletic legs out before him and fixing her with his light blue gaze.

'How are you settling in, Lucy? I imagine you find the splendour of Cranford and its extended tribe daunting after being in India.'

'It is certainly very grand, but I am very happy to be here. I don't think I've ever been made to feel so welcome.'

'The Lancasters are famous for their hospitality. I cannot get away from the feeling of family that I always find when I come to Cranford—more so when the children are present. At home in Devon, I find myself a frequent visitor to the nursery for tea.'

Lucy smiled. Tilly had told Lucy a little about Lucas's family, how his parents had drowned when the vessel they were on went down in the Channel when they were sailing to Jersey to visit friends, and how his sister had died in Spain shortly afterwards after giving birth to Toby.

'You have no other immediate family in Devon?'

'No. I have cousins and aunts scattered about the country, but no one close. I thank God for Tilly.' He grinned. 'I confess there were some ups and downs when we first met, my dear wife being as wilful and spirited as an unbroken horse, but I wouldn't have her any other way.'

His feelings for his wife were clear for Lucy to see. Tilly was a passionate, lively individual. They were well matched.

'And you and Charles are to return to India. Does that excite you?'

Lucy sighed. 'Yes, I have to confess it does. Like my father before me, I love India. Charles's work will take him far and wide. I'm looking forward to seeing places I haven't seen before.'

She looked past Lucas to where Charles was in conversation with William, having discarded his jacket over a nearby chair. With his hair falling over his brow, the recklessly dark, austere beauty of his face, the power and virility stamped in every line of his long body, she felt a familiar twist to her heart. They would be man and wife two days hence.

She was glad they were to leave for India soon. She could never be happy living her life in the metropolis. She did tell herself that she would be happy living anywhere providing Charles was with her. But—*India*? She was almost able to smell and taste the dust of the vast and beautiful Indian plains and feel the heat and smell the scents of that precious land.

Epilogue

It was a beautiful sunny morning for the wedding. The ceremony was to be conducted in the thirteenth-century church which stood in its own grounds close to the house. It contained monuments and effigies which reflected the ancient lineage of the Lancaster family. Anna, Tilly and Lucy had filled it with flowers from Cranford's glass-houses and the scent was intoxicating. The ceremony was to take place in the early afternoon and the guests would sit down to a splendid wedding breakfast on the wide terrace overlooking the gardens.

Shortly after midday, having been to see her son in the nursery, Lucy was ready, dressed in a gown of ivory silk overlaid with fine gauze and tiny seed pearls. Her lustrous fair locks were drawn back from her face into a chignon. Looking into the mirror at her reflection, it was not sentiment alone that brought tears to her eyes.

There was an ache in her heart for her father, who had not lived to see the day his daughter realised her own dream of becoming a wife to the man she loved, a situation she had thought could never be. For her it was both an end and a beginning. Never again would she fear that all she loved might be snatched from her by forces beyond her control, that fear would stalk her footsteps and make a mockery of her dreams. She would never look back.

Anna's image appeared in the mirror when she came to stand beside her.

'You look absolutely wonderful, Lucy. Charles has left for the church. Are you ready?'

Lucy turned and looked at her. 'As ready as I will ever be. Thank you, Anna, for all you have done for me. I feel coming to Cranford, being with the family gathered together and how you have embraced me as one of you, your presence and your company gives me peace. Peace and a sense of belonging I thought I would never know again when Johnathan died—and then my father.'

'I'm glad of that. It cannot have been easy for you leaving India alone to embark on that long sea journey back to England, but here you are—and about to be married.'

Now, standing beneath the chevron-moulded arch at the entrance to the church, Lucy focused her eyes on the groom dressed in dove grey standing at the altar with William beside him. Her heart surged with love. Charles's presence was like a tangible force, powerful and magnetic. They stood facing Reverend Bucklow, waiting patiently for the bride to appear.

Lucy was caught up in the moment as she moved slowly down the knave, her hand tucked into Lucas's arm. All the radiance in the world was shining from her large dark green eyes, which were drawn irresistibly to the man who was waiting for her at the front of the church, overwhelming in stature, his dark hair immaculately brushed and gleaming. His plum-coloured coat, dove-grey trousers hugging his long legs, matching silk waistcoat and crisp white neckcloth were simple but impeccably cut.

Every head turned to look at the bride.

'Oh, isn't she simply beautiful?' one of the maids seated at the back of the church sighed.

'Exquisite. And did you ever see such a gown?' whispered another as the bride passed through the south transept which housed an alabaster tomb chest and life-size figure of a knight and his lady.

Unable to contain his desire to look upon Lucy, Charles turned. The vision of almost ethereal loveliness he beheld, her face as serene as the Madonna's, her body slender, breakable, snatched his breath away. And he loved her. It was as simple as that. He loved her intelligence and her unaffected warmth. He loved the way she felt in his arms and the way her mouth tasted. He loved her spirit and her fire and her sweetness, and her honesty. My God, that he should feel this way about her. After a succession of meaningless affairs, he had finally found a woman he wanted, a woman, despite all her denials when she initially turned him down, who wanted him.

To have lost her would have been an appalling devastation too dreadful to contemplate. Lucy stirred his heart, his body and his blood to passion, to a love he could not have envisaged. He could not face a world without her in it, without her humour and fearless courage and angry defiance, that passion he had experienced in her arms, her lips smiling at him, her beautiful dark eyes challenging him.

Something like terror moved through his heart. Dear Lord, he prayed, make me cherish and protect her all the days of my life and give her the joy and happiness she deserves. With William by his side, he stepped out and took his place in front of the minister, waiting for her in watchful silence.

Lucy's eyes were irresistibly drawn to him, clinging to him, and she met his gaze over the distance without a tremor, surprised to find she felt perfectly calm, her mind wiped clean of everything for the moment. There was a faint smile on Charles's firm lips and her heart warmed as if it felt his touch.

When Lucy reached him, she looked up into his eyes, and the gentle yielding he saw in those liquid depths almost sent him to his knees. Still smiling, he took her hand, his long fingers closing firmly over hers. She responded to his smile—in that moment in complete accord, her marriage, too, seemed right. As he looked down at her, she saw his deep blue eyes were misted with emotion as he surveyed her. His smile said it all—that he adored her.

'You look adorable, Lucy,' he said quietly. 'And I love you.'

'And I you, Charles.'

Together, side by side, they faced the minister to speak the marriage vows that bound them together, the words reverberating through Lucy's heart—unaware as they did so of Anna and Tilly dabbing away their tears of happiness. Lucy could feel her eyes misting as she repeated her own vows and she lowered her gaze to the strong, lean hands that held hers in a gentle grip.

Suddenly it was over and she was his wife as long as they both would live. Charles bent his head and gently kissed his bride on the lips, unable to believe this wonderful creature belonged to him at last. They walked back to the house with a happy coterie of guests following in their wake.

The wedding breakfast, with everyone gathered around the enormous table that had been erected on the terrace and covered with the finest linen and shining crockery and bowls of pink roses to match those in the bride's bouquet, was a truly impressive affair, with course after course of elaborate dishes.

Charles leaned close to his wife, the sweet, elusive fragrance of her setting his senses alive. 'What are you thinking?' he asked quietly.

She turned and looked at him, her face lively and bright. 'About all this—our wedding. I never believed it possible that this could happen.' A cloud crossed her eyes and a note of regret entered her voce. 'My only regret is that my parents are not with us.'

Charles squeezed her hand comfortingly under the table. 'They will not be far away. I am certain that they are watching you from that mysterious place where we all go to one day.'

'Do you really think so?'

'Yes. Perhaps our children will produce their likeness,' he said softly, his eyes gleaming into hers, lazy and seductive, feeling a driving surge of desire at the sultriness of her soft mouth and the liquid depths of her eyes.

Lucy stared at him. 'Children?'

'At least half a dozen,' Charles replied, laughter rumbling in his chest. 'But you have to promise me one thing.'

'And that is?'

He stretched his arm possessively across the back of her chair without taking his eyes off her, slowly running his fingers along the back of her neck. 'At least one of them must look like you.'

She smiled, enjoying his caress. 'I'll do my best.'

After the meal which continued to early evening, when the sun was dipping in the sky and toast after toast had been drunk to the happy couple, Lucy rose to go upstairs. Seeing Charles about to follow her, she placed her hand on his shoulder.

'Give me half an hour, Charles, and then come up. I have a surprise—don't spoil it.'

Raising an eyebrow, he settled back in his chair and looked at her suspiciously, his lips curving in a half-smile. 'Then I will wait. What can it be, I wonder?'

'You will soon find out.'

And Charles did. Lucy could see he was not disappointed. When he entered their room, with bare feet she walked towards him dressed in a sky-blue silk sari finely threaded with gold, so fine yet so delicate that she imagined it would filter through his fingers like liquid when he removed it. It clung to her body like a sheath.

Memories of how she had looked in India when she had worn Indian attire came flooding back and Charles's heart turned over. She was exquisite. She was smiling up at him, a smiled that brightened the room, and the closeness and sweet scent of her heated his blood.

'The sari takes me back, Lucy. There is a radiance about you, a radiance I saw in India.'

'I dressed just for you—so that your eyes alone could see me like this. Although it's not the same, is it? Not the same as being in India.'

'It will be, when I take you back. It's a beautiful sari.'

'The material was given to me by Ananya before I left the palace—which I had made into a sari in London. I sincerely hope to see her again one day.'

'You will. I will make a point of taking you back to Guntal. Are you happy?'

'Ecstatic.' She ached with the happiness she felt. Slowly, deliberately, she leaned into him, the peaks of her thinly clad breasts pressed to his chest, rousing his blood to boiling as the heat of her touched him. 'The wedding was perfect. It's been a perfect day.'

'It's not yet over,' he said, his voice low and husky as his long-starved passions flared high as he folded her in his arms, crushing her to him. 'We don't have to return to the others right away.' His eyes shifted to the bed. 'There is time to seal our union—in bed.'

Laughing softly, she took his hand, drawing him in that direction. 'Then what are we waiting for? We aren't likely to be disturbed. I told Martha not to come back for at least—two hours.'

Grateful of the opportunity to be alone, they officially became man and wife in the best way possible, leaving them sated and warm and pulsating with pleasure.

Lucy lay exhausted and drowsy in her husband's arms,

her breath softly stirring the furriness of his chest. How she loved him and gloried in being able to respond to him in their bed. A warm and gentle breeze stole in through the open windows and cooled their heated bodies. Some moments later she lay on her stomach and, leaning on his chest, looked up at him, her gilded tresses spread in thick waves of silk over him, her eyes dark and sultry.

His expression held no laughter when he searched the hidden depths with his own. When he spoke, his voice was low and emotional.

'Thank God the past is behind us, Lucy, and you still have the capacity to love. I am so proud of you and all you have achieved.'

'I have you, Charles. A future with you and our son. That is all I want.' Raising her hand, she cupped his cheek and looked at him lovingly. 'Be assured that I love you. I love you in a way I never loved Johnathan. Yes, I loved him with all the innocence and the heart of my youth, but this, what we have, is something more, something deeper and more intense. Sometimes, when I think back to that night we were together, what we did, how you made me feel, the depth and fierceness of my feelings and emotions are disturbing—frightening, even.'

A great tenderness welled up in Charles and caught his throat. His hand moved out and gently touched her cheek. 'Then it is my responsibility to see that there is nothing to fear in the future. My attraction to you is both powerful and undeniable. I have wanted you from the moment I first saw you, one minute formal and strait-laced, and the next a woman filled with newly found passion. You are still full of strange, shifting shadows and I ask myself if I shall ever truly know who you are.'

'Know only that I am the woman who loves you, the woman you made love to. Your wife. That is the truth.'

He looked into her eyes, as if the only peace he could know would come from locking gazes with her. 'I'd like to gamble all I've got on the fact that I'll be the envy of every man who meets you.'

Charles's strong, lean hands left her face and folded round her, drawing her close to his hard chest and rolling her on to her side. Again, his lips were on her eyes, her cheeks, seeking her mouth. Trembling with a joy that was almost impossible to contain, Lucy abandoned herself to his embrace, pressing herself close to him and closing her eyes. No one could truly know what she'd gone through, how terrifying it had been for her and how it had influenced the path she had chosen.

'I can't wait for us to return to India,' she murmured, her lips kissing the hollow in his throat where a pulse beat rapidly. 'I hope it will be soon.'

'A week at the most, my love—so you'd better start packing. How will you feel, living the life of a nomad, travelling from one state to another—for I refuse to leave you and Edward behind in some far-away city to await my return.'

'It is what I want—more than anything.'

'Then in that we are in agreement.'

Lucy felt a rush of joy so intense she was sure she would faint. 'It will be like going home. What shall we do about the houses we own? It will have to be thought about now the wedding is over.'

'We will think of that later. I have a feeling Lucas would buy the house in Devon. The house in Chelsea I will keep on. It will be convenient for Lucas and Tilly to reside there when in London. Which leaves your house in Kensington.'

'I will sell it. I see no reason to hold on to it.'

'Whatever happens—if we do return, I shall see that we are together always.'

Fresh from their lovemaking, after looking in on their son, unaware of the importance of this day as he slumbered away, they returned to their guests. Ecstatic bliss glowed inside Lucy like golden ashes, long after the explosion was over.

Lucy was happy. The past was history and the future lay ahead, full of promise and hope.

* * * * *

Alliance With The Notorious Lord

Bronwyn Scott

MILLS & BOON

Bronwyn Scott is a communications instructor at Pierce College and the proud mother of three wonderful children— one boy and two girls. When she's not teaching or writing, she enjoys playing the piano, travelling—especially to Florence, Italy—and studying history and foreign languages. Readers can stay in touch via Facebook at Facebook.com/ bronwynwrites or on her blog, bronwynswriting.blogspot.com. She loves to hear from readers.

Visit the Author Profile page
at millsandboon.com.au for more titles.

Author Note

Each story in the Enterprising Widows series is about different ways people process loss. In Antonia's case, she wants to finish her husband's store as a way of completing his legacy. When this does not fill her with the sense of purpose she thought it would, she comes to realise that the most important legacies are not necessarily those of the brick-and-mortar variety, but ones of the heart. Her husband's legacy of helping others endures in the lives he's transformed, starting with hers and ending with that of his business partner, Cullen Allardyce, a man shunned by his own family. Together, Antonia and Cullen navigate the shoals of the past in order to plot a course into a future that honours their hearts and their memories, even though living their new dreams will come at a cost for them both.

I enjoyed the backdrops for this story. It was fun to research the London of the early 1850s. It was indeed true that women could eat out (a huge improvement), but there were only six restaurants where they could eat out at (there were other smaller venues and confectionaries they could go to, but in terms of a "real" restaurant, there were only the six). It was also fun to pick a hotel for Cullen to stay at. Mivart's has an interesting zoning history as to why it was allowed on Brook Street. Its founding was surrounded by much controversy, which was resolved by not having food services on the premises. But most fun of all was using Tahiti as Cullen's point of origin. This offered a little chance to look at Britain's presence in the South Seas in the mid-nineteenth century. There's a huge bit of nineteenth-century history unexplored there. Hmm. Ideas are brewing already...

Life is precious, my friends, and time is short—love deeply.

Bronwyn

DEDICATION

For B who always has the best ideas and who can recite disk seven of *How to Ruin a Reputation* by heart. Good luck at college. I am going to miss you.

Prologue

February 5th, 1852

There were some among society—mainly jealous old biddies with unmarried daughters—who would say Antonia Lytton-Popplewell was simply born lucky. Antonia would disagree. She'd been born with something much better than luck—optimism. Luck was haphazard at best and held one at its mercy without any indicator of when or where it would strike. But optimism was constant and that constancy made many things possible—like allowing oneself the pleasure of trusting others and believing that life would work itself out, which it invariably did.

Just like this current hand of whist. It had started out as an ordinary hand, but was working itself into a grand slam one trick at a time, thanks to her partner's extreme skill. If anyone could turn a mediocre hand into something spectacular, it was her friend, Emma.

To Antonia's left at the table, her other friend, Fleur Griffiths, gave a pre-emptive sigh of defeat. 'Four tricks to go. You're going to make it, Em. I can't stop you.' She tossed the seven of hearts on the pile.

Their hostess, Mrs Parnaby, matched her with a grimace and played a powerless card. 'Me neither.'

Fleur played her last heart and cast a wry smile in Antonia's direction. 'Once again, you have all the luck. Emma did all the work, but you'll win the night.' They'd played a round robin, rotating partners so that everyone had a chance to play with each other. As a result, Antonia had accumulated the most individual points for the evening, which had started hours ago after dinner. They'd sent their husbands home at nine. It was now after midnight.

Antonia laughed at Fleur's begrudging congratulations. 'I had complete faith Emma would see the potential in my little hand and maximise it.' Optimism always saw potential. Just as Antonia had seen the potential in the trio's friendship eight years ago when they'd been three new brides married to three powerful, older men who adored their young wives. Antonia had turned the wives of her husband's two best friends into her own best friends. Now, the three of them were as inseparable as their husbands, their bonds just as strong. The only bonds stronger were the bonds of their marriages.

'Well done.' Antonia applauded as Emma took another trick. She was genuinely enjoying herself. This evening was exactly what she'd needed. No matter how much she loved her husband, Keir, it was good to have some time with her friends, sans husbands. The last few months, she and Keir had been immersed in his latest business venture, an abandoned building in London he wanted to turn into a first-rate department store to rival the *grands magasins* of Paris. They hadn't had a moment to themselves since the project had got underway and it had taken a toll on them.

When Emma's husband had asked Keir to accompany him to check on the soundness of a mill in Holmfirth as a potential investment, Antonia had jumped at the chance to mix a little business with pleasure and turn the trip into a partial holiday. She hoped to rekindle a little romance between her and Keir. Between overworking on the new project and the looming disappointment of eight years of marriage in which he'd amassed a fortune but no family, Keir had begun to struggle in the bedroom of late. As a consequence, she'd felt the stress, too.

They'd begun to wonder if time had run out for them when they hadn't been looking. Where had the years gone? Keir had been forty-nine when they'd wed, a man who'd been determined to have a financial empire *before* he committed to marriage and a family so that his wife and children wouldn't struggle as he'd struggled growing up. She'd not been bothered by the age of her husband. Instead, she'd been optimistic that children would come eventually. But now, she wasn't so sure. The business and pleasure trip was going well in restoring her hope, though.

Antonia's cheeks heated at memories of last night. Perhaps she'd wake Keir up when she got back to their rented home on Water Street, crawl under the covers, slip her hand beneath his nightshirt and...

Someone banged on the front door, shouting, 'The river's in Water Street!' Emma's last trick went unplayed, their hands forgotten as the women exchanged a look of consternation and ran for Mrs Parnaby's lace-curtained windows. There was nothing to see, only to hear. To Antonia, it sounded like the whoosh and whirl of a roiling wind. But that made no sense…

'The dam!' Emma gasped, grasping the situation, wild panic lighting her grey eyes. 'It must have burst and the river's flooded.'

'The men!' Antonia cried, Emma's panic contagious. Their husbands had gone back to their Water Street quarters after dinner at the Parnabys', determined to make it an early night before the business meeting about the mill in the morning. Emma's gaze clashed with hers for a horrified moment.

'Garrett,' Emma whispered and then she was off, racing for the door.

'No! You mustn't,' their hostess cried. 'If you go out now, you'll be washed away, too.'

Washed away, too.

The terror of those words galvanised Antonia into action. She and Fleur grabbed for Emma, dragging her bodily from the door, Mrs Parnaby assuring them they would all go out in the morning for news. There was nothing more they could do at present.

Except to wait.

Except to think about the horror of Mrs Parnaby's words. Mrs Parnaby thought it was hopeless. She'd already consigned their husbands to death along with the other residents of Water Street, aptly named because of its location to the River Holme where Hinchliffe Mill preceded the town of Holmfirth.

The four women sank into the stuffed chintz chairs of Mrs Parnaby's parlour. A frightening silence claimed the room. No one wanted to speak the truth. No, it wasn't truth. Not yet. Antonia stopped her thoughts. She would not let herself go down that path—a path that led to the conclusion that Keir, Garrett and Adam were dead, drowned in a river that had flooded its banks when the dam above it burst. Antonia reached for Emma's hand. 'They're strong men. They can take care of themselves.' The idea that perhaps they could not was unthinkable.

Antonia let those words sustain her throughout the long hours ahead. She called on images of Keir in her mind as he'd been tonight. Happy. Laughing. Content. The way he'd looked at her from across the table had assured her that no matter what they faced in life, they faced it together and his love for her had not, and would not, diminish. Nothing could mar their happiness. Nothing could intrude into their private world.

But the world, like water, had finally found a way to seep in. When morning came, Mrs Parnaby led them through waterlogged streets choked with mud and debris. Animal carcasses, iron machinery wrested free of its anchorage, household odds and ends—nothing had been spared the river's wrath. Antonia had never seen anything as thorough as this destruction, all of it proof of how violent the flood had been and how dangerous. Waters strong enough to break down a building, to wrench iron equipment from its restraints and dismantle it, would have been unnavigable for even the most capable of swimmers. Her heart sank as they reached the Rose and Crown Inn where the displaced were gathering. If tons of steel had not survived, how could mere flesh and bone? And yet some had.

James Mettrick, one of the men they'd come to do business with, who was also a Water Street resident where they were renting, had survived. He was battered and bruised, but alive. He'd found his way to shore. If he had, perhaps Keir had as well. Perhaps Garrett and Adam, too. Antonia exchanged a glance with Emma and knew she was thinking the same thing. There was still hope.

Antonia clung to that hope as she threw herself into helping the bedraggled. She served hot drinks and food, wrapped warm blankets about shaking shoulders, toted lost children on her hip who'd come looking for parents, and held strangers' hands as they struggled to process the magnitude of the flood. Jobs, lives and homes had been washed away. Many were just starting to realise there was nothing and no one to go back to.

She stayed busy, but each time the door opened, her gaze strayed towards it, her heart hoping Keir would walk through it. Each time she was disappointed. She consoled herself in knowing that *when* he did come, it would be late. He would be out helping others, putting others first. He would not come until all who needed him had been helped. Then they would go home to London, to their town house, and this nightmare would be over.

At ten o'clock in the morning, it was not Keir who walked through the inn door, but George Dyson, the town's coroner. He was grey and obviously fatigued. Antonia's heart went out to him. What must the poor man have endured in these past hours! He'd spent the time since the flood bearing the worst news to friends and neighbours. She froze as she watched him approach Emma, a polite hand at her elbow as he said something to her in low tones. Colour drained from Emma as she gestured for Antonia and Fleur to join Mr Dyson in the inn's private parlour. For the first time Antonia could recall, her optimism faltered.

In the parlour, she gripped Emma's hand, the news falling like a blow despite Dyson's attempt to soften it. 'Lady Luce, Mrs Popplewell, Mrs Griffiths, I wish I was not the bearer of bad tidings. I will be blunt. Water Street never stood a chance. The river hit it from the front and the side, absolutely obliterating the buildings.' The man paused; his Adam's apple worked as he swallowed hard. She wondered how many times today had he already made the same speech? Antonia gripped Emma's hand tighter as if that grip could hold back the inevitable. Perhaps he only meant to tell them hopes were slim because of that damage? She did not care how slim the hope was as long as that hope still existed.

Dyson recovered himself and continued. 'James Mettrick's family and the Earnshaws, both acquaintances of yours, I believe, are gone. Their homes were entirely destroyed.' Antonia bit back a cry, her sliver of hope all but extirpated.

'James Mettrick survived. He was brought in this morning,' Emma argued, the jut of her stubborn chin saying plainly, *Don't tell me there are* no *survivors when there were*. Antonia had never loved Emma more than she did in that moment. Emma, who was willing to stand between them all and the Grim Reaper with her arguments and quick mind. But Emma could not out-argue, could not out-reason this. At the realisation, something turned cold in Antonia. She felt as if the very life of her was seeping away as she waited for the *coup de grâce*.

Dyson gave a shake of his head, his tone gentle with Emma despite her scolding. 'The bodies of your husband and his friends have been recovered, Lady Luce. Your husband was found in the Victoria Mill race. I *am* sorry.'

'No!' Antonia let a wail. Not Keir. No, this wasn't real. The world became a series of fragmented moments. She was on the floor, sobbing. Beyond her, Fleur yelled her rage and smashed a plate against the parlour wall. Then Emma was beside her and they were in each other's arms, each of them trying to support the other against the unthinkable. Fleur came to them and they clung together, crying, consoling, rocking, reeling, until they found the strength to rise and do what needed doing: identifying the bodies.

One of Dyson's assistants stood with Antonia in a tent acting as a makeshift morgue behind the inn. He drew back the sheet and Antonia gave a sharp cry at the mottled, cut face of her husband. She'd thought she was prepared. She'd seen death before. She'd been at her grandmother's bedside, her grandmother's passing peaceful, her hand in her daughter's, a serene smile on her face as she left the world. But *this* was nothing like that. Keir didn't look peaceful. He looked…angry, like a warrior who knew the forces arrayed against him were too many, that his best fight wouldn't be enough, but he'd fight anyway.

Out of reflex, Antonia reached to smooth back the dark mat of his hair and gasped at the gash revealed on his forehead. If she needed further proof, there it was. This had been a violent death. Something had struck him. She thought of the heavy machinery she'd seen in the street this morning. Had one of those pieces hit him? Had he been knocked unconscious? She reached for his hand. No, his hands were cut and scratched. He'd clawed at something, gripped something. He'd fought. Perhaps he'd clutched at a piece of furniture as he'd been swept into the current. Perhaps he'd clung to a branch at the riverbank, trying to hoist himself ashore.

She wanted to push the images away. She didn't want to think about Keir's last moments and yet she must. She would not be a coward, not when he'd been so brave. Had he been afraid? Keir had never been afraid of anything. No risk, no enterprise was too daunting for him. Her thoughts went to the inevitable. Had he thought of her at the last ? Had there been time to whisper a silent goodbye as he'd gone under? Had she been with him at the end at least in his mind?

'Ma'am? Are you all right?' the assistant enquired nervously. He was young and no doubt the day had been overwhelming for him, too.

She nodded the lie. How would she ever be all right again? All the light, all the love in her life, had just gone out. 'I'd like a few moments alone, please.' She'd always be alone now. It was a sobering thought.

The tent flap closed behind the assistant and Antonia

sank to her knees, Keir's limp hand still in hers. This would be the last time she saw him, held him. She willed the memories to come with their bittersweet comfort. 'I remember the first time I saw you,' she murmured. 'It was at the Gladstone Ball and you were my knight in shining armour.' She felt a soft smile cross her lips at the remembrance. 'We surprised everyone,' she whispered.

She'd come to London that Season armed only with a wardrobe that flattered and the Lytton optimism that her looks would be enough to save her from genteel poverty and spinsterhood. She'd done more than save herself. She'd married Keir Popplewell and lifted not only herself up financially, but her family as well. Keir had paid her father's debts, relieved the country estate of its burdensome mortgage, and purchased an officer's commission for her brother. More than that, though, she'd married a man she loved and who loved her in return.

As for Keir, he'd gained a foothold in society with his marriage to a baronet's daughter, something many had thought impossible. Who would tolerate the rough-mannered, blunt-spoken businessman despite his fortune? He didn't *act* like a rich man. He was notorious for talking to servants—his *and* the servants of others. That was just the tip of the *faux-pas* iceberg. He paid attention to the poor. Keir Popplewell had a heart for the outcast.

Antonia had fallen in love with that kindness. It was a rare man who knew when to be ruthless in business and kind in life. Now, that rare man was dead. Tears smarted in her eyes. He was gone and there was no heir left behind, no piece of himself, no legacy. There was no one left but her. She and Keir had indeed run out of time.

'I think it's time to go.' Emma's words pulled Antonia out of her own reveries by Mrs Parnaby's front window four days later. Most of those days had been spent in front of that window, thinking, remembering, crying, railing at a fate that had left her a widow before she was thirty, before she could be a mother. Keir was supposed to have died of old age; they were supposed to have had more time.

Antonia looked between Fleur and Emma in the silence that ensued. Emma's words were not far from her own thoughts. Somewhere in the sleepless darkness last night, Antonia had come to the twin conclusions that she had to pick up the pieces of this tragedy and, secondly, she had to carry on. She couldn't do either of those here in Holmfirth surrounded by strangers. She needed to be home, in London. Keir's business and his employees would be counting on her to continue the work.

Perhaps Keir himself was counting on her, too, from the Great Beyond: to go home and finish their dream. She nodded when Emma finished speaking. 'I need to return to London and see how things stand. Keir was in the midst of restoring an old building. He had plans to turn it into a department store.' Antonia drew a shaky breath, debating her next words. If she said them aloud the dream would become real.

'I think I'll finish for him. I think it's what I must do, although I'm not sure how. I'll figure it out as I go.' She looked to Fleur. 'Shall we all travel together as far as

London? It's a long train ride from west Yorkshire when one is on their own.'

Fleur didn't meet her eyes. 'No, I think I'll stay and finish the investigation Adam began on the dam for Garrett. There are people to help and justice to serve. People deserve to know if this tragedy was a natural disaster or a man-made one.' Eighty-one people had died that fateful night. It wasn't only their husbands that had been lost. So many families had been affected by the loss of loved ones and livelihoods.

Across the room, Emma spoke sharply. 'Do you think that's wise, Fleur? If it is man-made, there will be people who won't appreciate prying, particularly if it's a woman doing it. You should think twice before putting yourself in danger.'

'I don't care,' Fleur snapped and Antonia's head swivelled between her two friends. Something more was going on here. What had she missed? Fleur's tone was strident. 'If Adam died because of carelessness, someone *will* pay for that. I will see to it and I will see to it that such recklessness isn't allowed to happen again.' Antonia wished she had half of Fleur's courage.

'And Adam's child?' Emma shot back, the remark catching Antonia by surprise. She'd been so wrapped up in her own grief, she'd thought nothing of Fleur's hand finding its way to the flat of her stomach, a gesture she'd made several times over the past days. The thought of a child struck a chord of sad longing within Antonia. How wondrous it would have been for her to have one last piece of Keir, but there was no chance of that. Her courses had arrived that morning, not that she'd been expecting it to be otherwise.

Fleur shook her head, her voice softer when she spoke to Emma, her earlier anger absent. 'I do not know if there is a child. It is too soon.' But not too soon to hope, Antonia thought privately. Fleur suspected there was a chance.

'Just be careful, dear friend. I do not want anything to happen to you.' Emma rose and went to her. Antonia joined her and they encircled each other with their arms, their heads bent together.

'We're widows now,' Emma said softly.

There would be enormous change for each of them over the next few months—the death of their husbands was just the beginning. Widows lost more than a man when husbands died. Society did not make life pleasant for women who hadn't a man beside them even in this new, brave world where women were demanding their due. But amid the chaos of change, Antonia knew she could depend on two things: the friendship of the women who stood with her now and the realisation that, from here on out, nothing in her life would ever be the same again.

Chapter One

Late August, six months later

Eggs. Again. Antonia scooped a serving on to her plate and made her slow progress down the sideboard, adding the usual two sausage links and two slices of toast with a resigned sigh. Everything was the same. In the past six months since the flood had claimed Keir, *nothing* had changed. Not even her breakfast. The loose ends of the will were still, unfortunately, loose, and Keir was still dead, except when she lingered in the blissful state of half-wakefulness each morning when she wasn't quite conscious yet, when the day hadn't quite started and anything was possible. In those precious moments she forgot he was gone. She'd reach for him and then she'd… remember and the day would begin in full.

Antonia took her seat at the head of her lonely table and resolutely tucked into her eggs, her tongue hardly noting their creamy fluffiness. Her tastebuds had gone numb months ago along with the rest of her. Where once she'd enjoyed long meals with Keir filled with conversation and courses, she now ate quickly for fuel alone when she remembered to eat at all.

There was no pleasure in the meal. Meals, like everything she did these days, were for purpose only. In February, she'd returned from Holmfirth and got straight to work. She'd buried herself in that work, in fact, just as assuredly as she'd buried Keir in the ground at Kensal Green.

Her strategy had helped up to a point. She'd kept herself too busy working, too busy attending meetings with solicitors and city officials in charge of construction permits, negotiating with builders and buyers, to feel or to think about all she'd lost. She feared if she *did* allow herself permission to do either of those things— think or feel—the precarious house of cards she'd taken shelter in would come crashing down.

The illusion would be destroyed that she was all right, that 'things' were all right, that it was business as usual at Popplewell and Allardyce Enterprises, that the store was progressing as it should, that her life was 'getting back to normal', whatever *that* meant these days. In reality, neither was true.

The store was *not* progressing as it should be. Things *had* come to a screeching halt last week over a paperwork legality she could no longer overlook. As for her being all right and life getting back to normal, right and normal were not words that resonated with her these days. Her hands clenched about her coffee cup. The anger she kept close began to smoulder. Without Keir, her world would never be 'right' or 'normal' again.

The pain she could tolerate. In fact, she welcomed it. The pain kept her company. She wore it like a blanket, a second skin. What she could not tolerate was the ridic-

ulous snag with the store. It was why she was meeting
Mr Bowdrie, her solicitor, this morning. Since Keir's
property had transferred to her in the will, the agreements between her and Keir's silent partner needed to be
re-signed in order for the partnership to be legally official.

It was a mere technicality. Keir's partner had spent
the last several years content to leave the running of the
businesses to Keir. All she needed was his signature and
she could carry on with renovations. The problem was
that Keir's partner was nowhere to be found. Until he
was, she'd done as much as she could on the store. Without his signature, everything had ground to a halt. Which
had spawned another problem. If the store stalled, she
was in danger of having too much time on her hands,
time to do the two things she wanted to do least: think
and feel. If she didn't find another way to stay busy soon,
she wouldn't be able to avoid the twin devils.

You could have gone to France for Emma's wedding,
the voice in her head prodded gently.

The wedding had been earlier this week. Emma was
on her brief honeymoon now with her new husband the
Comte du Rocroi, Julien Archambeau. Emma was a
French countess now. In her letter, Emma had sounded
deliriously in love after having just lost Garrett months
earlier.

Antonia wasn't sure how she felt about that. She
wanted to be happy for her friend. But in all honesty,
she wasn't sure how she could be. On the one hand, Antonia was willing to admit to some jealousy. Emma had
done the one thing Antonia was desperate to do—move

forward. On the other hand, Antonia was in large measure appalled at the speed of Emma's new marriage. How was it even *possible* to love another so soon after losing the man Emma had proclaimed her soulmate?

It called into question the idea of having a soulmate at all. In doing so, it stole the romance right out of marriage and commuted it to something more pragmatic—that people could have successful relationships with multiple others as long as they had enough in common to start with. The optimist in Antonia counselled that she ought to find hope in that new revelation. She needn't be alone. Might she too also find a new husband? A new partner? A new love that could fill the void left by Keir?

Yet she wasn't ready to believe that. She could not imagine loving someone the way she'd loved Keir, of sharing the emotional and physical intimacy she'd experienced with him. It seemed…wrong, unfaithful. But *not* contemplating it meant she'd remain alone. Loneliness was not optimistic of her.

She had to stop such maudlin thoughts. This type of thinking was *exactly* why she stayed busy. Antonia pushed back her chair, scolding herself. One lapsed moment of not focusing on the store and her thoughts were already wandering in dangerous directions designed to drag her down into the morass of grief. She would *not* let the abyss claim her so easily. She called for the butler. Action was an effective buffer against the blue devils. 'Beldon, have my carriage brought around. I have an appointment with Bowdrie. He hates it when I'm late. Tell Randal I need my gloves and hat.'

She strode to the office she'd claimed as her own after Keir's death and gathered the papers required for the meeting, a sense of purpose resettling itself on her shoulders along with her resolve. *Today* she'd find a way around needing Keir's absent partner's signature. She had one last good argument to make to circumvent that need. Today, things *would* be different. She would not allow herself to think about it being otherwise.

Optimism was more difficult to maintain when faced with the inconvenient logic of the law. Twenty minutes into the meeting it was clear to Antonia that if the well-meaning but unimaginative Mr Bowdrie continued the conversation in this direction, today was *not* going to be different unless she found new answers, new solutions, to present to him. She suppressed a sigh as Keir's long-time solicitor explained yet again why nothing further could be done until they'd acquired Cullen Allardyce's signature on the paperwork.

'Simply put, Mrs Popplewell, the partnership between Mr Allardyce and yourself needs to be established since the partnership between Mr Allardyce and Mr Popplewell has terminated with Mr Popplewell's death. You are a *new* partner and that requires a new contractual agreement between you and Allardyce.' He gave a kind smile, tired resignation in his eyes that communicated he knew this was not the news she wanted to hear, but it was all he had to give.

Antonia felt his weariness. She was tired, too. This issue of a legitimate partnership had set the two of them at odds since the will had been read and not by choice.

Keir had trusted Bowdrie with the legal paperwork of Popplewell–Allardyce Enterprises for two decades, had hired him straight out of university. Antonia knew Bowdrie to be a good man. Keir had trusted him and she wanted to give him her trust, too. But trusting him meant delaying progress on the store. In her frustration, she had to remind herself that Bowdrie was not the problem, merely the messenger. Still, she had to try.

'I do not doubt your interpretation of the letter of the law. However, I am suggesting we approach this from a perspective of the spirit of the law.' She'd spent hours, days, poring over legal texts in the months since the will had been read. The letter of the law wasn't going to save her. 'I am not a *new* partner. There is nothing to re-establish. I've inherited Keir's shares in the company. I was married to him. By extension, I have become *him*. Marriage, in fact, makes that true. I am subsumed legally into my husband.'

It was not a law she liked, but it was useful at the moment. 'I am legally not a separate entity. I am a continuation of what Keir and Allardyce have already settled between them,' Antonia argued patiently from the edge of the red Moroccan leather chair set on the guest side of the wide, polished desk. She was careful to keep her words even and pleasant so as not to give vent to her own exasperation. 'The name of the company won't even change.' Perhaps she could help him see how pointless this exercise was in requiring a signature.

He shook a head just starting to show the first signs of grey at the temples. 'Mrs Popplewell, it is not me who needs convincing. It does not matter what I think about the situation.'

She leaned forward in earnest, warming to the argument. 'I disagree. *You* need to believe it more than anyone because you and my husband's legal team are the ones who need to defend it if my decision is challenged.' She had shocked him and she regretted that. She didn't want him shocked. She wanted him supportive, even if it was in support of upending centuries of English law.

'Ma'am, you can make all the logical arguments you wish, but that does not change the fact that the partnership needs to be re-established. That was made clear in February and it is still the case. The law has not changed.'

'Nor is the law going to. But our understanding of it can,' Antonia pressed on confidently. 'If questioned, we need to say that after further reading and research, we now believe that there is no need to re-establish the partnership because it is not terminated.' She'd known this moment was coming. She'd spent the last six months doing all that could be done at the building site without the required signature, hoping Allardyce would surface in time. Now, she'd run out of those things and Allardyce was nowhere to be found.

Bowdrie remained sceptical. 'That argument has never been made. There is no precedent.'

Antonia flashed a smile meant to charm. 'Then let's make one.'

'You intend to forge ahead without Allardyce's signature?' Bowdrie asked, his agile mind leaping forward to the consequences of such an action.

'Yes.' Antonia opted for directness. 'It's either that or do nothing. I cannot accept the latter.' Antonia flashed a stubborn stare in Bowdrie's direction to see what he made of the admittedly rash declaration. Sometimes rashness was the only way to break through an impasse.

'Allardyce won't like the idea you've decided to out-flank him in his absence,' Bowdrie warned.

'Then he can dissolve the partnership. In any case, I won't need his signature,' Antonia said staunchly. The more she talked, the more solid her grounds felt. If Allardyce returned and wanted to remain in partnership, he could sign the contract and all would be well. If he wanted to stay in the partnership he wasn't likely to complain over her decision to move forward. If he didn't want to remain in partnership, she would buy him out and all would still be well.

Bowdrie arched a brow. '*That* is desperation talking, ma'am. I would not recommend it.' He returned her stare with a look of long consideration. 'Do you know much about your husband's partner?'

'I know he's not here,' she replied smartly, truth-fully. She knew, too, that her husband had admired him, found him brilliant. But she'd never known him. Cullen Allardyce hadn't been in England for at least eight years. He'd not attended her wedding to Keir and he had not attended the funeral. That last was a definite strike against him. What sort of friend was absent for a decade of another's life?

'You might have more use for him than merely his signature. I'm not sure I'd be quick to terminate the part-nership,' Bowdrie cautioned. 'His pockets are deep as is his need for privacy, but that should not be a strike against him. Your husband trusted him and I think his presence may be reassuring to those investors who might prefer a more veteran presence at the helm.' Bowdrie pushed his glasses up to the bridge of his nose, a sure tell that he was uncomfortable with the conversation.

'You mean those who would prefer a man,' Antonia said plainly, reading between the lines of Bowdrie's well-intentioned delicacy.

Bowdrie cleared his throat and shifted in his seat. 'Well, yes. But there's more to it than that. To lose Mr Allardyce's support could send a message of uncertainty to the company's usual investors. They might question why he didn't stay on. If he leaves for whatever reason, it may encourage others to do the same. Especially since I do not believe it was Mr Popplewell's intention that the partnership be severed. His leaving would be viewed as a "shocking development".'

'You are inferring my husband's intentions on that front, are you not?' Bowdrie had given her an opening. 'Where does it say in any of Keir's papers that he means Mr Allardyce to be a permanent partner?'

Bowdrie shook his head. 'It doesn't, but I think it can be safely assumed.' He shut his mouth, but it was too late. He'd already walked into her trap.

Antonia smiled in victory, her point made. 'Spirit of the law, then? That *is* what you're talking about?'

'You are taking a risk, ma'am, with your argument.' Only because a woman was making it. In that regard it was the same risk she was taking heading up Keir's company.

'I have every faith my husband's legal team can defend my position.' She'd rather not have to test it, though. 'Have we had no luck yet? Do we even know if our letters have reached Allardyce?' The search for Keir's partner was the living embodiment of looking for a needle in the haystack. If Allardyce wasn't in England, that left the whole rest of the world. He could be anywhere, and the clock was running.

She'd prefer to act on plans for the store *with* his permission since she was cognisant that his funds were invested in the enterprise, too. But if she waited on him, it would mean she had to admit that without his signature she couldn't access the business accounts, she couldn't pay workers, she couldn't move forward on the department store. In addition, there was the possibility that they might never find him. If that happened, she didn't want to be in the position of having already admitted she needed his signature in order to operate legally. She would be stone-walled indeterminately.

It would be one thing if he was dead and that death could be proven. Then the company would revert to her, but if he wasn't conclusively dead, merely missing, it would take years for her to be given control and that was intolerable. No, she would not cede that ground easily. She had to push on as if she had every right to.

'We have sent letters to the usual places,' Bowdrie assured her. 'As you know, those letters went out the first of March.' Five months ago. She knew what that meant. The longer the letters went unanswered, the further away he was likely to be. At this rate, they could eliminate the Continent. He wasn't in Europe. If he were he could have been in England within a month of receiving word.

'If he's not in Europe, then where he is?' If she knew, it would give her a schedule of sorts. Africa? India? Those were far-off places. To reach them took more time than she had.

'Tahiti, Singapore. Burma, Ceylon. The last letter he sent to your husband came from Tahiti, but in it he mentioned his plans to travel between the islands on business.'

Antonia sighed. Such exotic locales. Usually just saying the names conjured up a yearning to see those places, but today, the words conjured worried. These places were outposts at the furthest reaches of the empire. No wonder they hadn't heard. She did the timetables in her head. If the letters had gone on the Steam Route through the mid-east and across the strip of land in Suez and on to a steam packet from Suez to Bombay, they would have reached India within two months, barring any delays.

It would take six months if the letters had gone around the Cape, but mail was unlikely to travel that route these days. Still, even on the Steam Route, one needed to add in another month at least for letters to arrive at the more remote outposts in the South Pacific that Bowdrie had named. That assumed a letter had found him directly. If it did not, it might take a ship several stops as it island-hopped to locate him. That would add months. Then there was the return trip to account for. If Allardyce left immediately, it would take him three months minimum to make the journey home, longer if he felt compelled to take ship around the Cape.

Her hopes sank. That meant she'd be lucky to hear from him by Christmas. More likely, she would not see him until after the new year, which seemed ages away from now. It strengthened her resolve, her belief in her position. 'Then it's a good thing we are not waiting for him. It could be another half-year before there's any word or chance of his arrival.' Another half-year before her decision would be contested. By then, who knew what might happen? What successes she might have to show him to prove her actions worthy of her decision? 'We will forge ahead.' She smiled broadly, but Bowdrie fixed her with a sad stare.

'Mrs Popplewell, waiting might not be a bad idea. Perhaps you ought to view this as a holiday interval? Might I suggest taking some time for yourself?' Bowdrie said, not unkindly. 'You've done admirably for your husband's holdings. As they say, you "hit the ground running".' His eyes were gentle and soft. They made her uncomfortable. She did not want his pity. It would tempt her to weakness, to give in to the grief buried beneath the surface of her life. 'But perhaps such efforts have come at an expense to yourself. Maybe now it is time for you to rest, to stop and draw a deep breath.'

Antonia blew out a short breath. She knew what he meant: she ought to take time to grieve, time to mourn. But if she stopped for even a moment, to consider all she'd lost, she would shatter. She'd never be able to put herself back together again.

'I appreciate the concern, Mr Bowdrie, but I do not think it necessary.' Forward was the only motion she knew. When the family had teetered on bankruptcy and everything depended on her ability to marry well, she'd not stopped to think about what would happen if she failed and she would not stop now. The key to optimism was much like the key to tightrope-walking: never looking back, never looking down, only looking ahead. There was only moving forward.

She rose to pre-empt any more of Mr Bowdrie's well-meant enquiries about her personal well-being. She had what she came for: the ability to move forward. 'Thank you for your time, Mr Bowdrie. Please let me know when you have word from Mr Allardyce.' In the meantime, the department store would move forward and so would she. Time and tide waited for no man and neither did Antonia Popplewell.

Chapter Two

Tahiti—October 1852

One, two, three. One, two, three. Reach, catch, pull. Repeat.

The tide was with them, the current at its quickest and the outrigger took full advantage, the six-man crew straining together as one, a fast, watery waltz. Cullen Allardyce's oar dug into the waves, his shoulders and arms burning from exertion even as the exhilaration of slicing through the water urged him and his crew to greater speeds.

'Ka hi!' The call came up from the steer man, his best friend, Rahiti, and Cullen executed a sideways stroke on his left, making a strong turn, using the speed of the waves to best effect , making sure not to break the team's rhythm and tempo. Big Puaiti in the power seat mid-canoe gave the call to change and Cullen shifted his oar to the other side. They were nearly there. The beach came into view, lined with people excitedly awaiting the outcome of the race. Despite his aching muscles, Cullen increased the crew's tempo as another outrigger pulled close, his nemesis, Manu, in the stroker's seat.

Cullen flashed a competitive grin at Manu across the water. They would not lose, not today! These races were in honour of Rahiti's marriage and Rahiti had selected his crew with an eye towards victory. Cullen was not only his best friend, he was also the best stroker in the village, although it galled Manu to no end that an outsider had taken the accolade away from him.

Cullen leaned forward and reached for the waves, digging his paddle in deep, catching turquoise water and pulling hard. Manu resented more than losing his oar position. Manu resented that Rahiti's sister, the lovely Vaihere, preferred Cullen's company to his own. The chief, Rahiti and Vaihere's father, had preferred his company, too. So much so, he'd made Cullen an adoptive son and given him a new name. Kanoa. The Seeker.

That had been years ago. He was one of them now. There was nowhere on earth he'd rather be and no other people he'd rather be with. Here in Maravati Bay, he was home, surrounded by family and friends and freedom. Freedom to do as he pleased, to *be* as he pleased. Which was all Cullen Allardyce had ever wanted.

The shore neared, turquoise waters meeting with a taupe line of sand. Cullen could see Vaihere on the shore standing beside Rahiti's bride, cheering for him. From the power seat in the canoe, Big Puiti called the change, his voice strong despite the gruelling length of the race. Their outrigger surged faster with each catch and pull. The soreness of Cullen's body was nothing compared to the sensation of this, of skimming across the waves, chasing victory.

With a final effort, they crossed the finish line half a

boat-length ahead of Manu's team. A joyous cry went up from the beach. Villagers splashed into the water to celebrate the victory. Vaihere was there and Cullen jumped out of the canoe, sweeping her into an embrace as she settled a hibiscus lei about his neck. 'You were magnificent, Kanoa.' She laughed up at him, the ocean-wet length of him dampening her *pareo*. 'I thought Manu was going to catch up,' she confessed with a mischievous glint in her dark eyes.

'His boat was too slow at the turn,' Cullen confided. 'Their steer man didn't read the waves as well as he should have at the halfway point. They spent themselves trying to catch up and had nothing left for a final sprint.' Rahiti had taken a great chance asking him to take the canoe out as fast as he had, but the crew was strong and had the endurance to hold the pace.

Rahiti, his new bride on his arm, waded through the surf and embraced him. '*Me tuâne*, you have brought me victory today.'

'Not me alone,' Cullen corrected. 'You made the choice to go out fast and Puaiti gave us encouragement with the strength of his calls. Truly, it was a team effort.'

Rahiti clapped his shoulder good-naturedly, his eyes dancing with happiness, not all of it attributed to his victory. 'But you were my stroker, you set the pace and you kept the team to it. Manu did not.' He grinned. 'Come and eat with me. We have a whole day of feasting before us.'

The *ahima*, the underground ovens, had been busy cooking suckling pig and the rich aroma of meat filled the air as they reached the village. Cullen and Viahere settled on a woven mat to eat, taking turns feeding each other from the collection of food and laughing. She listened intently as he recounted key moments of the race, but her gaze strayed often to where her brother and his new wife sat, eyes only for each other.

'You are happy for them,' Cullen said, letting his own gaze follow hers.

'They love one another. That is a rare thing.' She sighed and gave her hair a toss behind her shoulder. 'How wondrous for them that the person they're meant to spend their lives with was on the same small island as they.'

Cullen gave her a soft smile instead of disabusing her of the fairy-tale notion that people had soulmates. He didn't believe in soulmates any more than he believed in love—romantic love anyway. He had brotherly love for Rahiti and familial love for Rahiti's mother and father. But romantic love was merely lust. Quickly satiated. He'd slaked it often enough with different women to know it was not eternal, nor was it particular about whom he satisfied it with. But today was not the day to make that argument.

He shifted on the mat and fed Vaihere a bite of *umara* in an attempt to distract her. He was not entirely comfortable with the conversation. He was well aware that if he should offer for Vaihere, the offer would be welcomed by both Vaihere and her father. He was also aware that he would not make that offer. He wasn't a marrying man for philosophical and practical reasons. Philosophically, marriage was in direct opposition with his ideas of freedom. He liked women—plural. He loved their bodies, he loved exploring pleasure with them.

He could not imagine having only one lover the rest of his life.

Practically, there was much about his life, his past, that he would not willingly subject Vaihere to. This was her home and it was his, but his permanence here was not the same as hers. Some day in the far-off unknown future, if he should ever leave here, he would not willingly take her from this place, from her family, from the life she knew, and put her in danger. He knew what England did to unsuspecting foreigners from untouched corners of the world. He'd been six when the Hawaiian King and Queen had visited England and died there from measles.

He did not wish such a fate for Viahere. Nor did he wish other fates for her such as being tied to him. He did not think a woman like her who valued love, a sense of place and family would be happy with him for the long term. He was a man without a country, a man whose politics and scandal had alienated him from England. Family was important to Viahere and some would say he'd betrayed his.

He felt differently, of course. He thought it was the other way around: his family had betrayed *him*. Still, his own experience suggested that while he might crave the concept of a family of his own in theory, the practice of acquiring one was far less likely. Knowing that he would not offer her the things she wanted only deepened his guilt. She was waiting on him. He could not prolong her wait much longer. He needed to marry her or set her free. He could not see his way to doing the former, so it must be the latter.

Vaihere reached up a soft hand and caressed his cheek.

'I did not mean to upset you, Kanoa. Today is for happiness.' She took his hand and whispered, 'I understand more than you think.' Then her eyes changed, dancing with playful lights. She tugged his hand. 'Come with me to the lagoon. No one will miss us today.'

The lagoon was exactly what he had required, Cullen concluded hours later as he lay exhausted beside Vaihere. Despite the exertion of the race, his body had needed exercise. They'd swum in the aquamarine lagoon, dived beneath its waters with the sea turtles and lounged on the clean white sands of its hidden beach until the sun began to sink towards the horizon, a hot orange ball lowering into cool blue waters.

'We should go back,' Vaihere murmured against his shoulder. 'There will be dancing and food. I confess, I'm getting hungry.' She sighed reluctantly.

'One more swim.' Cullen pushed himself up with a grunt and brushed the sand from his legs. He waded into the water and executed a shallow dive. Of all the things he loved about Tahiti, it was the water he loved most. There was no water like this anywhere in England. A man could swim year-round here. Even if there were no politics, no scandal keeping him from England, he'd still choose to stay here for the water and weather alone.

He let the water cleanse him, letting it push back the long tawny tangle of his hair and wash the sand from his skin until he was ready to go back to the village, to join the wedding festivities and celebrate the perfection of this day: the tides, the weather, the racing, the victory, the pleasure of a full belly and a beautiful woman beside him. Life did not get more perfect than that.

He waded towards shore, his *malo* soaking and slung low on his hips, water sluicing from his hair as it hung down his back, his arm about Vaihere. He had his face turned to the sky, his gaze intent on the early stars peeping through now that the sun had settled, when Vaihere gave his arm an unmistakable warning tug. *'Aito,'* she whispered. Soldier.

He was instantly alert. Soldiers were a less welcome sight after the French-Tahitian war six years ago that had resulted in France establishing a protectorate that recognised Tahiti's sovereignty while reducing the Tahitian Queen, Pomare's, powers. The French Commissaire, Moerenhout, ruled alongside the Queen these days. Cullen was not fooled as to what it meant: Tahiti would shortly lose its autonomy. This was the way of empire building. The usual disgust he felt over the politics of colonisation unfurled in his belly at the thought. He'd seen such strategies before from the English in India.

Cullen squinted in the evening light and studied the man on the beach standing at rigid attention, taking in the navy-blue cut-away coat with its officer's gold braid. The man's bearing and uniform was that of someone who held significant rank. Cullen drew three immediate conclusions. First, that man must be incredibly uncomfortable in all those clothes. Secondly, he was military but a sailor, not a soldier. Third, he was not French, but British. Which meant the man was here for *him*. Cullen stepped in front of Vaihere, gently steering her behind him for protection although the man on the beach would think it for modesty.

'Lord Cullen Allardyce?' the man called, his stare unflinching as he gave Cullen the same intense perusal. Let him look. Cullen was not ashamed, although he could guess the direction of the man's thoughts. He knew how he must look to that proper European gaze, his long, sun-streaked hair hanging to his waist, his body tanned, half-naked, and tattooed. Well, the man couldn't see his tattoo *yet*, since it was on the back of his shoulder, but the man would see it soon enough.

Cullen strode from the water, ready to dispatch the man. Men had come to look for him before and he'd sent them away, but no one had come for years now. There were days when he almost allowed himself to believe he'd finally succeeded in breaking the chains that bound him to his old life. Here in Tahiti, neither his scandal nor his *outrageous* politics—that was his father's word for them—mattered.

'If you've come from my father, I have no wish for correspondence. Go back to your ship.' Cullen planted his feet shoulder width apart and crossed his arms over his chest. Let the man look. Let the man carry back heathen reports about his appearance and the news that the Marquess of Standon's son had gone native. Cullen was sure he wouldn't be the first to report on it. But he knew his assumption was wrong as soon as he spoke. His father had not sought him out for years now. There was no reason for him to do so. His father was as pleased as he, apparently, to have that tie severed.

'I've not come from your father,' the officer said

evenly. 'I'm Admiral Connant and I have a letter for you. It's come through many circuitous routes to reach you as no one was sure exactly where you'd be and I've been charged to put it in your hands whenever I found you. You're a hard man to find, my lord. We had the address in Papeete, but we were told there was no guarantee you'd be there since your business takes you all over the South Seas.'

Cullen shrugged unapologetically. He kept the small office in Papeete with its room overhead for the purpose of giving the rare letter a place to go and for himself on days when he had to see to the paperwork of the business, which was about twice a year—once when Keir's ship left and once when the ship came in. 'I am not often in Papeete, not since the war.' When the French had emerged the victors in the Franco-Tahitian war, Cullen had preferred the village in Ha'apape to the colonial centre.

The man offered a wry smile. 'I know. I gave you a week to show up while we resupplied.' The man was tenacious and intrepid, Cullen would give him that. Not everyone would travel the island, looking for a man who didn't want to be found. That piqued Cullen's interest and his concern. Who would mail him if not his father? He had few friends left in England who knew where to find him or, even if they did, who would need to go to the effort of doing so. It was too early for Keir's annual report. 'Who sent you?'

'Mr Bowdrie. A solicitor. He insisted it was urgent that you be found.'

He recognised the name. Bowdrie was Keir's solicitor.

Technically, *their* solicitor. For a moment the wariness eased. Keir must have money issues to discuss. Perhaps informing him money was being sent to an account, or informing him about an expenditure, likely a large one if Keir felt he needed permission. Perhaps there were papers needing his signature. If so, Cullen hoped Admiral Connant had had the foresight to bring them with him and not leave them in Papeete. He didn't relish the idea of going into the town just to sign papers that could just as easily be signed here and the Admiral sent on his way.

'Mr Popplewell has died, my lord.' The words snapped Cullen back to attention, the wariness returning.

'What did you say?' Cullen ground out. He'd heard the man clear enough, but what those words meant was too unbelievable to accept. Surely it wasn't possible. Keir was healthy, a big, strong man. He'd make a great power seat in the outrigger. But it had been ten years since he'd seen Keir.

There'd been the occasional letter and the annual reports from Keir regarding their investments, but all had seemed well. Very well. The man was besotted with his wife. Business was exceedingly good. Keir was always expanding, always looking for the next big thing, always depositing more money into accounts for Cullen that Cullen never looked at. Money didn't mean much out here.

Connant cleared his throat. 'Mr Popplewell has passed. The solicitor has written on behalf of Mr Popplewell's widow. I have the letter—if there is some place where we might talk?'

The question drew Cullen from his stunned stupor.

'Here, we can talk here. There are wedding celebrations in the village. I would not take this news into their midst.' He turned to Vaihere. 'Go to the village and quietly tell your father. I do not want anyone to worry.' To the Admiral he said, 'Allow me a few minutes.' He took those minutes to gather what wood there was and start a small fire. The swim and the news had left him chilled. Keir. Dead. The man who'd mentored him when his father had despaired of him. The man who'd respected his ideas, who had taught him about business and investing, who had encouraged him to see the world.

When the fire was going, Admiral Connant passed him the letter, the seal unbroken. He rose. 'I'll give you a moment of privacy to read it.'

Cullen slipped his finger beneath the wax seal. For a letter that had come thousands of miles, over sea and across desert, it was quite…short. It might as well have been a missive sent across town, one solicitor to another. There was the usual salutation for bad news.

> *I regret to inform you that Keir Popplewell has passed away.*

No mention of the circumstances leading to his death.

> *All his personal and business affairs have been left to his wife…*

Also not surprising. Keir had no children.

> *There are matters that require your immediate attention and physical presence in London in order*

for business to move forward since the partnership between Keir Popplewell and yourself needs to be renegotiated.

That part made him wince. He was being recalled to the last place on earth he wanted to be. Surely he'd find a way around that. He and Mr Bowdrie could exchange letters for years perhaps before an appearance was necessary. But it was the following lines that grabbed his attention and caused his heart and hopes to sink.

Failure to appear in person to resolve these issues will result in the eventual collapse of Popplewell and Allardyce Enterprises since the company will cease to be able to access bank accounts and conduct business as usual. Be advised such a situation would negatively affect Mr Popplewell's widow and those dependent on the company for their livelihoods.

That struck at the core of him. If it had just been about his money, he'd have let the company dry up. He had enough and he'd simply start over, build something from scratch if need be. One did not need money in Ha'apape. He might be a rogue, but he was not irresponsible. The operation here was for the benefit of others more than it was for him and Keir. They had set up the South Seas import branch of the company in order to find a way to assist those who struggled in the Empire, indigenous peoples whose ways of life were being squashed beneath the heal of colonisation.

Keir had been part of the Prometheus Club, headed by the Duke of Cowden, and the club had encouraged them to invest in people by buying regional arts and crafts from cloth to pottery to sell back in England. It was Cullen's job to traverse the South Pacific looking for things to send back to England and setting up relationships with clans and tribes in order to establish a regular pipeline.

Should the company dissolve, it wasn't just Keir's widow who would suffer, but hundreds of people who depended on the company for income—an income that wasn't always paid in coin but in goats and pigs, that allowed for trade and prosperity, that allowed people to feed their families.

Cullen sat beside the fire and stared out over the dark waters for endless minutes. There was no choice, not one that he could live with, anyway. He looked at the date on the letter. March. It had been sent a little over six months ago, almost double the time a letter should take to reach him. The urgency Bowdrie alluded to had grown old while Connant had searched for him.

He was cognisant, too, that, as a naval officer, delivering the letter wasn't Connant's only responsibility. Official military duties had likely added to the timeline. No doubt Connant had been charged with delivering the letter in India when he'd received orders. Nevertheless, Keir's widow would already be in the throes of worry, unable to do anything without his signature. There were workers counting on wages, ships unable to sail with their cargoes without payment. 'How long do I have?'

'My ship will dock in the bay come morning,' Connant offered quietly as if he could understand the magnitude of what leaving meant.

Cullen nodded. He'd have tonight to say his goodbyes. There was nothing in Papeete he needed. Material items had become less important to him. Everyone he cared for was here in the village. Vaihere would be strong. She would wait to weep until after he left. Her mother would pack an enormous basket of food and hand it to him with sad eyes. Rahiti and his father would argue with him, counselling him to find another way, to take time and think it through. He could not allow himself to be swayed by that very desirable, persuasive position. Too much time had already passed. People were counting on him.

He felt weighed down by the finality of the decision. How quickly everything had changed. The pleasantness of his life was upended, the distance he'd craved destroyed. Just hours ago, there'd been no thought of returning to England, a place that held only bad memories for him.

He'd gone to the ends of the earth and he'd still failed to outrun the arm of England. But England could not hold him. He would not stay. This was just a temporary inconvenience. He would sign those papers and see that all was taken care of. Then he would leave on the first available ship. There, beside the fire on the shore of the lagoon, he promised himself he would be back here, home again, this time next year.

Chapter Three

London—February 1st, 1853

He'd never thought to be here again. Lord Cullen Allardyce looked out the window of the train as it slowed, pulling into Charing Cross station, the South Eastern Railway locomotive completing its journey from the Channel terminus in Folkestone. A porter knocked on the door of his private compartment to let him know arrival was imminent. *Imminent*.

After three months of travel with its inevitable setbacks and myriad transportation experiences that included everything from steamers to camels and a night journey overland to the Port of Cairo, another ship to Marseilles, trains through France, the ferry to Folkestone out of Boulogne, and one last train from Folkestone to London, he'd finally arrived in more ways than the geographic.

Cullen tugged at his waistcoat, still accustoming himself to its tight fit. The journey had been one of transformation as well as transportation. He wouldn't do himself any favours walking around London sporting long hair and a *malo*. Besides, it was damned cold in this part of the world.

That last night in Ha'apape, he'd packed away his *malo* and said farewell to his hair. Vaihere performed a private version of the *pakoti rouru* ceremony and lovingly cut his hair to a more English length. Now his tawny waves skimmed his shoulders instead of his waist. He'd also said farewell to Vaihere. She need not wait for him. It wouldn't be fair and she'd understood that, when or whether he returned, their relationship, as it had been, was completed.

The farewells continued. At the Port of Cairo, he'd said goodbye to Admiral Connant and the culottes he'd worn aboard the ship. He used the delay at Shepheard's in Cairo to purchase two ready-made European suits of clothing and had worn them ever since. Cullen ran a finger between his neck and collar, missing the freedom of his *malo*. He'd not worn this many layers of clothing for years.

The train came to a halt and Cullen reached into his waistcoat pocket to check the address one last time. He'd visit Bowdrie straight away. Then he'd have to find accommodations. Thankfully, it was February and not the middle of the Season. A hotel room shouldn't be difficult to come by and a modicum of privacy. How long the privacy lasted would depend on discretion.

He'd need to visit Coutts and draw on his accounts, find a fast tailor and set up a meeting with the Duke of Cowden. It was inevitable word would leak out that he was in town, so he could only hope for a slow leak. He sighed and leaned back against the cushions of the seat. He'd not had to think of such things for ages, nor had he been this busy. The moment he stepped off the train, he would be absorbed into the hustle that was London, a place that was about as far from Ha'apape as one could get in ways that went far beyond geography. He rose and shrugged into his greatcoat—layer four—and exited his compartment.

He disembarked, fighting a wave of homesickness for the village, for slow days, for swimming in the lagoon, for blue skies and turquoise waters. But he could not regret his decision. He owed Keir. When his own family had despaired of him, Keir had not. He had once needed Keir, now Keir and the dream they'd built needed him. One month was all he'd need to see to business. He'd give himself until March and then he'd be back on board a ship heading home. Cullen drew a deep breath, and plunged into the melee.

'Welcome back, my lord.' Robert Bowdrie bustled out of his neat-as-a-pin Gray's Inn office within seconds of Cullen being announced. The speed was dizzying. The clerk had barely gone into the inner office when Bowdrie had come bounding out. Cullen speculated the usually reserved solicitor had likely leaped over his desk to reach him that quickly. Bowdrie pumped his hand energetically. 'What a relief it is to see you looking so well, my lord. Won't you come in?'

Cullen winced at the address. 'Mr Allardyce is fine, as it always has been.' It was one more thing he had to get used to all over again and one more reminder how far from Tahiti he was.

'Mr Allardyce then, will you come this way.' Bowdrie ushered him towards the inner office and shut the door behind them.

Cullen looked around the familiar space. He'd visited often with Keir. It was odd to think so much time had passed, time in which he'd lived an entirely new life, but this office had changed so little, hardly at all. Some folks said there was comfort in constancy, in knowing that things never changed. But Cullen found only sadness in such a premise. Change meant growth, learning, new places, new people, new thoughts. It meant testing the validity of tradition, something his father had been rankly against. His father would approve of Bowdrie's office.

With the exception of a few more grey hairs, Bowdrie looked the same. The office looked the same. The big desk still dominated the space, the red Moroccan leather chairs, a gift from the Duke of Cowden for long years of service, were still there for visitors. The sideboard still held the same four decanters—whisky, American bourbon, brandy and high-end gin from James Greyville, another of Bowdrie's clients.

Perhaps there were a few more books than there had been. Cullen tugged discreetly at his collar, feeling hemmed in. For such a small space, there were so many *things*. Shelves stuffed with tomes and masculine accoutrements, a compass, a globe, scales, paperweights. The English did like their objets d'art.

Bowdrie was at the sideboard, holding up a decanter. 'Would you like a drink? It's only eleven, but you've had quite a journey. A strong drink is in order as is a bit of celebration. I think no one would condemn our indulgence.'

Cullen shook his head. 'No, thank you.' Other than an occasional rum or a rare French brandy to keep up appearances in Papeete, he seldom drank alcohol any more. He'd discovered he had better things to do: swim, fish, train in the outriggers, and, of course, carry out company business between the islands for Keir. His days were full. He'd had to re-accustom himself to the prevalence of alcohol on his journey given that fresh water had been at a premium most of the trip. But his refusal had left Bowdrie feeling awkward and unsure how to continue the conversation. Cullen offered him a lifeline. 'Why don't we just jump straight into it? Tell me what's happened.'

Tell me what's happened since my friend died, since the one man in England who believed in me is no longer alive.

He'd had the whole journey to accustom himself to that, too, and he'd been as unsuccessful with it as he'd been getting used to the clothes and the alcohol. How was it possible he'd ever felt at home here? Or perhaps he never had?

Bowdrie returned to his chair behind the massive desk. 'I can update you, of course. The short of it is that Keir's death requires the partnership to be re-established, as I explained in the letter. But it is more than that. Banks also need reassurances that the company continues to be viable,' Bowdrie added meaningfully. 'I would never say this directly to Mrs Popplewell—she's had a difficult enough year as it is—but she is a woman in a man's world. Stepping into Keir's position as if she is Keir himself, the head of Popplewell-Allardyce Enterprises, does not help the business. The banks are concerned about a woman at the helm.

'It has not been an issue so far, but if there comes a time when loans are needed or short-term credit is required for purchases, or deals need to be brokered, it will be an issue. They will not do business with a woman. Any misstep on her part will be magnified ten times over because of her gender. Having you here will go a long way in offering reassurances.'

Cullen crossed a leg over one knee. Bowdrie was talking as if he would be here indefinitely. That would not be the case, but now was not the time to talk about leaving. 'How is the company faring now? Keir sent annual reports and from all accounts it looks to be thriving.' He hoped that was the case. The less of a mess there was to clean up, the faster he could be back on a ship. Keir had always been a fastidious bookkeeper so there was hope in that direction.

'The company is doing well at present. So far, we've minimised any financial backlash from Keir's death.' Bowdrie splayed his hands on the polished desktop, slightly hesitant. 'There are plans for growth. Mrs Popplewell has ideas, but I think it would be best if you heard them from her. She's the one at the helm these days and the one you'll need to work with to sort everything out. She is anxious to meet with you.' That was a warning sign if ever there was one. Very well, he'd been warned and he'd be on alert.

'I imagine she is. Without me, her hands have been tied. I am sorry for it. I am sure it's been an added difficulty,' Cullen offered. 'I hope not too much has come to a standstill. I will, of course, help her get things started again.' He meant it as a prompt, an invitation for Bowdrie to fill him in. Hopefully the whole supply chain had not been damaged yet. He and Keir had invested considerable effort in building it, one relationship at a time. But Bowdrie offered nothing. Cullen had the distinct impression Bowdrie was a little bit intimidated by Mrs Popplewell, if not more than a little. It did pique his curiosity about the woman Keir had fallen in love with.

Bowdrie shifted in his seat. 'Yes, well, she can explain all of that to you. I can have her meet you for lunch if that's not too soon. Where are you staying?'

'I don't know yet.'

'Mivart's on Brook Street would be my recommendation. It's not far from Mrs Popplewell's town house and Mivart's prefer long-term guests who stay for a month or more. It will be perfect for you, although there's no coffee room or club room on the premises. You'll have to eat out, but there are several restaurants nearby. I'll have my clerk make the arrangements and a reservation for lunch at two at Verrey's. Women can dine there,' he offered as an aside. 'That will give you time to settle in and unpack.'

He called for his clerk and gave instructions. 'Now that's taken care of, tell me what you've been up to. We have an hour or so before your room will be ready.'

Cullen gave a dry chuckle at the thought of condensing ten years into an hour. How very efficiently English. But perhaps it was possible when so few things changed.

Bowdrie raised his glass in a quick toast. 'Cheers.'

'Yes, cheers,' Cullen replied, offering a silent toast of his own. *Here's to being back.*

Chapter Four

Cullen Allardyce was back. Antonia stepped down from the town carriage at number two hundred and thirty-three Regent Street in front of Verrey's Café Restaurant and took a moment to gather herself. The news had put her emotions into a flurry since it had arrived three hours ago. There was the elation of relief—he was back, loose ends could be wrapped up, things could be finalised. The limbo she'd been navigating could be resolved at last.

But that relief was tempered against the anxiety of knowing such resolution would now require full disclosure on her part about what she'd done with *his* money *without* his technical permission. She was within her rights. *She* wasn't the one who'd ignored the business for years. If he disapproved of the current state of their affairs, he had to acknowledge his part in how they'd got there. He'd also have to acknowledge that she'd done quite well on his behalf in his absence. She'd spent his money, not lost it. There was a difference.

Antonia gave the skirts of her plum ensemble a final smoothing and stepped inside the restaurant. She approached the maître d' in his crisp black and white at the podium. 'I have a reservation at two o'clock for two.

It should be under Popplewell.' It was ten minutes to the hour. She was counting on being the first to arrive. She could stake out her ground.

'Yes, Madame. Right this way, your guest is already here.' Drat. She'd hoped to be early, to be able to study anyone who came through the door. It would have given her a little extra time to form a first impression. The maître d' wound his way through round bistro tables where a few groups of ladies gathered for a late lunch after shopping. Other than that, the heavy lunch crowd that gathered at Verrey's for its *dejeuner à fourchettes* had departed. He led her towards a table near the back wall with its mirrored panels that ran two-thirds its length, the effect making the restaurant look larger.

A man rose as they approached. The first thing she noticed about him was his height. He was a tall man and, up close, a large man. There was breadth to his shoulders and a muscled thickness through his arms that denoted developed biceps lay beneath the fabric of his clothes. And those trousers. They fit rather *well*, too well, something that the cut of his charcoal frock coat emphasised instead of hid.

Although it was shame on her for noticing. Antonia quickly brought her eyes back up, past the blue and white floral pattern on the grey waistcoat, to the sharp features of his face: the razor cut of his jaw, the precision-carved length of his nose and the tawny wildness of his eyes. Those eyes were mesmerising. It would be best not to look at them too long.

On first impression, he was a striking man, a man who possessed both physical and charismatic power to a point that he was almost overwhelming—but just almost. She'd never admit to being overwhelmed by anyone.

In truth, it was hard to know what to make of him. She'd never seen such a man who dressed as a gentleman, but looked more like a gentleman's ancient predecessors. The word feral came to mind, a term oft applied to an animal that had contrived to avoid domestication. The description suited him all too well, this man who had been gone from civilised London for over a decade.

'Mrs Popplewell.' He gave an inclination of his head. 'I'm Cullen Allardyce. I don't believe we've had the chance to meet.' He moved to the empty chair at the table and pulled it out for her. 'I took the liberty of ordering a tea tray so it would be ready when you arrived. But if you'd prefer something else?'

Antonia sat, her senses on full alert. Those manners could not hide the ways in which he was trying to control the interaction; the early arrival to claim the ground, the invitation to sit at the table as if *he* owned it, the ordering of the tea tray—although he'd been careful to balance that with an option. Still, she saw through the efforts.

These were subtle ways in which a man exerted dominance. The politeness of consideration easily created dependence in the recipient. Once people did things for you, you came to expect people would always do things for you and, before you knew it, you could do nothing for yourself. She knew. They were tactics she'd used often enough herself to know their effectiveness.

She leaned forward, a polite smile on her lips as her gloved hand brushed a feathering touch on his arm. It was time to establish some ground of her own. 'I *do*, in fact, prefer something else.' She turned to the maître d' with that same smile, never mind that she usually skipped lunch. This was about the principle of the matter. 'I'll have the *potage au vermicel et le petit pain du beurre* and a pistachio ice for dessert.' The maître d' left them and Antonia wasted no time grabbing the reins of the conversation. 'It is a pleasure to meet you at last, Mr Allardyce. I'm sure the journey was arduous, so your arrival is doubly appreciated.' Given that it had taken almost an entire year to effect.

He nodded. If he'd heard the nuanced critique of his tardiness, he made no sign of it. He merely offered, 'We were delayed longer that I would have liked in Cairo and the winter weather once we reached Europe was not in our favour.' His tawny eyes held hers, his voice sincere and private in its low tones as he changed the conversation. 'I am so sorry to hear about Keir, Madame. He was a true friend to me and he wrote glowingly of you. Your marriage made him happy.'

Antonia felt her throat tighten, the familiar lump form. How was it that after a year, after having officially left mourning behind, such words could still bring her to the brink of tears? There ought to be a moratorium on such reactions. It was hardly fair.

The trays of food arrived and their conversation halted until the dishes had been laid out. The respite was long enough to dislodge the tightness. 'He was a good man, the very best,' Antonia managed to say.

'I do not doubt it,' Allardyce averred. 'How are you getting on? I trust things have not been too difficult despite your need for my signature? If Bowdrie had sent the papers, I would have signed them and sent them back.'

And not come back in person. Antonia didn't miss the rebuke there. He'd not liked being summoned. He no more wanted to be in England than he wanted to be in that suit of clothing. 'If it could have been done, I would have done it. The documents need to be notarised, which requires you being here in person. You are not the only one who has been inconvenienced by these events.'

She would not have him thinking she'd asked for his return on the grounds of an uneducated, selfish whim. 'Bowdrie believes that we have to re-establish the partnership since it is no longer between you and Keir, but between you and a new entity. Myself.' She watched as he polished off his fifth triangle of a ham sandwich. Perhaps it was good after all that she'd ordered on her own. He'd already made quite a dent all by himself in the enormous, tiered tea tray. It would take loaves of finger sandwiches to fill a man his size.

He chewed thoughtfully, his gaze intent on her. 'Do you not agree with Bowdrie?'

Antonia braced herself. They were at the heart of the conversation now, the part that would decide how their relationship together might proceed amicably or otherwise, or not proceed at all. 'I feel there are more options. There was always a chance that we might not find you or that you were dead. In that case, I felt it best we have a contingency. To cede to the idea that we could not move forward without you would be to put ourselves in an untenable position, a ruinous position even, if the worst had happened to you.'

'You mean yourself,' he corrected. 'When you say "we could not move forward", you really mean *you*, singly, could not move forward.' He speared her with a stare, perhaps daring her to respond. She chose to stay quiet, letting her silence press him to continue. He clearly had more to say and she was not disappointed. 'Bowdrie is not a partner; he is an employee even if he was also Keir's friend. He serves at your pleasure. He offers opinions when asked, but he does not decide. There was no "we", Mrs Popplewell. There was only you and now there is me. So, when you use the term "we" from here on out, it means you and me. I think it's important we're precise about our terms. Don't you agree?'

Whatever was feral about his appearance, it did not extend to his mind, which was agile and well trained. Of course, she should have expected that. Keir had thought him a brilliant investor, a man with an eye for all the angles of a market. 'You're as sharp as Keir said you were,' she complimented. It couldn't hurt to sweeten the pot a bit before they went much further.

He sat back in his chair, the delicate teacup looking ridiculous but comfortable in his big hand with its surprisingly long, elegantly slender fingers. 'Sharp enough to notice that only Mr Bowdrie believed you needed to wait for me to move forward. Did you wait?' Those tawny eyes speared her again. 'You don't strike me as a waiting kind of woman, Mrs Popplewell.'

Part of her bristled at that—how dare he make such assumptions when he'd known her for less than an hour?—and the other part of her took fair warning. He was right. His instincts were unerringly accurate on this particular issue.

He set his teacup down and leaned forward, his tawny eyes intent on her. 'So, tell me, Mrs Popplewell, what have you spent my money on? After all, that is what "forging ahead" means in this discussion.'

She hid her surprise at the extreme bluntness of his question and at how quickly he'd decoded the carefully worded conversation. But she would not shirk from offering an equally direct answer. 'Wages, salaries, warehouse rents, cargoes. In short, the usual. I would welcome the opportunity to discuss the cargoes particularly with you so that I understand what the company is doing there. We could cut our overhead by manufacturing goods here at home—' she began to say, only to be almost vehemently cut off.

'No, that's not part of how it works.'

'Then you'll have to explain it to me.' She answered his heated response with her own coolness. 'Perhaps tomorrow we can start going over the accounts in case I've overlooked any nuances. Income from the property holdings continues to come in, as does money from investment dividends, and of course money continues to go out. Now that mourning is behind me, I intend to continue Keir's association with the Prometheus Club. I'd like to be up to speed on that by May when the Season begins and everyone is in town. I will appreciate any introductions you can make and, of course, I will appreciate your presence.'

Although at the moment she wasn't sure that was the

truth. Now that Cullen Allardyce was here she definitely had mixed feelings the longer she thought about what his presence might mean. She'd spent a year doing things on her own and while there was an element of the unknown when one learned as they went, she was now used to being independent, answering only to herself and occasionally Bowdrie. She would have to share now. Would he share? Yet running Keir's businesses was a lot of work. Sharing it with someone who already knew how the business worked would bring its own type of relief.

He frowned. 'The Prometheus Club is ambitious. I'll do what I can.' The non-committal nature of his response worried her. Was it non-committal because, like her, he was still assessing this new territory, still assessing her as she was assessing him? Or was it more? Had he thought of assuming Keir's position in the club? Would that be a first step in putting himself forward as the new face of the company? A first step in forcing her into an invisible role? She took a bite of her newly arrived pistachio ice to cover her worry.

'Is that all you've been doing? Paying wages? Maintaining the status quo?' he queried. 'That doesn't sound like moving forward.'

She wouldn't lie. If they went over the books, he'd discover it anyway and there was no way to hide a building. Antonia met the question squarely. 'There is one more thing. A few months before Keir's death, he'd purchased a building he meant to turn into a department store. I've decided to finish it, as a legacy to him. I can show you tomorrow.'

'A department store?' His brows went up, incredulity evident.

She couldn't decide if his incredulity was out of agreement, disagreement or merely surprise. 'Yes, one to rival the stores in Paris. Keir felt department stores were the way of the future, that eventually they'd come to replace individual shops. They certainly make shopping more efficient by having everything in one place.' *Keir felt*. It was still hard to talk about him in the past tense. She took a final spoonful of her pistachio ice to hide the emotion.

'That's another very *ambitious* undertaking, Mrs Popplewell.' He gave a sardonic lift of a sandy brow. 'Is there anything else you've done with my money in the last eleven months?'

'No, I think that covers it. As I said, we can tour the property tomorrow. I have a meeting scheduled with the site manager.' That seemed a good note to end on. The meal was finished, as was all they could accomplish for today which had essentially boiled down to taking one another's measure. She beckoned for a waiter. 'The bill, please.'

Allardyce leaned towards her and said quietly but sternly, 'Mrs Popplewell, I'll handle lunch,'

'Nonsense, this is a business meeting and you are my guest,' Antonia argued politely, determined not to be beholden or to give up one iota of the control she'd spent the lunch wresting back.

'I am your partner,' he corrected in undertones as the bill was brought to the table.

'Then you may pay your portion,' Antonia countered, 'if you feel that strongly about it.'

'I do.' Allardyce placed some money on the table. 'As apparently do you.'

'It's nice to see we agree on something. Hopefully this is the first of many agreements.' Antonia smiled and rose from the table. He rose with her and she was reminded again of his height, the largeness of him. She allowed him to see her out and wait with her while her carriage was brought around.

He looked out of place here with his longish hair and his busy eyes that constantly darted about the street. The bustling atmosphere made him edgy, she realised. He was having a bit of culture shock perhaps after being away so long. A thousand questions swirled in her mind about that time away. Why *had* he stayed away? Was there family who'd missed him? Keir had never mentioned any. She'd always had the impression Cullen was alone.

Her carriage arrived and she turned to him one last time. 'Mr Bowdrie's note mentioned you were staying at Mivart's. I will call for you there tomorrow at ten. Thank you for meeting me, especially when you've only been home for a few hours.'

He handed her into the carriage, his big hand engulfing her smaller one. 'I am "back", Mrs Popplewell. I am *not* "home".' There was a story there, perhaps answers to her questions, but not today. Or perhaps ever. He was her business partner now. Despite Keir's friendship with him, she needed time to form her own impressions before she decided to mix business with friendship.

Today had been a start, nothing more. As much as she liked to argue with Mr Bowdrie that this partnership was a continuation of something already in existence, it was a beginning, too. Cullen Allardyce was unlike any man she'd yet encountered. Dealing with him would require his very own rule book. One lunch was enough to know that working with him would not be business as usual. Well, she reasoned as the carriage pulled away from the kerb, she'd learned on the fly to manage Keir's holdings. She would learn how to manage Keir's silent partner, as well.

Chapter Five

⌒⌒⌒⌒⌒⌒⌒

Keir's wife would need some managing. Marvels usually did and Antonia Popplewell was definitely a marvel, a golden-haired whirlwind dressed in a deep green ensemble the shade of Tahiti's lush teak forests and, Cullen noted, a shade that also matched her eyes—eyes that sparked with energy. She was all brisk efficiency as she toured him through the establishment that took up numbers twelve and thirteen in Hanover Street. But that didn't stop the man in him from appreciating the sway of skirts up the steps. It was no wonder Keir had been enchanted by her. She was a twin wonder of brains and beauty. Not all men appreciated brains of course, but Keir had.

Inside, Popplewell's Department Store was well underway, though it was still something of a construction zone. They stepped around ladders and tools and cabinets waiting to be installed, but much of the hard work had been done. Individual departments were delineated with crisp wallpapers and protective sheets covered polished hardwoods.

'Let me take you upstairs to the third floor.' The heels of her half-boots clicked confidently on the polished oak stairs with its curved banister and elegantly turned spindles. It was no wonder mild-mannered Robert Bowdrie was intimidated by her. She was one part charming, with those golden English good looks and sparkling green eyes, and two parts unnerving with her shrewd intelligence.

He followed her up the steps, only half listening to her narrative. He was too busy processing the larger message of today's tour. She was absolutely on her game and he knew exactly what her game was: she wanted to show him she'd invested wisely in this project even if there was an emotional attachment behind it. She also wanted to show him that she was entirely capable of managing Popplewell and Allardyce Enterprises.

She understood that both the store and herself were on a trial of sorts. She knew he didn't have to renew the contract. He could walk away, which would create difficulties for her going forward, as Bowdrie had alluded to yesterday. What she didn't know, though, was that he'd not walk away. There was too much at stake, too many people's livelihoods.

This tour had shown him what she wanted. She wanted him to invest in the store and to invest in her, which meant signing the papers and leaving. Interestingly enough, that was what he wanted, too. Sign the papers, leave and let life go back to what it had been when Keir was alive. After Bowdrie's allusions yesterday, though, he wasn't sure those goals were mutually attainable. Without Keir there would be no going back to business as usual.

It *was* possible for *him* to go back, however. It would

require walking away and letting her find her own level until the banks pulled the rug out from under her or until they accepted her. She and the business that he and Keir had built would be the sacrifice required for his freedom, for finally cutting all ties to England. But that did not get her what she wanted—to keep Keir's business alive along with his store. In order for her to have that, he had a sneaking suspicion it would require sacrifice on his part. As if travelling halfway around the world wasn't sacrifice enough already.

'This will be the women's department,' she announced, turning to face him, her arms spread wide to embrace the entire floor. 'Ladies will be able to buy all the accessories necessary to complete an ensemble right here without having to traipse from one store for gloves and to another for shawls or...' she paused slightly, the first slight hesitation he'd heard her make all morning '...undergarments.'

Cullen decided to have a bit of fun with her. Could she be teased? He suspected she could. She was brisk, but not dry. All that charm had to have some humour with it, although she'd not had much to laugh about in the last year. Perhaps she needed to remember. 'You mean corsetry? Chemises? Pantalettes? Stockings? Nightgowns? That sort of thing?' He dropped each word into the conversation as if they were shockingly hot coals.

A hint of rose stained her cheeks, but she was up to the tease. 'Yes, exactly that sort of thing, Mr Allardyce. It's why we've devoted an entire floor to ladies only, so that they might have the freedom and *privacy* in which to shop,' she replied archly, giving him a smug smile that said she'd guessed his intention.

'*Touché*, Madame.' He flashed her a disarming smile and for a moment her eyes danced with a bit of laughter before she turned back to her tour, walking in that fast, brisk clip that matched her tone as she pointed out different areas.

'This will be where women can purchase ready-made gowns, some of which have been imported from Paris. We'll have alterations available on site. Here is where women can be fitted for their gowns just as if they were visiting a modiste on Bond Street.' Men were at work as they passed to install cabinets and shelves done in a soft, feminine ivory.

'This space has a woman's touch imprinted all over it. I can see your hand in all of this.' A good hand it was, too. She had an eye for colour, for creating an environment that would visually appeal and invite. But there was one thing that worried him. 'Women like to shop, Madame. This is all so efficient. It will shorten their pleasurable experience. Perhaps they would prefer to traipse from shop to shop, as you put it.'

She laughed and tossed him a smile full of womanly knowledge. 'Have you ever asked yourself why women like to shop? It's an excuse to get out of the house without needing a formalised reason, like attending an event or going to someone else's house. You do realise how few places there are for a woman to go in London while men have their pick of clubs and restaurants? For women, shopping is an *escape*.' The subject brought a different shade of pink to her cheeks, a passionate pink. This was a subject near to her heart. His friend had married a firebrand.

She wasn't done yet. 'We ate at Verrey's yesterday because it was one of six restaurants a woman can lunch at. One of six in a city this size,' she repeated for emphasis. 'Which brings me to the pièce de résistance of the ladies department.' She stopped before a space currently curtained off and drew back the draperies to reveal little tables and chairs and bakery cases still in need of installing. A bank of tall arched windows overlooking the street was hung with floor-long portières trimmed in elegant gold braid, letting in plenty of daylight.

'Popplewell's café,' she announced proudly. 'Ladies can lunch here or take tea. This way they can shop as long as they like, stop for tea, then shop some more without ever leaving the store. I want to make this one of the finest restaurants in the city, a place for women to come to when they want to escape their homes.'

'I like it.' Cullen nodded. He'd not thought of shopping as an escape before, although he could certainly appreciate the notion of wanting to be somewhere outside of the house. Growing up, school had at least been a chance to leave the archaic strictures of his father's domain. He looked about the space, seeing what it could be, what it was very close to being. 'It's a sound business decision. We want customers to keep their attentions on all things Popplewell. We don't want them leaving the premises to satisfy a need. We want to anticipate and satisfy those needs here.'

Passionate, intelligent, insightful—Antonia Popplewell knew how to make an impression. If he could see why Bowdrie was intimidated by her, he could also see why Keir had been captivated. Unfortunately, there were more Bowdries in the world than Keirs. Now, he also saw why Bowdrie was worried. Intimidated people often tried to squash out that which they feared. His father was like that. The man had spent his life trying to dampen his younger son's democratic zeal and sense of fair play.

She motioned that they should sit at one of the tables. 'You've seen the store, now tell me what you think.'

Cullen stretched out his legs. 'I am impressed that so much has been done under the circumstances. You have had a very difficult year and yet all this has moved forward. That is commendable.' He was not Bowdrie. He was not intimidated by a forthright woman with vision. He would give credit where it was due. 'All that remains is to hire staff, stock shelves and finish acquiring product. You should be able to open in July.'

That earned him a sharply arched brow. 'I mean to open at the end of April in order to take full advantage of the Season.'

He did not want an argument with her, so he said, 'What does your site manager say about that?' In fact, where *was* her site manager? She was supposed to have a meeting with him. Cullen had expected him to have been here when they'd arrived, but they'd completed the tour and there was no sign of him.

Her own response was equally evasive. 'I've got warehouses of cargo just waiting to go on to shelves and an agency that has already begun to hire staff for me. All that remains is getting the fixtures up so the store can be filled. Surely, if we started stocking shelves the first of March, we'd be ready by April.' It was a subtle argument to counter his timeline. Her timeline suited his plans much better. It ensured he could make a spring sailing. But his conscience pricked over his motives for agreeing to it. He felt compelled to offer a word of realism.

'*If* the final details can be completed. There's a lot left to do,' Cullen cautioned. Especially if her site manager made a habit of not showing up for work until noon. He asked the second question that had been prodding at him. 'Do you have a store manager in mind?' With a store this size, she'd need someone with experience. Department stores didn't run themselves. She didn't just need staff, she needed a manager and that manager would need his own department managers. There was a whole hierarchy that needed to be in place for each department.

He noted the subtle squaring of her shoulders and braced himself for her answer. 'I will manage the store.'

'Surely Keir didn't intend to run the store himself?' It was a terrible idea. 'Have you ever managed a store of any size before?' This was precisely the kind of thing Bowdrie had feared. 'Stores are time-consuming jobs that don't keep regular hours. A good store may *look* like it runs like clockwork, but that is an illusion only, a play if you will, for the customers' benefit. It takes considerable effort behind the scenes to make it appear "easy".'

'Have *you* run a store, Mr Allardyce?' she countered smoothly.

'Not one of this size. But Keir had me running his

fabric warehouses down on the docks for several years. Drapers would come to do the shopping for their stores. I know a little something about the concept of "retail".'

She gave a tight, polite smile. 'I appreciate the concern. I assure you, I have nothing but time.'

It was a poignant reminder that for all her charm, she had no husband, no children, to give that time to. It was a reminder also that although she'd approached the execution of the project with level-headed thoroughness, this was above all for her a passion project, a memorial for her beloved husband. To be at the store was akin to being with him, a way to hold on to what she'd lost. Beneath the honour and bravery of taking on such a memorial, Cullen wondered when such bravery became an obsession, when honouring a loved one became an unhealthy pastime of walking with ghosts?

There was rustling at the draperies that cordoned off the restaurant. A worker appeared, knit cap in hand. 'Mr Mackelson is here, ma'am. You wanted me to let you know when he arrived. He is downstairs.'

'Thank you, I'll be there at once.' She rose, but Cullen reached out a hand to stall her. She would think him out of line, but he'd risk it.

'On second thoughts, send Mr Mackleson up here,' he instructed with a stern look that sent the worker hurrying. Once the worker had left, he explained, 'Mackleson answers to you, not the other way around. When you go to him, you give him power. If he shows up for work at noon or whenever he feels like it, you've already given him too much of that.'

'Like showing up for lunch early enough to claim the table first?' she shot back.

He shrugged a shoulder. 'Something like that, indeed.' Then he smiled. 'You were early, too, as I recall, so perhaps you're familiar with the strategy?' That won him a little smile from her just as Mackleson came huffing up the stairs. Cullen took in the beads of sweat on his brow with distaste. A heavy man was a man with no self-discipline. No self-respecting warrior in Ha'apape would ever allow himself to look so slovenly.

Antonia Popplewell stood. 'Mr Mackleson, I wanted a report on the cabinetry for the men's department. When we last spoke, we'd determined they were supposed to be installed this week, but I see they haven't even arrived.'

Mackleson gave a long-suffering sigh. 'They'll get here when they get here. It's difficult to find enough delivery drays to haul a large order like that. I can't do anything about it.'

'We're supposed to open in two months,' she reminded him. 'Every delay creates more pressure the closer the deadline approaches.'

'I'll send an errand boy over again,' Mackleson grumbled. Cullen was not impressed. Something didn't ring true.

'That's not good enough,' Cullen interjected. 'They won't listen to an errand boy. You go yourself. You're the manager on this project. You should take responsibility. Who are the cabinet makers you're using?'

'Weitz and Sons,' Mackleson supplied with a sneer. Cullen knew them. They were very good, high quality. Unless that had changed in the last ten years. They'd done work on his father's town house when his mother had redecorated the library.

Cullen turned to Mrs Popplewell, whose eyes had narrowed to green cat-like slits. 'Did you pay full price?'

'Yes, absolutely. My husband always used them. They're a little more than other companies, but definitely worth it.'

Mackleson looked him up and down with another sneer. 'Who might you be, butting your nose into other people's business?'

'I'm Cullen Allardyce, Keir Popplewell's partner.' Cullen offered a cool smile, enjoying the looks of unpleasant surprise, then worry cross the man's bloated face. 'I'll expect a report by the end of the day and I'll expect that you'll return the money you've skimmed tomorrow morning, or you'll be removed from the job.' Cullen would like to remove the man altogether, but he had no one at present to replace him with. The moment he did, however...

'Now listen here, I haven't taken any money,' Mackleson blustered. 'You can't come in here making accusations like that, I don't care who you are.'

Cullen patiently cut him off. 'Then perhaps you can explain the delay to me. Weitz and Sons deliver their cabinets. It's included in their price. They have their own fleet of drays. Delivery is never a reason for delay with them. The only exception to that is for those who choose to pick up their own orders. Those folks get a fifteen per cent discount,' Cullen countered.

'The reason the cabinets are delayed is that *you* cannot find enough drays to pick them up without eating into the fifteen per cent you pocketed. Mrs Popplewell believes she paid them full price, but I would wager that when we look at the final invoice, it will show that you placed an order that specifies you will pick them up yourself.' Cullen paused long enough to let that sink in, his stare never wavering. 'If I were you, I wouldn't stand around. I'd hustle over to the cabinet makers and change my order and make sure those cabinets are here tomorrow morning.'

At least the man knew good advice when he heard it. Silence stretched long after Mackleson departed, but Cullen could practically *hear* Antonia Popplewell thinking. He didn't expect her to say thank you, but if she was angry, she had only herself to blame.

A thousand thoughts raged through her head, most of them inappropriate for voicing out loud, many of them beginning with *how dare he*. How dare he upstage her in front of an employee, how dare he thrust himself into the middle of her conversation, how dare he take things over. She wanted to rant at him, wanted to yell. But that was Fleur's way, not hers. She'd always prided herself on expressing her anger through more diplomatic means. She'd worked too hard today to show herself in the best possible light as a capable businesswoman. She wasn't going to ruin it with a rant.

Finally, Antonia found a collection of words she *could* say out loud and still maintain a modicum of professionalism. 'Do not ever do that again,' she ground out, pleased she'd kept her voice even when what she really wanted to do was scream. Keir never upstaged her. He'd always been conscious of boundaries.

Cullen gave her one of his sardonic brow lifts. 'Don't do what? Call out a man for stealing from us?' He rose from the bistro chair and began to pace. 'When a man steals from *me*, I have a tendency to want justice. When a man lies to me, I want justice. When a man is late to work and takes liberties with his position, I want justice. He was taking advantage of you and you were either too blind to notice, or you *did* notice and were unable to bring him to heel.'

The 'how dares' started up in her head again. She tamped them down. 'You have no right to speak to me that way. *You* have been absent for the entirety of this year. I have managed quite well on my own.'

'With *my* money,' he reminded her. 'With acting in my name as if you already had my signature *and* approval, two very large assumptions I would not tolerate from you if you'd not been Keir's widow.' If she was used to men backing down in the wake of her simmering fury, she would find that strategy didn't work with him. There was more than mere chivalry at stake. 'You have done well, all things considered, but you will need to do much better. You were not managing him.'

'And to be clear, Mr Allardyce, you are not managing me.' Antonia strode towards the exit and tossed him a look over her shoulder. 'Are you coming? We have books to go over. That's next on our agenda.' She set off down the staircase at a brisk clip, her self-sustaining mantra playing over in her head for strength. She was *not* going to let him get to her.

She was Antonia Popplewell, she'd come this far, she'd survived near-genteel poverty, the cats of the London Season, the tragic loss of a beloved husband, the first year of picking up her life without him. She would certainly survive the intrusion of Cullen Allardyce despite his commanding ways, piercing gaze and broad shoulders.

She *would* get through this. She *would* see the store opened. She would because she knew she would not give up. But she also knew Cullen Allardyce was right. If the store was to succeed, she had to do better. The truth hurt. She'd made some mistakes out of sheer naivety.

Keir had had a lifetime of business experience behind him when he made decisions—she had mere months of self-taught insights to fall back on. He had networks of people to consult. She had no one except Bowdrie, yet she was trying to run a business empire that required that lifetime of knowledge with the meagre experience she had. It was like trying to pull a coach with only one horse when one really needed four.

She'd not realised Mackleson had pocketed part of the cabinet money. She'd not picked up on the reason the delivery hadn't been made. She should have. Such things came with experience and time, neither of which she had at this point. Mackleson had been a thorn in her side almost from day one.

In truth, it was something of a relief to have Cullen deal with him since her methods had failed to obtain the desired results and she was running out of options. It was just one more way in which she secretly felt her inadequacies on this project, despite her efforts to learn quickly.

Her carriage waited at the kerb. She climbed in and a

moment later Allardyce joined her, his big body filling the space completely. 'Were you going to leave without me?' he asked as the carriage lumbered into motion before he was barely seated.

'No.' She wasn't ready for a full-blown conversation just yet. Apparently, Allardyce couldn't take a hint.

'How did you know I'd follow you?' He stretched his legs, his calf bumping against her skirts, making her aware of him on a less business-orientated level.

'Because I asked you to, Mr Allardyce.' She looked out the window, trying to make it plain she didn't want to talk.

'Cullen, please, Antonia,' he insisted. 'Since we are to be partners, perhaps it would be best if we dispensed with the formalities.'

'Fine.'

'But how could you be sure I *was* following? You never looked back to see if I was coming,' he persisted.

She turned her gaze, pinning him with a strong stare. 'I never look back, *Cullen.*' And she certainly wasn't going to start now.

Chapter Six

❦

The woman never stopped. A week spent in her company was more than enough time to confirm it. Antonia Popplewell was a tireless whirlwind of activity, somehow managing to be everywhere all at once, whether it was meeting the new employees sent over by the agency, discussing accounts with him, or taking delivery of the disputed cabinetry, which, Cullen was pleased to note, arrived bright and early the morning following his scolding of Mackleson.

Cullen wondered if she ever slept. Sleepless or not, she called for him with the carriage each morning at nine o'clock sharp at Mivart's, hair in a shiny, perfect, golden twist, her appearance immaculate, her clothing fashionable and above reproach. She favoured fine wools in darker colours—greens, blues, subtle purples—and ensembles with a military cut to the jacket, all designed to project an image of competent confidence—something that either impressed or intimidated, Cullen noted on repeated occasions. The latter continued to worry him. Many men didn't know how to respond to a competent woman in business, as Mackelson's situation proved. It further proved that Bowdrie was right to be concerned.

Did this morning's previously unscheduled meeting have anything to do with those concerns? Cullen stretched his long legs across the carriage and studied her. She'd broken with her usual attire this morning and worn a red and taupe plaid gown cut in the apparently timeless redingote style—a variation of a style he recalled from before he'd left. Taupe-coloured boots dyed to match peeped beneath the beige underskirt where the redingote fell away to allow one to appreciate the full skirt. Her tiny gold earrings were still in place as was her perfect twist.

The earrings and perfect twist wouldn't save her from his curiosity or his conclusion that the meeting with Bowdrie had her concerned. Everything about her signalled unease. She *was* worried. The red plaid was out of character for her, perhaps a hurried choice in order to accommodate Bowdrie's urgent summons. They weren't supposed to meet with Bowdrie until next week, but the solicitor had sent a note this morning that had them reorganising their day. It also had them setting out earlier than their usual nine o'clock.

'Did you eat breakfast?' he asked. Whirlwind that she was, she often forgot to eat. He had to remind her on several occasions to eat lunch and it made him wonder if she regularly ate dinner after she dropped him at Mivart's in the evening. She was pale today and her usual charm was absent. Her thoughts were clearly elsewhere. She'd not said anything beyond 'hello' to him since he'd got in the carriage and her gaze had remained fixedly straight ahead on the empty seat across from her.

'Coffee. That's all there was time for.' Ah, yes, her

coffee. She drank it religiously in the mornings instead of tea and she took it strong and black without any embellishment.

'That's not breakfast. We'll have Bowdrie's clerk go out for something. You need substance.' So did he. He was starving. When she said nothing more, he tried another prompt. 'Is there anything I should know before we get to Gray's Inn? I'd like to be prepared instead of surprised.'

She shook her head and he let it go, knowing it for a lie. He'd know soon. It was enough for now to recognise that any worry on her part meant there should be worry on his. That was how partnerships worked, whether those bonds were ready to be tested or not.

He was right. Bowdrie wasted no time ushering them into his office and shutting the door even though the clerk had been dispatched for breakfast and there was no one to overhear them. Bowdrie took his seat behind the desk and began without preamble. 'It's the bank. They are foreclosing on the loan Keir took out to buy the building. They're asking for payment in full.' He handed Antonia a letter, but he flashed Cullen a look that said, *This is what I've been fearing.*

This was what she'd been fearing—the other shoe to drop. Things had been going too well for the most part. Her emotions roiled, forming a pit in her stomach, her mind raced with consequences and conjecture regarding all she stood to lose if she lost the building at this point. No. She was not going to panic. Antonia took a deep

breath to steady herself. 'That is a twenty-year mortgage. Payments have been made on time. Keir has done
business with them before. They know he's reliable. Did
they say why the sudden change of heart?'

She didn't miss Bowdrie's swift downward glance as
he gathered himself for what was likely to be an unfa-
vourable response. She had her guesses, but she wanted
to hear it from him. 'Because Keir is not at the helm
any longer. Their loan was with him.'

Antonia scanned the letter. 'Why now? Why have
they waited this long to make a fuss?'

Bowdrie fidgeted with a paperweight. 'They wanted
to be fair, to extend you the courtesy of a mourning pe-
riod and a chance to get affairs in order.'

Antonia sat up a little straighter and curbed her temper. 'Fair? What about fair warning? That would have
been fair. What is not is this letter the moment I came
out of mourning.' She leaned forward. 'It is as if they
had a calendar in front of them and were counting down,
which suggests this was premeditated. They didn't just
wake up today and say, "Let's foreclose on the Popplewell building today." They've been planning this
from the start, ever since they'd learned of Keir's death.'
That property, situated as it was so near the Bond Street
shops, was highly lucrative.

Condemnation surfaced amid her emotions. She
should have seen this coming. Keir would have. But Keir
would never have been put in this position simply because he was a man. But she was female and that made
her fair game. 'We can pay them, or we can fight them.

We can take them to court for breach of contract and negotiating in bad faith.'

'Or perhaps there is a third option.' Cullen spoke,
splitting his gaze between her and Bowdrie. 'Please
don't forget I am in the room. I believe I was summoned from the other side of the world for exactly this
situation. They need reassurance that the company is
in good hands. Let them know that I am here, that there
is no cause for alarm.'

'Are you certain? It takes you rather into the public
eye.' Bowdrie looked almost apologetic, concerned in
a way that had nothing to do with the situation at hand.
A glance passed between he and Cullen that Antonia
could not decipher, some secret she was not part of. It
only served to fuel her anger. She was tired of men and
their secret, male-only lives she was not privy to.

This was too much. She was the aggrieved party
here. Antonia turned her anger toward Cullen. 'The
company is in "good hands" because a man is here?
Is that what you mean by giving them reassurances?
A man who has been absent from the business for ten
years is somehow *more* reassuring to the bank than a
woman who has overseen everything personally for a
year. Do you hear the ridiculousness in that?' She was
spoiling for a fight. After a year, her efforts had earned
her none of the respect she deserved.

But Cullen wouldn't bite. 'What I *hear* in my suggestion is *reality*,' he offered coolly.

Antonia wrestled her temper into submission. 'This
is how it begins. This is how you take the company from
me. I won't have it.' This was what she'd feared that first

day at Verrey's: he'd come to install himself in Keir's place and slowly relegate her to the background. She would lose the last piece of Keir she had left. She felt herself begin to shake, dangerous emotion overcoming her. She could not lose him, she could not. She'd fought so hard, so long, and she was almost there. The store was perched on opening in sixty days. Her mind grasped for her mantra.

I am Antonia Popplewell, I've survived the threat of genteel poverty, the cats of London...

She laced her hands together to keep them from shaking. If she could stop trembling, she could stop this wave, this *tsunami* of emotion that threatened the shores of her control.

'Antonia, are you all right?' Cullen's voice was somewhere in the fog.

'I am done here.' She heard her voice as if it came from someone else. She struggled to her feet.

Just put one foot in front of the other, through the outer office, down the stairs, to the carriage.

Her mind knew what to do, but her body was not willing. She made it to the outer office, bumping into the clerk who was valiantly juggling coffees and pastry before she collapsed. Only she didn't fall, not all the way. Arms engulfed her, caught her, lifted her with their strength, their wondrous, warm strength...

Strong, hot coffee. Was there any better smell in the world? Antonia struggled towards consciousness, lured by the aroma. But consciousness was confusing. She was in the carriage. How had she got there? She'd been in

Bowdrie's office... Ah, the bank, the foreclosure, Cullen asserting his blasted authority again as he had with Mackleson. She groaned. She'd let her temper get the better of her in there and the dam of her restraint had broken in front of Cullen Allardyce, whom she was desperate to impress.

She gave another moan of regret. Instead of impressing, she'd collapsed in his arms. Such hysterics would only give him grounds to challenge her authority. Someone shifted on the seat opposite and she knew when she opened her eyes, she'd see Cullen sitting there. She had to face him. She hated weakness, in herself more than anyone else. Optimists couldn't afford weakness or cowardice.

She forced her gaze open and there he was, in that damnably well-tailored new suit of his that showed off those broad shoulders, a reminder that she now knew first-hand what those shoulders were capable of. Genuine concern *for her* was etched on his face.

'Sip this, it's hot.' He passed her a tin cup full of steaming coffee. She wrapped her hands about the cup, the warmth seeping into her.

'Thank you.' Hopefully that would cover it without having to itemise what she was thanking him for.

'Here, there are rolls, too. You need to eat something. Did you have dinner last night after I left?'

'Yes.' But she knew she'd hesitated too long.

'What was it?' Cullen insisted.

'I don't remember.' Maybe she hadn't eaten. Some nights she didn't. There was so much to do and mealtimes were the hardest without Keir, that time of day when everything in their busy world receded and it had been only the two of them.

'Just as I thought.' Cullen gave her one of his raised-brow gazes.

She cleared her throat and took a begrudging bite of the still-warm roll. She tried for normalcy, something to restore equilibrium between them. 'That's a new jacket.'

He gave a self-conscious tug at the lapels of his dark jacket. 'My clothes order is starting to arrive. I can now expand my wardrobe beyond the two suits I came with.' He gave a low chuckle. 'I bought them in Cairo while we were delayed. They served their purpose.'

She hadn't known that. 'You came to London with only two changes of clothes?' She'd assumed he'd arrived with trunks, multiple trunks.

'One doesn't need a great many clothes in the South Pacific, although we've yet to convince the Europeans there of that. They insist on wearing all of this folde-rol.' He gave another tug of his lapels for emphasis this time. 'In the heat, it's downright absurd.'

It was on the tip of her tongue to ask what he did wear, but she thought better of it. Her mind had been surprisingly captivated by the words *'one doesn't need a great many clothes in the South Pacific'* and her stomach had given a queer, not unpleasant flip, at the images of Cullen Allardyce sans shirt and waistcoat. Was his chest as tanned as his face? Were golden hairs sprinkled along a tanned, muscled expanse of forearm? What about the rest of him? Did not needing a 'great many clothes' involve wearing something less than trousers?

She rapidly took another bite of the roll. She desperately needed to eat if that was where her thoughts were headed. No doubt those thoughts were brought on by multiple factors: stress, the lack of food, the growing list of questions she had about him and the amount of time they'd spent together.

She'd not spent so much extended time with another outside her family since Keir had died. The closest connection she had was her weekly meetings with Bowdrie. But Bowdrie never said anything interesting like not needing clothes. She knew without doubt in all the time she'd known him she'd *never* been tempted to imagine Robert Bowdrie without even a single article of clothing missing. But such imaginings were definitely a temptation when Cullen was around.

'I have an idea.' Cullen reached for a roll of his own, apparently satisfied she'd keep eating without his vigilant prompts. 'Let's take today off.'

She stopped in mid-chew and stared at him. Was he insane? 'The bank wants to foreclose on the store, didn't you hear Mr Bowdrie?' They had appointments to make, they had bankers to meet with, plead with, and if that failed, they had to go over the accounts and assess what it would mean to pay the loan in full. 'This is not a day to take off.'

'On the contrary, I think it's the perfect day to take off.' As usual, Cullen was infuriatingly unbothered by her hard words. Just once she'd like to get a rise out of him. He didn't strike her as a passionless man or a dry man, but he was definitely the master of his emotions. He gave nothing away. 'We've worked literally since the day I arrived.' He paused, his expression stern. 'When was the last day *you* had off?'

She didn't answer and Cullen gave her a smug *told-you-so* smile. But he misunderstood. It wasn't that she didn't remember. She *did* and it was simply too painful to say it out loud. She knew the answer. February the fourth, 1852. And she'd spent the evening playing whist with Fleur and Emma instead of being with Keir, thinking just how much she'd needed a girls' night. Instead, it turned out she'd wasted the last four hours of Keir's life being away from him.

'We've taken care of work, Antonia, but we've not taken care of ourselves,' Cullen was saying. 'It didn't occur to me until the bank's letter today that we should mark the anniversary of Keir's passing. I know I arrived after the official date, but I haven't been out to pay my respects. I would like to. He was more than a mentor to me, he was a friend—the best friend I'd ever had. A father figure to me, too, at times. I feel badly that I didn't think to go earlier.'

He reached for her hand and she was acutely conscious of his grip, warm and strong like the arms that had held her and the chest that had cradled her. 'Will you come with me? I would like your company. I would like to do this together.'

It occurred to her that she'd like his company as well. She nodded and drew a deep breath. She'd had flowers sent to the grave on the anniversary, but it was her secret shame that she'd not gone last week on her own. She had buried herself in work instead, telling herself that the work at the store was time-sensitive and she couldn't afford the day away. She'd been afraid if she went, she'd fall apart and not be able to put herself back together. But if Cullen was there, she'd have a reason to keep a rein on her grief. She could not afford another breakdown. This morning had been a close call.

He smiled and released her hand. 'To Kensal Green, then.'

Chapter Seven

Kensal Green made death look beautiful with its tree-lined avenues and elegant tombstones, a place of serenity located in the Chelsea–Kensington borough off the Harrow Road, at least three-quarters of an hour by carriage from Gray's Inn. There was plenty of time to prepare herself and yet her trepidation grew as they passed through the triumphal arch made of Portland stone that guarded the entrance. The carriage could go no further out of respect for the dead.

Cullen handed her down and she drew her mantle close against the chill wind. It had been grey and gloomy the day she'd buried Keir, too, a day not unlike this one. Cullen offered his arm and she took it, grateful for the chance to hold on to something, to someone.

The day of the funeral it had been her father's steady arm. Her brother was posted in Canada and had been unable to come. She had not cried at Keir's committal, understanding that any sign of weakness would be held against her by those in attendance. The funeral party had been made up of her father and mother and some of Keir's chief business partners, primarily the Duke of Cowden and members of the Prometheus Club. They would be watching her, judging her, and she'd need their approval.

'It's a beautiful place, very peaceful,' Cullen commented in hushed tones as they strolled the centre pathway, either side lined by Gothic-styled monuments of the wealthier citizens interred there. 'It's rare to see so many trees and so much *green* in town.' He was trying to put her at ease. It was kind of him. The optimist in her wanted to lean into that kindness, but her usual optimism had been tempered a bit this year. She'd been forced to ask questions about people's motives and forced to admit that not everyone had the best interest of others in mind.

She had to ask that question now in regard to Cullen Allardyce. What did *he* want? She was acutely aware that they'd not yet signed the partnership papers. After today's setback with the bank, perhaps he might not sign at all, perhaps he might rethink his words in Bowdrie's office. He'd seemed, at the time, quite willing to advocate against paying the foreclosure. Perhaps after further thought he'd change his mind and decide it was too much trouble. That worried her. She would be hard-pressed to buy him out and pay off the loan in full simultaneously.

'Keir is just over here.' She steered them off the main path towards a grassy space beneath a spreading oak. Her wreath of flowers was draped over the stone cross that topped his grave marker. The roses were already dried and withered, a reminder of how futile her gesture was.

Cullen studied the grave marker. She watched his eyes move over the big, etched letters.

Keir Catton Popplewell
Beloved Husband

Would he think she'd chosen rightly? Should she have chosen 'businessman' or 'friend of the Empire'? Goodness knew he'd made England enough money alongside his own. Cullen gave her a small smile. 'Beloved husband. He would have liked that. He had no family when I met him, except for the family he'd made with Luce and Griffiths, and then perhaps with me if I am not too bold to suggest it.'

'You are not. You were dear to him.' Her throat gave a tell-tale tightening. How odd to be offering comfort, assurances, to this man beside her, who was perhaps seven years her senior, who exuded strength and confidence as if he were untouchable. But in this moment, he was the vulnerable party relying on her for a change. It was the least she could do after what he'd done for her this morning.

'Thank you for that, Antonia.' Cullen bowed his head and she gave him a moment of privacy with his thoughts. For a fleeting second, she was jealous of those thoughts, of those memories that he had of Keir that she didn't. What did he know of her husband that she did not? Shouldn't a wife know a husband better than anyone? After a while, he raised his head. 'Did Luce and Griffiths come to the funeral?'

She pressed a gloved hand to her mouth as the terrible realisation hit her. 'You don't know, do you? No one told you.' Because that someone should have been her. She was his only point of contact to Keir, outside of Bowdrie. This was what they should have talked of that first day at Verrey's. But she'd done what she'd been doing for the last year—burying herself in work, moving forward, never looking back, trying to ignore what was behind her.

'What don't I know?' He looked seriously alarmed. As well he should be. Today had been full of alarming surprises for him: the foreclosure, the loan, and now this.

Antonia gathered her strength. She never talked about *it*, but she must talk about it now. There was no one else. 'They were all killed in the same accident.'

He had her arm again, leading her to the stone bench between the oak and the grave, his voice quiet and coaxing. 'Can you tell me about the accident?'

'It was more of a disaster than an accident. We had all gone to Holmfirth in the west Yorkshire dales, to look at a mill Luce wanted to buy. He wanted Keir's opinion, and Adam Griffiths came along to look into the environmental situation. There'd been concerns before about the safety of the dam upriver,' Antonia said slowly, but the more she talked, the more her words became like the River Holme, surging against the confines of that dam until the walls of her restraint could no longer hold them.

They flowed in torrents as she recounted how the flood had destroyed Water Street, how eighty-one people had been killed, how whole mills had been washed away, the mangled machinery she'd seen left in the streets the next morning, haphazardly deposited by the river, how the river had raged—she'd never heard water make such sounds.

'They took me to see his body after it was recovered.' Her voice softened now, her own rage receding and with it her strength. There was a tremble in her voice when she spoke next. 'He'd fought hard. He'd struggled against the river. His hands were torn, there was a gash in his forehead.'

Cullen's hand wrapped around her own at the first sign of trembling. Perhaps he was trying to stave off a recurring episode of this morning's tears. 'You don't have to say any more,' he offered quietly.

But she did. Now that she'd started, there was so much more to say. 'I should have been with him,' she whispered her shame. 'We had gone to Holmfirth because I'd encouraged it. Yes, Luce had invited him, but Keir had been reluctant to go. We'd just acquired the store and we'd been working non-stop on renovating the interior. He wanted to stay in London and keep working. But I pushed for it.' It was the first time she'd admitted it out loud. 'I was selfish. I was tired of sharing him with the store.'

She shot a glance at Cullen, watching his face for a reaction. 'We were trying for a child. It had been…difficult.' She would not say more in that regard out of respect for Keir's memory. She would not tell Cullen her husband had been semi-impotent at the end.

'We were trying for that family Keir had so desperately wanted and I thought some time away from London would help. Instead, it killed him. *I* killed him. If I'd let him do as he wanted, he'd have stayed in London. He would be alive right now.' She cleared her throat against the rising emotion. She needed to stop talking, but she couldn't and it was going to be her undoing. 'But he did as *I* wanted and he died for it.

'All I have left of him now are his dreams—his businesses, his store, his project in the South Seas with you—and if I lose those things I will have failed him in both life and death. I will have failed him entirely.' She choked on the last word. It was too late to save herself. Emotion rose fast and hard, an irresistible siege. Oh, God, she was going to lose the fight this time. But she was not alone. Cullen Allardyce's arm was around her, drawing her close, letting her head bury itself in his shoulder, her fists clinging to the lapels of his jacket as the sobs racked her.

She had not cried like this since those early days in Holmfirth, sitting by Mrs Parnaby's lace-curtained windows, staring into nothing. The cry left her exhausted, purged. She drew a long, cleansing breath. 'I've soaked your coat.' She straightened, finding herself reluctant to leave the shelter of his arms. He'd been patient. He'd not offered platitudes or tried to argue with her feelings.

'It will dry.' He smiled and withdrew a white handkerchief. 'And so will you. Feel better?'

'I'm not sure.' She took the handkerchief and dabbed at her eyes. It smelled of him, all vanilla and spice and warmth. 'I must apologise that I've gone to pieces on you twice today, but I fear I might do it again.' She offered a watery smile and a half-laugh. 'I've been afraid that if I let myself feel too much, I'll just go on feeling, hurting, and I'd never pull myself together. Seems like maybe I was right.'

'Perhaps crying it out is the best way to hold yourself

together. You can't *not* feel, Antonia. I think no less of you for it,' he assured her. The optimist in her wanted to believe him.

She drew a deep breath, trying to find her centre, still feeling the remnants of her tears. 'There is no crying in business, though,' Antonia reminded him. 'Everyone always says women are too emotional. It is the chain they bind us with.' And now she'd proven it.

'This isn't business, though, is it? This is life and I think grief is a way of savouring life, of commemorating it, as long as it doesn't drag us down.' He gave a nod towards the wreath. 'You were here last week?'

She shook her head. 'No, I sent the flowers, but I couldn't bring myself to come. It was cowardly, I know.'

'But then I made you come; I am sorry,' Cullen said quietly.

'I needed to come. I just didn't need to come alone.' She knew it was true the moment she spoke the words. 'How are you doing? I must apologise for not having told you sooner. It didn't occur to me that you didn't know. I feel horrible about it. I didn't stop to consider *your* feelings, what it must have been like for you to get the news.' She apologised, but he was quick to absolve her. She wasn't sure she deserved that.

'I had the whole journey in which to come to terms with it. I didn't have details, true. But dead is dead. I had months to process that. Although, I do admit, being here today makes it more final, more real.'

It was her turn to offer comfort. She reached for his hand. 'He was your friend.'

'He was also my family, just as you said.' He offered

her a smile and something akin to peace began to unfurl within her.

He'd been generous today, this man who was a stranger to her, known to her in name only and little else beyond her husband's affections, until last week. She wanted to reciprocate as a show of her gratitude. What could she offer him in return? She'd needed to talk—perhaps he needed the same? 'Tell me a story about you and Keir. How did you meet?'

'Did he never tell you?' Cullen laughed. 'I suppose not. It's maybe not a tale for a wife's ears.' It felt good to reminisce like this, with someone who'd known Keir. Admiral Connant had been a polite companion on the voyage and certainly had done his best to commiserate over his loss, but Connant had not known Keir.

He'd talked *to* Connant about Keir, but there'd been no one to talk about him *with*, no one who knew what he'd looked like, who knew how he laughed—a big expansive sound that started from deep within him and warmed anyone who heard it—who knew all the ways in which he had championed the underdog because he'd been an underdog, too, before he'd climbed his own way up the ladder to a fortune. Of course, Keir had already been in possession of a goodly amount of that fortune when Cullen had met him.

'Now you have to tell me. With a lead like that, my curiosity knows no bounds,' Antonia prompted. Her own eyes were shining with something besides tears. That gladdened him. Her grief today had been hard to watch, not because he knew her that well—he'd only known her a week—but because of her strength. What a year she must have endured—a year beyond his imagining. Perhaps she needed to hear a story as much as he needed to tell one.

'If you're certain you want to hear it? Don't say I didn't warn you. Prepare to be scandalised.' He teased a smile from her before he dropped his opening line. 'We met in a brothel in Wapping. We were both there on business, but different kinds of business, you might say. This was before he'd met you.' He gave her a wink. 'Don't worry, Keir was there to try to persuade the owner to sell. It was down in the London Docks area and Keir wanted a place he could use as an office and a kind of club where his buyers who came to warehouses could retreat to, a place where he could meet with his shippers and Captains without having to go very far.'

'I know that place. He told me about it. His acquisition was successful. Now it's the Captain's Club.' She cocked her head. 'And what were you doing there?' she enquired with mock solemnity. 'Distributing religious tracts?'

'Of course,' He grinned. 'Should I be hurt that you assume I was up to no good?'

She gave him a sly look, proof that she was feeling better. 'A young man in a brothel? You forget I had a London Season. I know what young men get up to.'

'I was half shot on gin and on my way to being entirely squiffed. I ran into a man and spilled my drink on him. Fisticuffs ensued. I won the brawl, but ended up being tossed out on my backside into the alley. I was too drunk to realise the danger of that. I ended up dozing off, only to be awakened by street thugs going through my pockets and none too gently.

'Let's just say, there were knives involved. One of those knives might have been more "involved" if Keir hadn't come along and taken the pair of them on. He chased them off and sobered me up. But the thugs had my money, my watch, anything of value. He'd seen me fight and offered me a job as a night watchman at one of his warehouses.'

He smiled at the memory and spread his hands on his knees. 'And that was the beginning of our friendship.' He hoped there wouldn't be too many questions. Like what had he been doing at the brothel? Why hadn't he simply gone home after the incident in the alley? He just wanted her to focus on Keir. His own past needed to remain there for as long as it could.

'You didn't stay a watchman for long, though, did you?' That was a safe question and he was glad to answer it.

'Keir was smart. He'd made me a night watchman to keep me out of the brothels. I didn't have time to visit such places, working nights. But being a night watchman gave me a lot of time to study what he did there and a lot of time to think. He also saw that I was good with people.

'Soon, he asked me if I wanted to work the warehouse, unload fabrics, assist with some sales. Pretty soon, I took over the sales and I saved my wages until I had enough to go to Keir and ask to buy a small share in one of his cargoes.' That had been the beginning of his own fortune and their partnership.

'You are exactly the kind of person Keir liked to help, someone who needed their potential polished, who just needed a chance. You are a credit to him.' Her green eyes were shining and Cullen felt a twinge of guilt. What she said was true. But he knew how she viewed it—that Keir had taken a young man with limited prospects because of his birth to the lower orders and made him into something. But this didn't seem the moment, after all they'd gone through today, to redirect those assumptions. His prospects had been limited by birth, he'd argue, but just not in the way she thought.

'You're a credit to him, too,' Cullen said, changing the conversation. 'I'd left to handle the South Seas venture before he even met you.' The less said about why he'd left for the South Seas the better. He quickly directed the conversation towards her. 'But when he mentioned you in letters, it was clear marriage made him happy, that *you* made him happy. I'd not seen many happy marriages in my lifetime, so I was doubly pleased for him.'

Perhaps even jealous that Keir Popplewell, self-made man, had the one thing that Cullen Allardyce, son of a marquess, born to have access to all nature of worldly riches if he wanted them—which Cullen did not—would never have. Love and loyalty could not be bought, not really. 'You are everything he said you were.'

Part of him had to admit that if it was possible to be envious of a dead man, he was—envious of what Keir had had. Objectively speaking, Antonia Popplewell was a rare gem, not that such a moniker worked in her favour. London often didn't know what to do with rare gems that didn't fit into the niches carved out for them.

'I'm hungry. That roll didn't last long. Why don't we find some lunch?' His stomach rumbled as if on cue. He laughed at the intrusion. 'I confess I miss Tahiti when it comes to food. It literally just hangs on the trees, waiting to be picked at leisure. When I was hungry, I picked a breadfruit, a banana, or a lime and just like that I had a meal. But here…' He rolled his eyes. 'Here, I have to really look for it and think ahead.'

'Tahiti sounds wonderful. Food at your fingertips instead of wondering if a restaurant will serve a woman without ruining her reputation.' She gave a wry chuckle. 'Lunch sounds good, though.' She rose and brushed at her skirts. 'We can discuss the foreclosure over warm soup.'

He put a hand on her arm in polite correction, a gesture he found himself making often where she was concerned. There were definitely rough edges between the two of them, each of them preferring their own ways of doing things. 'No, not today. No business. Let's have lunch, take a walk in the park. You can show me what's new in London since I left. No business today, just… friendship. I think Keir would have wanted that: for you and me to be friends.'

She put a hand over his and offered a soft smile. 'I think he would have wanted that, too.'

Chapter Eight

They dined at the Bristol on Prince's Street, savouring the quiet atmosphere and the warm soup after the briskness of the cemetery. She laughed as Cullen surreptitiously glanced at the nearby tables to be assured no one noticed them, then quietly put his hands about the curves of his bowl. He closed his eyes and gave a pleasant sigh.

'Is London so cold you're reduced to stealing the heat of a soup bowl?' she asked with a smile at this little slice of vulnerability he displayed.

'Yes, it absolutely is. I don't think I've been warm since the ship put into Marseilles and it's only got colder, greyer, damper and wetter ever since. The weather is more miserable than I recall.' He gave an exaggerated shudder. 'How *ever* do you endure it?'

'The promise of an English summer springs eternal.' She laughed at the doubting look he gave her. 'Have you forgotten how lovely June and July can be with strawberries to pick and wildflowers in the fields?' The memory was enough to make her smile and her words ran away with her before she realised where they were headed. 'We have a small estate in Surrey, not far from Emma and Garrett's.'

She paused, realising what she'd said. Her tone quieted. There was no 'we' any more. The estate was hers now, just hers. She reached for a smile to cover her gaffe. 'I should have you out when the strawberries are in bloom.' That only made it worse. An unmarried woman had just invited an unmarried man to her summer estate. She was making a hash of this. First, she'd invoked memories of Keir and then she'd invited a man to visit her.

Cullen looked uncomfortable, further proof she was making a hash of this. He shifted in his seat. 'June seems a long way from now when one looks out the window and sees all this rain.'

She drew a deep breath and made an ungainly about-turn in the conversation. She tried for some teasing of her own. 'Tell me about the weather in Tahiti. It must be outstanding indeed if it can erase the pleasures of an English summer. Perhaps talking about it will warm you up.'

As hungry as she found herself for soup and fresh bread, she was hungrier still for some piece of him, this man who'd met her husband in a brothel, whom her husband had lifted up and made into a successful business partner. The longer she was with him the more of a mystery he became or perhaps it was the more intrigued *she* became.

He gave her a grin and she wondered if the grin was for her or for his memories. 'The sky is impossibly blue. It's the colour of the deepest, brightest sapphire you've ever seen. The clouds are white, fluffy pillows. The water is a hundred shades of blue, green, teal, turquoise and aqua.' He leaned forward as if to impart a secret, tawny eyes dancing. She couldn't help but hang on his every word, and every picture those words painted. 'And it's warm. The water is warm, the beach is warm. But there's coolness, too. There are lush teak forests in the hills and mists in the mountains.'

'And food hanging from tree limbs?' she asked. 'What does breadfruit taste like?'

He gave a low chuckle. 'Would you believe me if I said it tastes like bread? It's not untrue. I think it tastes like a cross between bread and potato.'

'What do you do all day?' Her soup lay cooling and untouched, forgotten.

'Our days are busy, but not busy like here. There are no appointments, no bustling around. There are canoes to make, food to gather. People to meet with it.' He gave a grimace. 'European presence has politicised the clans, but that's a story for another time, not today.'

'You mentioned that you swim?' she prompted, unwilling to break the spell that wrapped their little table.

'Every day. We snorkel and dive, too.'

We. She noted that. It was the second time he'd used the term. She was curious. Who was we? She noted the presence tense as well. It was not 'we snorkelled and dived' as if those were activities relegated to the past, but activities in the present, activities he might resume shortly. But like the politicising of the clans, that, too, seemed a topic for another time.

'There are some divers who can go to extraordinary depths, down into the ocean where the sun doesn't reach. Pearl divers,' he said admiringly. 'There are others who are cliff divers, who jump into the ocean from great heights.'

'Did you? Jump off cliffs? Or dive deep in the ocean?' She couldn't resist the question.

He shook his head with a laugh. 'I don't do the deep-sea diving. That is a dangerous art. I do enjoy cliffs, though.' He grinned. 'It is like flying. But it's the water I like best, the canoeing, the swimming, the snorkelling. The fish are beautiful. They're blue and yellow and orange, such vibrant colours. Not like here where all the fish seem grey and silver. Some of the fish are very small, they're for beauty, not for eating. The tangs and the angel fish are too tiny for anything more than ornamentation. It's a beautiful world under the sea.' His wistfulness was obvious.

'You miss it.' Antonia said gently.

'Yes, I do miss it.' Their eyes met and held for a long moment, breaking only when the waiter came to remove the cold dishes.

Antonia looked around, realising for the first time the restaurant was empty. 'Oh, dear, I'd not realised it was so late. I fear we're on the verge of wearing out our welcome.' The waiters lined the wall, trying to hide their impatience over their two lingering guests, no doubt eager to get ready for the dinner guests.

'Perhaps it's a good time to take that walk we talked about.' Cullen rose and held her chair, offering her his arm, his gestures natural as was her own response to them. They'd not started this morning with such ease, but that ease was there now, a product of good food and even better conversation between them. It was something of a surprise to realise over the course of the day, they had become…amicable.

The optimist in her found the concept pleasing even as the caution she'd been forced to adopt over the last year warned her to be wary of amiability. He had more to gain from it than she did. But optimism won the day. Today there was no harm in walking beside this man who'd known her husband and enjoying his stories, enjoying his company. There would indeed be time to consider the foreclosure matter tomorrow.

They strolled Prince's Street on the way to the park at Hanover Square near the town house. He turned the collar of his coat up against the chill and she laughed, remembering his descriptions of the warm weather and the turquoise waters. There was nothing warm about a damp February afternoon in London.

'We don't have cliff diving, but we do have Berlioz,' she offered as they passed the rooms at number four Hanover Square. 'He performed last year and he's likely to direct something again this spring. England seems to agree with *him*.' The emphasis implied that she'd been keeping track of all of his dissatisfaction. He didn't like the food—it wasn't readily available; he didn't like the clothes—there were too many of them; he didn't like the weather—it was too cold. She slid him a sideways look, braving another question.

'Does *nothing* in London agree with you?' It was hard to imagine someone not finding *something* to like about one of the greatest cities in the world. She might not like the fog and soot, but she did love the fashions, the theatre, the balls and parties. At least she'd used to when Keir had squired her about.

He did not answer her directly. He favoured her with a thoughtful smile. 'Perhaps it is that I like Ha'apape more. I left behind a whole life in Tahiti to come here. I left a way of living that I appreciated, I left behind friends who are as dear as family to me. I left behind who I was to become someone I haven't been for a very long time.' He cocked his head to look at her. 'I even left behind my name.' She gave him a considering look, not quite following the last comment.

'In Ha'apape, I was called Kanoa, the Seeker,' he explained.

'Because you travel between the islands seeking goods or because you were looking for something more, ah, philosophical?' she ventured, intrigued by the idea of having a new life, a life apart from the one she had now, of having a different name.

'That's very astute. Both, I think. Rahiti's father gave me the name when he claimed me as an adoptive son.' She could see that pleased him, that he took pride in being this man's son. 'Rahiti is my best friend in Ha'apape. He's my brother in all ways but blood. He was married right before I left. There were canoe races to celebrate the wedding.'

The canoe races fascinated her and it took two rotations of the Hanover Square park to exhaust the topic. It was interesting to hear about the different positions in the boat, the importance of the tempo, of reading the waves and the tide. She'd never considered such things before. But the real treat was in watching his face light up as he spoke, the quickened cadence of his words as his own excitement grew.

This was *his* world and he was giving her a rare glimpse into it, into the things he did, how he lived, and the people he lived with, the *people* he cared for. Rahiti, Rahiti's mother and father. There'd been his words: *'I left a whole life behind.'* He certainly had. It begged the question of who else had he left behind? His friend had married. Had Cullen left behind someone who mattered to him in that way?

She did not dare ask for fear of having to examine her reasons for wanting to know and because it seemed too private, too personal of a question to ask despite the progress they'd made today. Or perhaps it needed to be asked for that very reason, because of the events of today.

He'd held her in his arms. He'd offered her his strength when she had none. He'd offered her physical human comfort, the one thing she'd craved in this year of loneliness; to be touched, to be held, to be comforted with another's body and not just empty words. And now a deep part of her didn't want to share that comfort, didn't want to think of others he might have comforted in the same way. That part of her wanted those moments to belong to her, to them, alone.

The more rational part of her said it didn't matter. If there was or had been someone, that person was thousands of miles away and he was here, her business partner now. Part of *her* world.

Your world is a place he despises, the voice in her head prompted unkindly. *He is here under duress, out of loyalty to Keir. Don't forget that. And don't forget your-self. You have a business to protect and sustain. Just a few days ago you were worried he might want to usurp you and now you're thinking the two of you might be-come friends.*

They reached the park gate and he ushered her out on to the pavement beyond the park. She felt deflated at the realisation their afternoon had come to an end. 'I'll see you to the town house, Antonia. I've taken up enough of your time this afternoon with stories of home.'

'I enjoyed the stories very much.' She wanted to pro-test. An evening of loneliness stretched before her, stark and empty—emptier than usual when compared to the company of today. 'Today started badly, but I think it's ending very well. Thank you.'

The town house was not far from the park and they reached her steps quickly. 'I want to thank you again for today.' For a moment she thought of inviting him in. But to what end? Her motives seemed amorphous and yet concerning to her. She had no business-based reason to invite him. A woman simply did not invite a man in without creating the wrong impression. There was an awkward pause while she looked for the right words to express her appreciation. 'Thank you most of all for your friendship, today.'

He bent over her gloved hand and kissed her knuckles in a show of gallantry that was only half playful. 'The pleasure was all mine.'

Then she climbed the steps and faced the long eve-ning ahead, already counting the hours until nine o'clock the next morning, when she could be with him again.

Chapter Nine

The offer of friendship to a woman was always a reckless proposition even when offered with the best of intentions. To offer friendship to a woman who was also one's business partner *and* the widow of one's best friend was perhaps dangerous living in the extreme. It combined proximity with memory and the combination evoked that most deadly of ingredients: emotion.

Cullen rolled to his back and tucked his hands behind his head, looking to the dark ceiling of his room for answers, for sleep, and, if neither of those were available, solace. He was used to dangerous living. Taking risks was what he did best. It was the feelings that came with this particular risk that he was not ready for. His risks were usually calculated with a clear understanding of what he stood to lose or gain. But this risk was neither calculated nor clear. This risk was motivated solely by emotional factors, all of which could be summed up in the phrase: this is what Keir would have wanted.

Now, he was lying here, unable to sleep because the driving force behind his reckless offer today was leading towards costly consequences. Everything he offered to do for Antonia came with complications. First, it pushed his return to Tahiti back, which led to the second complication: the longer he stayed in London, the more risk there was of his presence here becoming known to certain circles.

For himself, he did not care one iota if the old scandal was unearthed, but there would be consequences for those associated with him. He had to consider the potential damage it might do to Antonia and to the business.

That was *not* the sort of help Keir would want him to provide. Yet Keir would not want him to abandon Antonia or their venture. Keir would want him to see that the business they'd put in place to help victims of colonisation survive economically in a world that oppressed them politically was taken care of, too. That venture was as much Keir's legacy as the department store was. To abandon it would be like abandoning Keir himself and their friendship.

Returning to Tahiti before everything was settled was not the way to repay that friendship. Yet he wasn't sure that staying was appropriate repayment either. But perhaps Keir hadn't realised those two goals might well prove to be mutually exclusive. If Cullen wasn't in Tahiti the latter would suffer. In the immediate future, the solution was obvious. He needed to remain in London. If he wasn't here in London, Antonia and the business would both suffer. He couldn't be in both places at once.

The trick was in deciding how long he could stay here without undermining the good his presence could do. Part of him was relying on the old scandal as an escape route. He could use it as an excuse to leave, but what happened if it could be quelled? Or if it didn't surface?

Would the 'foreseeable future' become a slippery slope towards never being able to leave? Antonia needed him here whether she wanted to admit it or not.

The events of the last week had shown her strengths as well as the chinks in her armour. She was being asked to do the impossible—to run a business she had little experience with, to undertake a project where she was learning as she went and adjust to life without her husband. Any one of those items would be a tall order. But for her, impossible included futile. Yesterday's ultimatum from the bank suggested that no matter how hard she tried and no matter how much success she had, it would never be enough to satisfy banks and investors.

If there was one thing Keir had taught Cullen about business it was that successful businessmen had networks. No one went it alone. Yet Antonia was being forced to take that route. It was a route destined for failure at worst, limited success at best. It was not a route that could sustain the holdings Keir had put together. But that did not mean he was the man to hold it all together. If the old scandal surfaced, if it still had teeth, he would not be an asset to Antonia.

Cullen sighed and slid his gaze towards the long windows he'd left uncovered. Outside on the street, he could hear the early morning noise of London waking up— milk wagons rattling with their tin cans, vendors trundling their carts towards the markets. If he got up now, he could go for a run, something the hotel staff thought he was crazy for doing, but something he needed desperately. He and Rahiti used to run the beaches together and, since there was no place to swim in the middle of

London during winter, he had to settle for running the dark morning streets in a pair of loose trousers. He'd come back and do his exercises in his room.

He didn't want to return to Tahiti softened by city living. He'd lose his tan while he was here—there was no real sun in England to speak of—and he'd already cut his hair, but he was determined not to lose his strength. Perhaps it was vanity, but he was quite proud of the body he'd acquired while abroad. Swimming, running, canoeing in the outriggers, had all left their mark for the better on him.

There were, of course, places a gentleman could join that featured opportunities for fitness, like Jackson's boxing salon—if it was still open. Keir had mentioned in one of his early letters that Jackson had died. But Cullen was not interested in blatantly announcing his return to all and sundry. He'd avoid that as long as he could. Which might not be very long. Still, he took comfort in knowing that bankers and merchants didn't run in the same circles as peers. He had some anonymity yet.

Cullen levered himself out of bed with a grunt and reached for the trousers he liked to run in, a specially made pair out of flannel. The tailor had thought him crazy.

Being back in London had personal implications as well for him aside from the scandal. The longer he was here, the less likely it was that he could avoid his family. His father *would* hear he was in town, as would his mother, and they'd want what they'd always wanted from him: to settle down, to take his place in the marquessate beside his brother, the heir, do his duty to ensure that old, antiquated traditions were preserved. Especially now that his brother was still childless.

Cullen reached for his shoes. They were difficult to run in, but there was no question of running barefoot any more than there was the possibility of steering his mind away from thinking about the scandal that had earned him the appellation of notorious and had been responsible for sending him to the South Seas. London had a memory like an elephant. If he was in town, the scandal was in town. He'd prefer that scandal not to surface just yet.

Outside, he shivered in the cold. That wouldn't last long. He'd work up a sweat soon enough. He broke into a jog up Brook Street and headed towards Hanover Square, then over to Hanover Street. He'd made it a habit to run past the store. His mind plotted his route and ran through his day. After exercising, it would be time for breakfast and then Antonia would call for him.

They were visiting the warehouses today, his old workplace. That would be safe enough. He'd only ever been Cullen Allardyce there and no one in the warehouses read Debrett's. But soon they'd have to meet with the bankers and they knew who he was, who his father was. Before then, he'd have to tell Antonia who he really was so that she wasn't ambushed. But in the knowing, she might be disappointed.

His feet pounded the pavements in time with his thoughts. Why did he care what Antonia thought of him? He was her business partner. She need not like him. True, but *friends* usually liked each other. That's how friendship worked. It was something of a point of interest to him as he ran to realise that he *wanted* her to like him, that her esteem mattered. Perhaps it was only that she was the one person he was in contact with, outside of Bowdrie, who also knew Keir. If Keir cared for both of them, it stood to reason that they should *like* each other.

Yet he worried that she wouldn't like him when the whole sordid truth of his story came out. He wasn't exactly the protégé she thought he was. He turned up Hanover Street and focused his thoughts on his morning outing, which was a far more comfortable direction instead of wondering why it mattered to him if she liked him or not. After all, what difference did it make if he was just going to sail away again? But it continued to bother him that he wasn't the man she thought he was.

Cullen wasn't the man she'd thought he was. Or perhaps what she meant was that Cullen wasn't the man she'd drawn in her head all these months waiting for him to arrive. This was the theme of her thoughts as the carriage headed to Mivart's to collect him. She ought to be thinking about the foreclosure, about her strategy with the bank, but her thoughts had gone a different direction entirely.

When she'd begun the search for Cullen, he was nothing but a name. She'd thought only about getting that name on all the right papers, then he'd be more than welcome to go back to Tahiti and they would spend the rest of their association communicating with bi-annual letters. In her mind, she'd created a two-dimensional image. The man she'd imagined was nothing more than a place holder whose signature she needed. He was not a man with a story, or a past, or feelings.

But yesterday, he'd been all three of those things; he'd become not just a man her husband knew, but now a man she knew personally, a man who loved beaches, who swam in turquoise waters and paddled outriggers. In her time of need, he'd offered friendship and comfort, and, in his own way, he'd offered the protection of his name—to the business, of course, not to her especially.

The carriage turned on to Brook Street and she felt her stomach give a flutter of anticipation. What would he offer her today? Who would he be? The business partner or the friend? Or perhaps something in between? Being friends with a man was tricky business. Other than her brother, she didn't think she'd ever been just friends with a man.

Yesterday, they'd done well together, taking lunch at the Bristol on Prince's Street before strolling the park at Hanover Square. She'd hung on every word of his stories about Tahiti. They'd talked the afternoon away. It had furthered the ease between them, there was a comfort in being together. It no longer seemed odd to take his arm as she walked beside him. As a result, the earlier stiffness between them had softened.

By the time he'd bent over her hand at the townhouse steps, the stiffness had vanished entirely, replaced by something else. She called it friendship because that seemed appropriate and convenient. To call it something else would be less appropriate and certainly less convenient. For now, she would take the newfound ease although the question remained: ought she trust that ease? Was she being foolish? Was she putting aside too soon her earlier concerns about his presence?

The optimist in her always pursued potential when it came to people but being an optimist didn't mean being naive. He'd leapt to her defence yesterday, wanting to put himself forward as a means of discouraging the foreclosure and she was grateful. Having him here would quash the bank's misgivings. But what motivated his offer? Was this a way forward for him taking over the helm? Would he use the hand of friendship against her? Was it only a strategy? Or had his offer been genuine?

He was already outside waiting for her, dressed in a long wool coat, top hat and gloves when she reached Mivart's. He got in quickly, the wind blowing the carriage door shut behind him. He flashed her a smile and she had to remind herself how it would be easy, too, to forget that for herself, she knew little about him despite yesterday's stories. It would be a dangerous assumption to think she knew him well when she did not. It would be easy to let down her guard, to be ambushed by his kindnesses, by his handsomeness, by the quality of his relationship with Keir.

They worked the warehouse from the bottom up. The London Dock warehouses featured underground wine vaults and Keir had made good use of them, using them to store the red wine much beloved by the Duke of Cowden and the hard-to-come-by Archambeau *coteaux champenois* from Emma's new husband's vineyards, although Keir and Garrett Luce had been importing the wines for years. The wine steward Keir employed offered them a taste of a new barrel that had come in.

'Cheers,' Antonia offered as they each took a sip. The wine was good, it was an excellent *coteaux champenois,* sent no doubt courtesy of Julien Archambeau, but she must have grimaced unconsciously as she swallowed.

'Do you not like wine?' Cullen enquired.

'I do. This wine is quite good and somewhat rare.' She set her glass down on a nearby barrel.

'Then why the frown?' Cullen asked.

'This wine is from my friend Emma's husband's vineyards. Emma's *second* husband's vineyards.' She sighed and tried to explain. 'Emma was married to Garrett Luce.'

'Ah, I see,' Cullen said quietly, setting his own glass down next to hers. 'Garrett Luce, Keir's friend who also drowned. And Emma has remarried already.' He gave her a long look until she confirmed it.

'Yes. She married last summer, six months ago.'

'And you think it was too soon? You don't approve?' It was quiet and dim down in the wine vaults, just the two of them. The space invited intimacy, an exchange of confidences.

'I suppose so,' Antonia admitted. 'Emma was madly in love with Garrett. The night of the flood we had to hold her back so that she wouldn't rush out into the night. She *loved* him.'

'And you wonder how such love could be replaced so quickly.' This came as a statement, followed by a low-toned, private question. 'Do you think you will never love again, Antonia? Do you think you will be alone for the rest of your life? Do you *want* to be?' His tawny eyes gleamed lion-like in the dimness, the atmosphere charging like an electrical storm. 'The question makes you uncomfortable. Why?'

Antonia swallowed. 'Because we're supposed to find our soulmates. Soulmates implies there is just one person for us and when that person is gone…' She couldn't finish the sentence.

'We are humans, Antonia, not swans.' He gave a low chuckle, but she knew instinctively he wasn't laughing at her.

'Maybe some of us are, though. Perhaps it's possible that some of us mate for life and others do not. It's the only way I can explain it.' She picked up her wine glass and took another sip, suddenly finding she needed to wet her dry throat.

'Maybe not all of us are made for monogamy either.' He tossed the challenge out casually. 'Have you ever thought that monogamy goes against human inclination? If it weren't for missionaries, I think much of the South Pacific would be polygamous. Monogamy has always struck me as something socially enforced, but not naturally prescribed, a torture we give ourselves.'

Antonia nearly choked on her wine. She'd never had such a conversation before, not even with Keir. 'You are a scandal, Cullen Allardyce. Do you really think about such things?'

'Yes. It's hard not to when one reads travel accounts of other explorers.' He leaned close with a wicked smile. 'And what becomes clear to me from those gleanings is that an enormous number of indigenous cultures were not originally monogamous.' The smile faded to a hard line, his words wry. 'It's just one of the many consequences of European conquest. Europe has not been good for a large part of the world.'

'You don't agree with monogamy?'

'I don't agree with conquest, with oppression,' Cullen replied. 'People ought to be left to decide for themselves what behaviour best suits them.' She'd wanted to get a rise out of him, to see something finally get under his skin, and here it was. There was passion beneath his words. She'd never heard anyone speak like this, not even Keir, who held similar opinions.

Antonia met his gaze over the rim of her glass. 'How did we get from Emma's husband's wine to empire building?'

'It's entirely your fault.' His gaze did not waver and her stomach gave a little flip of awareness. Some women must find him absolutely devastating. 'You didn't answer my question,' he drawled. 'Do you want to remain alone? And if so, do you think that is what Keir would have wanted for you?'

This was getting entirely too personal. It was time to put a stop to it. She gave him a sobering stare. 'What I *think* is that it's complicated and we have the main part of the warehouse to explore yet.'

She headed for the stairs, aware of Cullen close behind and aware that he didn't find her answer satisfactory. Neither did she. But an answer was far *more* complicated than it might have been six months ago, or even two weeks ago when her answer would have been a resounding yes, she *did* see herself spending her life alone.

She could not imagine another's companionship in Keir's place.

But then *he'd* come and his coming was changing everything: the store, the company, even her. He infuriated her and challenged her. He challenged her decisions about the business and about herself. He made her feel and made her face all she'd lost, not just Keir, but also the loss of the life she'd had. Being with him for hours every day forced her to acknowledge how lonely she was and how long she'd be alone with nothing but work for companionship, an arrangement that was entirely antithetical to the social creature she was.

In the past, she'd been with Emma and Fleur every day and the six of them had been out together most evenings, taking in the theatre, concerts, or dining with friends and playing cards. Even before that, she'd enjoyed the formal events of the Season—the concerts, the Venetian breakfasts, the balls—even if not the people. This past year, though, there'd been no entertainments, none of the social life she'd once enjoyed.

She'd not thought she'd missed it, but Cullen's question was prompting her to rethink her answer. Apparently, she missed it more than she'd realised. It opened the possibility that perhaps Emma didn't have it wrong after all. Which led to a host of other new and confused thoughts that formed an inconvenient tangle in her head, no matter how hard she tried to push them away.

At the top of the stairs, Cullen came up close behind her, his voice a whisper at her ear, private but with an unmistakable undertone of decadence that set her stomach to flipping yet again. 'Just so you know, Antonia.

I'm not a swan.' Dear heavens. With the amount of flipping her stomach was doing this morning, maybe it *was* something she'd eaten after all. Perhaps her stomach had finally rebelled against eggs for breakfast because the alternative explanation available was unthinkable.

Chapter Ten

Directly paying the loan in full was unthinkable for reasons both of principle and practicality. They had to talk about it. It could not be put off any longer. Cullen sighed and sat back in his chair in the private office of the Captain's Club. They had retreated there after touring the warehouses instead of going to the town house—a place she seemed to seldom go unless she must. She slept there. That was all. The rest of her days were spent elsewhere—in warehouses and various offices Popplewell and Allardyce Enterprises kept around town. He could guess the reasons why.

He tucked his hands behind his head and watched the flames in the fireplace, mentally sorting through what he knew. He'd gone over the accounts again to be sure, hoping he'd missed something the first time that would allow them to pay the loan in full without damaging other aspects of the company. He had not. His conclusions were still the same.

It would dangerously deplete their liquid capital to pay that loan, which in turn would impact the payment of wages and the outlay of cash to pay for cargoes before the resale profits came in. Those expenditures would further shrink the ready cash in their accounts. Yes, Keir had a fortune, but it was locked up in property and ships, and cargoes that were somewhere in the various stages of being readied for resale. It was not what Antonia wanted to hear.

As if on cue, Antonia spoke from the desk across the room where she sat working through correspondence and invoices. 'I want to pay the loan in full. It will make us independent of the bank. They won't be able to harass us again.'

At least not until the next time they needed funds. Cullen pushed a hand through his hair. 'I advise against it. It's the riskiest choice you can make. It puts the company in a cash-poor situation, which, on the surface, sends the wrong message to investors. They will see the company as struggling. If they sense a struggle, they'll pull back on their investments and take a wait-and-see attitude that *will* truly put us in a struggling position.'

He rose and stood with his back to the warmth of the fireplace. Dear Lord, had London always been this cold? His bones were starved for Tahitian sun. From there he could see her, could watch her expression from behind the big desk as he continued his lecture.

She had a glass face that worked in her favour. When she was charmed, a man knew it. When she was vexed, a man knew that, too, her green eyes narrowing to sharp jade slits of displeasure. No wonder she'd taken London by storm during her Season. Her expressions were a source of encouragement and discouragement. A man could plan a courtship according to those glances, always knowing where he stood. That openness could do in a single honest glance what coy, hidden messages attempted to do in many.

At present, her face remained relatively neutral, except for her eyes. She was waiting, her clear green gaze resting on him, sharply alert in anticipation of his verdict. She looked good behind the desk in her high-necked white blouse, her jacket long since discarded, a loose golden tendril of hair curling softly against her cheek, the perfect combination of intelligence and femininity.

The sight of her stirred something primal and masculine in him. He wanted to be her...warrior. To fight for her, protect her. She wouldn't like that last part. She didn't think she needed protection. But she needed it all the more because of that. He'd been a warrior in Tahiti. He'd stood with Rahiti and his clan against the French.

But here, he needed to be a different kind of warrior in a different kind of fight that would require different weapons. Spears and outriggers could not help him here and the tools that would be of use were tools he was loath to employ. He was not in the habit of throwing his family connections around. It was antithetical to his personal beliefs about equality.

'With the exception of property, everything we do is based on a joint venture system,' he explained, unsure how much she knew about the inner workings of the company. It was one thing to read ledgers, it was another to understand the nuance behind the numbers. 'Our investors pool their funds in order for us to afford the voyages and the cargoes. It also protects each of us if the ship is lost. No one loses everything, as would be the case if the voyage was sponsored by a single individual. Fewer investors, however, means our burden and our risk increases as we shoulder what investors have left unfunded.' This had been one of the first lessons Keir had taught him when he'd invested his hard-earned savings in that first voyage.

Usually patience was a virtue, but not in Antonia's case. He'd learned that, for her, patience was simply a way of waiting him out until she could have her say. She gave a nod when he finished. But the nod did not signify agreement, only understanding. 'Perhaps I should have chosen my words more carefully. What I meant to convey is that we *can* pay the loan. Whatever their motive is behind issuing this foreclosure, we *can* call their bluff and we should. It will be difficult, yes, but it can be done.'

'And the danger, the financial insecurity we face if we do?' Cullen queried. Had she heard all of what he'd said?

She rose and came around the desk, the wide sweep of her blue skirts swaying gently. In general, Cullen found the current fashion for the wide cages women wore beneath their skirts the height of foolishness, but the style suited her. The fullness of her skirts emphasised the slim circle of her waist, her trim torso, the round, feminine curves of breasts beneath the pleats and tucks of her white blouse. Cullen gave himself a scold. These were hardly seemly thoughts given the context of conducting business and he forced himself to focus on her words.

'The danger you speak of is not the only danger, though.' She crossed her arms and fixed him with one of her hard stares. 'The other danger is what happens if we don't pay the loan. The bank will take the store and all the money that has been put into the building will be lost. We will lose money either way. But at least *my* way, we get to keep the store and we can recoup our investment over time.'

Cullen leaned against the oak mantel and gave a dry laugh. 'Is that what you're worried about? That the solution best suited for the company won't be *your* solution?' He paused. 'That's rather disappointing, Antonia. I thought we'd moved past that. I didn't expect you to be so petty as to risk the financial well-being of the company for your own territorial wars.' If that was the case, he truly was disappointed. He'd thought her capable of much better.

Those green eyes flared and he barely finished his set-down before she replied in clipped tones, 'How dare you think I would risk Keir's store and the business he spent his life building simply because I want to be "right".'

This was progress. He'd made her mad. Good. He preferred her mad, or sobbing, or arguing—anything but the brisk efficiency she usually evinced. She needed to *feel*. There was a reason she didn't spend time at home, a reason she worked without ceasing: so that she didn't have to *feel*. She'd *felt* at the cemetery and she'd *felt* in Bowdrie's office. She thought it made her weak, she despised it. He did not. He appreciated it was in those moments that she showed her real self. And it was in those moments that he understood her the best.

She was close to feeling something right now. What would she reveal? His curiosity wanted to coax that next revelation, wanted to push her for both their sakes. 'Well? Have you asked yourself the hard question? *Would* it be better in the long term to let the store go rather than put the rest of the business at risk?' Even as he made the suggestion aloud, he knew he spoke heresy and yet he wanted her reaction even if it came with a storm. Perhaps especially if it came with a storm. He was not disappointed.

'You have insulted me twice in two minutes. I will *not* give up the store.' Her tone was hot and insistent.

He pushed again. 'Even if the numbers suggest it's the better decision? Even if your business partner advises it?'

Green lightning flashed in her eyes. 'Is that what you're suggesting? If you were any kind of friend to him, you wouldn't even think it.'

'If I were "any kind of friend" I'd do my best to make sure his wife didn't bankrupt his business within the first year.' He was pushing hard now and she was pushing back with equal force, unguardedly and with brutal honesty. 'You have lost your objectivity, Antonia.'

'No, I have lost my *husband*, Cullen.' There was a bite to her words. 'I have lost my life, my love, my hopes and my dreams.' Her voice rose to a near shout, her hand making a fist at her side, eyes blazing. 'All I have left of him and our life together is that store. I will not lose that, too!' Her words ricocheted around the room in the silence that followed.

There! That was what he wanted, this admission of what drove her and why. His heart hurt for her, for the depth of grief that she carried even after a year. He would free her from it if he could. 'Even if it drags you down?' he persisted.

'It does not drag me down. It sustains me—' She stopped suddenly, perhaps realising how much she'd given away in the heat of disagreement.

'Gives you something to get up for in the morning?' Cullen finished for her, watching some of the anger leach from her.

'You make me say all sorts of things,' she accused.

'I make you say the truth,' Cullen clarified, gesturing for her to take the chair across from the one he'd vacated. Standing was confrontational. Sitting was conversational. Rahiti's father had explained that to him. The time for confrontation had passed. Now it was time to talk in the space that confrontation had created. 'I wanted you to *hear* the way you're approaching your decision from your own lips.'

She sat on the edge of the chair, the anger leaving her. 'So I am hoisted by my own petard?'

'Not hoisted. Aware. I want you to be *aware* of what is driving your thinking. You will not listen to me, but you will listen to yourself. You heard yourself, you are too emotionally attached to the project.'

'It's Keir's legacy,' she said, more quietly this time. 'The one thing I have left I can do for him.'

There was guilt in those words. He'd heard it before at the cemetery: guilt for family she'd not given Keir, the guilt for surviving, for having been at a whist game, for laughing with friends when the river had swept him away. This store was more than a legacy, it was a bid for absolution. What would she do when she realised it wouldn't work? That the store was only brick and mortar? That it wouldn't raise the dead or heal her self-inflicted wounds.

'It won't bring him back, Antonia,' he cautioned. She was on dangerous ground here, teetering on the brink of throwing good money after potentially bad.

'No, but in its own way, it will help him to go on and me, too.' There was a need for atonement in her words. 'I am not ready to give up, Cullen, simply because the bank has thrown a wrinkle in the plans.'

He nodded. Despite his arguments, which had been to push her to acknowledge her highly personal stake in the store, he'd like to see the store go forward. Keir was right, department stores were the new wave of shopping. Eventually, the store would make money as long as they could get that far. It was the in between he was worried about and the emotional toll it was taking on Antonia. 'Here's our situation then. The bank wants to be paid and we want to pay them without harming ourselves. Where does the money come from?'

'We need someone else to pay the bank,' Antonia said, half joking. She added more seriously, 'Unfortunately, my father doesn't have that kind of money.'

His did. But he'd crawl on his belly and beg in the streets before he asked his father for anything. Anything he took from his father would negate all the reasons he'd left in the first place. However, there was someone else who could help. 'I think we go to the Duke of Cowden and the Prometheus Club. We ask them to loan us the money to pay the loan. That way, we satisfy the bank, we keep the store and the company's cash flow isn't jeopardised.' Meanwhile, he'd devote his resources to determining who on the bank's board of directors had prompted the foreclosure.

Antonia nodded and some of the tension eased that had stalked her since Bowdrie had given her the letter. 'It's not how I'd prefer my first meeting with Cowden to go, but it's a good solution.' She smiled. 'For Keir.'

'For Keir,' he echoed, but he wondered how true that was. He was rogue enough to admit his motivation wasn't entirely for Keir. It was for her, to see her smile, to see her happy, this woman who loved with her whole heart. He would help her secure the store, although he wondered how happy the store would make her in the long term. No happier than he could. The store might help assuage her guilt in the moment, just as he might help her in the immediate future, but his presence here was not, could not, be permanent. He would leave. He'd promised himself he would. He didn't belong here.

Besides, if he stayed long enough he would disappoint her, just like the store would inevitably disappoint her. No matter how much money it made, that store could not be what she wanted any more than he could be. Only, she didn't see it yet. He hoped she would see it before it was too late, before the realisation destroyed her in a different way. But in the interim, perhaps he could help her move on and perhaps that would be held in the balance and weigh the scales in his favour when judgment came.

'I'll send a note and set the meeting up. Cowden is usually in town. If not, there's a train that runs near his estate at Bramble.'

'I want to be there, Cullen. You're not to go to that meeting without me,' she instructed.

'Of course, we are partners,' he assured her even as he felt the sting of her words. He was expected to treat her as a partner, but it was obvious she didn't see him in the same way. She still believed the decisions regarding the company were up to her. He was merely a counsellor, not a partner. One had only to look at her use of pronouns to see it. He couldn't help her if she didn't untie his hands. It was time to start working on those knots. 'Now that's decided, I must insist that I meet with the bank alone.'

'Why are you meeting with them at all?' she asked, instantly sceptical. 'I think a snub might do them good.'

'I want to figure out who pushed the idea of foreclosing on a loan against a reliable customer and I want to know why.' He wanted to confirm Bowdrie's suspicions that the bank was nervous with a female at the helm. 'I think it would also be *helpful* for them to see me. I can be more effective alone.'

The bank had treated her shabbily. They needed to understand this was his company, too. Treating her poorly was tantamount to treating *him* poorly, something he was sure they would think twice about if given the right inducement, if for no other reason than that he was a wealthy *man* with a proven track record of success. He would do his best to ensure it didn't happen again. As much as she wouldn't like it, this had to be handled man to man. Warrior to warrior. He would be her champion. Because it was what Keir would have wanted.

And it's what you want, whispered a little voice he was finding more and more difficult to ignore.

Keir was gone and he was here, and Antonia needed a man whether she wanted to admit it or not.

Chapter Eleven

Antonia did not like how things were being handled. It was Cullen who'd met with the bank, who'd brought home the dismaying news that the bank had foreclosed because it was uncomfortable with a woman being in charge of all that money, and it was Cullen who'd been in contact with the influential Duke of Cowden. It was Cullen who'd arranged the train tickets to Cowden's Sussex estate, Bramble, when the Duke proved not to be in town after all. But what she liked least of all was how she *felt* about it.

She *liked* having things handled. She told herself it was because it meant there was one less thing for her to worry over, but she suspected it was more than that. There was comfort in Cullen's competence, in letting him handle these things and knowing they would get done. Even more disconcerting was that there was comfort in his company. In the weeks he'd been here, she'd come to look forward to picking him up each morning and spending the day going over business with him. She could admit to that. She told herself liking his company was *not* the same as liking him, a condition that would require much more reflection should that ever become the case.

Even such a tempered admission, however, came with the classic tension between dependence and independence. By the time they made the all-important trip to Bramble, she was feeling distinctly *de trop* and worrying that her usual optimism had played her false. Cullen had done exactly what she hadn't wanted him to do and he'd done it exactly how she'd feared from that very first day at Verrey's Café: by making himself indispensable, by acting as if he was serving her interests, when in reality he was serving his own. He was being nice because it benefited him.

She stared out the window of the coach that had met them at the station, a coach sent by the Duke and arranged by Cullen—yet another result of how he'd inserted himself into her life.

He is a partner. He is doing no more than what a partner would do, the voice of optimism in her head reprimanded. *You've merely been alone too long. You are not used to sharing responsibility.*

She was making too much of his assistance. But that scold was always followed with a dose of self-doubt—he was doing all of this because she could not. The business with the bank's foreclosure proved it. She'd fallen short. She had not been enough on her own. Never mind that Keir had always depicted business as something best done with a small group of trusted participants, or that Keir had always collaborated with Luce and Griffiths, and Cullen. For her it was different, though. She had something to prove.

'You're troubled,' Cullen interrupted her internal monologue as the red-brick architecture of Bramble came into view. 'We're nearly there. I don't want to arrive with you angry. Cowden is sympathetic to us and he is a friend to Popplewell and Allardyce Enterprises, but he is also an astute man who is careful with his funds. If he senses there is dissension in the ranks, he will not put his money behind us. This visit is not a *fait accompli*.'

'Of course, my apologies.' Antonia pasted on a smile. She didn't need him to tell her how devastating Cowden's refusal would be. They'd be back to where they'd started: making a difficult decision about how to handle the loan payment. 'You needn't worry, I'll be on my best behaviour.' This was no time to let emotion interfere with decisions.

His tawny gaze rested on her. 'I know you will. You would never do anything to jeopardise the business.' He smiled and she was struck by how utterly devastating he looked today in a dark blue jacket and jade-green waistcoat paired with charcoal trousers. An emerald stick pin winked in his neckcloth, its gem matching the one set in the heavy gold ring on his little finger. 'Do I pass inspection?' he enquired when her gaze lingered too long.

She laughed. 'I was just thinking that for a man who a few weeks ago had only two changes of clothes to his name and preferred to wear as few clothes as possible, you go well-heeled.'

He leaned forward conspiratorially. 'Don't worry, I still prefer to wear as few clothes as possible, it's just so bloody cold here.'

He had to stop saying such things. It certainly wasn't

cold in the carriage, not after that remark. Antonia smoothed the wide skirts of her red and black tartan ensemble, casting about for something to say. She very unoriginally came up with, 'Do I pass inspection as well?'

'You always pass inspection.' His words sent her stomach flip-flopping. He reached for her hand as the coach rolled to a stop in front of the steep-roofed façade of Bramble, his touch sending a warm thrill up her arm. Drat, she should be more resistant to such things. Those stomach flips and warm thrills were two recent developments since the day they'd gone to the cemetery. She did not need any added complications. He squeezed her hand in assurance. 'Everything will be all right, Antonia.'

And it was. The visit went well. The Duke received them in his oak-panelled office with its view of Bramble's parklands and listened intently to their situation, something Cullen let her take the lead on explaining. She tried not to resent him offering input at key parts in her telling. 'I think it is important the bank understands that treating her shabbily with this arbitrary demand for payment in full is inappropriate,' Cullen shared when she finished.

The Duke nodded in assent. 'It's the principle I don't agree with. If they foreclose at will, then they cannot be trusted.' The Duke neatly flipped the situation. This was no longer about the credibility of Popplewell and Allardyce Enterprises, but the credibility of the bank. 'They make themselves no better than the moneylenders in St Giles. I'd be more than glad to have the Prometheus Club offer you backing.'

Antonia felt as if she could breathe again. They'd done it! The store was safe, their funds were safe, the business was safe. She schooled her excitement into professional gratitude lest her excitement indicate how desperate she'd been. 'Thank you so much. This means a great deal.'

'I am pleased to help, my dear.' Cowden's eyes lingered on her and she braced herself for the inevitable. The last time she'd seen the Duke and Duchess had been at Keir's funeral. She waited for *the* question. 'How are *you* doing, Mrs Popplewell? I thought of your husband the other day. He is missed.'

'I am doing well. I am very busy with all of my husband's holdings.' Antonia gave her standard answer and then deflected. 'I hope you and Her Grace will visit the store when you're in town. I would be proud to offer you a tour.' She had to stay strong. She could not let kindness undo her as it had in Bowdrie's office.

The Duke nodded and turned his attention to Cullen. 'And you, welcome back. It has been a long time.' Cowden gave Cullen a fatherly smile. 'Frederick is here with his wife and his children. I know he'll want a good visit with you.' Cowden rose, indicating the meeting was over. 'My wife has a luncheon planned for us and she won't forgive me if I monopolise your company. I hope we can talk later, though, Cullen, before you leave.'

'I hope we can, too.' Cullen smiled warmly at Cowden,and she gave him a long considering look, surprised at Cowden's use of his Christian name. She'd not realised he was so personally close to the Duke's family. She'd assumed his connection was simply through

Keir and the Prometheus Club. How interesting that he was friends with the Duke's oldest son, Frederick. It raised questions though, like: how did a man ditched in an alley know such people?

Luncheon was an enjoyable affair. It was hard not to like the Duke and Duchess of Cowden, both of them heading towards the end of their middle years. They were affable and considerate hosts. Within minutes of sitting down for lunch, Antonia felt at home. Of course, she knew them both socially and had met them briefly on several occasions. She and Keir had been regular attendees at the Duchess's annual November charity ball in town, which kicked off the holiday season. She hadn't attended this year because she'd been in mourning.

Even more compelling was the easy affability of Cowden's son Frederick and his wife, Helena, who took turns eating lunch with a toddler on their laps instead of sending him off with the nurse. Helena was so engaging, Antonia almost didn't mind when it was time to leave the gentlemen. Cullen tossed her a smile as she followed the Duchess and Helena from the room that said he knew what she was thinking—that they'd discuss business without her.

Outside, the day was fair, teasing the unsuspecting victim with the temptation of spring and the Duchess opted to walk in the garden. Helena set the toddler down where they could keep an eye on him as they strolled. There would be plenty of rain and mud, damp and cold, between now and the first blooms, but for today Antonia was determined to enjoy the country air and the rare sunshine. And the company. She'd not had feminine company since Holmfirth. She missed Emma and Fleur furiously.

'Frederick has told me all about the store. It sounds marvellous. You even have a children's department and a sweets counter. How exciting.' Helena looped an arm through hers with easy familiarity. 'You must start thinking about publicity if you mean to open in April. I had an idea. You must have a grand opening for the public, but also a private affair, something invitation-only for customers you especially want to cultivate. Something with champagne and cake.' Helena laughed. 'I'll go anywhere for champagne and cake.'

'It's actually a good idea and champagne will be easy. Emma Luce can supply it.' Antonia laughed with her, caught up in the idea of a party for the store. She was already making plans in her head before she recognised her error. 'I mean, Emma Archambeau now. She has remarried.'

'Ah, yes, to the man who ensures my husband has his red wine.' The Duchess joined them, coming up on Antonia's other side. 'I was so happy to hear of the marriage.' Her blue eyes sparkled, but her smile softened coyly. 'What about you, my dear? Will you be next to wed? Is there anyone special in your life at present?'

'Oh, n-no,' Antonia stammered, the bold question catching her by surprise. 'I am happy for Emma, but it is much too soon for me to think about such things.' It was a bald-faced lie. Ever since Emma had married, she'd done nothing but think and rethink such things. Cullen's presence had forced her to reframe those thoughts yet again as she grappled with her growing attraction to his…companionship.

'Too soon with the likes of Cullen Allardyce lurking nearby? That's hard to believe.' Helena gave one of her light, bubbling laughs. 'He's a handsome fellow. Most women would do nothing *but* think about remarriage with him nearby. Although I'm not sure that's a two-way street.'

He was indeed handsome, and he did raise…*feelings*… in her that she'd thought had died with Keir. But he was also dangerous to her position in the company. It would be all too easy for him to see her relegated to a back role. She might be an optimist, but she was not naive.

'If not Allardyce, perhaps we could suggest some other fine men,' the Duchess offered. 'With the Season just around the corner, we could have a list drawn up.'

Absolutely not! Antonia moved quickly to squash the idea. 'I don't think remarriage is for me,' Antonia said firmly.

'Perhaps an affair, then?' Helena said mischievously.

'That is not what I meant,' Antonia stammered, blushing furiously.

Helena patted her hand. 'Our apologies. We are making you uncomfortable. Her Grace and I misread the situation.' She slid a sly look Antonia's way. 'At lunch, we thought perhaps there was something between you and Allardyce.'

'There is.' Antonia maintained her firmness. This was her chance to dispel the notions of these two match-makers. 'It's business. We are partners whether we like it or not. Circumstances have thrown us together.'

Helena gave a light laugh. 'I didn't get the impression that Mr Allardyce minds being thrown together with you too much.' Helena leaned close in feminine confidentiality. 'No man looks at a woman the way he looked at you when he "minds it".' She made an airy gesture. 'I remember when Frederick and I were courting. I could feel his eyes on me from across a ballroom, any ballroom, it didn't matter where we were. I always knew when he was watching me. I still do. Now look at us. Married with four sons.'

Married *and* happy. One could not be in Helena Tresham's presence to know the future Duchess of Cowden was a woman exceedingly pleased with her lot. It made Antonia's heartache just a bit. She'd been that woman once. To be with Keir, to believe in the potential promise of children had filled her with an unmatchable joy. She would be lying if she said being with Helena this afternoon didn't make her yearn to have that joy again. Emma had found such joy, could she also? If she would just look for it? If Helena was right, would she even have to look any further than Cullen Allardyce with those piercing tawny eyes and delicious touches?

Oh, this was madness! What was she thinking of? Certainly not thoughts of marriage to a man she'd just met. An affair, then? A toe dipped in the pools of romance before taking the full plunge?

'I think it would be good for Cullen to settle down,' Helena was saying when Antonia finally corralled her thoughts. 'Frederick might have worn off on him a bit better if he'd stayed around. They've been friends for years.' She sighed. 'But *things* happened.' She said it as if Antonia knew what those 'things' were. 'Then Frederick got married and Cullen went to the South Seas instead.' Instead of what? Instead of marrying as well?

What a set of loaded comments that was, both of them so casually dropped into the conversation. Antonia's curiosity was notably pricked, especially after her earlier realisation that Frederick and Cullen had been friends before Cullen had met Keir. She'd not imagined it. Helena's comment confirmed it. What secrets lurked here? It was a rather vivid reminder that she knew very little about Cullen Allardyce. But there was no time to ask her questions. The garden gate opened, and the nurse bustled in with Helena's other three sons.

'My boys!' Helena beamed at the sight of them. She tugged Antonia along with her. 'Come meet them.'

The boys were charming, two years apart and replicas of their father, although Antonia thought if one looked closely, they were a fine blend of both their parents. They were full of energy, excited by the good weather and a chance to be out of doors. The rest of the afternoon was taken up with play. The boys had brought a small ball and a tag-style game, where the object was to keep the ball away from a designated player, soon ensued.

Everyone played, even the toddler and the adults. Her Grace the Duchess was promptly transformed into 'Grandmama' and the elegant Helena was simply 'Mama'. Antonia found herself rather quickly reduced to 'Toni'. No, not reduced, she thought, finding herself tagged and declared 'it'. Elevated. For a few hours she was elevated to 'Toni', to the status of a child's friend, and she loved it.

All of this laughter, the running and playing together, *this* was what it meant to be a family like the one she'd grown up in. *This* was what it meant to be alive. But if this was what it meant to be alive, what did that make her these days? She caught one of the boys and swung him around until he laughed. She laughed, too, because it was better than thinking about the answer.

Laughter floated through the open windows of Cowden's library where the gentlemen had adjourned after luncheon to talk some more business. But that had quickly degenerated into catching up. Ten years was a long time to be gone and, for the first time since he'd returned, Cullen was actually glad to be in England. He'd missed Frederick, and Cowden had always been a father figure and father fixture in his life since he'd been of school age.

'The boys are out,' Frederick commented with a chuckle as a particularly loud hoot penetrated their conversation. 'I don't remember us being that noisy growing up.' Us, being Frederick, his two brothers and their friends—Cullen, Conall Everard and Cam Lithgow.

Cowden laughed. 'At least you know where they are,' he commented sagely to his son. 'It's when you don't hear them that you should worry.' The two men chuckled, a warm look passing between Cowden and his grown son. Longing stirred in Cullen. What a wonder it was to see such a relationship, to see what was possible between a father and a son who cared for one another.

Frederick had shared that he and Helena spent most of the year living with Cowden and the Duchess in residence at Bramble with their sons, coming into town only for his politics during the Season. There were other ducal estates and Frederick could have raised his family on any one of them, but this had been their choice. There was genuine affection between the foursome despite the shared roof. Cullen couldn't imagine deliberately choosing to live with his parents. He'd gone as far away from them as he could.

There were shouts of 'Toni! Toni! Throw it here!' and Cullen's eyes went again to the window. The boys had roped Antonia into playing, it seemed. He couldn't help himself. He rose, unable to resist. He had to *see* what was going on down there. The sight that met him was glorious. The women had joined in the game, all concern for propriety having been set side. Antonia's hair was loose and, even at a distance, he could see her cheeks were red with exertion and laughter. She was carrying the youngest Tresham boy piggyback and helping him tag his brothers.

It might have been better if he hadn't looked. Cullen found he had to swallow around a thickness in his throat. This was a scene rife with potent images of family and love and of a life he'd never had, but one that he'd once craved, a life that had always been out of reach for him. The closest he'd ever got to it growing up was with the Treshams, then as an adult there'd been first the connection.

But a part of him had still been on the outside of that, belonging but not completely. Now, seeing Antonia playing and laughing, setting aside concern about the store, setting aside her grief and *living*, brought the need rushing back: a family of his own where no one worried about birth order and heirs, where there was only love. A family with a woman like her...

Eventually, Cullen was aware of Frederick standing next to him. How long had he been there? 'I could watch Helena play with them all day. She is indefatigable for her boys,' Frederick said softly. 'They are my greatest joy.'

Cullen slid a look at his friend. Pure love shone on his face, love and pride, and contentment. Frederick Tresham was a man at peace despite being a busy man who balanced his political responsibilities with the responsibilities of being a landowner and heir, father and husband. But it was easy to see which roles he treasured most.

'They are my great joy, too.' Cowden joined them, standing on Cullen's other side. He gestured to the play on the lawn. 'That is my greatest legacy, right there. What the Prometheus Club does for England's economic well-being, whatever I do to improve the land here at Bramble, all of that is worthy, but it pales compared to the people I leave behind to carry on.'

Cowden gave a nod towards Antonia. 'She's a natural with the little ones.' She was, Cullen agreed. She should be a mother. She *wanted* to be a mother. He recalled their conversation at Kensal Green and the disappointment in her eyes. Fate had been cruel there. Keir had been able to give her everything but a family. She felt the loss of it keenly, the incompletion of it.

They were both incomplete when it came to family. They had that in common. But they were incomplete for different reasons. He didn't dare reach for his dream for fear of attaining it only to ruin it. What did he know of creating a family like the one Frederick had when he'd not been raised to it himself? What did he know of being a parent when his own had, in his opinion, failed him? He would not father a child simply to revisit the mistakes of the ancestors on them.

'Thank you for this. She needed to get out, to enjoy herself,' Cullen offered as the men watched the children play.

'What she needs is a husband and children, a chance to have her life back. She tries to hide it, but anyone can see how empty she is and how much she has to give,' Cowden replied with a pointed stare.

'She says she's not ready.' Neither was he. He was certainly not ready for this conversation. Cullen was growing exceedingly uncomfortable with the direction the conversation was heading. Surely they didn't think *he* should be that husband? Frederick and Cowden of all people should know he wasn't marriage material and why. Now, bedroom material, that was different. He did have a certain prowess there. But marriage? No.

'She's young and she's had a year to grieve. If she was an equestrian who'd fallen off a horse, you know what I'd tell her to do,' Cowden mused. 'Losing Keir Popplewell was a blow to all of us. He was a good husband, a good friend and mentor and a man with sound social values. There's no question that his absence has left a gap in the many lives he touched. But the longer she waits, the harder it will be for her to let go.' Cullen could feel the older man's eyes on him. This message wasn't solely about Antonia. It was about him, too. He'd had ten years away, ten years in which to make his own peace with his family and with the scandal. But he hadn't.

'I am happy to back the store,' Cowden continued. 'Keir Popplewell knew a good investment when he saw it and I have no doubts the store will be a money-maker, but I am not convinced the store is good for *her*.'

A little trill of vindication flowed through Cullen. He'd thought the same thing. 'She sees it as Keir's legacy.'

Cowden nodded. 'Such a vision is worthy and ambitious, but she needs more.'

Frederick elbowed him in the ribs. 'She needs you and I think you need her. I saw the way you looked at her during lunch.'

'I was hardly ogling her.' Cullen felt suddenly defensive, trapped on all sides by Frederick, Cowden and feelings he hadn't quite sorted out. He knew what Antonia needed, but should he be the one to provide it? He thought of Cowden's endorsement of Keir earlier. He would never measure up to that.

'Of course not. It was the solicitude in your gaze. You were concerned about her comfort, her well-being. You were checking in with her with your eyes and she with you. There was that last look you gave her when she left the room, a private joke just between the two of you, perhaps? You've become close. There's no shame in that. It's a good start. There's something between you even if you haven't explored it fully yet.'

Did Frederick know how tempting his words were? How often had he thought the same? How he'd wondered what would it be like to reach over and stop her mouth with a kiss when she worried? Or to do more than take her hand and offer reassurance when what she needed was more than words to move past her grief? What she needed was a lover, someone to bring her back to life, to show her how to live again.

'Don't send an announcement to *The Times* yet, Frederick,' Cullen offered wryly. 'She needs to lean on someone at the moment while we straighten things out. Once I have her settled, I need to return to Tahiti.' Because Tahiti needed him and he needed Tahiti and while Antonia needed him, too, for the short term, he could not be what she needed in the long.

That got Cowden's attention. He raised a greying brow. 'You don't mean to stay?'

'No. I can't sustain the relationships we've grown in the South Seas if I'm here. I need to be on location.' It sounded logical, objective, when he said it that way.

'Surely you have an assistant, someone who could do that who is already in place there?' Cowden cleared his throat. 'I assumed that you were back permanently.'

Cullen felt distinctly uneasy. He feared for a moment that Cowden would rethink his support of the loan. Antonia would have his head if that happened. 'I don't think it's necessary and my life is in Tahiti now.'

'I think it could become necessary.' Cowden speared him with a hard stare. 'What happened with the bank could happen again and probably will. Whether it's right or wrong, Antonia Popplewell at the helm makes men nervous. Let me be frank—it will make even some men in the Prometheus Club nervous despite my endorsement.

There's a reason the one woman in the club is a silent investor and has an alias,' he said pointedly. 'If you're half a world away, you will be of no use to Mrs Popplewell. She needs you right here and that will not change, not in her lifetime.'

Cowden's words left him with a sinking feeling.

You can't go back.

All those promises he'd made himself about returning by September were useless in contrast to reality. He didn't want Cowden to be right, but he knew truth when he heard it. For the first time since receiving the news about Keir, he wasn't sad, he was *angry*. What the hell had Keir done to him? The feeling of being trapped persisted, all his freedom stripped away, everything he'd fought to achieve for himself lost.

'You know I can't stay. The longer I am here, the more likely it is I'll be a hindrance instead of an asset to her.' Even as he said the words, he felt the prick of guilt. His anger was selfish. Perhaps it was even cowardly. He'd left ten years ago, but what had he changed? What had leaving achieved?

Cowden's voice was quiet. 'I know very well why you left, Cullen. But perhaps it's time to face the fight, time to make your stand here where it can matter most. And time to make your peace before it's too late. Trust me, time will slip away and you don't want to regret it.'

'It's a lot to take in.' Frederick clapped him on the shoulder, intervening with an easy smile. 'Nothing has to be decided in the moment. Let's go down and join the women. They're having more fun than we are and I want you to meet the boys before you have to catch the train. Now that you're back, we can spend more time together.'

Now that he was back.

Cullen wasn't sure he liked the sound of those words. They were in fact downright ominous. Almost as ominous as the words, 'Antonia Popplewell needs a husband and children'. What made those statements ominous was that both of them were true.

Chapter Twelve

That sense of foreboding followed Cullen back to London. Clouds heavy with rain hung low in the soot-dark sky of the city, welcoming them back shortly after seven o'clock that evening. Even Antonia seemed to feel the effects. The positive energy and crisp country air of the afternoon seemed to belong to another day. It hadn't helped that the train had been delayed at one of the stations, turning a journey of less than an hour into two.

It had meant an extra hour trapped in a train compartment with his thoughts *and* the object of those thoughts. Far too much time to think. For her, too, he'd wager, based on the amount of time she spent staring out the window. Although he wasn't sure if her thoughts were driven by the meeting with Cowden, by plans for the store or by something the Duchess and Helena had talked about. Knowing Antonia's penchant for efficiency, it could very well be all three.

By the time they reached London Bridge station, lunch at Bramble seemed a lifetime ago. Both of them were tired and irritable. They'd set out early and the day had been long even if the results had been good. At least the coach was still waiting for them. He was thankful for that little luxury as he hustled Antonia through the crowd and into the carriage just in time to escape the first raindrops.

The storm didn't wait. Hard rain pelted the carriage roof before they were halfway to the town house. The loudness of the rain made it difficult to talk. But perhaps that was best. They might be better served with silence until they'd each had enough time to sit with the thoughts in their heads.

What would he say if she asked? That he'd spent the train trip back thinking of old hurts, old dreams and new acquaintances? That he'd been thinking of *her*, of how she'd looked in the garden with the children, how it had made his heart ache not just for himself but for her and how that ache had led to other more provocative thoughts. How might he comfort her? How might they comfort each other? How might he help her step out of the aloneness?

He could not save himself, but perhaps he could save her, show her that the time for her dreams was not yet past? Cowden said she needed a husband, but before that, Cullen thought she needed a lover. Someone just for her. A lover could be a bridge between the old world and the new, between loss and rediscovery, if she would allow it. Every day, he thought she grew closer to allowing it, every day the aloneness weighed on her a little more. He could be that lover. A lover needn't measure up to Keir. Only a husband needed to do that. A lover could be a fleeting fancy.

Cullen studied her in the dimness of the interior, her face turned in profile to see out into the evening streets.

There was a sadness to her gaze tonight and, despite his earlier advice to himself about silence, he could not let that sadness stand, especially if he had contributed to it in some way. 'Penny for your thoughts?' he ventured, aware that he might have left it too late. They were close to Mivart's. There was little time left for talk.

She flashed an apologetic smile. 'I'm not sure they're worth a penny. I was just feeling sorry for myself. I was thinking about how I'd given the staff the day off since I was gone and how quiet the house will be. Eating alone has little appeal.'

Especially after the Treshams. Cullen could guess what she was really thinking. What a stark contrast her evening would be compared to her day. 'If I go back to Mivart's I'll have to send out for something.' A thought that didn't appeal to him any more than her thoughts of eating alone. But finding a restaurant in this weather wasn't appealing either. 'May I make a bold suggestion?' He laughed to underscore that his use of the word bold was intended hyperbolically. 'Why don't we eat in? Neither of us needs to eat alone. I'm sure between the two of us we can put a meal together from whatever is in your pantry. Ham, toast, eggs.'

Antonia wrinkled her nose at the mention of eggs. 'All right, no eggs, then,' he amended. 'We'll improvise. As long as there's cheese and bread, it will be a feast.' He tapped on the carriage roof and gave the driver new instructions.

Cullen had never been inside the town house. Keir had purchased it as a wedding gift for his bride. Cullen had been gone two years by then. It was a three-storey home with pristine white trim about the door and windows. It was intentionally impressive on the outside and unintentionally oppressive on the inside. It was a mausoleum at worst, a museum at best, everything neat and orderly, all things in their places—places Cullen thought those objects had occupied for years. This house was not lived in any more. She was hardly here, hardly had the time to mess anything up. It reminded him of his parents' home. Elegant and empty. Soulless.

'It's beautiful,' he lied.

She tossed a doubtful glance his direction. 'Is it? It was when Keir was alive. I hardly notice it any more. The kitchens are this way.'

He followed her through a darkened dining room and down the stairs. The kitchen *was* better. It was clean, but obviously a lived-in, active place. Pots and pans stood at the ready for tomorrow's breakfast and the larder was stocked. Cullen gathered up a loaf of bread, a wheel of cheese and thick sausages. He slipped a bottle of wine beneath his arm. Out of the corner of his eye he watched Antonia tie on an apron and tuck up her hair as he deposited his finds on the long work table.

She handed him a knife. 'If you slice the bread for toasting, I'll slice the sausages for frying.' She paused and cocked her head. Domesticity suited her, he thought. 'You're smiling, I see it in your eyes. You're surprised I can cook.' She playfully brandished the knife. 'Well, I can, but don't tell anyone; it's my dirty little secret. Emma can cook, too. We used to sneak downstairs and make breakfasts for everyone when we were together.

Cook hated it, thought we were usurping his authority, but we loved doing it.'

'Yes, I *am* surprised.' Cullen picked up the knife and began slicing bread. 'You are a baronet's daughter. I thought such tasks were beyond a lady.' Surprised, but pleasantly so. She'd known struggle and difficulty and had overcome it—something else they had in common.

She gave him a long look. 'Before I married Keir, my family was struggling financially. We had to let our cook go. My mother and I spent a whole year cooking for the family and on a budget, too.' She laughed. 'I can make mutton taste like a four-course meal.' But there was seriousness as well. She'd not been pampered all her life.

'I approve.' Cullen reached for the wheel of cheese. 'Rank should not limit our need for basic life skills.'

She piled the sausage rounds into a skillet and gave him a soft smile. 'Keir rescued us both. You from the alley and me from genteel poverty. He rescued my family, too.' She set the knife down as if she had something important to tell him. Cullen waited. 'I loved *him*, though, not his money. It was never about the money. You might hear otherwise once the Season starts. It's a lie. I did need to marry well, but I loved Keir.'

The desire to be her warrior stirred once more. He knew too well how cruel *ton* gossip could be. If anyone dared to slander her, he would deal with them. 'I appreciate your honesty.' He was jealous of it, too. If only he could be that honest with her. Was that why she'd told him? Was she looking for him to reciprocate with a confession of his own? His confession would make hers pale by comparison. He moved to the stove to start it up and her next question caught him off guard.

'Keir *did* save you from the alley, didn't he?'

He nearly burned his finger on the matches. 'Yes.' Why would she question that?

'But you knew Frederick Tresham before you met Keir. Helena said you'd gone to school with him.' He could feel her eyes on him as he lit the stove.

'Even a poor gentleman's son attends school.' He knew where this was headed. It had always been the risk in taking her to Bramble, but there'd been no choice. She'd insisted on it and now she'd noticed certain things. He had to be careful. 'Your brother went, no doubt, despite the family straits,' he pointed out, taking a calculated guess.

'He did.' She nodded and went back to slicing sausages. Perhaps her curiosity was appeased. He hoped so. There were things he wasn't ready to explain. But his hope was misplaced. The afternoon had made her curious. She fixed him with a too-casual stare. That should have warned him. 'You're a gentleman's son, then, not a street rat.' There was no condemnation in it, but it was still a scold. 'When you said Keir rescued you from the alley, I assumed you'd been brought up in St Giles or something similar.'

'You never asked for clarification,' he answered.

'I was the one making assumptions. I will own that, as I will own there is always a certain danger with assumptions.' Her green gaze was intent and steady. 'But perhaps I was also deliberately led to those assumptions. You knew what I would think and you let me think it.'

The sausage began to sizzle, a rather apt physical metaphor, he thought, for the trill of tension buzzing between them.

'You never talk of your family,' she probed. 'Are they still alive?' She turned to the stove to move the sausage around the skillet and perhaps to give him some privacy in which to answer. He sensed he'd better make the answer good, or she'd just have more questions.

'Yes, they are. But we are not close. A gentleman isn't pleased to have his son in trade. My choices did not endear me to my father.' All true. He could say quite a lot about that relationship without naming names.

She turned from the stove for a moment. 'Then why did you do it? Why did you choose to enter trade if you didn't need to?'

He held her gaze as he answered, 'I do not think one man above another. To me, it is wrong to live off rents and the efforts of others while doing nothing. That is feudalism at its core and that social structure has outlived its usefulness in this new world where we tout equality and promote reform,' he said quietly. 'My father can't see that any more than he can see that his way of life is antiquated and on its way out, whether he believes it or not.'

'I'm sorry,' she said softly. 'Families should be close.'

'I'm not sorry,' he assured her. 'Families aren't always blood. I have the Treshams and in Tahiti I have Rahiti's family and I had Keir.'

'Father figures to stand in the void?' she said astutely. 'And Frederick? Does he stand in place of a brother who sides with your father?'

'Yes, I suppose he does.' He was a bit unnerved that

she saw so much, understood so much, and yet to be understood in that way was comforting. 'Frederick is a great champion of reform. He ran for his own Parliament seat in the House of Commons so that he could serve the interests of the masses and not the aristocracy.'

She smiled at that. 'And the South Seas? Is that about equality and reform, too?'

'Yes. Keir and I believe that economics is one way to foster equality across the empire.'

'That's what you're doing in Tahiti? Fostering equality?' She bent to put the grilled cheese in the oven, hips swaying.

'Yes. I do covertly what the French do overtly, only I offer a choice. The French offer only the illusion of choice.' That was all he wanted to say about the South Seas at present. It would be best now to direct the conversation elsewhere, preferably towards her. If today had raised her curiosity about him, it had also raised his curiosity about her. He leaned across the worktable and gave her a grin. 'Since we're talking about past lives, how is it you're so good with children?'

'I helped with the little ones back home. I taught reading at the church school in the village and I was always helping out with children's activities like the Christmas pageant.' She gave a little shrug. 'It just comes naturally. I like children. They're interesting and clever and so much more observant than people give them credit for.'

'You should have your own.' It was a bold statement. He watched her blush before she could turn away and put the skillet on the stove. 'Do you still want a family?' he pressed. 'You mentioned before that you and Keir had hoped for one.'

'I think that's out of the question now.' She checked the bread and cheese in the oven, suddenly busy. She rummaged a blue-checked cloth for the worktable and spread it over one end. She laid out pewter plates and found two wine glasses. He ought to help, but it was too much fun to watch her avoid the question or maybe it was the images that question conjured she was trying to avoid.

Within moments she'd transformed their corner of the table into a cosy eating space. She reached for a bowl on a high shelf and couldn't grasp it. 'Let me get that.' Cullen came up behind her, breathing in the soft, floral scent of her, an utterly feminine scent, the very promise of spring itself. Spring was nothing if not the season of hope.

He did not step back. Instead, he kept his voice at her ear. 'Why is it out of the question, Antonia? You are young. You have time.' Surely, an afternoon with the Treshams had reminded her of that, had brought such a thought to the fore. One could not be with the Treshams and not think about family, not hunger for a family of one's own.

'Because it would require remarrying and I don't think... Oh! Please back up. Hurry, we're burning the grilled cheese.' She bent swiftly to retrieve the rack with their melted cheese and bread from the oven. Cullen retreated to the table and retrenched, popping the wine cork and lighting a thick tallow candle. When she turned with the platter of sausages and grilled cheese in her hands, her eyes lit with pleasant surprise. 'You've made our table look lovely.'

'I think it's you who makes it lovely. Good meals start with good company.' He took the platter from her and set it down between their plates. He passed her a glass of wine. 'Here's to today. A long day, but a good day.'

'Thank you for this.' She took a sip of the wine.

'You did most of the work. I should thank you.' Good lord, she was beautiful by candlelight in her apron. No ballgown could look finer.

'I mean for the meal, for eating together. I did not want to eat alone.' She paused, looking thoughtful, as if she were about to tell him something important. 'It's dinner time I miss the most, and breakfast. Keir and I made every meal a celebration. Now, meals hardly mean anything at all.' Beautiful *and* lonely, Cullen amended. He would chase that loneliness from her if she would let him.

'You are alone, too much.' Cullen took a bite of juicy sausage, his eyes resting on her, forcing her to look back at him. 'In all seriousness, have you ever thought of taking a lover?' He barely got his question out before she spit her wine all over the blue-checked cloth.

'I beg your pardon?' she managed between gasps.

He had to stop doing that—saying such audacious things. *Do you want children? Have you thought of taking a lover?* How was a person supposed to respond? With the truth? Hardly. The truth might send him running for the door, might jeopardise the business partnership he hadn't quite signed for yet. She couldn't afford the truth. He had to stop looking at her the way he was right now, with the full intensity of those lion eyes. And she *had* to stop looking back or the truth would tumble out, that, yes, she would consider it if the lover was him.

'Truly, Antonia. Why not take a lover? It would be good for you.' He took a sip of wine and she remembered too late it wasn't his drink of preference.

'Would you like cider instead? We probably have some.'

'No, I would *not* like cider. I would like an answer to my question.' How could he sit there and discuss lovers so casually? 'A lover makes perfect sense, the best of both worlds.' He carried on the conversation calmly. 'You can have companionship, you can have physical intimacy without needing to give your heart.' He helped himself to a cheese sandwich. How could he eat when he'd managed to tie her stomach into knots with such a decadent discussion? 'That's what's holding you back, isn't it? The idea that you have to love someone again?'

Dear lord, he read her like a book. 'Am I that transparent?'

'Only in the best of ways, Antonia.' He leaned across the table, his thumb dabbing at the corner of her mouth in a gentle motion. 'You had a bit of cheese there. I got it.' He smiled, the casual intimacy of his touch easy and natural. 'I didn't mean to upset you, but I did mean to make you think. What are you going to do for the rest of your life? Keir died, not you, but you've buried yourself along with him. You can still have a life if you would just claim it.'

'I do have a life. I have the store, the businesses. I am very busy,' she reminded him.

'Busy isn't the same thing. I saw you today on the lawn. You were *happy*.' He moved his head to catch her gaze, to bring it up to meet his, his eyes boring into her, into her soul. 'Don't you want to be happy?'

His warm hands closed around hers as they rested on the table and she thought, *I want happiness. But not the consequences.* How did she explain such a thing to a man who feared nothing?

'I cannot risk it. Happiness has its costs. *I* simply can't be hurt again, I'd never survive it.' She feared not being whole, but she wasn't whole now, with all of these protections she'd mentally put in place. She was empty. She was realising belatedly that part of being whole was being filled.

'Let *me* fill you.' He came around the worktable in a slow movement, his eyes never leaving hers, his intent written openly in their tawny depths. 'You needn't marry to not be alone.' He pushed an errant curl back behind her ear. 'Tell me you're not tired of being alone. Tell me you don't want to be touched and I'll stop.'

But she did not stop him. She could not tell him a lie. He bent his mouth to the space below her ear, pressing a kiss to her skin. Her breath caught; her pulse leaped. She *did* want to be touched and she wanted *to* touch. To have and to hold.

'Yes, I want those things,' she breathed her confession into the candlelit darkness. She was tired of being alone, of not feeling for fear of what would happen if she did. Today had driven it home to her just how alone she was.

'You can have them,' he murmured against her skin, his mouth kissing the corner of her lips. 'I can give them to you. For a night, for a week, for a month. It needn't mean anything; you needn't attach your heart.' It was the perfect temptation—all the benefits, none of the cost.

It would mean something though, it would be a step back towards living, towards feeling, and it beckoned like the light beyond a dark room. Oh, this was a wicked lure. To take what he offered required a certain bravery. 'This is not as easy as you make it out,' she whispered her resistance. She should step away from him before this went too far. But, in truth, she didn't want to step away, didn't want to stop this.

'It can be.' His eyes were half lidded as his hand cupped her jaw, his mouth inches from hers. 'Let me show you. Let me be your lover, let me bring you back to life.'

'Yes,' she whispered, reaching for his mouth with hers.

Chapter Thirteen

He tasted of sharp tannins and cheese. He smelled of vanilla and spices and exotic places she'd only dreamed of until she'd met him. This was madness, delicious, outright madness, and she was wilfully drowning in it after treading water alone for so long. She gave her mouth to him, her neck, her throat, a little moan escaping her as his teeth nipped the tender skin just beneath her jaw, the rough pricking defining the rules of this engagement. This would not be gentle. It would be fast and cathartic.

Her mouth sought his with a hard kiss to seal the contract of his teeth. She'd given her consent with a single word: yes.

Yes, kiss me in the kitchen, yes, wake me from this half-life, show me how to live again. Yes, touch me. Yes, take me. Yes, tear my clothes, exorcise my ghosts. Set me free.

From here on out the pace would be fast, the passion fierce and given free rein to consume them at need.

He lifted her to the worktable, his body finding its way to her, amid the volume of skirts and crinolines, to stand between her thighs, to press proof of his own want against her, the hardness of him straining and evident even though layers of fabric separated them.

It was evidence, too, that this was not all for her, that he needed, wanted, this, as well, for himself. An afternoon at the Treshams had shaken something loose in them both. Their mouths sought each other, tongues tangled, lips devoured. Her breath caught, her hands fisted in his hair, anchoring her to him in a swirl of passion's torrent.

'Too many damn clothes,' He swore against her mouth, his hands seizing the bodice of her gown and ripping— freeing. Yes! Her blood pounded in primal joy.

Take them all, she thought. *Take every last petticoat, untie every ribbon, set me free.*

Her own hands tore at his neckcloth, fumbled with the buttons of his shirt, of his jade waistcoat. Clothes piled on the floor, desire riding them hard, leaving her only in her chemise and he in his trousers. She made short work of those trousers, feeling his eyes on her as she freed him, baring the hot, long length of him as he'd bared her. His voice was a growl at her ear. 'Shall I take you upstairs?'

Her resolve wavered, passion cooling for a moment as rational thought asserted itself. Not upstairs. Not in Keir's bed. She drew him close, defying the ghosts that pressed hard. 'No, here. This cannot wait.' She would not survive stairs. Her passion was like lava, burning fast and hot and just as quick to cool. She needed this, but she didn't trust it to last, not quite yet.

'Here then it is.' His own breath came ragged. His hands gripped her hips and pulled her to the edge of the table until she would have fallen if not for him. He was her strength, her pillar, her arms wrapped about his neck, her legs wrapped about the lean muscles of his hips, their bodies perfectly aligned for intersection.

The first thrust took her hard and she gloried in it, her neck arching back while a primal groan climbed her throat. Release stalked her, she wanted to explode, wanted to shatter into a million pieces. He came into her again. She would get her wish. It would not be long now. Her hands dug into the muscles of his bare shoulders, feeling the tension of his body as it gathered for its own completion.

Then completion was upon her and he left her with a force equal to how he'd entered her, his own satisfaction occurring against her thigh, both of them sagging against one another, sated and exhausted, the sudden fury of their want spent, the storm blown out. She leaned into him, her head against his chest, marvelling that he could keep his feet at all. She could barely stay upright. For the first time in ages she felt as if she could sleep the night away, so complete was the sense of peace that flooded her.

Despite her surroundings, she must have drowsed any way, her body vaguely aware of being lifted, of being carried and then laid down, of Cullen's weight beside her on a mattress, of being drawn into his arms, the murmur of nonsense words at her ear until sleep claimed her entirely.

Watching her sleep claimed the attentions of both his body and mind. His body could relax at last, the tension within him satisfied. Peace was not something he experienced often, but it was here with him in this big bed, with this woman. His mind, however, did not share that same peace. As much as his body wanted to join her in slumber, his mind had other ideas. The heat of the moment had passed and he was left with the reality of what he'd proposed—that he'd be her lover—and the consequences of what he'd done.

The proposal had been intended solely for her and yet that had likely been a lie from the start. He'd wanted her for himself, this brave, beautiful woman, who'd taken on the world, who fought for those she loved even at the expense of herself. And so he'd persuaded her that she needed this when in truth he'd needed it, needed *her* just as much. It was poorly done of him. He could offer her nothing. Whether he stayed or left, he would disappoint her on all fronts—as a business partner, as a friend and as a lover.

She stirred and he gently pushed back a strand of hair from her face. Her eyes opened and for a moment she tensed and looked about the room. He heard her exhale. 'Ah, good. A guest room.' She closed her eyes with a sigh heavy with relief.

'*Our* room,' he murmured in understanding. 'Our place.' He'd had enough wits left after their explosive lovemaking not to take her to the main bedroom, but was that because he was a coward, afraid of offending Keir's ghost where it was most likely to linger? A thought intruded. What would Keir think of what he'd done? Was this the action of a friend? He pushed the thought away.

Antonia snuggled against him, her breasts taut against

the fabric of her chemise as they pressed to his chest, her hand tracing the curve of his shoulder, slipping around to his shoulder blade. Her fingers traced and stopped. 'What is this? I feel something.'

He chuckled. 'My tattoo.'

'Tattoo?' She sat up and tugged him upright so she could study it in the lamp light. He felt her fingers trace the dark ink of the bird in soft, gentle strokes. 'Were you a pirate?' she teased as they settled back down beneath the blankets. Her drowsiness was gone and her eyes caught the light, glinting like emeralds hiding in the dark. She was doubly charming like this, alive and curious and unguarded.

'A warrior,' he corrected, wrapping a long gold curl around his finger. 'In the South Seas, the bird is a messenger from the gods. Some even believe that the bird has its own powers. The bird on my back is a tern. One island I visited, the elders said terns are symbols of safe return because they never spend a night on the water.' He propped himself up on one arm, his hair falling to one side. 'It's more than a symbol. It's true. If you're at sea and you see a tern, you can follow it. It will lead you to land.'

'So, you're a messenger?'

'Yes, I thought it was rather fitting given the job Keir sent me to do, which was to establish trade relations between our company and the island clans. Twice a year, I journey between the islands collecting cargo and then I ship it back here out of Papeete. Tapas cloth, necklaces and bracelets made of shells, pineapples, coconuts, teak, handwoven baskets, vanilla, seeds of exotic plants to be grown in English greenhouses—' He broke off with a chuckle.

She ran a hand down the length of his arm, the stroke of her fingers pleasantly rousing him with their warmth. 'What a life you must lead. It sounds…wonderful. Different beyond anything here. I think I might be more than a little envious.'

'It is different.' He gave her a soft smile. 'And I am a different man there.'

She laughed. 'Ah, yes, the man who wears few clothes.'

'That's right.' He grinned. 'In Tahiti, I wear a *malo* around my hips and it's very freeing. I can run, swim, climb, without restriction. A good English jacket would rip at the seams the way these tailors sew them to be skin-tight.'

'Form-fitting, I believe that's the word you're looking for.'

'Ridiculous is what it is. A man can't move in these clothes.'

'Try a corset and crinolines.' She slid him a teasing look. 'Sometimes there are doors I can't get through all in the name of fashion.' Then she remembered the original thread of the conversation. 'How else are you different in Tahiti? You have a tattoo and wear a *malo*, what else?'

'I am barefoot. I hardly ever wear shoes when I'm not in Papeete. I go everywhere in an outrigger.' He did his best to describe the canoe to her. He dropped his voice to low conspiratorial tones. 'I used to have hair down to my waist.'

'No!' Her eyes were wide in disbelief.

'Yes, it's true. I cut it when I came back.'

She threaded her hands through his hair. 'That makes me sad somehow. It must have been magnificent. But this is nice, too. You look like a lion.'

He laughed. 'How so?'

'Your eyes, your hair like a mane and you're large, quite intimidating really. The day I met you it was your height I noticed first, and I thought to myself, "He's a big man."'

'The first day I saw you, I thought, "There's a beautiful woman, she's everything…"' He stopped himself. He was going to say she was everything Keir had said she was, but they were doing so well, making such progress in bringing her back to life, moving her forward, he didn't dare risk it. There was no place for Keir in this particular bed just now. So he said instead, 'Lovely. I thought you were everything lovely.' He kissed her softly and whispered against her mouth, 'This is good, Antonia, us, together. *We* are good.'

'We are,' she whispered back, her hand seeking him beneath the covers, his phallus rising at her touch. 'What if we try it again, this time more slowly. I want to savour you.'

He smiled against her mouth. 'And I want to savour you.' Good lord, but this felt right. Too right, truth be told. There was no way he could hold on to it. Eventually he would disappoint her, but before he did, the interim would be glorious.

Chapter Fourteen

She had a lover.

It was the most glorious, most decadent thought to wake to and she held it close as she drifted slowly to the surface of consciousness. The day would come with its challenges and inevitably tarnish these moments, but for now she floated in pure bliss. Her body bore witness to the truth of it from the exquisite, sated lethargy that kept her in bed long after the usual time she rose to the delicate soreness in the most private of places, reminding her she hadn't dreamed it, but lived it, *felt* it to her bones—all of it: the heat, the passion, the overwhelming, reckless desire to throw caution aside. Last night she'd done just that—on her kitchen table no less.

Oh, no, the kitchen! Her eyes flew open, last night's fantasy connecting to this morning's reality. Her clothes were still down there. So were his and it was too late to do anything about it now. Cook would be here, would have seen the clothes, the two place settings. Cook would tell the housekeeper. The housekeeper would tell her maid, Randal.

Antonia let out a groan. She could not hide this. Or him. Which raised the question, where was Cullen? Had he gathered his clothes and gone home before dawn? If so, perhaps she could cobble together some sort of explanation that might appease Cook's curiosity. Her brain began to work. Perhaps she could say she'd been caught in the rain and left her wet clothes downstairs. That wouldn't explain the two place settings, though.

The jingle of approaching china in the hall broke her concentration. Her door opened and she braced for Randal with tea and questions, but it was not Randal who slipped inside. It was Cullen, bare chested *and* bearing morning gifts with delicious smells, a feast for the senses on all levels. 'You're shirtless.' She was at once aroused and horrified by the sight of him. 'Did Cook see you like that?'

Cullen grinned and carefully set the tray on the bed. 'She did.' He gave a playful waggle of his brows. 'Don't worry, I'd got my trousers on before she arrived. I don't think she minded.' He gave a casual shrug to indicate it was of no import. She disagreed. As for the not minding? Probably not. One could do worse than to start their day with a half-naked Cullen Allardyce in one's kitchen. But there'd be no hiding it now.

'I told Cook I stayed over because you weren't feeling well last night.' He reached for a slice of toast and buttered it. She watched the butter melt on the heated bread, her mouth watering. The explanation wouldn't hold for long, but at the moment she was too hungry to worry.

'I'm starved.' There was a sense of wonderment to that. How delightful to be ravenous in the morning, to crave food. How *different* after a year of lacking real appetite.

He tore off a bit of the toast and fed it to her, his fingers brushing her lips. 'That's what an active night of lovemaking will do for you, my dear. Restores your appetite like that.' He snapped his fingers and laughed.

'What else did you bring?' She glanced at the tray.

'Sausage, toast, tea. No eggs.' He fed her another bite and set about buttering his own toast. 'Why don't you like eggs?'

'I like eggs,' she clarified, 'they just became symbolic, that's all.' She reached for a sausage link. This was how breakfast should taste: hot and delicious with a touch of spice. Not unlike the man who sat cross-legged on the bed wearing only trousers, stubble lining his jaw, waiting expectantly for her to continue. 'When I came home from Holmfirth, I thought everything would change, but it didn't.' She tried to make light of it, but couldn't quite pull it off. '*I* had changed. A terrible tragedy had happened to me. *My* world would never be the same, so why was everyone else's?'

She played with the toast, sorting through her thoughts before she spoke them. 'Every day was the same, the same thing for breakfast, the same things needed doing—menus, instructions for the housekeeper. I thought—how was it possible those things still needed to be done? How could things be the same after what had happened? I wanted to move on and I couldn't.' She gave a shake of her head. 'Am I making any sense?' He probably thought her a raving lunatic.

He offered a disarming smile. 'You make perfect sense.'

She looked down at her toast. 'I was mad at you. It

was easy to blame you, to make you the embodiment of my inability to move forward. I needed your signature and without it everything was held up.'

He took another sausage. 'Yet you found a way to muscle through that detail until I arrived. I disagree. Everything *had* changed. You had new responsibilities with the businesses. You've done marvellously.'

'I've made mistakes Keir would not have made. Mackleson, for instance.' If she was confessing her faults, she might as well confess all of them.

Cullen grimaced. 'How were you to know? That's why I am here. That's why we have partnerships—to fill in each other's gaps. No one person is good at everything. No one expects it.'

'I do. I expect it of me.'

'Then you expect too much. It's a sure path to disappointment,' Cullen warned. He rose and moved the tray to the bureau. He turned and stepped towards the bed, his eyes burning hot, his voice a low husky drawl. 'What shall we do today?' He took another step, stalking her, intention in his gaze that made it apparent this was a rhetorical question only. A trill of anticipation rippled through her. She could do a little teasing of her own, too.

'We need to meet with the designers for the ladies' department to go over the plans for the displays,' she said, as he took another step closer. She wet her lips, teasing him. 'Then we need to oversee the transporting of goods from the warehouse so those displays can start being set up. Then—'

'Stop it, Minx,' he growled, putting a halt to her list of tasks with a kiss that was soft, playful, a gentle invitation to sensual exploration and she took it. Making love in the morning, surrounded by daylight, was a new delight. The mystery and shadows of the night were gone and in their place was a quiet open honesty, one's body entirely on display, entirely at the mercy of daylight, and Cullen was taking full advantage.

She stretched beneath him, giving a small moan as his lips pressed kisses down that body, raising heat and desire in their wake. This was a delicious, wicked worship and she wanted more, more of this play, this pleasure, this slow burn that would sear her as assuredly as the wildfire of last night had seared. He reached the juncture of her thighs and there *was* more, a whole new level of desire unfolding as his mouth sought her innermost source of pleasure, ratcheting her need from languorous satisfaction to the active seeking of fulfilment.

He licked at her core, she arched her hips upwards, anchored her hands in his hair in a desperate attempt to be closer, to push the pleasure further, all gentleness gone from the interaction now, replaced with a need to seek and find completion. He knew her need and he answered. She could feel the heave of his shoulders, hear the panting of his breath as the shudder of her own release claimed her with no small sense of awe. She'd not known it could be like this, that lovers could lay abed fully naked in the morning light, doing wondrous things to one another's bodies. What a discovery…about lovemaking, about herself.

Cullen stretched beside her, his eyes half-lidded. 'Did you like that?'

She gave a throaty laugh that hardly sounded like her.

She was becoming wanton. 'You know I did.' A wicked idea came to her. What was good for the goose... She slipped her hand beneath the sheet and flashed him a coy glance. 'Perhaps you'd like a bit, too?'

Cullen grinned and rolled on to his back. 'I thought you'd never ask.'

It was her turn to explore with her mouth, her teeth, her tongue. Not only his body, not only this new passion between them, but her own power. To know that she could rouse and control, that in this bed without the world between them, they were true equals. It was a heady realisation indeed, one that excited her as much this passion play did. When his release came, she took him in hand, revelling in the pulse of his pleasure. His eyes were the colour now of rich amber, dark with his desire, proof that he, too, was pleased by the power politics in this bed.

'We are good together.'

Yes, they were.

She sighed, curling up against him. 'I don't want to leave this bed.'

'We'll come back, I promise.' He laughed and pressed a kiss to her hair, but neither rose from the bed with any haste, in no hurry to move on with their day.

Last night she'd taken the next step in moving on and she'd been floating on air all day. It was, perhaps, inevitable that she would crash. One could not float on air for ever. The guilt came late in the afternoon as she climbed the stairs to change for dinner. The work of the day was done, the goods moved from the warehouse to the store where workers could begin the long process of unpacking and arranging, Cullen had returned to Mivart's to change as well. Now she was alone with her thoughts, which were not only reflections about last night, but also about the guilt.

A whole day had passed. Should she have felt guilty sooner? Was it wrong that she only just now contemplating that guilt? She passed by the door to the room, *their* room, guilt pricking at the sight of that closed door, the chamber of their secrets. Was it wrong that she'd enjoyed herself so thoroughly? That she'd not thought about Keir in those moment of extreme pleasure, but rather of the man she was with? Of herself? Had it been wrong to live in those moments and let them consume her?

She wished heartily that Emma was here. Would Emma tell her she had also felt guilty at first with Julien Archambeau? But Emma was across the Channel and even if Fleur was in town, Antonia saw little of her. Between her own commitments to the store and Fleur's commitments to the newspaper and the publishing house, there was little time for social visits and in the beginning there'd been too much grief, both of them hiding away, burying themselves with work in their private sorrows as they mourned. She would have to come to terms with this latest development on her own.

He had come to terms with last night, and with this morning. Cullen gave his neckcloth a final tug and inserted a topaz stickpin. They were dining out tonight at the St James's, then perhaps taking in a play, but Cullen could think of other things he'd rather be doing with her than sitting in a theatre box risking potential notice by early arrivals in town and wasting time that could be better spent in bed. He was hopeful he could change her mind.

The anticipation of changing her mind made him smile. Antonia was a passionate lover. She'd thrown herself into lovemaking with an abandon that had matched his own. He'd meant it when he'd said they'd been good together. Not just physically good, but there'd been a mental, emotional connection as well that belonged just to them. Not to Keir. He was no part of it.

That had been the piece he'd had to come to terms with. There'd been moments last night when he'd felt like a cad. The question that had guided his decisions to date had reared its head: what would Keir want him to do? It had been the question he'd asked himself upon leaving Tahiti, certain that Keir would want him to come back to England and ensure the company's survival. It had been the question he'd asked himself in regard to the decision made since then, too. What would Keir expect of him when it came to the business? When it came to watching over Antonia?

Answering those questions had come with sacrifice—leaving the life he'd built in Tahiti. Now with developments at the bank and Cowden's warning, another sacrifice loomed—that of being unable to return. To save the business might require him permanently staying in England as might watching over Antonia. Was it fair to ask that much of him? Perhaps he ought to stop asking the questions what would Keir do? What would Keir want? In the quiet of the late afternoon in his rooms, Cullen had decided he could not let that be the sole criteria of his decision-making. It would lead both him and Antonia to leading lives lived for a dead man instead of themselves.

Cullen checked his pocket watch. Antonia and the carriage would be pulling up to the kerb soon. He gathered up his long wool coat, slipping it on as he headed out the door. The decision had given him perspective on the affair with Antonia, but by no means did that decision make anything simpler. The affair itself had its own complications.

What did she expect from him? By necessity, it needed to be short term if he stood any hope of returning to Tahiti. Would that be acceptable to her? Perhaps he might suggest that once the store opened they would ease their need for daily contact. After all, Keir and he had not seen each other every day even when he'd been in England. Business partners needn't live in each other's pockets. That would give them this month to enjoy one another.

It seemed a good plan, one that made sense for five minutes, right up until he climbed into the carriage and saw Antonia dressed for the evening. Then, all rational thought fled. She'd chosen a gown of midnight-blue velvet with a sweetheart bodice, a thin, sparkly silver belt at her waist, a wrap of soft white fur about her shoulders, her blonde waves done up high in an elegant coiffure that exposed the slimness of her neck—a neck his mouth knew very well the heat in his blood reminded him. 'You are stunning,' He reached for her hand, encased in long white gloves, and kissed her knuckles.

She laughed. 'You look well yourself considering you were hauling crates and entirely dusty a few hours ago.'

'And loving every minute of it.' He grinned. 'It brought back old times, old memories of working in the warehouses. It felt good to do manual work. On the island, life is full of exercise. We're always fishing, swimming, sailing, hauling, hunting, building. I worry about growing soft here. I don't know if calisthenics in my rooms and running the streets before breakfast are enough to keep me in shape.'

'Running the streets?' She gave him a glance that was part worry and part curiosity. 'Where do you run? Wherever it is, I hope you run fast. London streets are not the safest even in good neighbourhoods.'

'Yes, I run fast.' He smiled at her concern, aware of how that concern made him feel—cared for, included, as if there was a place for him here in a city where he'd never quite felt at home.

'I wouldn't want to lose you,' Antonia offered softly, barely loud enough to be heard. Perhaps she hadn't meant for him to hear it.

What could he say to that? He could not say 'you won't' because that implied promises he was not comfortable making and it implied a permanence he wasn't willing to contemplate. Yet for her, something deep within him yearned to say those exact words, yearned to be a man who could stay, who'd want to stay, who could tolerate London and its hypocrisy. So he said instead, 'I hear St James's has a spectacular steak.'

St James's was empty given that it was the middle of a week in winter. A few year-round politicos dined at various tables, too busy with their discussions to notice them. Cullen preferred it that way. It wouldn't be long before he'd have to tell her…something. London would slowly start filling up. Someone of import would notice him and word would get back to his father. That would lead to a confrontation he'd rather avoid because it couldn't change anything for him, but it could make things worse for Antonia.

Perhaps things were already worse? Other than the little bantering exchange in the carriage, Antonia had been quiet. Something had dampened a bit of her joy. Not second thoughts, surely? Not after her remark about not wanting to lose him. Guilt, then? Perhaps she, too, had spent some time this afternoon grappling with the terms of their relationship.

He did not broach the subject until after their meals came—steak for him and fresh, grilled trout for her. 'What's on your mind, Antonia? Are you not having a good time?' He could not bring himself to use the word 'regrets'. He didn't want her to have regrets—regrets about what they'd done, what they wanted to do, or regrets about him.

She put down her fork and gave him a solemn look. 'I think the problem is that I *am* having a good time. I am, perhaps, enjoying this too much.'

Ah, so it was the guilt then. He had felt some of that, too, and found a way to dispose of it. 'You are entitled to happiness. You do not owe the dead your life.'

She shook her head, the diamond earrings sparkling in the lamplight. 'It's not that. It's more that I have guilt *about* the guilt. Primarily, I feel guilty because I didn't feel guilty at all until much later.' She played with the stem of her wine glass, her voice low and private. 'You should know that being with you was unlike anything I'd ever experienced before.' She glanced up at him, her green eyes shimmering. 'It both thrills and frightens me.'

He imagined those fingers doing to him what they were doing to the wineglass. They should have stayed in. 'Frightens you? How so?' Having such a discussion in public was its own aphrodisiac and it ratcheted his desire to be home with her early tonight. Time was wasting indeed.

'Because all good things end. I know that now. I also know they end sooner than one would like. I don't want to wake up one morning and suddenly learn that you're gone. If you're going to leave, I at least want to prepare myself for it.' There was a sharpness added to her gaze now that had him alert, his steak forgotten. 'You *are* going to leave, aren't you, Cullen?' It was more statement than question. They'd never spoken of it aloud, but it had been implicitly hinted at in his comments and she'd noticed.

'That hasn't been decided.' And it was much harder to decide staring at the decolletage of her blue velvet gown.

'There's no need to prevaricate, Cullen.' Somehow this had gone from a pre-seduction dinner to a business negotiation. He did not like this one bit. It was starting to look as though he might not get a second night, let alone a month.

Antonia responded to strength and truth, so he would give her that. He sat back in his chair and fixed her with a stare. 'I would *like* to go back to Tahiti. My life is there. But you are here and my obligations are here. It is not clear to me that I can leave without jeopardising the company.' Only that he must leave at some point before his past caught up with him. Leaving her would be far more difficult than he'd anticipated.

'Things will not always be unsettled. The company will not always need you so close at hand.' That was debatable according to Cowden, but Cullen would not argue that point with her tonight when there were other battles to win. 'Let me ask you point blank, Cullen. If those are the only things holding you here, how long do we have?'

'If those are the only things...'

He'd caught the phrase. They most certainly weren't, but they were the only things they'd discussed. They'd tacitly avoided renegotiating their affair.

Well, so be it. He'd given her truth. Now he'd give her honesty. 'We have until the store opens. We have March and a couple of weeks beyond.' Even if he stayed, they wouldn't have any more time than that before someone unearthed his scandal and trotted it out. Town would be full of aristocrats by then. He'd need to have his defences in place so that the scandal didn't hurt the business.

He had become a silent partner and gone to Tahiti in order to disappear the first time scandal had reared its head. Disappearing had worked wonders. People had forgotten him. But this time he was no longer a silent partner. This time he was the one standing in the breach, convincing investors and banks their money was in good hands.

'A month and change.' She nodded slowly, thinking.

'I won't trap you, Cullen. You needn't stay here. I won't steal your life. We have a month to open the store and a month to ensure you can return to Tahiti, to the life you want. I promise you, when the time comes, I *will* let you go.' That promise should have thrilled him more than it did. Her voice took on a coy edge that pleased him far better. 'But if time is of the essence, I might recommend going home. Now.'

'I couldn't agree with you more.' Cullen signalled for a waiter. 'The bill, please.'

Chapter Fifteen

Time was indeed of the essence—the essence of life, the heartbeat of the living and Antonia's pulse beat in time to its rhythm in the heady days and weeks that followed. Antonia felt as if the world around her was signalling spring. The long winter of both season and soul was giving way to better days, darkness giving way to light, grief giving way to joy, death giving way to life.

Her cup was running over with happiness. The store was coming together brilliantly. Cullen had replaced Mackleson with a new foreman by the name of Maxwell and things had run smoothly since. Each day the departments took further shape, displays were finished and more shelves were stocked until one could see the store come alive. It was rich and vibrant, the merchandise visually appealing, and it exceeded her expectations.

Her days were spent at the store while Cullen divided his time between the store and the warehouses, having taken over the office at the Captain's Club down on the docks. She loved the days best, when they worked side by side, solving problems and making plans. But nothing topped their nights.

The nights were just for them. They made a pact not

to bring work home and their evenings were spent dining in or out as the mood struck them. If they stayed in, they spent the post-dinner hours playing two-handed whist or backgammon before heading up to bed. If the staff was scandalised that Cullen spent more time at the town house and only the guest room gave signs of being used, no one said a thing. She liked to believe everyone was simply happy for her, that no one was judging.

That guest room had indeed become their place. Cullen had a few items stashed in the bureau drawers and she had a dressing gown in the wardrobe. But it wasn't the things in the room that made it theirs. This was the place where they made love, where she lay in his arms listening to stories of far-off Tahiti, falling in love with the South Pacific, its sandy beaches, turquoise waters and sunshine, as much as she was falling for the man who told those stories. Her happiness would be complete if not for the reminder that time was passing.

As plans moved forward for the grand opening of the store, an unexpected anxiety gripped her. Instead of feeling a sense of accomplishment in knowing that she'd preserved Keir's legacy, she was filled with dread. Dread about what to do next. The store was complete and she could manage it as she'd suggested to Cullen. But that did not fill her with the same anticipation it once had. It was simply more work to get up and do in the morning. Something to fill her days with until... until what?

Did she really want to spend her days with ledgers and accounts and contracts? But if she didn't, how would she fill those days? She needed purpose. She needed *something*. There was dread, too, in knowing that the completion of an old dream also meant the ending of a new dream, a dream she hadn't even known she wanted until six weeks ago. Despite her promises, she did not want Cullen to go.

She'd hoped having time to prepare for the loss of him would offset the hurt, that it would give her a way to protect herself—if she needed it. She'd hoped to not need that contingency. She'd not begun this affair with the intent of indulging her heart. She'd meant to believe Cullen's wicked promise that first night in the kitchen— that physical intimacy, physical satisfaction, didn't require the engagement of emotions. But it had followed none the less.

She often wondered if it had happened for him, too, or if he was just counting down the days, filling them with a trifling affair? There were times when she'd catch him looking at her with intense longing and she would think that he'd fallen, too, that he was no longer keen on leaving, that he might stay, that they might have more of these early spring days together when anything was possible. But at other times, she wasn't so sure. His gaze seemed far off as if part of him was already in his canoe paddling his blue waters. How she would love to see that sight in person!

She would remember him that way, she'd decided, imagining him in his *malo*, out on the waters he loved, his hair growing back to its former length, his deep tan returned, and she would know he was happy, that she'd been right to keep her word. To keep him here was tantamount to the keeping of the lions she'd seen as a girl in the cages at the Tower of London menagerie. He was not meant for town.

There was still time, though. The optimist in her wouldn't let her dwell on such sweet sorrow for long. There was still the now. She wouldn't ruin the present by looking too far ahead. Although every day, the increasing quantity of mail in the silver salver reminded her that time was running out. Invitations mounted. The Season was nearing and with it the end of her affair. The store would open and Cullen would leave, his promises fulfilled. The way that made her feel inside was worrisome indeed.

'You seem pensive.' Cullen rolled the dice and moved his pips on the backgammon board.

'Why would you say that?' She rolled and grimaced. A two and a three would do her no good. She had a pip on the bar and Cullen had all his home points blocked out except the sixth. She couldn't get in.

Cullen grinned and rolled again. 'Because we're a week away from our grand opening gala and you've missed three opportunities tonight to put me on the bar.'

'That is all true.' She laughed and rolled again, a six and a five. At last, a roll she could use. She moved her pip in to play. 'But to be honest, that's not the whole reason.' She rested her elbows on the game table. 'An invitation came a few days ago. I've been thinking about how best to approach it with you. Lady Camford is hosting a ball and I'd like to go.'

She paused and then continued, launching into her carefully crafted list of reasons. 'It should be a small event, not a lot of folks have come up to town yet for the Season. It's meant to be a practice ball of sorts for her goddaughter who came out last year. Apparently the girl is a bit shy and Lady Camford wants her to have a bit of a warm-up before the larger affairs.

'Lady Camford is a friend of my parents, which is why I've been invited,' she explained the connection. 'I thought it would be good practice for me, too. Perhaps I need a bit of a warm-up after a year out of society. I thought it would be good for the store as well, a chance for me to promote it, to encourage people to come by.' She clasped her hands together, readying herself for the larger request. 'Would you come with me?'

Come with her? He'd like nothing more and yet it was the thing he should do the least. Who would have thought six months ago he'd relish the idea of a ball with an English woman on his arm? That his body would thrill at the prospect of seeing her in a ballgown, of waltzing her across a crowded floor. Yet, giving in to the prospect tempted fate when he'd nearly fulfilled his promise, when he might be able to leave England undetected and without doing harm.

But one look into the emerald eyes, sparkling with hope and even with nervousness as if she were a young girl putting herself on the line for a boy she liked, when they were neither, had him rethinking the wisdom of refusal. On what grounds could he refuse, though, without exposing himself? If she knew everything about him, she might decide he was not the escort she needed, or even the partner she needed. 'I appreciate the offer,' he said gently, 'but perhaps you should think about what it might mean for us to be seen together socially. Lady Camford is a family friend, so your parents will be there, yes? Are you ready to explain me to them?'

'I will tell them it's business.'

'Do you think your mother obtuse enough to believe that?' Cullen asked bluntly. 'In my experience, mothers are endowed with a sixth sense when it comes to their children's romantic inclinations.'

She laughed a bit at that. 'It sounds like there's a story there, something you know first-hand?'

'Yes, and it's a story I'd rather not tell if you don't mind,' he answered soberly. He wanted to make it clear he could not be teased about this, that this was not a topic open to probing.

'All right.' She reached a hand across the table and placed it on his, her touch warm and encouraging. 'I won't push you on it. I will, however, push on the ball. It is my first social appearance since coming out of mourning. People are going to speculate no matter what. Have I come out because I am looking to remarry? What kind of situation did Keir leave with me? Am I a wealthy widow? The fortune hunters will be on their game. Having you with me will spike their guns for a while even if I proclaim it is strictly business between us.

'Think of it as your civic duty to me and to the store. While I don't like the idea that a male presence at the head of a business steadies investors' nerves, I understand it is an unfortunate truth in our present world. With you beside me, we can bolster confidence in Popplewell and Allardyce. Peers may not dirty their hands in the daily running of companies, but they *do* invest. The Prometheus Club is proof of that. And their wives shop. I want their patronage.'

'You are far too persuasive for your own good.' Cullen shook his head in defeat. If he didn't go now, she'd ask again later when it truly was out of the question. His father was always in town for the Academy art show and his mother made appearances at all the balls.

It was not that he was a coward. He'd gladly face his father in a crowded ballroom, but now he had someone to protect, someone who could be hurt by that relationship and the old scandal, and that someone was her. And, perhaps, that someone was him. It would hurt him to cause her pain after she'd already endured so much. It was unlikely anyone of note would be at Lady Camford's. This might indeed be fortuitous, after all. If not fortuitous, then certainly the lesser of two evils.

'If you think you're up to it, then I am up to it.' He smiled. 'I would be pleased to stand beside you as you make your return.' He gripped her hand in a supportive squeeze. 'You will dazzle them as always. Perhaps so much no one would look twice at me.'

She laughed. 'If you think that, you underestimate your appeal. Every woman in the room will notice you.'

'Perhaps the appeal you underestimate is your own.' He rose and raised her with him. 'I seem to have lost all interest in this game when another, more enchanting game awaits me upstairs.'

She gave him a flirty look of mock bashfulness. 'But, sir, you were winning,' she said coyly.

He stepped close, letting his mouth hover tantalis-

ingly near her own and whispered, '*Now* I am winning.'
He claimed a kiss and all thoughts of ballrooms fled in
exchange for bedrooms.

Ballrooms had not changed much in the ten years
he'd been away. Cullen had not expected they would.
The aristocracy didn't like change much. They clung
to their traditions, their rituals, and both were on in-
tentional and unintentional display in Lady Camford's
ballroom. The parquet floor was polished to a walnut
sheen, its soaring Doric columns that lined the room,
separating the dance floor from the perimeter and supporting the soaring ceiling, were draped in pale pink
silk swathes and baby-pink rosebud garlands in honour of her goddaughter who was dressed to match in a
white gown and pink sash. The six-piece orchestra was
sequestered in a musicians' balcony that overlooked the
top of the ballroom.

In an adjacent room, the usual refreshments were laid
out—orgeat in a giant silver punch bowl, trays of pret-
tily iced biscuits done in pink and white, lobster patties
and finger sandwiches. In his younger days, he and his
friends would bet on who would eat the most lobster
patties. The one saving grace was that footmen were
circulating with glasses of cold champagne—a drink
that was always in season, not that Cullen intended to
partake of it much. Still, it would be better than warm,
watery punch if a man needed a drink.

'Nothing has changed,' he whispered at Antonia's
ear as they passed through the ballroom, looking for her

parents. Lady Camford had mentioned in the receiving line that the baronet and his wife had arrived earlier.

She gave a light laugh over her shoulder. 'Did you think it would?' No, he hadn't and in that moment he keenly felt the comment Antonia had made to him that first night together—that she'd thought the world would change because she had. He supposed part of him felt that way, too, hoped for that, too. But the broken system seemed to find a way to limp along, outliving even itself.

'Have I mentioned you look stunning tonight?' He had his mouth close to her ear, using the crowd and the noise of conversations as an excuse to keep a hand at her back and his body near. She smelled of vanilla and flowers and he wanted to breathe her in, the scent a reminder of the freshness of spring, the infinity of hope and possibility. She wore emerald-green silk tonight, a shade that brought out her eyes and drew attention without being ostentatious. A diamond choker sparkled at her throat, matching earrings sparkled at her ears and a wide bracelet sparkled about the wrist of her long white gloves.

'Perhaps you are biased,' she demurred with a private smile that said she was remembering how long it had taken them to get dressed and why they'd arrived later than planned. He thought the late arrival might work to their benefit, though—there would be fewer people to notice them. People were already partnered off into their preferred groups of friends and acquaintances, immersed in catching up after a winter apart.

He growled. 'I am not biased. Every man we've passed has looked at you.'

'Don't be jealous. Every woman we've passed has

looked at you,' she parried with a laugh. 'I don't mind. Because I know a secret.'

He gave a low chuckle, liking this flirty game of hers. She was happy tonight, joy spilling out of her. She was made for this, to be among people. 'Tell me,' he cajoled. He was already glad he'd come if being here gave her such joy. He'd promised to bring her back to life and this evening was proof that he had. Truth be told, as long as she was beside him, the evening was enjoyable for him, too, something he'd not expected. He'd not realised how much of a difference her presence made to him.

'I get to go home with you. No matter how much they flirt with their fans and flutter their eyes, you are mine.'

Her confidence aroused him. What a spark she was! It was a treat to see that spark unveiled in surroundings outside of business. 'Maybe we don't have to wait until we get home.' His gaze was already quartering the ballroom, looking for an alcove, old habits dying hard, or not really dying at all.

'Look! There are my parents.' She shot him a teasing look.

'Minx.' He groaned. 'You are a such a tease.'

'And you are wicked. Now, be on your best behaviour,' she scolded with a laugh.

He would be, for her, because tonight meant so very much to her personally and professionally.

Her parents were delightful as far as parents went. Antonia had her mother's looks, which had aged well, and her father's charm. But Cullen didn't think he and Antonia were fooling either of them no matter that Antonia introduced him as Mr Cullen Allardyce and emphasised repeatedly his role as Keir's partner in the company. He'd hoped to escape any further inquisition when the music began, but Lady Lytton was too quick. 'Perhaps you might do me the honour of a dance? I am afraid my husband doesn't dance as often as he used to.'

Cullen bowed and offered his hand wryly. 'How can I refuse?' The baronet and his wife were much cannier than he'd given them credit for. He should have known better. Antonia had to have come by her talents somehow. Years of watching them had no doubt rubbed off on her in some degree and she'd merely refined them. In anticipation of the evening, Cullen had been prepared for the potential of interrogation, but in his imaginings it had always been man to man. He'd not anticipated the interrogation coming from her mother, that was his fault, his oversight. After experiencing Antonia's bluntness, he should have known better.

The music began and he led Lady Lytton through the opening movement, but she led the conversation. 'You and my daughter are having an affair.' She smiled as he tried to hide his surprise. 'I see you're the one who is used to doing the shocking. But let's not have any coyness between us. My daughter has had a difficult year. The world is not kind to widows, especially young ones. I see her sparkling tonight and if you are the reason for bringing her back to life, than I don't much care how you've done it.'

'Yes, ma'am.' What else could he say? He was entirely off script here, feeling his way. Usually these sorts of conversations ended in duels.

They began the next pattern, Lady Lytton as sharp on her feet as she was on conversation. 'I wonder though if my daughter knows who you are?' Her smile was a little colder now and his own was more formal, more guarded. 'She made much of your partnership with her late husband, but does she know you? I admit my husband and I did not. It was not our business to poke into Keir Popplewell's business. However, now that his business is our daughter's business and there's a silent partner that's surfaced, we did our research, Lord Cullen Allardyce, second son of the Marquess of Standon.'

He'd been braced for that. He was ready. 'That ought to please you. Even a marquess's second son is quite an elevation for the daughter of a baronet.'

She shot him a sly look. 'Only if you marry her. Is that your intention? It was not my understanding that you were a marrying man, that you had no interest in the trappings of the peerage and that was the reason you went abroad.' She speared him with a hard stare reminiscent of Antonia on her mettle, challenging him about the store.

'My husband and I go about society only a little. We prefer our life in the country with our horses and innovating around the estate.' She arched a blonde brow. 'Perhaps I do not have the story correct? I do understand society can get the facts wrong on occasion.' The overture was skilfully done. She was giving him a chance to correct the narrative attached to him. He also wondered how much she knew? Or if this was a veiled request for information? Was she inviting him to spill the whole sordid tale?

'I do not think your daughter is looking to remarry,' he offered diplomatically.

She gave a short nod. 'How convenient for you, then. But that's your business, that's between the two of you. Frankly, I do not care if you're a marquess's second son, or a duke's heir. What I am most concerned about is, you do not immerse her in scandal now that she's clawed her way back to the land of the living.'

She paused and leaned close as the dance ended. 'Mr Allardyce, if I know, others know. I just want my daughter to know before it comes back to haunt her. I am sure you can imagine the damage it would do her and I hope we agree that neither of us wants to see her hurt.'

'Of course, my lady. I appreciate your candour.' He gave a short bow and escorted her back to Antonia and Sir Jonas. The next dance was a waltz and he led Antonia to the floor, desperately wanting these minutes with her, fully aware that everything between them was about to change and he'd be the one to change it for better or worse, although he wasn't sure at present what the 'better' would be. Right now, he could only see 'worse'.

Chapter Sixteen

He would find a way to make it better, Cullen vowed. He would give her this moment, he would let her shine, he would let London see her sparkle. Cullen placed his hand at the small of her back and positioned them for the dance. She looked up at him in anticipation as if she'd been waiting all night for this one dance. He would not take that from her even as his mind was already rife with all the ways in which his scandal could do exactly that.

He moved them into the dance, unable to look away from her and she from him. 'People will talk,' he warned.

'Then let them. It would be a waste to spend this dance staring into the blank space over your very broad shoulder,' she bantered in private tones.

At the top of the ballroom the tempo of the music picked up and he accelerated coming through the turn, the pressure of his hand at her back urging her closer, giving him better control over the dance until they were flying, soaring, together without their feet leaving the floor.

Exhilaration glowed in her eyes, there was exquisite joy in her smile and he savoured it. If London was looking, so be it. There was just this moment and it was his, theirs. He would remember it long after he returned to Tahiti: the night he'd held the most beautiful woman in his arms, a woman who cared for him, and he'd given her the waltz of her life, the perfect bookend to the promise he'd made her—that he would bring her back to life. Now his work was done. He could leave in good conscience, his debt to Keir paid. There was no longer any pretence of a grey area there, nor any hope that they might choose to renegotiate that departure.

After speaking with Lady Lytton, it was clear that the hurt he would inflict would not be just the social fallout or the ways in which his past could hamper the department store. One might be able to ride out those particular storms. But there would be internal scars, too. She had not undertaken their affair lightly. She'd battled guilt and grief for this, and she'd be repaid with scandal if he stayed any longer. He was risking much even now.

She would feel betrayed, misled and she'd blame herself. She'd think she ought to have known better, just as she felt she ought to have known better about Mackleson. To stay would risk destroying her confidence. He would not be responsible for that. Her optimism was one of the things he loved about her best. It was an integral part of who she was, a part of her charm, what set her apart from others.

He leaned close to her ear. 'Did you know the waltz was a metaphor for sexual congress? The man in pursuit of the woman, the closeness of our bodies, the heightened risk that your breasts might brush the lapels of my coat, or that our bodies might touch below the waist,' he whispered naughtily.

'There's little chance of that, not with crinolines. A man can't get within twelve inches of a woman in petticoats and hooped skirts.' She gave a low, throaty laugh. 'And I dare say that's still six inches too far for most men.'

'What a vixen you are.' He grinned at her bawdy humour and suddenly wished they were anywhere but a public ballroom for what he had in mind. 'I'd like to dispense with those petticoats and crinolines forthwith,' he growled.

'And I'd like to dispense with your jacket, your waistcoat, your shirt...' She laughed up at him. Was she aware of how lovely she was? 'Based on all this naughty banter, I'd say the waltz is not a metaphor for sex but foreplay.'

He grinned down at her, taking a final turn. Soon the magic would be over. 'What do you know about foreplay?'

She was up for the challenge. 'I know your nipples are sensitive to tongues. I know—' Her eyes broke from his for a moment and when they returned there was shock in them. 'Cullen, everyone is watching us.'

That was unfortunate. There should have been anonymity on the dance floor. He'd meant for this dance to be for them, for her, not for public display. And yet it had become that. He leaned close once more. 'We can't stop them from looking, so we might as well give them a show. Eyes on me, love, and keep smiling. They can look, but they can't come into our world.' Not yet. He wouldn't be able to keep them out for ever.

'And then?'

'And then we'll go home and finish this.'

She gave a mischievous smile. 'Ah, so I was right. The waltz *is* foreplay.'

She'd not been this glad to get home in quite a while. They'd finished the waltz with a flourish amid applause from the perimeter. Cullen had taken a bow and she a curtsy. Never, even at the height of her debut, had she cleared a dance floor. It had made leaving a little more difficult than she'd have liked, everyone wanting an introduction as they made their way through the ball-room to make their farewells to Lady Camford who was certain they'd made her early pre-Season ball the talk of the society pages. Antonia had laughed, saying, 'As long as they also mention the department store', but Cullen had been surprisingly reserved or perhaps he'd just been wound tight with desire and eager to be away.

Subsequent events certainly bore the latter out. They'd been halfway undressed by the time they were halfway home and they only made it halfway up the stairs in the empty town house before all restraint was lost with the rest of their clothes.

He took her there on the staircase, balanced between his body and the wall, her legs wrapped about his hips, her hands tangled in his hair, her pleasure a gasping chorus of sobs, so great was the release that swept her when climax shuddered through them both. It had been rough and glorious and fulfilling. And yet, something was off because when something was too good to be true, it usually was—even an optimist knew that.

He lifted her in his arms and carried her the rest of

the way to what was now *their* bedroom. He laid her down and stretched out beside her in what had become his usual post-coital pose—his long body on its side, his head propped in his hand. 'An amazing night,' he murmured, his voice still husky.

She pushed a length of his hair back behind his ear, giving his jaw a soft caress, and gently ventured her theory. 'It was. I will not forget that waltz. Nor will anyone else who was there, I dare say. Are you all right with that?' It had seemed that he was. After all, he'd suggested finishing up with a show for the onlookers, but afterwards, he had been tense. She'd not misread that. Some of the unease she'd noted in him then was still there, lingering in his eyes.

'You were dazzling. People will always notice a beautiful woman.' He smiled, but it did not convince her. A thought occurred about the source of that unease.

'How was your dance with my mother?' Perhaps she had said something to upset him? 'She can be rather headstrong at times.' And protective of her only daughter.

That earned her a chuckle. 'Like her daughter? I see where you get your personality. Your mother loves you, she cares about you. I cannot fault her for that.'

'That sounds suspiciously like another way of saying she was hard on you.' Antonia raised up, mirroring his position, her head on her hand. 'Tell me what she said.'

'She wanted to make sure I didn't hurt you.'

'You won't,' Antonia assured him. She saw now what it was. He, too, had been thinking about the timeline they'd laid out. The store was set to open within days and she'd made a return to society. His promises were fulfilled. All that remained was to ensure the company was able to function with him halfway around the world without investors panicking. She and Bowdrie had been working on that. She would keep her promise, too, and let him go.

'We knew this was coming. We never meant this to last for ever, only to enjoy it. We've had our time. I admit it will be hard to let you go and perhaps I would choose differently, but we made promises and we will honour them.'

It took all of her courage to say those words. She did not want to let him go, but it was the honourable thing to do. He'd come halfway around the world for her and now she had to let him go back. His part of the deal was fulfilled. But she was touched that he was worried about hurting her—perhaps it proved that this had meant something to him as well, something more.

He shook his head. 'Leaving you will indeed be hard…'

'Leaving can be renegotiated,' she said, but he pressed a finger to her lips.

'It's not that, Antonia. I could not stay even if I wanted to. I left the first time so that I would not be a liability to Keir and I will leave again so that I am not a liability to you. You will have my money and my name, and I hope it will be enough to see you through. But you cannot have me—indeed, you do not want me anywhere near.'

She stared hard at him, trying to understand. His tone sounded ominous, not unlike Mr Dyson's quiet tones when he'd come to tell her that Keir was dead. 'What are you talking about, Cullen?'

'I am talking about the scandal that comes with me and the fact that after tonight you and I are living on borrowed time before the Marquess of Standon comes knocking.'

'I don't even know him. What does he have to do with you? With us?' Her stomach tied itself in knots.

'He's my father and I am a stain on the family name and, by association, you will be dragged into it, too. He's been wanting his revenge for quite some time.' She understood now. The marquess would go through her to get to his son. She and the store were at risk. She reached for patience, for steadiness in the face of her anger. How dare he hide this from her, how dare he drag her into this? The little voice in her head asserted itself. This wasn't solely about her, but Cullen, too. He was hurting.

She got out of bed and fetched their dressing robes. This was not a conversation to have naked. She slid her arms through hers and tossed his on the bed. 'You'd best tell me everything if we're to figure a way through it,' she said calmly, but inside she felt as if her world was about to fall apart just when she'd put it back together.

She sat in the chair beside the bedroom's small fireplace, watching Cullen pace the length of the chamber, his robe open, offering tantalising glimpses of nakedness every few steps. She did not rush him. He was choosing his words, perhaps considering where to start. Her eyes never left him. Her own mind was a riot of thoughts. How was it possible that they'd been so happy a few hours ago? The ecstasy of the ball seemed far away. But only for her, came the sharp reminder. Whatever it was he was about to tell her, he'd known all of it the entire time and he'd withheld it. At some point, there'd have to be an accounting for that.

'I find it best, Cullen, to start at the beginning,' she prompted after a while. 'Tell me why you went to Tahiti. It wasn't only for the promotion of trade, was it? Not only because your principles demanded it?' She did not doubt they were part of the reason. But neither were they the entire reason as he'd implied that night they'd fried sausage and eaten grilled cheese. 'What was so awful that you had to leave England?'

'Are you sure you want to know?' He turned from the window. 'Once you know, it will be the beginning of the end for us.'

'We were always going to end, Cullen.'

'But not like this, not with you hating me. Tonight, your mother insisted that I tell you before you heard it from someone else, somewhere else.'

She nodded, her heart twisting. She detested seeing him like this, tortured and troubled. Even more, she despised the idea that he thought her hate was so easily acquired, that she had no tolerance for error. 'Cullen, I care for you. I have given you my body, my heart, and you have brought me back from the dead. Nothing will put you beyond my love.'

He gave her a hard look. 'Are you sure about that, Antonia?'

'Whatever it was, it couldn't be that bad. You had a wild youth, many young men do. My own brother had plenty of scrapes before he joined the military. If it was gambling, or drinking, or lightskirts—' she thought of the brothel and the night he'd met Keir '—or brawling, it is not so terrible.'

He faced her squarely and the rest of her assurances died on her lips. 'Antonia, it was murder. I killed a man. Illegally. In a duel. He was the brother of the woman I was supposed to marry.'

There was nothing to say that wouldn't make a mockery of her words. She'd asked him to trust her love. She couldn't back out now because the words were frightening or because they held heinous connotations and she would not do him the disservice of trying to mitigate them with platitudes like 'I'm sure you had good reason'. Was there ever a good reason to take a life, let alone to take it on the duelling ground in the heat of misunderstood honour? But she could do him the service of listening. She settled deep into the chair, her feet curled under her. It was going to be a long night.

Chapter Seventeen

He'd given her enough to go running from the room or to send him out of the house or both. Perhaps that's what he'd been hoping for. It would make things easier for him if she were angry, if she simply banished him. He wouldn't have to explain the whole sordid mess to her, wouldn't have to see her face fall in shock and horror when she heard the truth about the man she'd let into her life, into her bed. But if that was what he'd hoped for, he was sorely disappointed. Antonia's optimism was made of sterner stuff.

'There's certainly a lot to explain to me, Cullen. A duel, a death and a debutante,' she said solemnly. She looked so damn serene, so beautiful, sitting by the fire, her hair loose, her silk robe flowing over curves, and it hurt to know that the serenity was a hard-won façade. It was an illusion only and it was his fault.

A man had to know where to look to understand that: in her eyes where anger and worry sparked like embers; at her hands where they lay tightly clenched in her lap. No, she was not calm. Right now she was probably wrestling with her anger and with her need for self-preservation. 'I suppose, though, the only question that matters is why? Will you answer it?'

He would answer it if for no other reason than the truth was all he had left to give her. But where to begin? With his father? With the marriage? He gave a short nod of his head and opted for the latter. 'I didn't want to marry her. I made it clear to her, to her father and to mine that I found the match unsuitable and I had no intentions of honouring it no matter what inducements it came with.' He grimaced in remembrance. It had come with several inducements: two estates in the country, a home in town, a carriage, horses, a significant allowance from his father.

Antonia looked thoughtful. He knew what she would ask before the question came. 'Many men would find those inducements sufficient to overcome marital reservations. Is it wrong of me to ask why you refused?'

'They assumed my integrity was for sale. Only my father and I disagreed on what a man's integrity ought to consist of. I felt integrity lay in being true to my own personal beliefs and he felt that a son's integrity lay in being loyal to his family, to his family's line, especially when that line came from the peerage.'

He stopped before the window and stared out into the dark garden behind the house, remembering those difficult days. 'It was complicated. I can't explain why I refused the marriage without also explaining my father. He and I were always at loggerheads. He is a Tory to his core. Traditions, family lines, rituals—those things matter to him. They are worth fighting for, sacrificing sons for. Change concerns him, change undermines the things he treasures, the things he protects.'

Antonia cocked her head to one side, considering.

'But not you. Change excites you. New places, new people, new ideas. It's why you like Tahiti so much.'

'Because it's new to me, not because it has no traditions.' He chuckled. 'Sometimes I think Rahiti's father would get along well with mine. He and his clan have their rituals and traditions, too, and they are as equally important.'

'But they're new to you and that's why you love it there,' she surmised.

He nodded, some of his anxiousness easing. He couldn't spare her the consequences of his tales, but it felt good to be understood as he told it, a reminder that she understood *him*. 'My father felt it was within his rights to arrange a marriage for his second son that would benefit the marquessate. He wanted the alliance that would come with me married to the Earl of Southberry's daughter.' He shook his head. 'Selfishly, I didn't want to be married yet. I was only twenty-five, I'd been working for Keir for two years and loving it.

'My father spent those two years ignoring me, ashamed of what I was doing—working in trade and supporting reform wherever I could. I stood against everything he stood for. To him, it was worse than whoring and running up gambling debts. Those at least were a gentleman's vices. He could understand them. What he *couldn't* understand was the pleasure it gave me to work in the warehouse, to talk with captains, to meet people from all over the world.'

He diverged for a moment. 'The docks *are* dangerous, but they are also full of ordinary people having extraordinary adventures, everyday sailors making modest wages, but who speak two or three different languages not because they've been to a fancy school, but because of the experiences they've had. It's amazing to me, but men like my father don't see the value in it.'

He shrugged. 'Anyway, my father felt this marriage was a way for me to redeem myself and come back into the family fold. He told me, "You've had your fun, now it's time to come home and serve the family. I need you and your brother needs you." What he really meant was that the marquessate of Standon needed me. My brother had been married for five years and had not produced a child.'

He studied her for a long moment, gauging how she was taking the news. This was the good part. It was going to get worse. 'Perhaps you think it was indeed selfish of me? After all, you were much younger when you came to town looking for a husband and a way to save your family.' She'd not flinched at the sacrifice while he'd baulked entirely.

'I don't think that at all, Cullen. I made my choice willingly and no one was forcing me. My whole family was in on the plan together and I don't think it occurred to any of us that I would fail to find someone who was both acceptable to me and to our needs.' She gave a soft chuckle. 'We Lyttons are like that. Optimists to the core.'

She was encouraging him with those words, he realised. Encouraging him to go on with his tale, letting him know that she was listening to understand, not to judge, that his story, no matter how terrible, was safe here in this room, with her. He hoped she wouldn't regret those very generous offerings.

'Was your freedom and your disagreement with your father the only reasons you didn't marry her?' Antonia prompted gently.

He blew out a breath. 'I was suspicious of just how sweet the pot was. I was getting a lot for doing what my father classified as my duty, as what was expected of me. It wasn't like him to be so generous. So I started digging. I discovered that the generosity was prompted by the Earl. I also discovered his daughter was pregnant with another man's child, a reprobate of an officer in the army who'd made false promises and left, but not before damage was done.

'The Earl was willing to offer my father votes and seats in the House of Commons and to promote my father's political ambitions as well as setting me and his daughter up with considerable wealth if I took her off his hands and claimed the child.' He gave a short huff of dry, wry laughter. 'Of course, I wasn't supposed to know about the child. I was supposed to think the child was a wedding-night conception and an early birth.'

'That's terrible.' Antonia wrinkled her brow. 'I am surprised a man like your father who is so concerned with his line would tolerate an illegitimate child as heir.'

'My father felt his odds were fairly well hedged. My brother might still have a child, the child my bride carried might be a daughter. Any son that came afterwards would be mine and we had proof that this bride was fertile, if nothing else. Of course, the plan was that I was not to know any differently. Appearances are everything to men like my father, the Earl and the Earl's son.'

He watched her thoughts work behind her sharp eyes.

'That's why there was a duel. Word got out you'd refused the marriage, but once the child became apparent, everyone would assume it was yours. The dishonour of abandoning her would be yours, too.'

'I was a convenient target. To be fair,' he said solemnly, holding her gaze, 'I don't think the brother knew what his father was up to. My biggest regret is that the brother believed he was defending his sister's honour.'

'You were both victims then,' she offered quietly. Then anger got the better of her. 'Men and their stupid culture of honour. I didn't think anyone duelled these days. It's a ridiculous way of settling things.'

'In 1840 the Earl of Cadogan killed a fellow officer. In 1845 two men named Seton and Hawkey duelled fatally. Last year, apparently, two French émigrés, Barthelemy and Courmet, also duelled,' he recited in rebuttal. He'd just heard about the latest from Frederick during their visit. Duelling might be less fashionable than it once was, but it was not *out* of fashion.

'I don't excuse what I did,' Cullen said sombrely. 'I am not telling you any of this for absolution or in hopes of you softening it for me. I simply want you to know why I can't stay, why there must be distance between us. Death by duel is murder even if the courts are not likely to apply the term. I won't sugar-coat it. I murdered the Earl of Southberry's heir in order to save myself.' His throat tightened. After all these years he still couldn't talk of it, think of it without emotion. 'If I could take back those seconds, if I could stop my hand on the trigger, I would.'

Antonia came to him, not with her body, or her touch.

Perhaps she knew physical contact would bring him to his knees. She came to him with her eyes, those green flames locked on him, her words soft but stern with the command, 'Tell me.'

Cullen closed his eyes, but it didn't stop him from reliving every moment as vividly as if it were yesterday. 'He was nervous. I'd seen his hand shake when he'd picked up the pistol. He was younger than me by a couple years and in over his head. When it came to worldly living I definitely had the edge. But when it came to righteous indignation, he had me there. He was furious about his sister and what he perceived was my despicable behaviour towards her. If he could shoot me, he would. The real issue was the question of his talent. Did he have the skill, the cool hand and head to make the shot? Or would he delope and feel satisfied? He was an unknown commodity to me and I wasn't sure what he'd do.'

He paused and opened his eyes. 'Keir was my second. When step nineteen was called, Keir saw him turn. He cried out a warning. I pivoted on my heel, and let instinct, let self-preservation take over. I fired. The shot took him in the thigh and, two days later, he died.'

'Keir was your second?' Antonia's eyes had widened.

'Keir saved my life that day and in the days that followed. He was the one who got me on a ship and out of the country before anyone might think to arrest me. He was the one who sent me to the South Seas.' He gave a short chuckle. 'Even in the midst of crisis, he believed in me. He turned that crisis into an opportunity. It got me through the shock of what had transpired, of what I'd participated in.'

'Thank you for telling me,' was all she said for a long while. When she did speak again, it was out of concern for him. 'Can you still be arrested?'

'Technically, I suppose so, but I doubt anyone has that kind of interest in the event. Southberry cannot push any legal claims without risk of exposing himself or his daughter. Legal claims must be investigated and proven with incontrovertible evidence. Southberry would not risk it. Nor would he risk standing up publicly against the Marquess of Standon and the Duke of Cowden.'

'Then what is there to worry about?' Antonia asked bluntly.

'Gossip. Rumours. This might not be tried in the court of law, but it most assuredly will be tried in the court of scandal where things need only to be spoken of to be breathed into being. They don't need to be proven. Keir and Southberry's heir might be dead, but there are others: the other second, the doctor, the house servants at Southberry House, the gentlemen at the club the night the challenge was issued.

'It was no secret we were going to duel. Plenty of people knew. Twenty men must have heard us, but they were only party to the public story: that I was refusing to marry an honourable earl's daughter. I was already the villain, having eschewed *ton*nish life for life with Keir in trade. I was only at the club to meet with my brother in some attempt to negotiate a way out of the situation. I was already "the Notorious Lord Cullen Allardyce"—this just added to my notoriety.'

He took the chair across from her, slouching. Telling the story had come with its own mental exhaustion and there was still the fallout to deal with. 'Do you understand now why I can't stay? How I have put you at risk? Once that story starts to circulate, reminding people why I've been away, you will be attached to the scandal, too.'

'It has not hurt business before,' Antonia was quick to point out and his heart swelled at her effort to protect him when he was the one who ought to be protecting her, had in fact been sent for to do just that. Now the shoe was on the other foot.

'Then, Keir was the face of the business. I was a silent partner and the *ton* does not pay much attention to trade. Keir handled the bankers, so I was of little consequence except to him. It was very much a case of out of sight, out of mind. You know how society works, a scandal only lasts until the next one rolls along. But now I *am* the next scandal. Notorious Lord Cullen Allardyce, too wild for London, raking around the South Seas half-naked with long hair and a tattoo.'

'I see. I can't be at the public helm of the company and neither can you. I am scandalous because I'm a woman in business and you are scandalous...'

'Because I am me. Yes, your analysis is correct.'

He watched her think for a moment. 'I've heard it said that any publicity is good publicity. Perhaps this works in our favour. We open the store, the story gets around about your return and people flock to the store to get a look at you. And then once they see that you're not so notorious after all and once they see that a woman can run a department store, all this will be forgotten.' It sounded overly optimistic, even for her. He wished it could be so, but it was too much of a fairy tale to hope for. Some day a world where such an ending was possible might exist, but not yet.

She rose. 'You've given me much to think about, but not tonight.' She extended her hand. 'Come to bed, Cullen. I do my best thinking in the morning.'

He took her hand and let her lead, but not before their eyes met, communicating silently what they refused to say out loud, but what must be mutually understood. This would be the last time. The end had come.

Chapter Eighteen

Antonia had known he'd be gone in the morning. It had been implicitly agreed upon and the knowledge had underscored the slow, savoured lovemaking that had lingered through what remained of the night. But knowing had not prepared her for how it felt to wake up without him. He was not in her bed, his warm body wrapped around hers, nor was there any sign of him in their room, no reminders that he'd ever been here. His clothes were gone, the trifle dish where he kept his cuff links was empty. It was like waking from a dream one had thought was real, only to discover it wasn't. Had he even been here at all?

It was for the best that he was gone. This was only ever meant to be a fling, a chance to put mourning behind her, to prove to herself that she could move on. She rationalised it all as Randal helped her dress. She'd known it would hurt, she'd been aware that she'd engaged her heart despite her best advice to self that she not do that nor was she required to do that. She'd done it anyway.

If she felt sadness over the end of the affair, she had only herself to blame. She'd been warned. It would pass.

The affair had been temporary. She would get over it. She *would* get over him. In the long run she would be glad for the distance. She understood the reasons for it. It had not been done unfeelingly, but out of a need for protection so that Keir's legacy could go forward untarnished.

All of this excellent, logical reasoning got her downstairs, but it was no match for the newspapers that waited beside her breakfast plate. The society pages had not wasted a moment picking up on Lady Camford's ball. *Waltzing into Scandal!* declared one page. *An Alliance with a Notorious Lord!* another touted. They would have made her laugh if they hadn't been about her.

Antonia scanned each of the articles. That beautiful waltz, those precious heady moments, had been reduced to gossip fodder. But it could have been worse. Neither story had brought up the old scandal. There was no mention of the duel, of jilting Southberry's daughter. There was only the mention that Lord Cullen Allardyce, known for his notorious exploits about town and his scandalous tendency to work for a living, had been spotted at Lady Camford's ball after a ten-year absence from English shores where it was posited that he'd lived and traded among the indigenous peoples of Tahiti.

She took a swallow of hot coffee. Yes, it could have been worse. There was hope in the fact that it wasn't. An idea came to her. What if she could keep the newspapers' attentions turned on other issues besides Cullen? Idle hands were the devil's workshop, as the saying went. Perhaps the same could be said of idle minds in the press. If she could keep those minds full of other things, they might overlook pursuing more about Cullen.

Antonia read the articles again, something else striking her. The articles had mentioned her only once as Cullen's dance partner and had said nothing about the store. That was where the attention ought to be. They'd attended the ball to promote the store. If she could get Fleur to help, her idea might help them both.

She sought out writing materials and dashed off a quick note to her friend, asking for an appointment later that morning at the *Tribune* where Fleur had taken over in the wake of her husband's death. Fleur might not have time to socialise, but she always had time to discuss business.

'Antonia! It is so good to see you.' Fleur came around the desk in the editor-in-chief's office to envelop her in a hug. 'Look at you! Yellow was always a good colour for you. You look wonderful.'

Fleur smiled, genuinely pleased to see her. Fleur was always authentic, she never faked emotion even when she should. She was dressed in grey serge with white cuffs, an apron over her bodice and skirts. For half-mourning or out of workplace necessity? Antonia wondered.

'Come in, how can I help you? You must be swamped with the store getting ready to open. I have reporters assigned to the gala tomorrow night and to opening day.' Fleur was a whirlwind, hardly drawing a breath.

'You are a marvel, Fleur. Editor of the newspaper? Head of the publishing house? Two jobs in one. I'm impressed,' Antonia complimented, looking around the cherrywood-panelled office done in deep greens and cream with its polished bookcases, plaques denoting accolades hung on the walls and long windows with a view of the street. It was a professional, masculine domain. But it was a woman who sat behind the desk these days. 'Do you ever sleep?'

Fleur laughed and tucked an auburn curl behind one ear. She flashed a smile. 'That's rich coming from you, the business magnate running an import-export company, overseeing property investments *and* opening a department store.' She paused for a rare moment. 'And yet you went dancing last night. Is that why you're here? Do you need me to investigate your mystery partner?'

It took Antonia a second to realise Fleur didn't know she'd not met Cullen at the ball. She glanced down at her hands briefly. 'It wasn't the first time we'd met. He's not a mystery to me.' She was fumbling for words and making a hash of it as she tried not to give too much away. 'He's been here since February. He was Keir's silent partner. We've been trying to sort some business things out—contracts, things like that.' She was talking too much now, overexplaining and overjustifying.

She stopped and clenched her hands together in her lap. She drew a deep breath to reorientate herself. 'I am here because I am wondering if you could run a story tomorrow about me. Perhaps a human interest story about me and the store. You already know me so it would just be a matter of writing it up. I know it's short notice, but it would focus everyone on the gala tomorrow night.'

Fleur leaned across the wide desk, reaching for her hands and taking them in her own. 'Of course I'll do it. We've been friends a long time. I'll do anything I can to help your endeavour succeed. What good is it to run a publishing empire if you can't use it to help your friends? But will you answer a question for me in return?'

Antonia hesitated a moment too long. 'It's just about publicity for the store.'

Fleur gave her a strong stare. 'Not deflection? You want this story to draw people's attention away from the notorious Lord Cullen Allardyce waltzing you about the ballroom last night? Deflection would be good for both of you.'

Antonia sat up a bit straighter, feeling put on alert. 'You'll have to explain that to me, I'm afraid.' She'd not been ready to discuss him with anyone. She'd rather liked having him all to herself. He was her secret.

'You're mixing business with pleasure. How long do you think it will be before someone figures out what you just told me—that he is your deceased husband's business partner? Waltzing is not signing contracts.'

'We were at the ball to promote the store. We thought it might be a good idea to be seen together for business reasons,' Antonia explained.

Fleur nodded. 'You were thinking that his face and his name would shore up any questions about the company being in good hands. It's a sound strategy even if it's unfortunate we have to take such measures at all. Or it would be sound if he was the partner you needed. Is that it?'

Antonia said nothing, not wanting to impugn Cullen. Fleur gave a dry laugh. 'He's a walking scandal, isn't he? When a man is gone for ten years without a word, there's a reason, usually a pretty big one. So now, here you are, with a silent partner who cannot publicly be of use to you, and you cannot get the credit you deserve.' In more ways than one. Antonia thought of the bank and their attempt to foreclose on her early.

'I think it will help if people are reminded that the store is Keir's legacy. That I am finishing this for him.'

'And Allardyce? Where will he fit in to all of this?' Fleur persisted.

'He will go back to Tahiti once the store is open and our new partnership agreement is signed. Society will forget about him.' But she wouldn't.

'Will the company survive once your investors realise he's gone?'

'Will it survive once they realise the depth of his scandal if it comes out?' Antonia countered. Fleur had already guessed there was one, she needn't go into detail.

'You're damned if you do and damned if you don't.' Fleur gave a sigh of sympathy.

'I did meet with the Duke of Cowden and I do think I'll have some support for the company from the Prometheus Club even if Cullen is a partner only on paper. I am optimistic,' Antonia said.

Fleur smiled. 'Of course you are.' Silence stretched a bit too long. Fleur played with a paperweight. 'You called him Cullen,' she said quietly. 'You've become close? Is there a chance that waltz was more than a waltz?' Fleur stared and Antonia knew her face had betrayed her.

Fleur nodded in realisation. 'Dear Heavens, Antonia, you've taken a lover. Well, that explains the glow.' Then she gave a heavy sigh. 'You could have chosen a more discreet lover. You don't want word of this to get out. It will destroy whatever bit of credibility you have—sleeping with your husband's business partner who comes with his own full-blown scandal already included.'

Antonia chewed her lip. 'I know it sounds bad, especially when you put it that way, but it won't get out. He's leaving. He'll be half a world away. I'll likely never see him again.' The enormity of that finally swept her. She'd been ignoring it all morning, all last night, burying the realisation with practical concerns like the gala and Cullen's revelations. It was not, she realised, unlike the way she'd handled Keir's death—burying it beneath work, burying it so deeply she didn't have to face it. But now, Fleur was forcing the issue.

Fleur's face softened. 'Oh, my dear girl, you love him.'

'Yes, yes, I think I do.' Antonia swiped at her tears. 'But it doesn't matter. He has to leave. He can't stay.'

'Do you think he feels the same way about you?' Fleur asked hesitantly. 'I know it's a delicate question. Sometimes love only runs one way in these affairs.'

'You mean when a woman loves a rake?' Antonia gave a watery smile. 'He has not said as much, but I do think he cares for me, deeply.' She thought of the many things he'd done for her since his arrival. He'd delayed his return to Tahiti, he'd fired Mackleson for her, he'd helped her through her grief when she could not help herself. Sometimes actions spoke louder than words.

She'd seen the genuine look of regret and hurt on his face last night as he'd shared his scandal. He'd not wanted to tell her, but telling her had been done out of love, out of a desire to protect her so that she was not ambushed by it, so that she understood what needed to happen next and why. But she did not tell Fleur that.

Last night was still too new, too private, and it was not her story to share.

'If he feels the same way, why not go with him?' Fleur posited. Fleur could not know how those words gave life to her own nascent fantasy. She'd been captivated by Cullen's stories of Tahiti, of the sun and sand and white beaches of palm trees and fruits she'd never tasted, of turquoise waters, waterfalls and warm lagoons, a place where cold winters and soot-filled skies became fictions. To be in such a place with Cullen would be Paradise. But Paradise had a cost.

She shook her head. 'It's impossible, Fleur. There's the store to think of and the company. I must be here to oversee everything.'

'If it's an anchor about your neck that is keeping you from happiness, then perhaps you should sell it. Sell it all, Antonia.'

The thought bordered on heretical. 'I couldn't. Keir spent his life building all this.' She couldn't even begin to wrap her head around the idea of selling the company, the ships, the warehouses, the property spread around town, the town house, the store she'd just fought so hard for.

'Are you to spend your life being a dead man's care-taker?' Fleur did not mince words. 'Who is this legacy for, Antonia? There is no son or daughter you are holding this for.' Antonia heard the anger and the truth in Fleur's words. There'd once been hope that Fleur might be carrying Adam's child, someone to take over Adam's empire. Sadly, it was not to be.

Antonia looked about the office. 'Would you sell the newspapers, the publishing house?'

'I think it is different for me. I am not in love and facing separation, risking a second chance at happiness,' Fleur said honestly. She steepled her hands. 'I'm sorry. I've made you uncomfortable. I'll write up the story immediately and make sure it runs in the evening edition. I'll talk about who you are and remind people of all of your and Keir's philanthropic work in the city. It will do what you hope. And I'll see you tomorrow night at the gala. We can drink Emma's champagne and celebrate your success.'

Antonia rose. 'Thank you, Fleur.' She smiled and hugged her friend goodbye. It had been good to see her, good to talk to someone at last, but it had not given her the clarity she'd been hoping for. She could not be distracted by such things at the moment. She had a heart to mend. She'd best mend it by tomorrow night when she saw him again. People would see them together and she couldn't afford to give anything away. She had a store to open.

Chapter Nineteen

$\mathcal{O}\!\!\sim\!\!\mathcal{O}$

$\mathbf{S}$he was at the store helping with last-minute displays in the ladies' department when the evening news came, delivered in person by Cullen, which was a surprise in itself. She had not been expecting him. After last night, she'd not thought to see him until the store gala tomorrow and, even then, she'd only thought to see him here-after in a professional capacity. From the stormy look on his face, something more had happened. She tried not to panic. It could be anything—a problem at the ware-house perhaps? But in the back of her mind, she knew the look on his face was not commensurate to a prob-lem at the warehouse.

She set aside the lacy underthings she was folding and went to him, drawing him aside before he could draw too much attention from the other clerks working nearby. 'What is it? What's happened?'

Cullen slapped down the papers beneath his arm. 'This is what has happened, what I told you would hap-pen. Someone has dug up the scandal. The society pages are full of it. Except the *Tribune*, which had the good sense to cover the real story.'

Antonia flipped through the *Tribune* first, noting the

half-page story about Popplewell's Department Store and the Popplewell legacy, just as Fleur had promised. Then she flipped through the other papers and grimaced.

More than one ambitious reporter had gone straight to work after last night's ball, not content to simply note Cullen Allardyce's return. Three other papers had dragged out the scandal in some part. No one paper had the whole story and none had it right. Antonia tried to look for the silver lining. 'Most of this is just speculation.'

'The average reader doesn't make the distinction between speculation and fact,' Cullen said grimly.

'The *Tribune* has a wider circulation than these papers. Perhaps that story will offset the others.' She said it for herself as much for him. She gave a heavy sigh. 'I know how damning this is, Cullen, for you, for us and for the store, I won't pretend otherwise. But I *will* hope, because what else can I do?' She held his gaze, wanting to lend him some of that hope. He was grimmer than he'd been even last night.

'There's something else.' He reached for her hands— deliberately or out of reflex? Was he finding it as hard as she was to transition back into being partners only? It was difficult being this close to him and not touching him. Only they were touching now and that made it even worse. His touch reminded her of other touches, touches she would never have again from him.

'Have you thought of going with him?'

Fleur's heresy came to mind. She pushed it back and tried to focus on the next crisis. There was a new cut above his eye, she noticed just then, and she wondered if that next crisis had something to do with it.

'I found Mackleson lurking in the unloading yard when I came in. I dispatched him.'

'Violently, it appears. He took a swing at you.' She couldn't help but raise a gentle finger to the cut. 'Does it hurt? Do you need ice?' Then she remembered he was a brawler. It was how he and Keir had met.

'Ow.' He flinched. 'It doesn't hurt unless *someone* touches it. I'm fine. He looks worse.'

'What was he doing here?'

'I don't know. I looked around, I didn't find anything out of order. He's gone now.'

She knew he meant to be reassuring, but it wasn't. 'Gone where, though? Do you think he'll come back? Do you think he'll try something disruptive at the gala? Do you think he'll go to a reporter and tell some story about how you beat him up? That would be damning because it would fit with the apparent history of violence associated with you and it would make the rumours easier to believe.'

Cullen shook his head. 'I don't know. I will tell everyone to be vigilant about strangers though, just in case. The loading bays and the yard will be busy and well populated tomorrow night. It would be easy for someone to slip past unnoticed.'

'That worries me,' Antonia confessed. 'We'll have a lot of important people here. I don't want them to be in danger.' Doubt crossed his face, and she retraced her thoughts. 'Do you think we won't? Do you think the gossip will deter our guests from coming?' It was a horrible thought. To be so close to the finish line and then to falter, to be brought down by rumours before they even had a chance.

She gathered her resolve and every ounce of optimism

she possessed. 'No, I think people can't stay away from a rumour. They'll come to see if it's true, to judge for themselves.'

'You will need more than one night of success.' There it was. *You*. No longer *we*. No longer *us* or *our*.

'When are you leaving?' She swallowed hard. Asking the question made it real, no longer a theoretical date on an invisible calendar.

'I stopped at the ticket office on the docks this morning. There's a ship that sails the day after tomorrow.'

This morning. He'd gone from her bed to the ticket office. Her heart sank. Perhaps she'd been a bit too optimistic when she'd told Fleur she thought he felt the same. 'You wasted no time.' She tried for a smile. 'You did not want to wait until after opening day?' Had he picked that day because he knew she couldn't possibly see him off? She'd be needed here from open to close and hours before and after.

'I thought it best that I be gone as soon as possible.' He gestured to the newspapers. 'I think I was right. The store doesn't need me anywhere near it. I am wondering if I should even come tomorrow night.'

Anger flared. She tamped it down. 'People would be disappointed. You might be the main attraction.'

'If I am, I am sorry for it, Antonia. Sorrier than you know,' he said gently. 'I only meant to help.' He gave a rueful smile.

'You *have* helped, in ways I can't begin to express,' she argued.

'I should go.'

If she didn't tell him now, she might lose her chance.

The ship might not sail until the day after tomorrow, but it was clear that in many ways he was already leaving. There might not be another opportunity to be alone with him without interruption.

'No, you should come with me. We are not done with our conversation.' She drew him into a storage room, the most privacy she could arrange on short notice. The storage room was filled with boxes and she wished she could have done better. She'd never dreamed she'd be having one of the most important discussions of her life surrounded by lacy underthings.

'Antonia, I don't think this is a good idea,' Cullen moved a box of French stays aside and took a seat on the packing crate. He knew what she wanted. It was what he wanted, too. He simply couldn't give it to her. All he could give her was bad news, bad press. Wasn't today's taste of that proof enough? And this was just the start. It would get much worse.

'I disagree. I think it's a great idea. We've talked about what the store needs, but we haven't talked about what I need. I need you. I need you to be here tomorrow night to help me handle everything. I did not do this alone. You helped me finish the store. You fired Mackleson. You got the inventory moved from the warehouse. You got Cowden to manage the loan for us.'

She was making him out to be a hero when what he'd actually done was put her ambitions in jeopardy. Her eyes shone with their green fire. He wished he was worthy of it. She stepped towards him, and his thighs parted of their own accord to accommodate her so that she could

stand between them. It was the last thing he should have
done. He needed distance, he did not need to be touching
her. It only reminded him of all he couldn't have. Her
arms wrapped loosely around his neck and he had the
suspicion she had already made a decision unilaterally.

'You have been an integral part of this. I can't stand
in front of the guests tomorrow night and pretend it
was all me, not when Cowden knows the difference. It
would make me a liar.' He watched her throat work as
she swallowed. 'I promised I'd let you go when the time
came, Cullen. I mean to honour that, but I have to ask:
do you really believe we are done, that there is nothing
more we can give each other?'

He was aware that his own arms were about her waist,
that her hips were tucked firmly against his groin and
his body did not believe for a moment that this conversation was neutral. 'How am I supposed to answer that,
Antonia?'

'Truthfully.' When had their mouths come to be so
close that each word was nearly a kiss? That a whisper
was all that was needed in order to be heard?

'I need to leave England. I need to be forgotten in order
for you to thrive here. I can be the most help to you if I
return to Tahiti.'

'And we exchange letters twice a year?' There was
some heat to those words. He silenced them with his
mouth.

'You'll be fine. I've signed all of Bowdrie's paperwork. My name is on all the financials,' he managed to
say between slow kisses. Her hands were in his hair, now,
her tongue teasing his lips, making talk more difficult.

Her hand reached for the fastenings of his trousers. It would be tempting to let her have her way, to make naughty, half-dressed love in the storage room knowing someone could walk in at any time—which would put paid to both of their reputations for good—but he couldn't allow it. He covered her hand, stalling her progress. 'One more time won't change anything, Antonia. We decided that last night. We are just prolonging our hurt.'

'Our hurt? Or just my hurt?' She stepped back, but her temper flared. He adjusted his trousers. Maybe a fight was what they needed to establish some distance. 'If you believe in us, why won't you fight for us?'

Did she truly not realise she was breaking his heart? 'I *am* fighting for us, Antonia. I am fighting for you, I am giving you every chance you wanted and I am sorry that I am imperfect, that I'm not Keir. That I am not enough.'

It was the story of his life. He'd not been enough for his father and now he was not enough for Antonia, the woman he loved. The realisation that he loved her was like a thunderbolt and the reality of it sizzled through him, but not the surprise. The reality was that he'd loved her long before this moment. He'd simply not been willing to name it.

He could see she wanted to argue. He moved towards the storeroom door with a shake of his head. 'You don't have to say anything. You don't have to disagree. I don't belong in your world. I belong in mine and after tomorrow night, that's where I'll be.' In Tahiti, where he was Kanoa, the Seeker. The one place in the world where he was enough.

'What if I belong in your world?' Antonia challenged softly, her words stopping his hand on the door. God, he loved her optimism, her hope that somehow all the imperfect pieces of the world could be made to fit together.

He glanced back at her briefly. 'I would never ask it of you.' He slipped out the door, quashing the fantasy that flared in his mind of them on the beach at Ha'apape, her hair down, a hibiscus tucked behind an ear, the warm water gently lapping at their bare feet. There was no time for dwelling on impossibilities, not when there was real work to do.

He had people to visit to ensure tomorrow's gala was a success, starting with Frederick and Cowden and the Prometheus Club members. If they came, others would follow. Cowden would use his leverage to strong-arm attendance if needed and Frederick would know just how much damage the news stories had done to drive away invitees. It was the least and last thing he could do for Antonia.

Chapter Twenty

Cullen checked his pocket watch as he made a surreptitious tour of the exterior of the building. Twenty minutes to go. Popplewell's would open at eight o'clock for the evening gala. A sense of relief filled him at the sight of the front of the building. A red carpet had been rolled out for the occasion and carriages had been delivering guests for the last half-hour. People had come and were coming. Guests stood on Antonia's red carpet, sipping chilled champagne, the party starting even before the doors opened, everyone admiring in advance the giant crystal chandelier that hung in the entrance and was clearly visible from the outside.

Cullen smiled to himself as he went around back for one last check of the unloading yard. His evening visit with Cowden and making the club rounds with Frederick, even though it meant significant personal exposure of himself, had paid off. He'd not been sure it would until this moment. This morning, there'd still been some cancellations. Not everyone had been persuaded to overlook the rumours and still make an appearance.

He'd been partly right that the rumours would put some people off. But Antonia had been right, too. Some people couldn't stay away from scandal. There'd also been others this morning who were jockeying for a last-minute invitation and Antonia had been more than happy to accommodate, or so he'd been told. He'd not seen her since last night. They both had separate obligations to complete today if the gala was to go off well. Separation was for the best, though, if they couldn't keep their hands off each other.

Cullen surveyed the unloading yard, sweeping it with his eyes for any security concerns. He nodded to the men stationed there. 'Anything to report?' he asked.

'No, Sir. There was a bit of an altercation earlier while the caterers unloaded some food, but we sorted it out, just some drivers fighting over who got to bring their wagon in first.'

Cullen used the door at the rear of the building to let himself in. Despite Antonia's insistence that he be here, he'd debated coming tonight all day. Would he do Antonia more harm or good by coming or by staying away? If he came, he might inadvertently reignite the notice he hoped to avoid. But if he didn't come, she'd be on her own.

That had decided it. Who would stand with her if reporters asked tough questions? If one of the many investors with Popplewell and Allardyce voiced concerns about her ability to sit at the helm of the company? Or what if simply one of a thousand things went wrong? She couldn't be everywhere at once, putting out little fires. She had to be the gracious hostess, greeting guests and giving every appearance of enjoying her own party as if she hadn't a care in the world, as if this project hadn't been a year in the making. In the end he decided it would look odd, as if there was indeed something to hide if he was absent from his company's own grand opening. Besides, she would need him for moral support if nothing else.

Inside, it was organised chaos. He strode through the first floor where the hat and glove counters gleamed, their glass-paned display cabinets clear without a smear or fingerprint on them, the merchandise inside them laid out in exacting perfection: gloves were fanned out to show each colour available, jewellery glinted. The displays were captivating, drawing the eye so that each department was a feast for the senses. It had taken weeks to get the goods unpacked and arranged. The time had paid off. There was even a section that showcased the goods imported from Tahiti. It was beautifully done with rattan furniture and tropical fixtures so that shoppers might feel they were in Tahiti itself.

Cullen fingered one of the delicate shell bracelets on display. That had been the dream, hadn't it? To bring the world together—the woman on the beach who'd gathered the shells and strung them with the woman in faraway England who would wear the bracelet and dream of another place. He picked up a carved statue. Or the little boy who might put this statue in his room and be inspired to learn about where it came from, where that place was on a map and perhaps some day he might go there; some day in a future where it didn't take months to make the journey.

Already travel time had dropped from six months to three. Already, it was no longer necessary to go around the Cape. He knew there were plans to make the Steam Route even more efficient. There were men who were dreaming of a canal in Egypt. It would make the process a journey of weeks instead of months. He'd spoken with Cowden about it, last night. He'd like to be part of that process when the time was right. He set the carved figure down. This was how change was made. One generation at a time. Not for the first time, he wished his father understood that. Cowden did.

He moved on to the men's department, decorated like a gentleman's club with its walnut panelling, dark maroon wallpaper and tall leather-covered wingback chairs. Artwork featuring riding to the hunt hung on the walls. He focused on the decor; no detail had been spared. It was better this way, better to keep his mind busy with thoughts of the future—the trip back, the chance to meet with some men in Cairo on the return. A busy mind meant no time to think about Antonia, to think about the things she'd said last night in the storage room.

'What if I belonged in your world?'

But she belonged in this world. This was what she'd worked for.

He stopped to talk with the clerks, dressed in well-tailored suits that complemented the quality of goods they offered for sale. He gave a smile and encouragement, a piece of advice where needed. He'd helped Antonia train many of them. He knew them by name. 'Remember to let gentlemen know they can get all of their wardrobe handled here. We can keep their measurements on file so they can have something made up quickly, or so that we can find something of excellent quality for them already on the rack,' he coached.

'You look sharp, gentlemen. You'll be meeting men tonight who will appreciate that. They don't want to be served by someone who is slovenly—' He broke off in mid-speech, feeling the energy of the department shift. He looked about and found the source of the distraction.

Antonia stood there, dressed in an ice-blue gown whose skirts shimmered when she moved, like light on snow. She wore her diamonds at her ears, her neck, the bangle about her gloved wrist, her golden hair pinned up as it had been at Lady Camford's. Had it only been two nights ago that he'd held this enchantress in his arms on the dance floor? It seemed a lifetime ago. She swept forward.

'Gentlemen, you do us proud. By the end of the week, Popplewell's will have a reputation for the most handsome clerks in the City.' She held out her hand to him. 'Mr Allardyce, it's time. Shall we go greet our guests?'

He tucked her hand into his elbow and felt her tremble. 'Nervous?'

'Yes.' Antonia laughed and then sobered. 'Do you think Keir would like it? Would he be pleased with the store?'

'Absolutely. He'd be so incredibly proud of you, Antonia.' As he was. For the first time in a long while, he thought, everything was going to be all right. The last words he whispered to her before the doors opened were, 'You are beautiful, too.' He would hold this picture of her in his mind, of his lovely, fierce Antonia, when he was back in his world.

They received the guests together as if they were hosting a grand ball, sending each group off with a guide to offer a tour of the building, making sure the guide highlighted departments of special interest to each guest. Cullen made a mental note that several guests were the men he and Frederick had talked with at the clubs. Frederick and Helena passed through the receiving line, Helena gushing over how elegant everything looked, the string quartet playing from one corner so that everyone could shop by music. When Cullen asked about Cowden and the Duchess, Frederick promised his father would be along later.

Eventually, Cullen had to leave Antonia's side. They needed to mingle, he with the men and she with the women. He was in the men's department, shaking hands and keeping an ear out for any conversation he needed to nip in the bud, when a familiar but cold voice spoke behind him. 'So, this is what you've been up to instead of visiting family.'

Cullen turned, stiff and startled, but ready. 'Father, what a surprise. I was unaware you were in town.' It was only a bit of a surprise. With all the newspaper coverage, he'd half expected it, assuming his father was indeed in town, something he'd not bothered to ascertain for himself.

'As I was you.' His father's tones were as pointed as ever, his tone highlighting all nature of disappointment. Cowden was with him and Cullen understood the situation immediately. This was the Duke's doing. This was why Cowden had come late. He couldn't blame Cowden for trying. The man meant well.

Cowden gave a broad smile, purposely ignoring the tension between the two men. 'When a man's son pulls off something as spectacular as this, one doesn't want to miss it.' He extended his hand to Cullen. 'The store is spectacular. The Duchess is going to want to redecorate the town house after seeing this.'

'Well, if she does, our house goods and furnishings department stands ready to assist.' Cullen shook the man's hand. 'Have you seen the teak furniture we have from Tahiti? One-of-a-kind pieces.'

'You've become quite the trader,' his father drawled, his eyes sharp on him. There were wrinkles around those eyes, more than Cullen remembered, and grey hair that went beyond the temples.

'It's the way of the world these days, Standon,' Cowden put in jovially. 'The aristocracy isn't what it used to be. It's the beginning of the end of life as we knew it. Besides, a man shouldn't make his fortune living off the backs of others. It's exciting, too, don't you think? So much potential to explore, a chance to recraft our legacies. Self-made men like your son are the future.'

But not even for the sake of the Duke's approval would his father bend. He merely gave a short nod of his head. 'A gentleman never goes out of style, Cowden.'

'Let me show you the section dedicated to the South Seas and you can tell me how Mother is,' Cullen intervened. 'Did she come tonight?'

His father scowled. 'To something as plebian as this? A merchant's trade show? I should think not. You can dress it up with crystal chandeliers and champagne, but that's what it is. If you wanted to see any of us, you could have called at the house where it is appropriate.'

Cullen exchanged a look with Cowden. He was glad Antonia hadn't heard the remark. It would have devastated her. This was her palace, the place she'd sunk her heart and soul into; her happiness, her grief, all of it had been poured into this and tonight was meant to be her triumph. As far as he could tell, the triumph was well under way. He would not let his father steal that from her all for the sake of their personal feud.

He was showing Cowden and his father a teak desk when he heard the first scream, followed by another. He looked up at the wide staircase leading to the third floor, women spilling down it, awkward in their wide skirts. Someone fell. Good God, there was going to be stampede. Then he smelled it. Smoke! 'Cowden, take my father, get out of the building.' Cowden hesitated, no doubt thinking of Helena and the Duchess. 'If they're upstairs, I'll see to them; if they're not, they're already safe.' He gave Cowden a push. 'Go, please.'

Whatever was happening, was happening on the third floor. Antonia was up there. He knew he'd never make headway on the crowded staircase, so he darted for the backstairs the clerks took when they hauled inventory, taking the steps two at a time. When he reached the floor, shrieking chaos was in progress. Flames raced up the elegant floor-length draperies until they were sheets of fire, rapidly spreading to the wallpaper.

He spied her in the thick of things, helping women to the stairs, encouraging people to stay calm. But it was a losing battle. People were pushing and panicking.

'Antonia!' He cut through the crowd, desperate to reach her. The fire was spreading with alarming speed, the air filling with smoke. A third-floor fire would be difficult to reach with water and hoses. Someone pushed at him in their haste and he nearly tripped. The place was in full stampede now out of fear the fire would chase them down—and the greater fear that the fire would outrun them. He watched in horror as Antonia fell and struggled to get up. She fell again. He clawed his way to her side, shielding her with his bulk until he could get her on her feet. The last of the guests were gone from the floor, the smoke thick now. 'We must hurry.' He glanced around at the destruction—where beauty had reigned just hours ago in immaculate displays there was now only disaster. Flames licked at dress forms, tore through bolts of fragile fabric. The third floor was lost.

'Steady on, we'll get out of this,' he said fiercely, his voice hoarse. 'Whatever you do, don't look back.'

Too late. She glanced over her shoulder and saw it all—the fire eating up everything, the beautiful, carefully arranged floor where a woman might shop and find feminine sanctuary burning with abandon. Whatever might be saved, it would be nothing here. Fabrics were incinerated, the creamy fixtures marred with ashes and soot and the ravages of flames, a dream going up in smoke.

Her eyes stung with smoke, with tears of loss. She never looked back and tonight she'd broken her cardinal rule. That was when she stumbled, her ankle twisting in her skirts before Cullen caught her. She hobbled once. Cullen swore and swept her up into his arms.

'Turn your head into my chest, you'll be able to breath better,' he instructed as he descended the staircase. But she couldn't look away, her gaze riveted on the conflagration burning over his shoulder.

There was only smoke on the second floor and Antonia thought there might be some hope, after all. If the fire brigade came quickly enough the fire might be contained. They might save something. Empty of people, the floor was eerily quiet as if it was already resigned to its fate, all the beautiful furniture prepared to be sacrificed as kindling to the fire that raged above. But then came a crack and the roar of flame as the ceiling began to falter, flame licking through in hot, red, streams.

Cullen's grip on her tightened and he lumbered into an awkward run, burdened as he was with her weight. That was when she knew: they were going to lose the whole building. She turned her face against his chest, the first sob breaking loose as he reached for the last flight of stairs and fresh air.

Outside, Helena and Fleur ran to her. 'I think she's hurt her ankle. She took a fall.' Cullen set her down gingerly, but she clung to him, instinctively knowing he meant to leave, to turn back towards the danger.

'Stay with me,' she said fiercely, gripping his lapels. His face was sweaty and streaked with smoke and ash. She felt Fleur and Helena try to disengage her. No. She would not let go. There were two nightmares in her mind now: the sight of her beloved store in flames and the night of the flood—the night she'd let Keir go, how she'd unwittingly given him up without a fight. She would not make the same mistake twice.

'I have to join the men, Antonia. Every hand is needed if we are to save the building.' He peeled her dirty, gloved hands from his lapels with gentle force. 'Let me go fight for you.' She felt Fleur's arms about her and then he was off, running to join the newly arrived fire brigade. It would be all right. He would man a hose and it would be all right, she repeated, never letting him out of her sight as Fleur and Helena helped her to a place where she might sit. But then it wasn't. A cry went up and there was a commotion at the front of the hose line, men gathering around, Cullen among them, and then Cullen darted into the building.

She exchanged a horrified look with Fleur. Fleur was on her feet before Antonia even had to ask. 'I'll find out what's happened.' But Antonia knew what had happened. Cullen had run back into a burning building and for the second time she stood to lose the man she loved.

The minutes passed like hours as she waited for Fleur, as she waited for Cullen to reappear. The fire seemed to be getting worse, the dark flames lighting up the London night sky. Why was it getting worse? Why wasn't the water having any effect? Perhaps it was only her imagination. She had too much at stake. Damn her ankle. She was tired of waiting. She was grateful for Helena's grip on her hand.

Fleur returned breathless, her face pale. 'Someone reported a clerk was still inside, in the second-floor stairwell. Apparently, too panicked to move.' Too frightened to think rationally, Antonia thought. 'Cullen went in after her.' Her mind immediately went to the image of the second-floor ceiling slowly cracking apart with a river of flame.

'He'll be trapped in there; the ceiling was going to go,' she murmured, mostly to herself. Beams would fall, charred timbers would block off exit points. She squeezed her eyes shut, trying to shut away the images of Cullen overcome with smoke, or worse, burned alive by flame.

'Don't think about it,' Fleur whispered and hugged her close. Surely the fates would not be so cruel as to take both men from her. She would give up everything to see him safe—the store, the company, her reputation. She didn't care what the papers wrote, what scandals they unearthed or if he sailed for Tahiti without her. She only cared that Cullen walked out of the inferno alive, because knowing he was alive in some part of the world was better than knowing he was dead in hers.

A cry went up at the entrance and Antonia strained to see. She rose, leaning on Helena and Fleur. A man emerged, tall and broad, a black-clad woman in his arms. Profound relief swept her and she sagged against Fleur. 'It's him. He's all right. Help me get to him.'

It took a while to reach him. Cullen was the hero of the hour, having rescued the trapped shop clerk from the stairwell. She reached him with her eyes before she could make her way through the crowd. He saw her and began to move, cutting through the crush and taking her in his arms. 'I'm all right, I'm here,' he murmured into her hair, and she held on to him for dear life. How would she ever let him go in the morning?

Chapter Twenty-One

Morning was a subjective term. They didn't leave the fire until after three that morning. And they only left then because it was impossible to see anything of merit in the dark and because the town house was only a couple of streets away. They could rest, recover and return. Rest and recover were subjective as well. There was food and clean clothes waiting for them—someone on her staff had the foresight to go to Mivart's and fetch a change for Cullen—but even after washing up and food, sleep remained elusive.

'Come lay down with me,' Cullen encouraged from the bed where he lay stretched out an hour before dawn. 'At least close your eyes. You don't need to sleep. Just close your eyes, Antonia.'

'I can't stop seeing it, eyes open or shut.' But she did relent and lay down beside him.

'I know.' He combed his fingers through her hair with a sigh. 'What a night. My father was there. Cowden brought him.' He gave a hoarse chuckle, his voice still carrying the effects of the smoke. He'd said nothing of the ordeal once he'd gone back inside and she didn't ask. Saying nothing confirmed for her just how bad it must have been and how close. Maybe she didn't want to know, at least not yet.

'I was with him on the second floor when I heard the noise.' Cullen's fingers were gentle in her hair.

That was how he'd got there so fast, she thought. 'The noise sounded like fireworks the closer one was to it. Then there was fire everywhere and flames running up the draperies.' Antonia squeezed her eyes tight. She did not want to relive those moments of panic before she'd taken charge and tried to organise a retreat before it became a full-blown stampede. 'At the outset, I was scared to death.'

She paused. She'd never spoken these next words out loud, but perhaps a near-death experience brought them to the fore. 'A thousand things flashed through my head all at once. I had no idea I could think of so many things at one time. I thought I was going to die like Keir, in a freak accident. I wondered if Keir had felt like that—knowing without question that he was down to the last minutes of his life,' she whispered the words in the dark. 'But then I thought to myself, last minutes or no, how do I make them count? It's what Keir would have thought. How can I help others? Who can I save? And then I thought about you and suddenly you were there, and...'

'And you're safe, Antonia. You were brave tonight.' His grip about her waist tightened. 'I was scared tonight, too, when I saw that woman push you and you fell, and I lost sight of you. I know why you stayed and helped everyone, but in that moment I wished you had fled, that you'd been the first one down the staircase.'

'A good captain always goes down with the ship,'

she murmured. 'You scared me, too, going back into the building. You were a hero. Margery owes you her life. You went into a burning building to save someone you didn't even know.'

She felt him smile against her neck. 'It's what Keir would have done. He saved us both so that we might save others. I think that's his real legacy.'

Antonia turned in his arms, facing him, her arms wrapped about his neck. 'I think you're right.' She smiled into his tawny eyes. Sometimes the best way to defeat a ghost was to invite him in. For the second time Keir had been part of their conversation without haunting it. The first time had been at the cemetery. The realisation came to her that they could be themselves and they could still celebrate Keir, the man they had both loved and the man who'd brought them together. Why had she not seen it before? Why did she see it now when it was too late?

'I love you, Cullen,' she whispered, letting her eyes droop closed. There was always the chance things would look better by daylight.

Things did not look better in the morning. She and Cullen returned to Hanover Street when she woke. Smoke was still rising from the fire and its grey tendrils could be seen at a distance high in the sky. The smoke was only a prelude to the shock of seeing the building. The solid, square building looked like the jagged Gothic remains, the roof gone, the façade jutting into an empty sky. The structure remained, mostly, it having been heavily constructed out of brick, but the wood used to brace the internal structure had burned.

She leaned on Cullen's arm for support, her ankle still paining her. 'It's gone, all gone. Who would do such a thing? I cannot believe this was an accident.' Accidents were candles being left lit, or oil spilling on a stove and getting out of control, or a cigar left burning unattended. Accidents were not explosions that sounded like fireworks and draperies going up in flames.

The man in charge of the fire brigade and an inspector approached them. 'Do we have any insight into what caused this?' Antonia asked.

Both men looked tired. They'd been working all night. 'We do. We found the remnants of small explosives that were likely planted on the third floor near the draperies, probably behind the draperies, which is why they went up so fast and why they weren't detected.'

Antonia felt her stomach clench. 'This was deliberate?' It was one thing to assume it was deliberate in theory and another to have it be truth. It meant facing the fact that someone had wanted to destroy her store.

'Yes, Ma'am. This was arson,' the inspector replied solemnly. 'I am sorry. It is a great loss and while I understand that this is a difficult time, time is of the essence. Do you have any idea of who might have set the fire?' His gaze had drifted to Cullen, expecting a man to have the answers, but Cullen said nothing, his own gaze making it clear that she was in charge and the one of whom questions ought to be asked. Under other circumstances she would have revelled in the authority he conferred on her. After all, it was what she'd wanted in the beginning. But now she knew what it meant. He was leaving. This would be hers to handle.

'Possibly,' she said. 'We had a disgruntled site manager by the name of Mackleson. He was fired two months ago for skimming money, among other things. We caught him on the premises a couple days ago.' It wouldn't be 'we' much longer. Just 'I'. It was ironic to think that was something she'd once wanted.

When she finished, Cullen said, 'There was a disturbance last evening when the caterers arrived and our security were occupied with that long enough for someone to get into the building. That disturbance could even have been orchestrated on purpose.' He glanced at her, apologetic. 'I didn't have time to tell you and it seemed inconsequential when it happened.'

She nodded. 'Is there anything left worth saving?'

'The structure can be salvaged. If you're asking if you can rebuild, Ma'am, the answer is yes. It will take time and money, but you are insured,' the inspector offered. 'If you would like, I can walk you through it.' He extended his arm. 'We'll take it slow.'

She hesitated and shot a look at Cullen. 'Go on,' he said softly. 'I want to remember you like this, walking towards your new dream, hope springing quite literally from the ashes, because that's who you are,' he whispered for her ears alone.

He was saying goodbye. She'd step away with the inspector and he would be gone. His ship sailed in a few hours and she'd promised to let him go. Perhaps goodbye was better like this—simply stepping away, stepping into the work of the day so that she wouldn't feel the loss of him so keenly. She nodded, filling her eyes with the last sight of him.

'I'll write when I get there. Antonia, go build your store and whatever you do, don't look back.'

She swallowed against the thickness in her throat and took the inspector's arm. Her ear was only half tuned to the inspector's report. She felt Cullen's eyes on her as she limped towards the rubble, watching no doubt to make sure she kept her word. They'd had an incredible interlude. Now it was over. Eyes forward, eyes on the future.

By mid-morning, Antonia was up to her neck in work, in decisions and in people to help. The newly hired staff came to sort through the rubble. Robert Bowdrie came to handle insurance paperwork. Fleur came for mental and emotional support and to ensure the fire got a fair reporting in at least one newspaper. The architect came with the blueprints. The Duke of Cowden came to lend his gravitas to the process and seeing everything was done right. He came out of friendship, but also because his money was involved. In many ways it was as much his building that burned down last night as it was hers. Still, there was hope in the air after a night of disaster. But it did not inspire her as it once might have.

'Are you all right?' Fleur pressed a mug of coffee into her hands. 'You've been going non-stop.'

'Just overwhelmed.' Antonia found a smile for her friend. 'It was good of you to come.'

'Where's Cullen?' Fleur asked.

'Gone. He left this morning.' But it seemed longer than a handful of hours.

'Gone as in…?

'Gone to his ship, as in going back to Tahiti.' Gone,

as in not in her bed. As in his arms not waiting to hold her. 'It was what we agreed upon. It's what is best.'

'For whom?' Fleur interrogated fiercely. 'For him? For you?'

She didn't have an answer for that. 'He thinks it's best for the company, it will protect us from losing investors and having to contend with the old scandal.'

Fleur gave her a thoughtful look. 'So you're both willing to give each other up for the sake of the company? For an inanimate thing built by a man who is now dead?'

'Fleur, please, you're not making it better. It was very hard to let him go,' Antonia begged.

Fleur took her hands. 'I don't mean to make it better because you are making the wrong decision and what is worse is that you *know* it is the wrong decision.'

'Fleur, I have work to do,' Antonia said. She had to stay busy or she would lose what was left of her sanity.

'Yes, you always do, don't you? Why do you work, Antonia? To build a legacy or to bury the hurt?' Fleur challenged. 'How is that working for you?'

It wasn't working. She missed Cullen and she knew instinctively that she was repeating the pattern she'd used with Keir. The harder the work, the deeper she could bury what mattered without confronting it, without feeling anything. Only this time, she wanted to feel. She didn't want to forget the feel of Cullen's body, the sound of his low voice at her ear, the look of him, all broad-shouldered elegance in those jackets he claimed were too confining. 'It doesn't matter. It's too late now.'

Fleur looked at the little watch pinned to her bodice. 'No, it's not.'

'What are you suggesting?' But Antonia knew what her heart was suggesting—that she hail a cab and run to the ship, metaphorically, as her ankle hurt too much for any literal running. It was a half hour across town. An hour and a half until the ship left. 'I have a business to run, Fleur. It would take months to turn it all over. And there's the store.' She had responsibilities. She couldn't hare off to parts unknown at a moment's notice.

But thoughts of the store did not fill her with the old joy. She stood, hands on hips, and looked up at the blackened brick structure. When had this stopped being her dream? Before last night, she realised. It wasn't the work that daunted her, it was that she no longer had the heart for it and it no longer seemed important.

Keir's real legacy to us is that we have the power now to save others.

And perhaps they had the power to save themselves if they would simply take the risk. Keir's whole life had been about taking risks, taking chances on people as well as investments.

She spied the Duke of Cowden talking with the architect. 'Fleur, help me limp over there. I have an idea.' Her pulse began to thrum as new excitement took her. 'Then, be a dear and get me a cab, a fast one.' Fleur grinned and hugged her.

A half hour later, she climbed into a cab and urged the driver to make haste. She settled back against the cracked leather squabs with a smile of satisfaction. Apparently, she could drop everything on thirty minutes' notice. But she wasn't home free yet. She still had to convince Cullen.

* * *

He was going home. Cullen leaned against the rail of the ship, trying to interest himself in the busyness of the dock. He tried to convince himself that the feeling in his stomach was one of excitement. He'd promised himself he'd be back in Tahiti by September and he would easily make that. It was a good time of year to sail, fewer storms in the spring. He'd done what was needed, signed the papers, helped where he could. To stay now would undo that help. He had a life waiting, a place where he could do the work he was best at and work that made a difference.

Antonia would be fine without him. He'd seen her today with the inspector, taking charge. In fact, she would be better without him. If he stayed, she'd constantly be putting out fires of another sort and all set by him. He didn't want to stay and watch her respect for him turn into something else. And it would. One could only live with a troublemaker for so long before they got tired of the trouble and its consequences. But damn, he'd miss her. More than miss her because this wasn't about missing. It was about loving. He loved her too much to stay.

Down below on the wharf they were getting ready to pull up the gangplank, the last of the cargo loaded. Good. Soon it would be too late to do anything about. Soon, life would start again—life without Antonia Popplewell and he would navigate it. Someone gave a call that they were minutes away from getting underway to make the most of the afternoon tide.

Just then, there was a commotion on the wharf, a

carriage driving recklessly. Foolish driver. Horses near the water on the wharf was bad business if something startled them. As the carriage slammed to a halt and the door opened, a woman exited, her movements brisk— well, somewhat brisk; she was limping. It was the limp that made him look more closely.

'Antonia!' he called out and she looked up, shading her eyes against the light. He waved. He called again, but the ship's horn sounded, alerting the docks to its departure. No. Cullen raced down the stairway. He had to stop the ship.

'Wait! Wait!' Cullen sprinted towards the sailors at the gangplank. He could see Antonia gamely limping through the crowd as fast as she could. 'That woman is coming.' He gestured towards her. But what had she come for? To beg him to stay? Or— His heart gave a leap. Had she come to come? But that wasn't possible. She had work…

'Sir, we have orders, we have a schedule. Sir, the tide,' the sailors protested.

'Antonia!' He ran to the centre of the gangplank, knowing it made it much harder to move a gangplank when a man was on it. 'What are you doing?' he yelled into the crowd as she struggled to reach the ship.

'I am coming with you!' she shouted back and his pulse leaped with the confirmation.

'Sir!' It was the captain now, his tone strident and insistent. 'Perhaps you would prefer another ship at a better time? We must go!' He would not lose her now, but if he got off the ship, he'd miss the tide.

'Just a moment longer, she's almost here.' Then she

was there, breathing hard from her exertions. He grabbed her hand and pulled her aboard. Only when she was safe in his arms did he say, 'We can go now, Captain. I have everything I need.' Then he was with her, and they were laughing in each other's arms.

'You crazy girl, what are you doing?' He laughed down at her.

'Right now I'm just trying to stand up. Between my ankle and my corset, I'm done for.'

'That's what I'm here for.' He swung her into his arms. 'To prop you up when you need it.' He carefully navigated the steps, carrying her to the ship's rail.

'You're always carrying me.' She laughed as he set her down.

'That's what partners are for.' Cullen smiled. 'Seriously, though, do you know what you're doing? What you've done? You've jumped on board a ship bound for the South Seas with nothing but the clothes you're wearing.' The enormity of what she'd done was starting to sweep him now that the exhilaration of the dash was receding.

She flashed a wide smile. 'Isn't that how you did it? Only going the other direction? I have it on good authority there's clothes to be had in the Port of Cairo. Two sets ought to be enough.' She laughed. 'After all, I am told one does not need many clothes in Tahiti.'

'But one might need a husband.' He watched her eyes shine with tears.

'One might,' she said carefully.

'It can be arranged in Port Cairo.' He raised her hand to his lips. 'Will you be my wife, my partner?'

'On one condition,' she said solemnly. 'I want to marry you in Tahiti, on the beach you love, with the people you love. Can we do that?'

'Yes, we can do that.' He tugged at the ring on his finger. 'But perhaps I have a condition, too. For the sake of propriety, might you wear this until we get there?' It would solve the problem of a cabin and the inconvenience of enforced celibacy, something he was not looking forward to if she was nearby. Now that she was his, he had no intentions of wasting a moment. Life was short, happiness must be grabbed whenever it could be.

She smiled and slipped the ring on her finger and held her hand up to admire it. 'Compromise, hmm? I think that is a great start to this partnership.'

He bent his mouth to hers, stealing a kiss. 'Speaking of partnerships, do I dare ask about the business? Do we still have one?'

She wrapped her arms about his neck. 'Yes and no. I have sold my shares to the Duke of Cowden. The Prometheus Club will oversee everything. You maintain your shares until which time you'd like to part with them, if ever. Cowden expects you to continue with your South Seas operation and I will receive my own dividends quarterly as an investor. Satisfied?'

'The real question is—are you satisfied? You have given up everything.' Over her shoulder, London was fading as the ship began the long slip down the Thames towards the sea.

'I think you should rephrase that, Cullen Allardyce. I am satisfied because I have *gained* everything.' Of course she would think that, optimist that she was. She took his hand and led him to the prow of the ship.

'There's nothing to see here,' he murmured at her ear, drawing her close against him as they stared out over the water.

'There's the future,' she replied. 'We'll never look back, Cullen. We'll only move forward. Together.'

Epilogue

Tahiti—September 1853

The four long, clear notes of the *pu*, the conch shell, blew in the directions of the four winds, the sound calling the gods and the Mana to the beach. The significance of that sound sent a rill of excitement through Antonia. Today was her wedding day. She tightened her grip on the bouquet of island gardenias she held in her hands. The sweet fragrance of the flowers soothed her nerves as she stood on the beach, Rahiti's wife, Raina, on one side, the newly married Viahere, Rahiti's sister, on her other. About her was assembled the clan Cullen called family.

Her gaze was trained on the aquamarine waters, waiting to catch sight of her groom. The sun shone with pleasant warmth in the piercingly blue sky. Her bare feet luxuriated in the sand.

A light breeze feathered the fabric of her white *pareo* against her body. Cullen was right. There was less need for clothes here. Her crinolines and corsets were packed away in Papeete. Today, she wore the clothes of his clan, a simple single garment draped not around cages and hoops but just her own body. It felt both decadent and free, an outward expression of how she'd felt since the moment she'd jumped aboard the ship. She was free now, no longer weighed down by grief and limitations.

'They're coming!' Viahere whispered excitedly. 'Do you see them?'

She did see them and her pulse raced at the sight of Cullen at the front of the outrigger, the wind off the ocean in his hair, which had grown during the year he'd been away from the islands. It was still not down to his waist, but Antonia was sure it would get there. She positively adored making love with a long-haired man.

'He's a fine man,' Raina whispered appreciatively. 'Almost as fine as my Rahiti.' She laughed, squeezing Antonia's arm. They'd become good friends in the short time Antonia had been here. The clan had welcomed her warmly and rejoiced over Cullen's return. Rahiti and the men had immediately set to building a house for them in Tahitian fashion. The women had helped her set up that house yesterday with a housewarming ceremony and hand-made gifts that had made her cry at their generosity.

The outrigger reached the beach and Cullen jumped out to stride ashore. He was bare-chested, wearing a white *pareo* draped about his hips in a short skirt that showed off his exquisite legs. He was tan now, his hair sun-streaked the colour of honey. She liked this iteration of him very much. She liked this iteration of herself as well. She'd been busy learning the language, learning how to cook traditional foods and learning the customs. She especially liked the idea that meals were communal. Dinner was eaten together by the whole clan.

There were many hands to prepare the food, and there was always good company to eat with. No longer were meals lonely ordeals.

Cullen came to her and took one of her hands. 'Tahiti becomes you, my love. You look ravishing,' he whispered as Rahiti and Raina acted as their escorts and led them to the flower circle laid out on the sand. She passed her bouquet to Raina and Cullen took her other hand. The *tahua* raised his and the ceremony began.

It was unlike any wedding she'd imagined for herself and certainly nothing like her former wedding. Antonia's bare feet curled into the warm sand as the *tahua* began the handfasting blessing and bound their wrists with auti leaves. 'For spiritual protection, healing and purity,' Cullen whispered. 'I guess we need that last after all the time we spent in the cabin on the voyage.'

She smiled at him, letting her eyes say all that she could not: how much she loved him, how much she was looking forward to the life they would make together and every adventure they would have in this paradise. As optimistic as she was, she'd not imagined such a man or such a land existed or that they could be hers, that she would be allowed two grand, but different passions in her lifetime.

The priest bound their wrists together and poured out the water of purification over their hands. Purification, a beginning, a new start. There were many new starts ahead for them. Cullen gave her a sharp look and she knew her glass face nearly gave her away. She needed to be careful. She intended to keep that news for later tonight.

They exchanged flower crowns of island gardenias and leis of hibiscus as they exchanged their vows, pledging their commitment and devotion to one another in their own words. 'You brought me out of darkness, you showed me how to love again,' Antonia said, her eyes glistening with tears of joy. 'I pledge my heart to you for ever, in times of plenty and in times of paucity, I will stand beside you as your wife and your partner.'

She did not think the words adequate to express what he meant to her, but they shook him. She could see it in his eyes and then he reached for her, crushing her to him and holding her as if he would never let her go, never mind that the village looked on. She felt the slight tremble of his broad shoulders as he buried his face in her hair, letting emotion claim him for a moment before he found his voice.

'I may have brought you from darkness, but you brought me to life. You showed me what real love can make possible, what real love can forgive. I am yours for ever. I will spend my days worshipping your body and serving your happiness.' He barely waited for permission to kiss the bride before his lips found hers in a long kiss full of promise, full of passion.

The *tahua* offered the nature prayer to bless the marriage and then Rahiti's mother came forward to wrap them in a *tifaifai*. It was the blanket the women had given her yesterday at the housewarming and it would be the blanket they slept beneath every night. A perfect start to a loving marriage.

Rahiti's father came forward. 'You have married Kanoa. Now, we present you, our newest daughter, with a Tahitian name. You shall be known as Tereva, which means beginning.' She nodded, too overcome with emotion to speak. It was perfect.

Cullen took her hand and stepped with her out of the flower circle to lead the procession back to the village for the celebration. She had never known such happiness as that which followed—the feasting, the dancing. This was her new life, her new world. She and Cullen would live here as much as possible, with the understanding there would occasionally be business to look after in Papeete. She would stay here in the village while Cullen travelled the islands twice a year, but they would manage.

'Come with me, Wife,' Cullen whispered, leading her into the evening shadows. 'No one will mind if we slip away.'

Night in Tahiti was dark. There were no street lamps, only stars to light the way, but very shortly flames came into view from a bonfire on the beach of a lagoon. 'I thought you might like to swim before we go to our home.' He pressed a kiss to her mouth.

'I'd like that very much.' She'd taken to the warm turquoise waters with verve. There was nothing she liked as much as an evening swim with her husband. She reached for the tucked end of her *pareo* and unwound the cloth, letting fall to the sand, standing before her new husband naked in the new-risen moonlight, watching as he did the same. He was glorious nude, even more so in Tahitian moonlight. She moved into his arms, her arms about his neck, her body pressed to his. 'You're right. Clothes are overrated,' she whispered.

'Are you happy?' he asked, searching her eyes. 'It's so much all at once.'

'It is everything I could hope for. *You* are everything I could hope for, a dream I didn't even know I had.' She smiled up at him. The time had come. 'It is so much blessing all at once, but it's about to be even more, Cullen.' She took his hand and pressed it to her belly. 'This time next year, you'll have been a father for a couple of months, at least.' She smiled at the stunned look in his eyes. 'Now, I've overwhelmed you.' She laughed.

He laughed with her. 'You overwhelmed me from the start. One would think I was used to it by now, but I think you will never cease to amaze me.' She followed his gaze where it travelled to their hands at her stomach. 'A child, Antonia? Truly?' There was awe in his voice. 'I did not ever dare to let myself dream of being a father, or of happiness, or of love and now I have all three thanks to you.'

Antonia smiled softly at her husband. 'Don't you know by now that love always finds a way?' Overhead, the stars came out. It was hard to believe those same stars would be shining over London although no one would see them through the soot. Some people thought she was merely lucky, but Antonia knew better. She wasn't lucky. She was loved. 'Cullen, it's going to be a grand life,' she whispered. And they would live it to the fullest because life was too precious to waste a single moment.

* * * * *

HISTORICAL

Your romantic escape to the past.

Available Next Month

How Not To Propose To A Duke Louise Allen
The Marquess's Year To Wed Paulia Belgado

....

A Season With Her Forbidden Earl Julia Justiss
A Wedding To Protect Her Fortune Jenni Fletcher

4 brand new stories each month

HISTORICAL

Your romantic escape to the past.

MILLS & BOON

Keep reading for an excerpt of a new title
from the Historical series,
THE EARL'S CINDERELLA COUNTESS
by Amanda McCabe

Prologue

For love is a celestial harmony
Of likely hearts compos'd of stars' concent,
Which join together in sweet sympathy,
To work each other's joy and true content
—Edmund Spenser

1808

'*I'm afraid you cannot return to school in the New Year, Eleanor dearest. With your mother sadly gone, there is so much for you to do here at the vicarage. I do so rely on your good sense...*'

Eleanor St Aubin could hardly bear it another moment. Could hardly bear the walls of the old vicarage, whitewashed and hung with gloomy old paintings, the sound of her father humming to himself as he wrote his sermon in his library, where he stayed almost all the time. *Humming!* As if he hadn't just brought her world—what was left of her world after losing dear Mama—around her very ears.

She'd clung to the idea of going back to Mrs Meecham's School for Clergymen's Daughters in the bustle and colour of Bath, with her sister Mary. Clung to the thought that soon she would be with her friends, her books and her music lessons, walks across the hills and parks of the town. She would not be alone.

Now there would be no school. No Bath or music or friends. Papa needed a housekeeper, and Mary was only ten, no use at all. She would go back to school. Eleanor was fourteen and 'sensible'. So she would stay home.

Eleanor stood in the middle of the small drawing room, among her mother's dark-green-cushioned furniture and the scent of beeswax polish, woodsmoke and tea cakes, which she would now be responsible for providing. She listened to her father's humming and the thud of his books as he stacked them on his desk. She could hear the cook in the kitchen, clanging pots and pans, and imagined she also heard her chores in the still-room, the jam and potpourri and herbs calling to her. She imagined the parade of parishioners coming endlessly to their door, through the tangled garden pathway that also needed her urgent attention. They would want tea and cakes and would need placating as they waited for her father, who was always late.

Eleanor sighed. She didn't mind talking to the parishioners, really, even when it was about dull altar flowers and fetes to raise coin for the roof. In fact, she quite enjoyed that part, the organising and helping and the solving of problems.

Mama had been so splendid at it all, the church matters *and* the housekeeping. Chatting with people and bringing a tea tray in once in a while.

Eleanor's old chores were far from those she had being the lady of the vicarage and she already felt as if she was drowning. She had no idea how to do any of it! No idea how to manage their few servants, see to meals, tidy the garden and be gracious and smiling all the time.

She'd always half imagined that she might one day marry a curate herself and keep her own vicarage just as Mama had. But that was in some hazy 'someday', when she was older, more learned and not so very awkward and unsure. Not now, when she was still a school-girl.

Her frantic stare fell on a barley twist side table, its books and porcelain vases covered with a film of dust. Without her mother's close eye on every detail, things were descending into chaos. And now Eleanor was the one who had to pay the attention.

She closed her eyes against the dust. Against the windows that needed washing and the curtains that needed mending. She did not *want* to be the grown-up! She wanted to go back to school, to the pale houses and crowded streets of Bath. She wanted a little more time to decipher out her life, not have it thrust upon her without her say-so. She wanted to cry and kick some-thing and rail about unfairness! She wanted…

She wanted her mother. That was what she wanted. She wanted Mary Ellen St Aubin to hug her close and tell her all would be well. But it would not. Not now.

'Eleanor,' her father called out plaintively. 'Have you seen my spectacles?'

The cook shouted at the scullery maid and Mary

shrieked from her chamber upstairs. Eleanor couldn't bear it another moment. The chaos *she* was meant to control now, the absence of Mama, the realisation that this was her every day now and there was no escape— she was suffocating.

She spun around and raced out of the drawing room, through the small, flagstone-floored foyer, and yanked the door open. Luckily, there was no one on the pathway, no poor soul seeking solace from the vicar and tea and cakes from the housekeeper—from her. She heard a hum of conversation from the churchyard just beyond the garden hedge, but she couldn't see anyone. She clutched at handfuls of her grey muslin skirt and ran. She ran down the overgrown path, veering a bit towards the church, its old Norman stone tower stretching towards the cloudy sky as if it watched her. She dashed through the lych-gate into the lane.

She didn't stop running.

Rather than head towards the village, a small but pretty place lined with shops, where everyone knew her and where someone was bound to see her and report her hoydenish behaviour to her father, she went to the woods that stretched in the opposite direction, cool and green and quiet.

The woods were part of the estate at Moulton Magna, the grand property of the Earl of Fleetwood, the greatest lord in the neighbourhood. Since the Earl was friends with her father, indeed had bestowed on him the living in the first place, no one in the Canning family—the Earl, Countess and their sons, plus a vast staff—cared when the vicar and his daughters walked there. It was a beautiful spot, with groves and streams, smelling of the fresh, green air and Eleanor usually loved it.

She enjoyed the company of the Canning brothers, as well, she had to admit. Especially the younger, Lord Frederick, he of the glowing sky-blue eyes and easy laughter. His teasing ways that made her blush and stammer, made her close her eyes and picture him at night and wish she had said something different to him, been someone different. She always sought him out there when they were both home from school, even if she told herself she did not.

But today she hoped she wouldn't see Fred, or any of them. She could feel drops of moisture at her temples from her mad dash, dampening her dark brown hair. Curls escaped their pins and clung to her neck, and she was sure her eyes must be red from crying, her pale cheeks blotchy. She would be a terrible sight, a disgrace to the vicarage. And she couldn't bear for Fred, of all people, to see her that way! To tease her and laugh at her, even in his light, joking way. She didn't want him to remember her that way.

She saw no one as she ran down a winding, mossy path, towards a small summerhouse that topped a rolling rise. It had long been a favourite spot for her, as well as for Mary and the Canning brothers. The view from its colonnaded portal stretched for miles—meadows and trees and the grand, glowing house of Moulton Magna. They would chase each other there, laughing and teasing. Today, she wanted to be alone. To not have to be the strong, sensible one everyone said she was. She had the rest of her life to do that.

She stumbled up the steps of the little, round, domed building and into the single room. Greyish sunlight filtered through the skylight high overhead, dappling the dried leaves that drifted over the mosaic floor, reminding her that autumn was lengthening and when winter came she wouldn't be at school. She'd be here. Alone in the summerhouse, which echoed now with old laughter.

She sat down on a wrought iron chaise, its cushions taken inside now. She didn't feel the hard press of the bare slats, though, or the chill of the marble walls. She let that silence wrap around her and drew her knees up to press her forehead against them. The tears fell then, until she had no more of them. There was only a sort of tired resignation.

She wanted to blame Papa, to curse at him, even though she couldn't. It was not his fault, not really. Her mother had been so superb at her job of keeping the vicarage and he couldn't begin to do all she had done. He didn't know how, and he had his own tasks of sermon-writing and consoling the bereaved, comforting the dying, celebrating marriages and new babies. She was the female. She had to cook and clean and manage servants. It was how the world worked. She was the eldest daughter. The duties were hers, along with helping Mary, and they had to be done.

But, oh! She had loved school and her friends and books. Loved Bath, glowing like honey in the light, the Avon bubbling past, laughter and people and shops.

She reached under the chaise and found the basket

of books she'd left there still waiting. Novels and poetry—things not suitable for the vicarage library. She took out her favourite, Spenser's *The Fairy Queen,* with its etched illustrations of the Redcrosse Knight and his true love Una.

The door cracked open, letting in a bar of light and a breeze that stirred at the leaves. Her stomach lurched as she was suddenly dragged out of her fantasy world. She dropped her feet to the floor and wiped at her damp cheeks. Had her father caught her? She didn't want him to feel even worse! Didn't want to put her tears on anyone else.

But it was not her father or sister, or a Canning gamekeeper come to lecture her against racing through the park. It was Fred. The last person she wanted to see. The only person she wanted to see.

He stood there in the doorway, half in the wavering shadows, and studied her with a worried frown. Eleanor felt her tense shoulders ease at just his presence and she clutched the book close to her with a sigh.

Fred, though he was much older than her at nineteen, and *very* handsome indeed, with his waves of amber-gold hair and sharp cheekbones, his bright blue eyes filled with laughter was much sought after by every eligible young lady within miles and miles, had always been such a friend to her.

There was the flash of a deep dimple when he smiled at her. He spoke to her not as if she was a silly child or a sensible housekeeper, but as a lady who understood poetry and history and who loved to run and dance even when she shouldn't. He raced her through the woods, taught her the rules of cricket, read with her, teased her, laughed with her. He was always quick to make her giggle when life at the vicarage was too dour, to run with her, read poetry with her, tell her tales of the world outside.

Yes—he was her friend. And if, in the quiet of her dark chamber at night, she dared to dream he might be more, might one day kiss her and hold her close—well, that was *her* secret. She knew he never would, not really. He was handsome as a god, as a prince in a poem, and the son of an earl. But the dreams were so lovely.

'Ella,' he said softly, kindly. 'Are you unwell? I was riding by and saw you running.'

Eleanor ducked her head, hoping he wouldn't see those red eyes and splotched cheeks. She was plain enough in comparison to him already! 'I—I'm all right, Fred, really. I just—my father told me I cannot return to school. He needs my help at the vicarage.'

'Oh, Ella. I am sorry,' he said.

His voice was full of sympathy and understanding and she feared it would make her cry all over again. He was one of the few who knew how much she really loved it at school, for she confided in him about her friends and studies. They read *The Fairy Queen* together while he told her about his own school and his hopes for the future away from his own family.

He gestured at the book she clutched. 'You could be Una.'

She felt her lips tug at a reluctant smile, even though she knew he flattered her just to cheer her up. 'And you shall always be the *parfit gentil knight*. The Red-crosse Knight.'

He smiled in return, but Eleanor sensed something rather sad and dark in the gesture. Something not like Fred, who was always so merry and ready to run and laugh.

She sat up straighter. 'Is something amiss?'

'Of course not. It's just...' He stepped closer, into the glow from the skylight. He wore a red coat, glittering with touches of gold.

'Fred...' she whispered, a cold knot forming in her stomach. 'Are you— That is...'

'I'm also leaving, yes. I have my commission in the Grenadiers and we're leaving for the Peninsula tomorrow. I was looking for you to say...'

'To say goodbye?' she choked out. Her eyes prickled and she warned herself sternly not to start crying again.

She had long known Fred was meant for the Army. His older brother, the dashing Henry, was the heir to Moulton Magna. Their destinies sorted them as surely as hers did for her and Mary. Fred would surely go far in the Army, flourish there where his bravery and gift for friendship would be valued and she was happy for him.

But—oh! He was one more loss, after her mother and her school and any foolish hopes she might have dared harbour about the future. That one day a miracle would happen and Fred could be hers, even though he was the Earl's son and she the vicar's daughter.

She rose slowly to her feet and took a step closer to him. He smelled wonderfully of sunshine and lemon soap and just *Fred*. She was suddenly achingly aware this could be the last time she saw him. It was certainly the last time she would see *this* Fred and be *this* Eleanor. So many images scrolled through her mind in a great flash—his smile, the blue glow of his eyes, the freedom of laughing with him.

She gently touched his hand. It was warm and slightly rough, so alive under her fingers, and she longed to clutch at him, hold on to him and this moment for always.

'I shall miss you,' she said simply. She could think of no other words.

He smiled at her, a flash of his old teasing grin, and turned his hand to hold onto hers. 'And I will miss you, Ella. Will you keep the book for me? Think of me adventuring when you read it?'

She gave him another smile in answer. It felt rather watery, weak, but she yearned to put all she felt into it. All she thought of him in her secret heart. All she hoped for him. She couldn't bear to send him off with a vision of red eyes and miserable weeping! 'Of course I shall. No one could ever read the lines as you do, though. Really, you should have been one to tread the boards rather than march in the Army!'

'I'm glad your father is here to keep an eye on Moulton Magna for me. I have the feeling my parents and brother will need all the prayers they can find!'

Eleanor shook her head, thinking of the Earl, of Henry and their carelessness. But it was Fred who would be in danger. She had the gnawing, anxious sense that it was Fred who needed the prayers, needed someone to look after him. And it could not be her.

To her horror, she felt those tears well in her eyes again.

'Oh, Ella,' he said, his sharply carved face crumpling in worry. 'Don't cry, please! I can stand anyone crying, but not you.'

'Because I am sensible and strong?' she whispered.

'You are that. But also because of your dear heart, your laughter and poetry. Your kindness. No one is kinder than you, Ella. I need you to keep watch for me here. You're the only one I can really count on.'

Eleanor nodded, cherishing those words. Trying to remember them for the long days ahead. But she hated the hint of worry in his voice, the tinge of some foreboding, and it made her shiver. She longed to cling onto him even closer, to not to let him leave her side. 'You *can* rely on me, Fred. I'll be—thinking about you a great deal and sending you all best wishes wherever you are.' Sending him her heart, even though he would never know it.

He gently touched her cheek, tracing the last of her tears. 'So, friends always, Ella?'

Friends. Such a pale word for what she felt for him, for her secret dreams. But it was a precious gift nonetheless. One she hugged close. 'Yes. The best of friends.'

To her shock, he took her hand in his, holding it tight and bent his head to press a soft, gentle kiss to her fingers. Then he turned and left and she was alone again.

Eleanor curled her fingers tight, as if she could hold

on to that kiss. The thrilling sensation of it all. The bright, sunshiny tingles. She wanted to remember it always, remember *him*.

She smoothed out his handkerchief, running her fingertip over the embroidered blue *FC*. She fancied she could smell his lemony soap there, the essence of Fred and his golden glow.

'The best of friends,' she whispered. She folded up the handkerchief carefully, tucked it in the pages of the book and stepped back out into the real world to face the future, carrying with her the memory of Fred and his kiss.